T0367417

Other publications by Young Park

The Life And Times of A Hyphenated American
Shootout at Grove Street
Korea And The Imperialists
The Korean From America
Tiny Holes

CHOICES

a novel

Young Park

iUniverse, Inc.
Bloomington

Choices
A Novel

iUniverse books may be ordered through booksellers or by contacting:

iUniverse
1663 Liberty Drive
Bloomington, IN 47403
www.iuniverse.com
1-800-Authors (1-800-288-4677)

ISBN: 978-1-4620-2880-1 (sc)
ISBN: 978-1-4620-2818-4 (e)

Printed in the United States of America

iUniverse rev. date: 7/15/2011

FOR:

GARY
HENRI
CHICK
KEVIN

In
Memory

KAM WAH

1 ————————————————

SPRING HAD NOT BEEN a smashing season. After two weeks in Guangzhou and Beijing a giant deal collapsed and I was returning to San Francisco with nothing. The only positive part of the trip was a quick visit to Harbin to see BJ. I hoped the coming Summer would be better. Considering the gas mask fiasco, anything would be better.

The Eva Air flight left Hong Kong at 3 PM and landed at SFO five minutes after its scheduled 4 PM arrival time. It was an overnight trip with an hour stop over in Taipei. The Super Business Class in the upper deck was very comfortable and the food was good. No single malt, but blended scotch was available. I slept most of the way from Taipei.

While waiting in line to clear immigration, I decided to take a taxi from the airport. The Bart ride was too much like being a nine to five commuter at that time of day. The trains were crowded with bored and tired workers. No Giant game was scheduled at the new Pacific Bell stadium so traffic was not abnormally heavy.

It was early evening and the freeway traffic into the city was light south of Candlestick Park. It jammed up just past hospital curve with commuters trying to get across the Bay Bridge, going east to Alameda and Contra Costa counties.

The stream of end-to-end traffic coming out of the city going south on 101, north across the Golden Gate, and east over the Bay Bridge was rushing along at five miles per hour. It would be an hour or more before many of them reached their suburban homes. If there was an accident or other mishap it could be three or four hours. They were the commuters who spent a good part of their lives sitting in their cars on the freeway. Looking at them sitting in their cars reminded me of the time many years ago when I spent hundreds of hours on the Santa Ana Freeway, driving my MG from Orange County to UCLA. In more recent times I spent my commuting hours on airplanes. I swore I would never do that again.

Some drivers busied themselves texting messages or talking on their cell phones. I saw a woman putting on her makeup while driving. She was using the rearview mirror and steered with her knees. I could never do that because I wasn't agile or brave enough. These women have no fear.

One of the differences between freeway commuters and me was that they had a permanent home to go to. For me "home" was one of a dozen or so stopovers in foreign countries and San Francisco, where I lived for a couple of weeks at a time. My "home" was a state of mind.

Another difference was that most commuters sitting in their cars on the freeway had regular salaries and probably made more money than I did. If my last trip was any indication, everyone in the western world made more money than I did.

As an independent international business consultant, a title I listed as my occupation, I really didn't make a lot of money. I didn't actually consult with anyone and business clients didn't always ask for my advice. My primary function was as a "go-between" – a "fixer." I found connections for people who needed them to complete business deals. That was how I spent my time. It wasn't much of a profession, if it could be called a profession. My business and I were temporary. Nothing about me was really permanent.

Whenever I thought about things like this I wondered if I was in the wrong business. I could have stayed in education and learned how to live a sedate life. But, many of us go off on tangents because we didn't want to deal with a normal life. Living a normal life was far more difficult than doing what I was doing. Those who stick it out and raise a family were much tougher than I was.

I conned myself into believing that being a consultant had possibilities because I didn't risk any capital and the returns could be gigantic. Could be. That was what this latest deal could have been – gigantic. It was a once in a lifetime thing. But, as most of those once in a lifetime things, it didn't happen. So who's fooling who?

It cost sixty bucks for the taxi ride. Bart would have cost about six or seven dollars. Well, it was my coming home present. I checked the mailbox. As usual, there was nothing but a few bills and reams of worthless advertisements. I threw everything but the bills in the overflowing waste basket placed next to the mail boxes. No one wrote me letters or even sent a postcard. My only means of communication was Email and via my cell phone. There was something called Skype, but I haven't gotten up to speed with that. I was dragged into the new world of Internet kicking and screaming.

I gathered the three bills and went up to my second floor apartment. The apartment smelled a bit musty because I had been gone for a couple of weeks. I opened a window and let the cool San Francisco Bay breeze in. No one had broken in so my computer and television were where I left them. I found my half full bottle of single malt scotch, which was as valuable as the television set. I found some ice cubes and poured a good drink.

There were several messages on the answering machine. Andre, Chick, Megan, Peter, Gary, and my children left messages. Some were over a week old. I figured most of them would call again, so I didn't return any of the calls. I turned on the computer and checked for Email messages. There were a couple of dozen of them and it took almost an hour to read them all. I promised my computer I would answer them tomorrow.

It had been several hours since I last ate on the plane. With great foresight, I had thought ahead and emptied the refrigerator before I left. There was nothing to eat. So, my careful planning wasn't all that clever. I should have stashed a couple of frozen TV dinner in the freezer. Oh well, next time.

I found a bag of Orville Redenbacher popcorn and a couple of cups of rice still in the five-pound bag. If I cooked the rice, what would I eat with it? I could order some Chinese or pizza. Ah hell, I wasn't really that hungry. I'll have to go to the grocery store sometime. Tomorrow.

I decided to pop the popcorn in the microwave. I poured another drink and forgot about eating real food. I watched the news on the television for a while. The news depressed me so I played a Helen Reddy CD and that always made me feel good. Delta Dawn was the last song I heard before I drifted off to sleep.

An hour or so later the phone rang. With some effort I got up from the sofa, went to the desk, and answered the phone.

"Hello."

"Ah, you're back. Welcome home, my friend."

"*Bonjour*, Andre."

"How are you?"

"Some jet lag. You know how that is."

"I won't keep you. Let's have lunch and catch up on things."

"Fine. How about day after tomorrow. Give me time to get acclimated."

"That's good. Come to the house about eleven-thirty and we'll go from there."

"Okay."

"Listen, my friend. You did a great job."

"Not so great. The deal died an agonizing death."

"You had no control over that. Don't worry about it. Really. Not to worry. See you day after tomorrow."

"Okay."

Andre was an exceptional person and few could match his expertise with international commercial procedures. He could speak three different languages fluently and knew more about guns and ammunition than anyone in the business. I've known him almost as long as I've known Kam Wah. He was a true friend.

I showered and settled down with another scotch. My third one since I came home. Am I drinking more and enjoying it less?

I surfed the television, looking for a program with which I was familiar. I picked one with actors I had seen in other shows. It was a new crime series. Television shows were living proof we lived in a violent crime ridden society. So much crime and so little time. A half hour into program the phone rang. A call from overseas?

"Yes?"

"Well, you're finally answering the phone."

"Chick?"

"Who else?"

"I thought it might be God. You know how he, or is it she, always calls. Of course, not at odd hours like some people."

"Are you saying this is late? This is not late. It's not even midnight here so it's only about nine there."

"The last time you called it was five in the morning."

"When did you get back?

"Today."

"Do any good?"

"Not really. Whatta ya need?"

"Have a request for canned Jack Mackerel. Can you contact your people in China for this?"

"You have some specs? They come in different size cans, you know. And do they want them in tomato sauce or brine?"

"I'll send the specs today."

"Okay."

"Oh, another thing. Peter's been trying to get in touch with you. He's been calling you for days."

"What about?"

"I think it has to do with some surplus army trucks."

"Haven't had too much luck with Peter's contacts. The last time his contact was looking for flame throwers for Pakistan and that turned out to be a dud."

"Well, I told him I would call him if you were back so you can expect a call right after I hang up."

"Is the mackerel for that woman in Boca Rotan?"

"Yes."

"Oh."

"Hey, she's all right."

"I've never been able to connect with her. She never buys anything. The price is always too high she says."

"She's okay. I've done business with her before."

"But I haven't."

"Do what you can. Okay?"

"I'll make some inquiries. Send the specs."

"Talk to you later."

Chick was a long time friend and business associate who lived and worked out of Tallahassee. I had known him for fifteen years or more. He was instrumental in putting together a beta glucan plant in Georgia and the beta glucan business was what first took me to Harbin. That's how I came to meet BJ. So in a round about way, I owed Chick. But, that's another story.

As forewarned, Peter called ten minutes after Chick hung up. Peter was located in San Antonio and was an expert with vehicles and other transportation equipment. He dealt in everything from bullet proof luxury limousines to helicopters.

"Hello."

"Hi. It's me, Peter."

"Hello, Peter."

"Chick says you were in China?"

"Yeah. I hear you have some surplus army vehicles."

"There are twenty-eight of them. Manufactured in Poland and none have more than eleven thousand kilometers. I have specs and pictures that I'll send. I also have eight Agusta A109 helicopters, military version, 1992-1994. All have low hours."

"How old are the trucks?"

"Made twelve years ago."

"Twelve years ago and with only eleven thousand kilometers? That's only about seven thousand miles."

"That's right. Never really been used. Have verification on all that."

"Verification by the broker or the owners?"

"The owners. The source is reliable. I've worked with them before. Check the papers I send."

"Okay."

"One other item. Just got word 200 military jeeps are available. Brand new. All according to US army specs made at the US Chrysler plant. These were slated for Colombia but the deal went sour. Price is $24,000 per unit. There's a thousand in it for Chick and me. We can include you in that thousand."

"Are these Wrangler jeeps?"

"Yes, but with military specs. I'll send you photos and specs."

"The price is too high."

"But these are military specs."

"Price is still too high. But, I'll ask. Let's just hope this isn't like that Pakistani business."

"Haven't you heard from Akim?"

"No. I haven't and my associate hasn't either. Listen, Peter, we went outta our way to find flamethrowers, night vision equipment, and sniper ammo."

"I'll check with Akim."

"I don't think anyone is going to take him seriously."

"I'll tell him that."

"There won't be a next time if he doesn't have up front official documentation from the government, Peter."

"Okay. I hear you. But, look at the specs on the trucks."

"I will."

"Thanks."

"Not a problem to look."

"I'm sending them now."

"Fine. I'll ask about the helicopters and if there's an interest you can send me the specs."

"Thanks. I appreciate the help."

Peter's deals were specialty items and of value only to people in that business. Unfortunately, most of these deals rarely worked out for me. There were so many things that could go wrong and they usually did. A lot of my time was spent with these spot sales that went nowhere.

———

Thinking about canned Jack Mackerels and surplus army trucks was depressing. The gas masks were supposed to take me away from these makeshift deals. I really had to quit spending so much time dwelling on how the gas mask deal collapsed.

I went back to surfing the television and stumbled on to a new medical series. Other than the inane comedy sitcoms and reality shows, there were always medical, police, and legal shows on television. If the good shows lasted more than one season, the plots became bizarre. Of course, sex was always a part of the story.

Half of the medical program hour showed lots of blood and gore before, during, and after surgery. The other half of the program involved doctors and nurses groping each other. I wondered if sex was an integral part of medical internships. Lawyers in legal shows were also heavily involved with sex. Sex and gore and crime, that's what sells. Made more sense to rent a porno flick, which was sex without a contrived story.

I quickly lost interest in watching television and found a Spencer novel I had read over a year ago. The book, my fourth scotch drink, and an Ella Fitzgerald CD helped me get through the night.

2

I SPENT THE NEXT day cleaning my apartment. Most of my clothes had been laundered at the Guangzhou hotel, so I didn't have any laundry to do. I restocked my cupboard with food and bought another bottle of fifteen year old Glenfiddich single malt scotch.

I had dinner that night with my children at the Casa Orinda steak house. The boys each ate at least twenty-five ounces of beef. The girls shared a chateaubriand. They like their beef too. For a change, instead of prime rib roast I had the fried chicken.

I got home about ten and sent inquiries to China for Chick's Jack Mackerel and to Kevin in Vietnam about Peter's trucks and jeeps. After that and a couple of scotch drinks, I decided to get a good night's rest.

I got up early the next morning and walked around the neighborhood for an hour. I should have gone to the gym for a proper workout, but didn't. I'll go tomorrow.

At about a quarter to eleven I left to meet Andre in Foster City. I was looking forward to lunch with Andre because I always enjoyed his company and it was time to put the gas masks to rest.

We didn't go to Anderson's Black Angus steak house as we usually did. We went instead to a seafood restaurant on the waterfront at the southern tip of the bay. It was not too crowded but the outside tables on the patio were all taken. We were seated indoors at a window table.

"Was the restaurant business really getting that bad?"

"All businesses are slow lately. People are not buying lunch as they did before, so Anderson's quit serving lunch. Now they only serve dinner. But, this place is okay. Seafood is always fresh. Only drawback is no lady waitresses to charm."

"Well, can't have everything."

Our waiter brought menus and gave a verbal rundown of the day's specials. It took me more than ten minutes to read the eight page menu. Prices were high, but everything was supposed to be fresh. As usual, Andre was planning a big lunch.

"So, what's your heart's desire today? The sole is good. Also the mahi mahi."

"I'll have the trout. And hope it's really fresh."

"All the entrée are guaranteed to be fresh. Haven't heard any complaints and they do a good business. How about we share a salad?"

"You know salad and bread without the entrée would be enough for me."

Andre ignored me and pointed to the lunch specials.

"There's also soup with the lunch specials."

"Andre, this is a lunch, not a dinner banquet. And I know you're gonna push dessert at me."

"You've been in Asia for weeks, my friend. You need good nourishing food. I want you to eat and get well."

"Get well? I haven't been sick."

"You need to revive yourself with good food."

"Okay." I wondered how I was going to eat all the dishes Andre would order. This was similar to the giant dinners Kam Wah ordered in Guangzhou and Hong Kong.

"How about some wine?"

"A glass will be fine for me." I knew I would end up drinking more than just one glass.

"Red or white?"

"Whatever you think is good."

"Also I think we should have a side dish of salmon *sushi* and a Caesar salad we can share."

"Okay. I'll stay with the trout."

"I'm going to have the sea bass. I think it's from Chile. Ah, here's the waiter."

We gave the waiter our orders and Andre asked for a bottle of Bordeaux. The waiter brought the bottle and poured some in his glass. After he tasted the wine and gave his approval the waiter poured a glass for each of us. Andre raised his glass and made a toast.

"Here's to buyers of gas masks, whoever they might be." Andre raised his glass and I touched it with mine.

"A curse on them and may they all go to hell," I added.

"Well said."

If there was a fireplace handy we would have thrown the glasses into the fire. I was tempted to just throw my glass on the floor.

"Not too many of those deals around."

"We came close," he said quietly.

"Close only counts in horseshoes."

"Whatever, it was worth a try. I appreciate what you did in China. I know it wasn't easy."

"It didn't happen, so I'm a failure."

"No, my friend. You made the contact. No one else could do that. If there were no defects, you could have made the deal. That's the way I see it."

"Have you heard what happened after we pulled out?" I asked.

"I've heard nothing after I told you the deal was off."

"Did you know Hoover was working for the US government?"

"Hoover?" He thought a moment. "It's possible. You know, I only met him once – just before we went to Paris to meet with the Prince. Hoover came down from Seattle on his way to China to prop up the Premier's nephew."

"My Chinese army liaison told me Hoover was an American agent. I guess most officials on that level know. That's why he'll never get close to real decision makers."

"Ah – so it wasn't only because his grandfather stole all those bonds and went to Taiwan."

"There were a lot of people in this deal that we didn't know about. Several American agents contacted me before I left China. They wanted me to give them the name of my army liaison. They were pissed when I told them no. The day I left Hong Kong, my Chinese army liaison called and told me a new set of players was driving the deal. The Saudis weren't the only buyers and the gas masks were only a part of a bigger transaction. Overnight, everything changed. It wasn't the deal we started with.

"A million gas masks are not everyday common goods and we found them for those who are involved in bigger deals. We got used, Andre. It wasn't planned that way, but we got used."

"If the gas masks were not damaged, we would have finished the deal. I think when I decided to pull out, all these other elements came into play."

"I agree. There is something of interest – my Chinese army liaison hinted that a rumor would be leaked that a million defective gas masks were sold to buyers in the Middle East."

"That should cause some nervous moments for someone."

"Would it have been worth the money to run the risk, Andre?"

"Makes no difference now. It's finished."

He looked out the window. He still thought about how close we had come to eight-five million dollars. About as often as I did.

Andre finished his wine and refilled our glasses. Two glasses of wine at lunch was usually my limit because after several glasses I got sleepy. Andre could drink the whole bottle and never feel it.

The salmon *sushi* was served, followed by salad. Thankfully, Andre decided to not order soup, but he did order another *sushi* dish.

"Do you think the Chinese will really leak that information?" Andre asked.

"Yeah. I think so. It will embarrass the Americans and some people will feel real heat. Middle Easterners have money to burn, but some of them won't like being made fools of. If it goes as orchestrated by the Chinese, a few heads will roll. The buyers may end up just dumping the million gas masks."

"So be it." Andre wanted to forget it or at least not talk about it.

The main dishes arrived and the waiter filled my glass with more wine. The trout was very good and Andre was more than satisfied with his sea bass. Another basket of San Francisco sourdough bread was brought to the table. I avoided eating more than a half a slice, knowing Andre would order dessert.

"How did your other business go?" he asked.

"Other business?"

"You had some personal matters to attend to, right?"

"Oh, yes. Thanks for your help. It worked out fine and you helped save someone's life."

"Nothing wrong with doing good deeds."

"I think I'm better at doing good deeds than being a money maker."

"What's bothering you, my friend?" He looked at me with raised eyebrows.

"I don't know. There was a lot of money on the table. Why didn't I take advantage of that?"

"Do you mean a side deal with Hoover? I wouldn't have opposed that. I don't think anyone would have objected, except the buyers when and if they learn the gas masks are defective."

"So why didn't I?"

"You have high moral standards and I'm grateful you're on my side. I can trust you. Still, I would understand if you made a side deal."

"I don't know about moral standards. I do know I passed up a lot of money. I've asked myself why and I really don't have an answer. I did what I thought was right, but what the hell is right? You did the same. You passed on the deal. Do you have an answer?"

"You think I haven't lost sleep over this?" He shook his head and sighed. "There are no answers."

"I've thought some about this. The gas masks were defective. People who used them could die. From a business point of view, we didn't sell goods because we knew they were defective. Are we such moral capitalists?"

"Both are good reasons not to buy or sell defective goods. Has nothing to do with capitalism."

"Is one a moral decision and the other a business decision?"

"Does it make a difference?" he asked.

"I guess not. Still, we trade in goods that are used to kill people. We're amoral about all this. So why didn't we do the gas mask deal?"

Andre looked at me and buttered a piece of sourdough. He took a bite and a sip of his wine.

"You've had a difficult time on this trip, my friend. But, you know the business we're in. There is no right or wrong. Don't talk about morality and try to deal in guns and ammo. That's a dead end street. If it's a problem for you, best to get out of the business."

"You're right. Anyway, my real value in the business is in dealing with the abstract, not material things. I called in a favor to get to the person who could make the deal on the gas masks. And I wouldn't give his name to others. Why, I ask myself."

"Are you all right?" he sounded concerned.

"Not to worry, Andre. I'm just recovering from a couple of things that happened on this trip. And I'm pissed about losing out on an eight-five million dollar deal."

"Is there something personal?"

"Isn't there always?"

Andre sipped his wine and looked at me and frowned.

"You need to get away for a while, my friend. Come to the Philippines with me. Some very nice ladies there to help you forget."

"Very tempting, but I really should get on to the Vietnam deal."

"When are you going to Vietnam?"

"Soon. Trying to get a fix on the army contact."

"Do they have our proposal?"

"Yes. The problem is making the right contact. In Nam, even a twenty-five million dollar proposal doesn't always get everyone's attention. Then there's the red envelope."

"An ammunition plant will make millions of dollars for everyone and Vietnam would end up with a thriving industry. A few thousand dollars to pave the way is okay, but a personal retirement fund we are not going to create."

"I agree."

"When you're ready, let me know. I'll be in Panama in a couple of weeks and then back to the Philippines." He paused and looked at me. "I worry about you. I'm serious. Take some time off. I don't want to lose you."

"I'm okay."

"We don't have to do this thing with Vietnam now. It can wait a few months."

I sighed and wondered if I should call off the business in Nam. But then, what would I do? This was the business I was in.

"No. I need something to do. Vietnam will be a good change for me."

We set the gas masks fiasco aside and talked about other business. Andre was concerned with problems involved in shipping gun powder and the insurance costs. But things were working out in Panama for transshipment to Europe. Andre was a wizard in figuring out that sort of thing.

Over my objections, Andre ordered dessert. An ice cream sundae this time with coffee. After we finished the dessert and coffee, he paid the bill and walked me to my car.

"You're too smart. You ask too many questions and when you can't get the answers, you ask more questions. Don't go too deep with all of this. There are no answers. We do what we think is right. Doesn't always mean what we do is right, but we tell ourselves that it is."

"Guess that's really all we have."

"Believe me. It's more than what others have."

"Call me when you're back from the Philippines, Andre. Take care."

"*Adieu,* my friend."

Andre was right. I can't dwell on moral issues and trade in arms and ammunition. I made that choice when I entered the business. There were only a few options available and I exercised one option with the gas masks. Being able to exercise an option was the only real freedom I had. Morality was never the criteria for a decision in my business. It was what was "right" at the time, whatever "right" means. Why am I getting hung up on this?

I went home and took a nap. Wine with a big lunch did that to me. Later that evening I sent an Email to Kevin in Ho Chi Minh City and asked about the ammunition proposal. He answered within an hour and said there was a positive response from the army. We could push for a meeting within the next two or three weeks.

There were two reasons for making the trip to Vietnam. One was the ammunition proposal and the second was Yasha's proposal to develop a resort in Vietnam. If permitted by the government, her project would include a casino. I had promised to help her with this when I was in

Beijing. It could be a much bigger project than the gas mask deal or the ammunition proposal.

I had given Kevin a run down of Yasha's resort proposal several weeks ago and asked him to make inquiries. I was anxious to get this to the attention of decision makers because it was the only immediate source of cash I had. It was a very good plan, but being good didn't mean the Vietnamese would agree to pursue it. However, Kevin was positive about the reactions from his contacts.

As with most of these proposals, much depended on the decision makers in government. This dependency made my life unpredictable and plans were always temporary or put on hold. I had become accustomed to this, but lately I was becoming dissatisfied with being at the mercy of some government agency or private financial entity. Was it time to change my life style? Again? But, change to what? Was this a mid-life crisis?

3

THE NEXT MORNING I went to the gym and worked out for a couple of hours. I paid a monthly fee to use the facility, which was close by and worth the expense. When I joined the club they asked if I wanted a fitness consultant. I told them I didn't need one. Many of the women members seemed to have need of this kind of consulting. There was probably a good deal of positive support provided and maybe other side benefits no one talked about.

Around noon Gary called and suggested we have lunch before I left the country again. We agreed to meet the next day. Gary was one of my all time favorite friends. We had not been involved in any business deals because Gary was not in my kind of business. His business, other than education, was real estate and he did rather well with this. We met during my last job with a community college some years ago. He was the Director of Community Services in the college district. He was always positive about things, even when his own life was in chaos.

Our lunches usually lasted three to four hours. We met in Pleasanton, a nice town where the Alameda county fair was held every year. A variety of ethnic restaurants catered to the tourist trade and we tried them all. We spent most of the time talking about the political and social state of the union and how screwed up our personal lives were.

He gave me a run down about his problems with an investment he had made in a mini-shopping mall in Fresno. He also brought me up to date on the strained relations with his present wife. It was our usual lunch therapy session. We spent an equal amount of time discussing the state of world politics and our need for a good woman. Whenever the opportunity presented itself, we made careful assessments of the women walking by. In the spring and summer many wore shorts and halter tops. One reason we ate at restaurants with sidewalk tables.

I always got an emotional lift after the lunches with Gary. I felt better about things in general after the lunch.

It was a week with little happening so I decided to check on how Meilan was doing. Meilan was the daughter of Guangzhou police Chief Wu. She was at Mills College and I promised her father I would look in on her from time to time. The last time I saw her we went to dinner at Jack London Square in Oakland. I decided to see how she was doing after her first two quarters in school.

I wondered if some young man had come into her life, which I knew was going to happen. She was beautiful and being from China, real or imagined, she had an exotic aura about her. Meeting members of the opposite sex would be part of a normal and healthy social evolutionary process but there were could be problems with boy-girl relations between people of difficult cultures. BJ would say such encounters were a part of her *karma* and not to worry. But, I was still concerned. Paternal instincts?

I called her dormitory and left a message, asking her to call me back. She called the following day.

"Hello."

"Hello. It's me, Meilan. I'm so glad you called."

"How are you?"

"I'm fine."

"I called to say hello and ask if you would like to have dinner with me."

"Oh, yes. That'll be wonderful."

"If you're free, how about this coming Saturday?"

"Saturday will be great."

"This time I thought we could go into the city for dinner. There's place in the city called the Carnelian Room. You might have heard of it."

"No. But, I don't know too many places."

"Well, I think you'll like this place. What time would be convenient for you?"

"Any time is okay."

"How about six-thirty?"

"That's fine," she said.

"Okay, I'll pick you up at the dorm on Saturday at six-thirty."

"See you then."

I made reservations at the Carnelian Room, located on the 52nd floor of the Bank of America building. It was one of the better restaurants of the city's thousand plus dining places. It was also unique because of the fantastic view of the city lights. I also liked their rack of lamb.

To make the evening really special I bought Meilan an orchid corsage. I wore a tie for the occasion. I didn't do ties much, but I figured, what the hell, why not. I arrived fifteen minutes early and went into the front entrance of the dorm. She was waiting for me in the dorm lobby. She gave me a dazzling smile, and kissed me on the cheek.

I was amazed. In the short three months or so since I last saw her, she had changed. Or was she the same lovely girl and I just didn't notice how beautiful she was? Or maybe it was because she was all dressed up. She had on a form fitting, ankle length, blue *cheongsam* with white cherry blossom designs. Mandarin collar, cap sleeves, and frog enclosures were all in place, as the classical design demanded. It had a slit on the left side, showing enough leg to make all male hearts beat faster. She wore heels and looked stunning.

I stood back and looked at Meilan. Seeing her made me think of BJ. The *cheongsam* was the modern version of the traditional dress worn by the Manchu women during the Ch'ing Dynasty. I've never seen BJ in such a dress.

"Meilan, you're beautiful."

She smiled and blushed.

"Thank you. It's the only dressy dress I have. I'll have to get some western style clothes. My mother insisted I bring this dress. But, it worked out because otherwise I wouldn't have anything to wear tonight."

"Your mother couldn't have been more right. Nothing you can buy would match what you have on."

She blushed again. Her innocent manner was very appealing.

I took the corsage from the box and pinned it on her dress. She thanked me and gave me another kiss on the cheek. It was worth every penny. Sorta like a prom date.

She turned and motioned to a young lady standing behind her. A pretty girl with dark brown hair and large brown eyes. She wore the top of a baseball uniform with the number nine on it. It had a San Francisco Giant logo on the upper left side of the shirt. She was in shorts and barefooted. Painted red toenails. The coeds at Mills were as lovely as the ones I remembered from USC. Or was it just that I was at the age when all young coeds looked beautiful?

Meilan pulled her toward me.

"This is Sue, my roommate."

"Hello, Sue." I extended my hand. She shook it, smiling.

"I've heard all about you. Meilan talks a lot about you."

"Well, I'm really not as bad as some people say I am."

Both girls laughed and looked at each other. They giggled some more.

"It's all good, believe me," Sue said. "The corsage is beautiful. I should be so lucky to have someone give me one."

"Oh, I'm sure you have one or two who will."

She stood with her hands behind her and finally said, "Well, you guys better get going. Nice to finally meet you."

"My pleasure."

Meilan gave her the smile and a nod. It was a girl thing and only they seem to understand what that meant.

"See you later."

"Bye. Have a wonderful dinner." Sue gave us a royal side to side wave of her hand and watched us leave the building.

It was a pleasant night and traffic into the city wasn't too bad. I parked in the underground garage and we took the elevator to the street level floor. From there we rode to the 20th floor and transferred to the express elevator that zipped up to the restaurant on the top floor.

We were seated near the large glass wall on the east side and had a magnificent view of the city, looking toward the Bay Bridge. Wisps of white fog floated by. She was excited and enjoying the evening.

The waiter brought us menus and asked, "Would you care for a cocktail?" He avoided looking at Meilan.

Meilan wasn't twenty-one so if she ordered a drink she would be hard put to show any identification proving she was of age. The Carnelian Room was not about to serve minors and the waiter knew she was under the age limit. As everyone else in the room, he might have wondered how someone as old as I would be with someone as young as Meilan. But, he wasn't hostile, so he must have guessed it was a family thing.

"The young lady will have a glass of ginger ale and I want a single malt scotch, neat."

The waiter breathed a sigh of relief, nodded, and went to fetch the drinks.

He brought the drinks and withdrew, giving us more time to look over the menu.

"Here's to you," I said and raised my glass.

She held her glass up and smiled. She wasn't really interested in the ginger ale.

"You know, I don't know what to call you," she said.

"Anything without a title. No titles please."

"Well, I've thought about it and you're younger than my father and obviously, older than I am. If I treat you as if you were from my parents' generation, I would have to be more formal – like I am with my Dad's friends. So, I thought you could sorta be like family – closer to my generation. I can call you *shu fu*."

"Well, I am younger than your father and definitely not young enough to be in your generation. But, if you feel comfortable thinking of me as an uncle, *shu fu* is just fine."

"Oh, good. That way we can be kind of related and also be good friends."

"I'm your friend whatever you call me."

"Thank you. I'm relieved that's settled." She looked around the room. "It's so exciting to come to the city for dinner. Sue said this was a very classy restaurant."

"It's a good one. The real treat is the view of the city at night."

"That's what Sue said. I think she's been here."

"There are lots of nice places in the city and I'm sure you'll see most of them before too long."

"Well, I don't know anyone who will take me. Except you, of course."

"Oh, there will be others."

"You think so?"

"I know so."

"Really?"

"Really."

She was a winner. Her girlish charm was most disarming and one could so easily fall under her spell. I wondered if she knew what effect she had on people, especially men. Yeah, I think she knew. She'll use her beguiling ways to get her way with many things. That was okay, as long as she played the game straight. I thought she would.

It was a simple but elegant menu and Meilan took her time and read it from cover to cover.

After a time, I asked, "Do you mind if I ordered appetizers?"

"Sure. Anything is fine."

The waiter sensed that we were ready. He came to the table with pad in hand and stood waiting for me to order.

"We'll start with a small antipasto platter. Prosciutto, pastrami, roasted peppers, marinated mushrooms, olives, and artichoke hearts."

I didn't think the pig's feet and other exotic items were necessary. The waiter nodded and wrote on his pad.

"And the Caesar salad we'll share." I looked at her and asked, "Have you decided what you want?"

"Yes. I would like the squab."

"A good choice," the waiter said. He approved of her choice and was ready to help all he could, as most men would be. "And you, sir?"

"I'm going to have the rack of lamb. Medium rare."

"Another good choice." He nodded and collected the menus. Then he asked, "Would you care for wine with dinner?"

The waiter turned his eyes up and pursed his lips.

"Yes. I'll have a glass of Pinot Noir. And please bring me an extra glass?"

He nodded and smiled a "yes sir."

It was a beautiful night and we looked at the city lights and sparkling lights on the Bay Bridge. The view was extra special that night.

She told me about the classes she was taking. A good sign she had adjusted to the American college scene was the stories she told of typical dorm antics. She was a foreign student who fitted in nicely with her American classmates.

The waiter brought the wine. The glass was almost full. He set an extra glass next to mine, as if it were the customary thing to do and left. I poured half of my wine into the glass and passed it over to her. Her eyes opened wide and she flicked her eyes to the left and right. Then she grinned.

In America and Europe, most young women her age would have had wine at home or at a family dinner. But, she was from China and brought up in a traditional house. I thought it was time all that changed.

"Here's to you and your success," I toasted her.

I raised my glass toward her and she touched my glass with hers.

"Thank you." She smiled and took a sip of the wine. "My first real glass of wine."

"There's time for everything. No need to rush."

"I know. And I'm glad you will help me."

"Well, I'm not going to be there for all the wonderful events of your young life. Many things will come to you in time and you'll have to handle them yourself. But, I'm always here to help, whenever you need me."

"I don't think my parents would be that liberal."

"They shouldn't be and you shouldn't expect them to be so easy. They love you and want the best for you."

"You know you sound just like an uncle would sound."

"You'll have to get used to me."

"I already have. And I'm glad you're that way."

The waiter brought the antipasto I requested arranged on a three tiered plate stand. The prosciutto and pastrami were excellent. Meilan took a taste of everything. She enjoyed it all.

The Caesar salad was almost a meal in itself. The waiter mixed it on a cart wheeled next to the table. He was showing off for Meilan and went through the ritual of tossing the ingredients in the air for her benefit. She was the center of attention. Something she would have to become accustomed to.

She watched with great interest as the waiter performed. Then she turned and gave me that beautiful smile that will melt a thousands hearts. Ah, I thought, just twenty years too late.

"Tell me, how did the quarter end?"

"I had a four point GPA."

"Wow! That's great. Have you told your parents?"

"Yes. They called yesterday. I also told them you were taking me to dinner. My mother was worried that I didn't have a formal dress to wear."

"You look lovely. The dress will cause many people to stare. In fact there are some in this dinning room who have been admiring you."

"Oh? Really, do I look okay?"

She looked slyly around the room, smiling. She played the part well.

"You look just fine. Your mother didn't have to worry about anything. But, the four point GPA is just great."

"Well, I got an A- in my English lit class."

"Hey, an A is an A. With or without the minus."

"I know. But, I'm going to get all straight A's this quarter. Some A pluses too."

"I know you will. How's everything else going?"

"Everything is fine. The people in the dorm are great. The instructors are all very helpful."

"Have you been able to get away from the campus? Meet people who aren't students at Mills?"

"You mean have I met any boys," she grinned.

"Well, there is that. Lot of them around."

She looked down and hesitated. Then she looked up at me and smiled. So, she's met someone.

"There is this one guy who I met at a joint computer science meeting between Mills and Stanford. He was with the group that came over for a daylong conference. He's in his second year. He's a computer science major."

"When was this?"

"About a month ago."

"Have you seen him since?"

"Once. He asked me if he could come to visit and I said yes. He came back and we went out for coffee. We spent a couple of hours just talking. But, I haven't been on a date with him or anything like that."

"Do you like him?"

"He's very nice. Sue met him when he came over. She thinks he's hot."

"Hot?" I laughed. "I guess that's good."

"His name is Andrew. Andrew Parker. People call him Andy."

"Has he asked you out for a date? I mean a real date?"

"Yes."

"And you said what?"

"I said maybe."

"Maybe? And how did he respond to that?"

"He said he would call back and ask again. He called and wanted to go out tonight. I told him I had a date."

"A date?"

"Well, this dinner is sort of like a date."

I laughed and shook my head. She smiled broadly.

"Okay. I count as a date. What did he say?"

"He said he would call me again next week."

"You want to go out with him?"

"I guess I do. But I don't know."

"Maybe you can double date with your roommate. Does she have a boy friend?"

"She knows a couple of guys. She dates once in while. Not every weekend. About once a month."

"That sounds reasonable for a student in a high powered college."

"I guess she and I can work something out. It would make it easier."

"Whatever you do, I know it will be alright. But, if you start to see this Andy on a regular basis, I would like to meet him."

"I knew you would say that. I want you to meet him if things go that way."

"That's fine. Also, know that I will not say anything to your parents about this."

"I appreciate that."

"I'm sure you'll tell your parents about your many friends when you're ready."

"I will."

"Good. I'll probably be going back to Asia soon and if I'm in Guangzhou I'll visit with your parents. I've never met your mother. This time I'll ask to meet her."

"Oh, you'll like her. She talks about you as if she's already met you, but she only knows about you because my father tells her everything. She says she feels better knowing you are here. I know I feel better."

"Always here for you, Meilan. Never doubt that."

We finished the dinner and shared a *tiramisu* with coffee. She talked more about her spring quarter classes and new instructors. Over half of her instructors were women. She was learning more about the library and how to use it.

"I was thinking about getting a bicycle to ride around campus. It'll help me get to classes on time."

"I think that's a good idea."

"I'll ask dad to send me money and then find a bicycle shop."

"I'll get one for you. I'll have one delivered to your dorm in a couple of days."

"Hey! In a couple of days? Wow! That's great. But, are you sure it'll be okay? I mean you'll done so much."

"Not really."

"But, a bicycle. I don't know what my father will say."

"Not to worry. Remember, I'm part of the family now."

"You are part of my family. In this country, you're the only family I have. I'm glad I have you."

I was pleased she felt that way. Being her family was fine with me.

It was a little after eleven-thirty when we got back to the dorm. I walked her to the front entrance. She put her arms around me and gave me a peck on the cheek and a hug.

"Thank you, *shu fu*. I really appreciate all this. You will never know how much."

"My pleasure. Take care and if you need anything call me. Good night, Meilan."

"Good night, *shu fu*."

———————————

Driving home I wondered about this Andrew Parker. I guessed it was her first real opportunity to meet a young man. So he's willing to come all the way across the bay to see her. Lust or just a good guy? Why do I look at the bad side? He's probably an All-American good guy.

There were benefits to being at a women's college. But then again, it might have better if there were male students around as classmates. Whatever, one way or another, she was going to have lots of them around. I hoped she finds the good ones. I didn't want to think about the alternatives.

She was special and I really felt like an uncle. So, add one more to the list that Kam Wah says was my collection of women I felt obligated to help. The "wayward monk" he called me, which I probably was. Wayward monk was better than being a not so successful capitalist.

On Monday I went to a bike shop. It had been about fifteen years since I had even been on a bicycle. As everything else in the world, bicycles had changed. The prices ranged from $350 to $6,000. As a good uncle would, I didn't think a thousand dollar bicycle was what she needed.

The different types and makes were endless. I described to the guy in the shop the bicycle would be used on a college campus and not on mountain trails. He had names for each of them, which meant nothing to me.

There were a few Schwinn brand bicycles and it was a name with which I was familiar. They had a woman's model, seven speeds, with fenders and a rack on the back. Extras included a bag, chain cover, and kick stand. I picked a blue one. It cost $649. I negotiated it down to $585. I also paid cash, which meant he could list the sale for whatever he wanted.

I asked that it be user ready and delivered to her dorm. I wanted him to provide verbal instructions when it was delivered and to make certain she was satisfied. If she did not want it, he was to take it back and she could come to his shop and pick one out. The bicycle could be delivered the following day. That was an extra fifty dollars.

I said I would call him the day after tomorrow to check.

It wasn't easy being an uncle.

4

WHEN I FIRST WENT to Vietnam the business environment was similar to China's about ten years earlier. The paranoia of the Vietnamese leaders didn't help the economy develop with any speed, but in the years since I first went there, things had changed significantly.

Vietnam was a centrally controlled economy attempting to compete against international capitalism while maintaining communist party control over the economy. In spite of the big brother environment, the evolving economic system, and newly created sources of wealth, inevitably led to corruption. In many cases this created obstacles to real commercial progress.

In practical terms, operating in Vietnam meant knowing people who knew how to manipulate the system. It also meant lining the pockets of people who had access to those who sat in smoke filled rooms making the final decisions. Elaborate systems of "shared profits" were designed by experts who had years of experience in such matters. It was a way of life and we all accepted it.

Lan Le Bui, AKA Kevin Le, was my major Vietnam contact. We had worked on a number of projects and developed a solid personal and business relationship. Several years earlier, his father was known as the "Tobacco King" of Vietnam. Kevin was also in the tobacco business but had his cigarettes produced in Thailand. He could speak, read, and write English fluently.

His major value as a business contact was his entrée into various departments of government. He was well known and could get into offices not open to everyone. In the developmental phase Vietnam was experiencing, there was a certain frontier atmosphere and many, such as Kevin, practiced a cowboy style of business.

Kevin was married to a Korean woman and, at the last count, had two children. When they were born, he sent me photos via Email. He was a very proud father. Kevin had social and personal habits of many affluent Asian males, especially when it involved members of the opposite sex. He was also loyal to those he called friend. Fortunately, I was one of them.

I asked him to help with my proposal to remodel an ammunition plant in Vietnam that would produce 9 mm ammunition for domestic use and export. It was a twenty to twenty-five million-dollar project. The income from the sale of ammunition could be well over a million dollars per month. More, if production capabilities were modified to keep up with demand.

The procedure was to first obtain an official introductory form – not always a simple process. The second step was to submit the completed form and a copy of the proposal for further consideration by the appropriate bureau. An even more difficult process. If the proposal was thought to be feasible and would help Vietnam's economy, a meeting was arranged.

A project of meaningful size was classified as a Foreign Direct Investment and could be a joint venture or a hundred percent foreign investment. In more recent times, many projects were totally foreign owned and financed. Yasha's resort/casino project was one of these.

I hoped for a joint venture with the Vietnamese army for the ammunition plant proposal. The funding, technology, and world marketing would come from a Philippine arms company in which Andre was the VP and international marketing director. The Vietnamese would provide the plant, labor, and required certifications. The required forms had been submitted and a meeting with appropriate officials had been approved.

Yasha's resort proposal required a similar process. Kevin sent me a form for Yasha's proposal and I passed it on to her. She called me when she received it.

"This form is ten pages long."

"It shouldn't be too difficult to do. There is one consideration that might be important. Do you have a European branch? Big enough to finance a major project?"

"Well, there are branches, in the UK, Paris, and Germany, but they don't have the money to finance this kind of project on their own."

"Can one take the lead with financial assistance from the parent company?"

"I think so. The one in Hamburg is a good bet. Why is this important?"

"I think it's best to have an entity outside China make the proposal. An all Chinese proposal might not be well received."

"It's no secret the China parent company is involved."

"I know, but the foreign name makes it seem that others are involved. Everyone knows, but it's the façade that's important. Kinda dumb, but we all make believe."

"I see. I'll talk to the board about it."

"When you get it completed, have the Hamburg office send the form to the office in Hanoi. Have your name and title identified as the director of the project. Make certain of that."

"When will we hear from them?"

"I don't know. Depends on what they want to do in the next fiscal year. Also, when the decision makers figure out how they can make a buck."

"Do we offer them something now?"

"No. But, my contact will impress them that the project means big bucks. Speaking of big bucks, have your Shanghai bank get an understanding with Deutsche bank that will allow you to draw up to twenty-five thousand dollars in US dollars via their branch in Vietnam."

"Why the Deutsche bank?"

"I've worked with them before. And I know the manager of the Hanoi branch. They're trustworthy."

"What's this for?"

"To fill the red envelopes and other emergency expenses. You may not need red envelopes for all the people you meet, but there'll be several stages. Each one will send you to the next level. If you're lucky, there'll only be one or two levels. The lower levels won't cost much, but remember it takes money to open the doors."

"Okay. When will you and I meet?"

"Why do we need to meet?"

"So we can plan. We have to plan, don't we?"

"We can plan when and if they ask you to come to talk. Remember to send me a copy of the introductory form you sent to Vietnam."

"I can hand deliver a copy to you in the US."

"Send it UPS. Get to work on the proposal. We've discussed the major points and you should build on those. Just make certain you check the data you use. Shouldn't take more than a week to write the proposal, if that long. Get this done and we might be going to Nam next month."

"I can be in the US in twelve hours."

"Good bye, Yasha."

———

Yasha, AKA Alice to her non-Asian business associates, had become one of my favorite people. She was in Beijing when I was working on the gas mask deal and during that time she and I became good friends. She was a whole lot brighter than others in the business and her career goal was to become a successful business tycoon. She had the financial support of an extremely wealthy Shanghai banker and a giant financial empire.

I didn't have any prior business projects with her and the Vietnam resort proposal was one of the largest I had been involved with. My consulting service for this project was the only source of income I had in the coming year. What I didn't know was that getting involved with Yasha was to become very important to me, in more ways than one.

5

IT WAS ABOUT TWO-THIRTY in the morning when my cell phone woke me up. Who would call at this hour? Callers from overseas knew the time difference. I had a bad feeling about this call. Someone was calling on the cell phone and not on the land line. I looked at the small screen. It was a number in Harbin. It wasn't BJ's number. It had to be Ahn.

"Hello."

"This is Ahn."

I knew it was something about her.

"What is it, Ahn?"

"I have some bad news. Very bad news."

"Tell me."

There was a long moment of silence and I thought the signal had been disrupted.

"Ahn, are you there?"

"Yes. I'm sorry to have to tell you this, but Bi Ju Ma is dead."

"What? What did you say?"

"Bi Ju Ma is dead."

I didn't really understand. Did I hear him correctly?

"Did you say that she is dead?"

"Yes." He paused and sighed. "She was killed in an auto accident."

My mind went blank.

"Hello. Are you there?" he asked.

"Yes. I'm here. Forgive me, but I need a minute."

"Okay. Take your time."

BJ was dead. Stay focused, I told myself. Be calm and focus on the facts. I knew I had to keep talking. I tried to be detached and asked for some information.

"Hello. Ahn? I'm here. When did this happen?"

"Two days ago."

"How did it happen?"

"She was driving her father's car. She was coming back from a visit to Yuan's farm. She went off the road and crashed into a concrete wall."

"Anyone else involved?"

"No. She was the only one in the car."

"Was there another car involved?"

"No. Only her car."

"A single car accident? How did this happen?"

"I don't know."

"How are her parents doing?"

"Having a difficult time. And there is the boy."

"Yes. I know."

"There will be a burial ceremony day after tomorrow."

"I'll come as soon as I can. It'll take me about two days to get there so I'll miss the funeral."

"Let me know when you'll arrive. I'll meet you at the airport."

"Please tell her parents I send my condolences and that I'm coming."

"I will."

"Thanks, Ahn. I'll call as soon as I make arrangements."

"I'm sorry to be the bearer of such bad news."

"Thank you for the call."

———————————

I always called him Ahn – his surname – not by his given Korean name, Ho Kun. Ho Kun Ahn was an up and coming entrepreneur who came to Harbin at a very early age from North Korean. Resourceful and clever, he started with one taxi and now had three taxis and two large trucks. He was married and had two children.

He was a survivor and street smart. He knew everything about the city and about the Korean community in Harbin.

I met him when I came to Harbin last December. Soon I came to rely on him for everything I needed during my visits to Harbin. A very strong bond existed between us and I trusted him with my life.

I sat with the phone in my hand and stared at the wall. The news was so unexpected. I was aware that something happened to her but I couldn't think about her being dead.

I had known her for a little over seven months and our relationship had become serious. I didn't make any commitments and that was alright with her. She said she loved me and she knew this right away because it was her *karma*. She believed our spirits coexisted in harmony, resulting in a state of happiness. That was our *karma*, she said.

But, other forces had interrupted and disrupted that harmony. That was also *karma*. What were those forces that brought her to this end?

Suddenly I felt very weary. I fell into a dejected state and stayed that way for the entire day.

It was late afternoon when the cell phone chimed. Was Ahn calling again? I picked up the receiver, unsure of what to expect.

"Hello."

"Hey. Thought you might be out. But I let it ring hoping you were coming out of the shower or something. How are ya?"

It was Megan.

"Well, I've had better days."

"What's the matter?"

"Some really bad news today."

"What?"

"My friend in Harbin is dead."

"Oh, no. My God, I'm sorry. What happened?"

"All I know is that she died in an auto accident."

"Auto accident?"

She was silent for a long moment.

"You're going to Harbin, aren't you?"

"Yes."

"When will you leave?"

"As soon as I can work things out."

"Is there something I can do?"

"Not much anyone can do."

"When did you hear?"

"About two this morning."

"God, I am sorry."

"Well, I have to get myself together."

"Will you call me before you go?"

"I'll try."

"If you can't I understand. But, promise you'll call me when you get back."

"I promise."

"I know she really meant something to you. If I can help, please let me know."

"Thanks."

"Call me."

"I will."

———————

Megan was from Chicago and I met her in Guangzhou last year. She was on her first trip to China and was getting her business together. She brought small business people to the Fair and they purchased a variety of consumer items they sold in their shops in Chicago malls. She needed some help with the intricate business maze and I was able to provide some assistance. The last time I saw her was at the Spring Canton Trade Fair.

She was an unusual woman who was just emerging as an independent person. Her family was very wealthy and she didn't have to earn a living, but she wanted to do something of value. Coming to China was her escape from what she believed was a meaningless life.

We started a friendship that became one of those surprise happenings. What might have been never got started because I met BJ. Megan was from another part of American society and I didn't know how our different worlds could coexist. But we remained very good friends. Well, actually more than good friends.

6

THERE WAS NEVER A doubt about going to Harbin. I had to go
and find out what happened. It was something I had to do.
To do this I had to think in more practical terms. To get
to Harbin I needed some cash. My only potential source of income
was Yasha – based on my promise to help with her resort proposal in
Vietnam. Payment for my consulting services would include expenses
and fifteen hundred dollars a day. I could ask her for an advance.

Given the time difference, it was about ten o'clock in the morning
in Shanghai. I figured she would be at her office at the corporate
headquarters. I called the number on her name card.

"Hi. I knew it was you. Your name and number flashed on the
screen."

"Hello, Yasha. How are you?"

"Getting things in order for our trip to Vietnam. I sent a copy of the
proposal with the application form. So hoping to hear soon."

"Well, it's one reason I'm calling."

"Are you going to back out of this?"

"Calm down, Yasha. If you can do what I ask, going to Vietnam
will be an absolute certainty."

"You had me worried there for a second. So, what is it you're going
to ask me?"

"I have a personal problem and need about five thousand dollars now. You can deduct this from my consultant fees. I'll sign a note or contract or whatever you want. But, I promise, we will go to Nam."

"You have a personal problem? What kind of personal problem? Are you going to tell me or are you going to say it's none of my business?"

"If you can give me the money I need, you have a right to know what it's for. I have to be in Harbin as soon as I can get there. It has to do with a person who was very close to me."

"Was?"

"She died several days ago."

"She?" There was a long pause. "Was she your woman?"

"Yasha, I don't have a woman. But, she was very close to me."

"I see." She didn't say or ask anything else. "Of course, you can have the money. More if you need more. Just tell me."

"Thanks, Yasha. I just need enough to get a plane ticket and expenses for a couple of days in Harbin."

"I can arrange your plane tickets. I'll get you on Air China from San Francisco to Shanghai and then a connecting flight to Harbin."

"I don't want to burden you with all this. If you send the money via bank transfer I can buy the ticket here."

"No. It's quicker for me to do it. I can use the company account."

"Okay. Whatever you can do will be appreciated."

"I'll send an Email with the flight schedule."

"I appreciate this, Yasha. I'll make it up to you."

"Well, finally something you need me for." She paused. "I want to help."

"Your help is gratefully accepted."

"What time is best for you?"

"I want to be in Harbin as soon as I can. I have a visa, so I can leave anytime."

"Alright. I'll be in touch in a couple of hours."

"Thank you."

"Just take care," she said. "You mean a lot to me."

"You mean a lot to me also, but remember what I said about us."

"I remember. But, that isn't going to stop how I feel."

"Let's not get into that right now."

"It's how I feel."

"Do I have to start calling you Alice?"

"God, I hope not."

"So, I'll look for your Email."

"It's how I feel."

"Behave, Yasha."

"Regardless of what you say, that's how I feel."

"Get the plane reservations, Yasha."

"In a couple of hours."

"Thanks."

"You asked me for help, so you remembered we're friends."

"Yeah. We're friends." I couldn't help but smile. She was something else.

It was one of many times when Yasha would come to my rescue. Without her, my life would have been in continuous state of chaos.

Without any questions or explanations, she was willing to help me get to Harbin. She didn't make an issue about my relationship with other women and it didn't effect how she felt about me. I was trying to keep our relationship on a friendship basis but she wanted something different. I told her that wasn't going to happen. But, that didn't deter her. She had plans of her own.

In ninety minutes, I received an Email from her telling me I had First Class reservations on an Air China flight leaving SFO at 1:19 PM the next afternoon. I assumed her company had some pull with the airline. I was scheduled to arrive in Shanghai at 6:45 PM the next day. I was also booked First Class on an Eastern China flight that left Shanghai at 9:00 PM and arrived in Harbin at 11:50 PM. She said she would meet me at the Pohong airport. Yasha was an organizer.

I called my children to let them know I would be overseas for a week or so. I also called Megan and told her I was leaving the next day and promised her I would call when I returned.

I caught up with Kam Wah in Hong Kong.

"I called to tell you I'm coming to China."

"Are you coming to Guangzhou?"

"No. I'm flying into Shanghai and then go to Harbin. Be there for about three or four days."

"Why are you going to Harbin?"

"My very close friend was killed in an accident."

He was silent for a minute and I could hear him lighting a cigarette.

"Is it the Manchu lady you told me about?"

"Yes."

There was another minute of silence while he smoked and thought about me and my Manchu lady.

"After Harbin, come to Guangzhou. I will be there."

"I'll try to make it."

"Don't just try. Come to Guangzhou. You need anything? You have money?"

"Yes."

"I expect to see you in Guangzhou. Call me when you arrive in Harbin."

"I will."

"Remember to call me."

"I will.

I would return via Guangzhou from Harbin because Kam Wah's counsel was always welcome. And I needed all the help I could get.

Kam Wah and I were as close as brothers might be. We had traveled all over China, visiting places in the western interior provinces that didn't have paved roads as well as most of the major cities in China. Two years ago we went around the world on a business fact finding trip. It began in San Francisco with a stopover in Frankfurt then on to Moscow, St. Petersburg, Hamburg, and Berlin before coming back to Hong Kong. We didn't make much money, but we certainly learned a lot.

We were in Moscow and St. Petersburg just before the collapse of the Soviet government. The decayed state of the government and society in general was apparent. Looking at the empty shelves and long lines at the markets and other places, I wondered why America was in constant fear of the Evil Empire. It was neither evil nor an empire. Russia was just a place where a lot of people were trying to survive. Not too unlike other places.

7 ————————————

WHILE I WAS PACKING and getting ready to go to the airport, a draft copy of Yasha's resort proposal arrived via special UPS delivery. I spent an hour going over the document. It was very well done. The final finished copy should be impressive.

It was my first time on a transpacific Air China flight. I usually flew China Air that stopped at Taipei and then on to Hong Kong or other cities in Asia. People were often confused about Air China and China Air. Air China was the national airline of the People's Republic of China and China Air was the national airline of the Republic of China, Taiwan. There was a world of difference.

It was a little less luxurious than First Class on Taiwan's China Air, but was very comfortable. The food was not as good as China Air and scotch was not available, but they had some good Chinese wine.

I tried to sleep but couldn't. Thinking about her was all I could do. I went from being depressed to an angry state of mind and the flight attendant knew I wasn't a happy camper. Still they tried to make my trip comfortable. First Class passengers on most airlines are pampered by the flight attendants whether they're amiable travelers or not. Flight attendants had a tough job.

————————————

The spectacular airport at Pohong easily matched the ones in Hong Kong, Singapore, or airports anywhere in the world. It was one of the showcases of the new China and its growing power.

Yasha was waiting for me at the arrival gate. She gave me a hug and peck on the cheek.

"How was the flight?"

"It was fine. They need some imagination with their food and better selection of drinks, but it was fine."

She tilted her head and frowned.

"Don't mind me. I'm just bitching. It was a very good flight."

"You look tired." She grabbed my arm. "Let's go to the VIP lounge."

She led the way into the lounge and we found seats in a corner, away from the central seating area. At the refreshment counter she got a cup of hot green tea and I found a bottle of Tsingtao beer. We sat without much conversation.

"I didn't know if you wanted to come back to Shanghai or go to Beijing, so I left your return open. Actually, I didn't know when you wanted to come back."

"That reminds me. I have to call my contact in Harbin and let him know when my flight gets in."

"You can use my cell phone."

"Thanks, but I have my China cell phone."

I dug out my China cell phone from my bag and called Ahn.

"Been waiting for your call."

"I'm coming in at 11:50 PM on Eastern China from Shanghai. Sorry it's late at night."

"Not a problem. I'll get you a hotel."

"Not the Victory this time."

The Victory Hotel was where BJ and I had spent our time.

"Okay."

"You have my China cell phone number?"

"Yes."

"Good. See you tonight."

I shut the cell phone and stared at it. I was going back to Harbin and she wouldn't be there.

"You okay?" Yasha touched my arm.

"Yeah. Now, as to my return, I'm going to Guangzhou before I go back home, so I'll just go straight there."

"I'll meet you in Guangzhou."

"Not necessary. I won't be staying more than a day."

"Whatever, I'll be there," she said firmly.

I didn't give her an argument. After all, she was paying for this.

"What are you going to do in Harbin?"

"The burial will be over, so I'll meet with her parents and a few friends."

"Just that? No business."

"This is not a business trip. As I said, it's personal."

"You never mentioned this woman before. How long have you known her?"

"Not very long." I thought a moment. "I've known you as long as I knew her."

"I met you last December in Guangzhou. That's only about seven months ago. I guess she was special to you."

"Yes, she was."

"Will you tell me about her?"

"Not now."

"That's okay." She hesitated. "I want you to know I'm sorry."

"Thank you. I really appreciate your concerns."

We sat for a while and looked out the window, watching the planes landing and taking off. She reached over and took my hand. This had not been a usual part of our relationship, but I felt better holding her hand. We held hands and didn't talk for a while.

———————

"I sent you a copy of the final draft. Have you had time to look at it?"

"Haven't had time to really study it. Just a brief glance, but, what I saw was good. It has some very good ideas and it's well organized. I think the Vietnamese will be impressed. It'll be expensive, but if that's what your bosses want, they should know it will cost."

"So far there haven't been any objections. Do you have any suggestions?"

"Send a first class finished copy to Hanoi. Also, prepare about a half a dozen copies of the proposal to take with you. Find a real language expert who can translate it all into Vietnamese. Make it very professional and printed on good paper. The cover must be first class. You might put the Vietnamese flag on the cover. Pin your name card on the cover and have it very prominently displayed on the title page. Try to keep the final copy around forty pages. Some illustrated pictures of the proposed resort will help. Also have a couple of copies printed in English. That will be the neutral language, in case there's a question about definitions. Send a copy in English and Vietnamese to Hanoi. I'm sure you'll have some printed in Chinese for your people in the company. Do not take a Chinese copy to Vietnam."

"Anything else?"

"Yes. Have name cards printed for me with my name and title as an advisor for your company. In English and Vietnamese. Use the same format as you do for your own name card."

"You want a title as an officer in the company?"

"No. I'm only a consultant, not an employee of the company. You're the boss in this affair. After this first go around, I doubt that you'll need me."

"I'll always need you," she said softly. "You trust your contact in Vietnam?"

"I trust him as much as I trust you. He'll set up meetings and introduce you to certain people. But, remember, neither he nor I can guarantee anything will happen."

"You do a lot of business with him?"

"Yes. Have done business with him for years."

"I really feel good about this."

"So do I. You do your part and things will work out."

"How long will you stay in Harbin?"

"I don't know. But, I'll call you and let you know."

"I can come to wherever you will be."

"No need."

"You might need me. I can help."

"We'll see."

"Well, I have three thousand US dollars for you." She reached into her bag and extracted an envelop. If you need more, let me know."

"With the airfare, I'm using up my consulting fee."

"Not to worry."

"Thanks, Yasha. Plane leaves at nine. I'll have to find the gate."

"I think it's two gates over."

"Well, better get going."

———————————————

When we got to the departure gate she put her arms around my neck and kissed me. It wasn't just a peck on the cheek. It was a real kiss. That was a surprise, a very pleasant surprise, but still a surprise. Should I put a stop to this or did I suddenly need care and comfort from someone like her?

"Call me," she said.

"I will."

I watched her walk away. She turned and waved. Was this another situation over which I was losing control?

8 ———————————

I HAD THE CHICKEN dinner and Tsingtao beer. It was pretty good for airline food. I tried to relax and think what I would do in Harbin. I would go see her parents, which was the most difficult part. I also wanted to find out exactly what happened and how she died. For that information I had to see police Superintendent Hong. We didn't part on good terms when I last saw him. I had to eat humble pie and make amends. I didn't know if he would talk to me.

The plane was delayed so the plane arrived in Harbin International Airport at midnight. Otherwise, it was an uneventful flight. I was one of two First Class passengers and the one flight attendant had time to be more than attentive.

———————————

Ahn was waiting at the gate. He had a grim look as he shook my hand and gave me a hug.

"It's not a good time," he said.

"No, it isn't."

"I booked you into the Shangri-La Hotel this time."

"Thanks. How is your schedule for the next few days?"

"As before, I'm here when you need me."

"Thank you, Ahn."

"How long do you plan to stay?"

"I don't know. Did the burial go well?"

"Yes."

"I hope her parents are okay."

"They're doing as well as can be expected. She had lots of relatives and they were all there. They know you're coming."

"I'll try to see Mulan and her father before I leave."

"You want to go out there?"

"We'll see. One person I want to see is police Superintendent Hong. He can give me the official version of what happened. I'll try to meet with him tomorrow. Have you found out anything about this accident?"

"Not too much. All I know is that her car crashed into a concrete wall."

"She was a good driver, wasn't she? She didn't drive when I was here, but I assume she had driving experience."

"She's probably been driving since she was a teenager."

"The road she was on was the same road we took when we went to Yuan's farm, right?"

"Yes."

"I remember it's a good road."

"Yes, it is."

"You said she ran into a wall. What kind of wall?"

"It's one of those concrete walls that are on top of tunnels that goes under the road. You know, to let the water flow from one side to the other. Helps control flooding in the rainy season."

"She must have been traveling very fast. I can't imagine her speeding. Did a tire blow out?"

"Not that I heard. There might have been some kind of mechanical break down in the car. Steering wheel or something like that. Maybe the gas pedal stuck."

"Hong should know. The police have the car now, right?"

"Yes."

"So, they must have checked it out. They should know something."

"There has been no word from the police about these things."

"Then, I'll have to ask."

While Ahn parked the taxi, I went into the hotel and registered. My room was on the seventh floor. The Shangri-La room was an upgrade from the one I had at the Victory hotel. It had a well-stocked mini-bar and a king size bed. Very comfortable. The gym was on the eleventh floor.

I opened a mini-bottle of gin and drank most of it in one swallow. I opened another bottle. I was tired and feeling down. I tried to freshen up with cold water in my face. It really didn't help.

I met Ahn in the lobby and we went into the hotel coffee shop. They were closed, but no one objected to us using a table.

"I'll call her parents tomorrow morning and see if they are okay with a visit about ten or so."

"I'll be here about ten."

"If you can, make it a little earlier. I want to get a plant. Do you know where I can get a good sized flower pot?"

"Yes. No problem. We can pick one up on the way."

"Good. In the afternoon, I want to meet with Hong."

"He may be surprised you're calling him."

"I have to make amends. I wasn't very pleasant the last time we met. In fact, when we parted he was very angry."

"He will not easily forget."

"I know. I'll have to beg a little."

"Maybe beg a lot."

I sighed. "Yeah. A lot. Whatever it takes, I want to know why she crashed into that concrete wall. I hope Hong will have some answers. He seemed to be a competent police officer and he would ask the same questions we're asking. I only hope he will be willing to share his information."

"If he doesn't, we might look for someone else to ask."

"Who?"

"Maybe there's someone who works in the police department who has seen a report or has heard something."

"Do we know someone?"

"I'll ask around."

"If you do, do it as quietly as possible. I don't want to get Hong all up in arms."

"He won't know."

"I don't know where all this will lead, Ahn. It may be a dead end or it can become very involved."

"I know."

"Don't get yourself into a bind. This is my problem and I don't want you, or anyone else, to suddenly have troubles."

"Well, if there was something wrong with her death, some of us think it's our problem too."

"That's good to know."

"Well, I have to get going. I was on the late night shift tonight."

"I'm sorry. I forget you're working."

"No problem. I'll see you tomorrow."

It was after one when I bid Ahn good night. I went to the hotel lounge for a drink. The stools at the bar each had a short back rest and were built for comfortable sitting. Facing out was the usual mirror with rows of liquor bottles lined in front.

The bartender was getting ready to close the bar. I introduced myself and noted his name tag had Paul printed on it. I asked if he was Korean. He was. He said his surname was Yim and he had adopted his English name while a student at the university. The bartender at the Victory Hotel was also Korean. Were all bartenders in Harbin Korean? Why not?

"Sorry, but it's time to close."

"I just got in from a long flight and need a night cap. Can I get one before you shut down?"

"Okay, one while I clean up."

If I wasn't Korean I wouldn't have gotten a drink. Was that racist rationale?

I remembered a Japanese single malt scotch made by Suntory.

"A couple of months ago, I had a single malt scotch made by Suntory. Do you have that?"

"Yes. But we also have another single malt. Brand name is *Yoichi,* made in Hokkaido by Nikka distillery. It's twenty-five years old. Want to try that?"

"Okay. I'll have one. Neat."

It cost a fortune. I took a sip and then a real swallow. It was worth every penny.

I stared at my tired reflection in the mirror. I was in Harbin again and she was not here. I continued to wonder about her death. A one-car accident explanation was too simplistic. It would be more reasonable if another vehicle were involved. What difference did it make? Would knowing the cause make her death easier to accept?

Paul finished his chores and said, "Time to close shop."

"A quick one for the road."

"This is it."

"Thanks."

He poured another drink and put the bottle away. I finished the drink in one gulp. The trans Pacific jet lag and drinks were taking their toll. Paul looked at me and probably thought he shouldn't have given me the last drink. He knew I had been drinking before I came into the bar. I put up my hand.

"I'm okay. That was a helleva scotch, Paul. Can you put all this on my room tab?"

"Sure. No problem."

He watched me with some concern as I made my way out of the bar and to the elevators. I think I was weaving. With some effort I made it to my room. I took my shoes off and fell on to the bed. In a few minutes I fell asleep with my clothes on. So much for my return to Harbin. BJ would not have been pleased with me.

9

I MADE IT TO the gym a few minutes before eight in the morning. I started slowly on the tread machine and worked my way up to a fast walk. I stopped several times and drank some water. Alcohol dehydrates the body and I was plenty dry. After an hour or so of this torture I went back to my room and stood under a hot shower for twenty minutes. I made some coffee and finished my morning routine with a shave using a razor provided by the hotel. The electric shaver just didn't do it.

I put clothes in the laundry bag and called for housekeeping to pick it up. One of the great services of major hotels in Asia was the laundry service. If they picked it up before ten you could be assured of clean clothes by six that evening. This included dry cleaning.

It was after nine in the morning, so it was reasonable to assume that Hong was at his desk. I dialed the hotel operator and asked to be connected with police headquarters. A telephone receptionist answered the call. I said I wanted to speak with Superintendent Hong. She asked me who I was and the nature of my business. I gave her my name and told her Hong would know who I was. She asked me to wait. In a minute Hong answered his line.

"Welcome back to Harbin."

"Thank you."

"I was told you arrived last night. I guessed you would be coming to Harbin. I'm sorry about Ms. Ma."

"Thank you."

"What can I do for you?"

"I need your help."

"My help? As I remember, you did not want my help before."

He remembered. Time to grovel a little.

"Please accept my apologies for my behavior the last time I was here. I was wrong and I acted badly. But, this is a different situation."

He was silent for a minute. I imagined he was wondering whether he should accept my apology.

"What kind of help?"

"I want to know how and why Ms. Ma was killed."

"She died in an auto accident. She's been buried. What more is there to know?"

"It'll be easier for me to accept her death if I knew something about the incident. Get the closure I need."

Another moment of silence. I hoped he was a reasonable man. Fortunately, he was.

"I will meet with you, but in an unofficial capacity."

"I understand. Can we meet this afternoon at the Shangri-La hotel lobby?"

"At three o'clock."

"Thank you. I'll see you at three."

What did unofficial capacity mean?

I called Kam Wah to let him know I had arrived in Harbin. He always wanted to know where I was in China. I think he was worried I would get in some kind of trouble because of my American habits and attitudes. He would feel better if I was more Chinese in thought and action. Of course, being Chinese meant being his version of what a Chinese should be.

"How long do you intend to stay in Harbin," he asked.

"I don't know. A day or two."

"What do you plan to do?"

"I will visit her parents."

"Is that all?"

"I don't know. Depends on a number of things. I want to find out how she died."

"Find out? What is there to find out?"

"I won't know until I ask."

"Who will you ask?"

"Anyone who will talk to me."

"You said she was killed in an auto accident. What is there to find out? Why are you doing this?"

"I want to know what happened."

"Do you think something is wrong?"

"I don't know."

"The police must have investigated the accident. Have they said there was something wrong?"

"I haven't asked them yet."

"I see."

He was silent and I could hear him lighting a cigarette.

"I have to know what happened, Kam Wah. She was very special to me. I have to find out."

Another moment of silence. He puffed on his cigarette.

"Do not do anything foolish. Ask nicely. Not wise to upset the authorities. Remember, if something happens, the closest influence I have is Beijing."

"I'm just going to ask what happened."

"Call me when you are ready to come back. Do you need anything? You have money?"

He always asked whether I needed money.

"I'm fine, Kam Wah. Thanks. I'll call in a day or so."

"Be careful. Remember, you're in China."

"I will."

I called the Ma house and asked if I could come to visit in a couple of hours. Mrs. Ma said I was welcome any time. Seeing them was not going to be easy.

I went down to the restaurant and ordered bacon and two eggs, over easy. A big breakfast for me. As I was finishing breakfast, Ahn came into the restaurant.

"Did you get a good nights rest?" he asked.

"I had a few drinks last night and overslept."

"Good. You looked beat last night."

"Want some coffee or something to eat?"

"No thanks. Had breakfast a couple of hours ago."

"Guess I'm going to be late for a meeting with the Ma family. Well, better late than never. You know a place to get a plant and some flowers?"

"Yes. There's a place near by."

I signed for the bill and followed Ahn through the lobby and out to his taxi. It was a nice day. Warm and sunny. We stopped at a shop that had a good assortment of plants and flowers. They catered to tourists so the plants were fresh. I picked a plant called Astrantia – Star of Summer. I also bought a bouquet of mixed flowers.

Armed with these tokens of sympathy we went to BJ's home. I didn't have to apologize for being late. It didn't matter. Mrs. Ma gave me a hug and cried a little when she saw the flowers. I shook Mr. Ma's hand and did the same with BJ's son, who only vaguely remembered me. He was holding the toy truck I had given him.

Mrs. Ma invited us into the living room where she served tea and biscuits. I ate one of the biscuits and sipped the green tea. She said how much BJ thought of me and how they all looked forward to my visits. I had only been there twice, but she made it sound as if I had dropped by on a weekly basis. Mr. Ma said he was honored that I had come all the way from America to pay my respects.

"You know Meiling came for the funeral. She flew up from Singapore," Mrs. Ma said. "She talked about you and Bi Ju. She is very sad for you."

She looked down at her hands. I held her hand while she softly cried. After a few minutes, she looked up at me and smiled. She patted my hand and blotted her eyes with a small handkerchief.

I took a deep breath and wished I knew what to say to comfort her. Nothing was ever going to be the same in this house. I tried to fight off the dispirited feelings and thought of more practical things. I asked Mr. Ma about the car BJ was driving.

"Was the car an older model?"

"No. Not that old. A good Nissan four door sedan. It was only five years old. I bought it over a year ago. The company I work for sells their used cars to company employees. The company mechanic there looked after it for me and we had it completely checked just three months ago."

"Did Bi Ju drive it often?"

"Yes. When I did not take it to work, she often drove herself to school, and when she went shopping. She visited many of her friends and drove to her cousin Mulan's farm at least twice a month."

"I guess she was an experienced driver."

"Oh yes. Bi Ju has been driving since she was fifteen. She drove in all kinds of weather. Even when it was snowing. Bi Ju was a good driver."

"Do you have any idea what might have caused that accident?"

"There's no reason I can think of. It was night, but the road is good and there are lights on the road. It wasn't raining and the weather was clear. The tires were almost new. And she doesn't drive fast. She has never driven fast."

Mrs. Ma looked from her husband to me. Her eyes wondered why I was asking these questions. We all sat quietly sipping our tea. No one said anything for a while.

My thoughts were on the car. Nissans were reliable vehicles and thousands were used as taxis in all major Chinese cities. She was driving a five year old company car that was well maintained.

Mrs. Ma poured more tea and said, "We're having a family gathering tomorrow afternoon. Please come. The rest of the family will want to meet you. And that includes you too, Mr. Ahn."

Ahn smiled and said he would come.

"Thank you, I will," I said.

We stayed for about an hour and half, talking about nothing in particular and occasionally Mrs. Ma would comment on something BJ did or said. I finally said I had to get going. They walked us to the door. She grabbed my arm and pulled me back. She had tears in her eyes. She took my hand and looked up at me.

"You were the one for her. She loved you very much. I think of you as my son, even though you and she were not married."

"I'm honored that you think of me as a son."

"She is buried with the necklace and ring you gave her. She never took off the ring. She wore it always. I thought it should stay with her forever."

"So do I."

"When I think of her I will think of you," she said.

"Thank you. Please take care."

She hugged me. I put my arms around her and whispered, "I will make this right."

She looked at me, puzzled at what I said. I couldn't explain what I meant because I didn't know myself.

Fortunately, I didn't have to explain myself when Mr. Ma took my hand.

"Thank you for coming," he said.

What did I mean when I said I would make things right? The sadness and loss felt by her parents reinforced my feelings that there was something I should do. What that was, I didn't know. I only knew she was a beautiful person and should not have died alone in an auto accident.

As I got into the taxi, I looked back at them standing at the door. Chu Yen crowded between them and waved at me. I wondered how life would have been if I had stayed in Harbin to live with BJ.

I hoped Hong would have some answers. If he wouldn't tell me what he knew, I would have to find out myself. But, this was Harbin and there were lots of people who wouldn't want a foreigner nosing into things. On my side there was Ahn and myself. We were definitely outnumbered.

We decided to have a quick lunch in the hotel restaurant. There was a crowd at the buffet luncheon, many locals, as well as hotel guests. I had a salad and chicken rice, a favorite Singapore dish. It was not genuine Singaporean, but close enough.

"According to Mr. Ma the car was in good shape."

"I have three taxis and two trucks. Two of my taxis are Nissans. They're good cars. And Mr. Ma's company mechanic would know how to keep a car well maintained. Especially if the car owner is a manager in the company."

"So, right now the only thing we know for certain is that the car was in good working order. She was certainly not a reckless driver. There has to be another reason her car crashed into that concrete wall."

"What other reason?"

"Someone else could have been involved," I said.

"Who would want to harm her?"

"The only unusual thing about her was her relationship with me. Is someone trying to get at me by killing her?"

"You mean the North Koreans?" he asked.

"When I was here a couple of months ago we talked about double agents and immigrants who might be working for the North Korean police."

"Yes. But not only the North Koreans. Remember the American agent? He was also using Koreans for his own purposes."

"Everybody wants to use the Koreans here," I said.

"You had something to do with the American agent leaving, didn't you?"

"I mentioned him to someone in Beijing. But, the Chinese government won't ask the North Koreans to leave, even if they have a network here."

"I know most of the Koreans here and I don't think anyone has connections to the North Korean police. Of course, it might be someone who has recently arrived."

"Maybe not a recent immigrant. Planted moles can stay inactive for years and are used primarily to get information."

"All of that requires a network. Very secret and carefully controlled."

"Yes. That was what the American agent wanted me to help him with. Create a network."

"But, She was killed. That's more than just getting information."

"Yes, it is. More to think about."

"Well, what do you want to do tonight?"

"I think I'll eat a light dinner at the hotel and try to get to bed early."

"I'll be here around nine in the morning. If you need me tonight, call."

10

I WONDERED HOW MY meeting with Hong would be. Has he forgiven me for my bad attitude? Whatever, I needed his help if I was going to find out what happened to BJ.

I came down to the lobby a few minutes before three. There was a fair amount of people traffic, including some European tourists. I guessed they were German. There were also a few Japanese meeting with local businessmen.

Precisely at three, I saw Hong come into the lobby. I was surprised to see him in mufti. He had on a black suit, white shirt, and no tie. He didn't wear a hat and had on a pair of fashionable sunglasses. He was taller than I remembered. He looked around the lobby and saw me. I rose and extended my hand.

"Hello, Superintendent Hong. I certainly appreciate your taking the time for this meeting."

"Not at all. It's a pleasure to see you again."

Well, his greeting was more congenial than I expected. How much have I misjudged this man?

"May I suggest a cup of coffee?" I said. "I don't know if you have had lunch, but we can get a bite if you wish."

"Thank you, but I've had lunch." He looked around the lobby. "If you don't mind, can we go some place where it is quieter?"

"Of course. Wherever you wish."

He gestured toward the door and led the way to a car parked on the street. It was a Chery four-door sedan, not a police car. I assumed it was his private car.

We drove for about a half an hour and stopped at a small business mall. There were three small shops and a café. The shops included a grocery store and a store that dealt in hardware and other items needed in the home. The smallest was a bicycle repair shop at the end of the complex.

The man behind the counter knew Hong and gave him a knowing nod. Hong nodded back and led the way to a table against the wall, toward the back of the room. Casserole dishes were the major items on the café's menu. It was not a place one would come for just a cup of tea. But apparently it was normal for Hong.

Without ordering it, a pot of tea and two cups were brought to the table. Hong poured the tea and raised his cup.

"Welcome to Harbin."

"Thank you."

"I'm sorry about Ms. Ma."

"That's the reason I wanted to meet. I want to know what happened."

"Her accident is under investigation."

"Can you at least give me some information?" I asked.

He took a deep breath. "It seems you have some powerful friends in Beijing, as well as in Guangzhou. There have been inquiries and requests for information from these people about the Choi matter. The death of Ms. Ma has also become a concern to them because of her relationship with you. More questions have been raised."

Friends in Beijing and Guangzhou could only mean Chang, Lai, and Chief Wu. Hong was talking to me because of the pressure from them. Something I didn't expect, but was grateful for their intervention.

"I didn't know this."

"These people speak on your behalf."

"They are very kind. I appreciate their help."

"Because of their interest, I will, unofficially, tell you what I think happened. Ms. Ma was killed in an auto accident that may have, I say may have, been caused by another vehicle. A large vehicle, like a truck, could have struck the rear of the car she was driving. There were skid marks on the road and the rear of her car was badly damaged."

"You mean someone forced her car into that concrete wall."

"That is conjecture at this point, but very possible," he said.

"If what you say is true, it had to be a very heavy vehicle going at a high rate of speed to push her car into the concrete wall."

"Yes – if that is what happened."

"Do you have any idea who might do this? And why?"

"It had to be someone who knew her car and where she would be that night. As to why – who knows? There could be many reasons."

"Including her association with me."

"It was not a secret that she was your woman."

"I don't claim anyone to be my woman."

"Whatever, it's what everyone believes."

"I didn't think I had enemies here."

"You're right. People in the Korean community think very highly of you."

"The only person I had problems with was Choi and he's not a part of this community."

"And you were implicated in the assassination of Choi."

"Do you think a North Korean agent did this?"

"More probably someone was hired to do it."

"Hired?"

"Yes. And it would be a Korean."

"Why a Korean?" I asked.

"I don't think Koreans would hire Chinese to do this kind of work."

"That's reasonable. Koreans would hire Koreans."

"There is still the question of why. There is no apparent motive or reason for killing her," he said.

"Except her relationship with me."

"But, it would be a mistake to think the North Korean government is directly involved. I don't believe anyone in any official capacity would do any hands-on hiring. The job would be contracted by someone not in the government."

"So there's a network working for the North Korean government."

"Most countries maintain some kind of network in neighboring countries. North Korea has covert agents in China and most certainly in this province because of our proximity to the North Korean border."

"Other countries also play that game."

"Yes. I know about the American agent who wanted you to help establish an intelligence network here."

"Oh?"

"When he was asked to leave, I was the one who gave him the message. The order came from Beijing." He frowned and sighed. "Why didn't you come to me?"

"If you remember we did not have a good working relationship then."

"I was just doing my job. Nothing else."

"I know. I was angry then. I'm sorry about that," I apologized.

"Are you angry now? About Ms. Ma?"

"Yes. I'm angry. I'm angry because I'm beginning to believe this was not an accident. She was targeted because of her relationship with me and my problems with Choi. But why her? Why not kill me? I can be easily reached. My visits to various cities in China are not secret."

"You must remember we are only speculating that Choi's death has any bearing on this. I hope your anger doesn't lead you to misguided action. I am warning you to not pursue any course of action that is in violation of Chinese law. Your friends in Beijing cannot help you if you break the law. It will be even more dangerous if it involves a foreign country."

"I don't intend to break any laws."

"I certainly hope not."

He poured more tea into my cup.

"Well, I'll be here only for another day."

He handed me his name card with a number written on it.

"Here's a telephone number where you can reach me, day or night. If you need me or learn anything, call me."

"By the way, the Ma family is having a family gathering tomorrow. Will you provide some security for them?"

"Yes. I know about the event. We'll be there."

"Good. I'm very pleased we had this talk. It makes things clear."

"I hope you understand everything is supposition. We cannot prove anything."

"Well, at least, you've confirmed who the opposition is."

He started to say something, and then stopped. He heaved a sigh.

"Heed my advice and let the police handle this matter."

He raised his hand at the cook behind the counter, waved, and put some money on the table. The cook waved back. We drove back to the hotel without much conversation.

"I probably won't see before you leave. Have a good trip."

"Thanks. And thank you again for this meeting."

"I think you deserved to know what I know."

"It helps," I said.

"But, not enough?"

"For what happened to her, nothing is enough."

11

I T HAD BEEN OVER six months since I last saw Meiling. She was born in Harbin and has family here so she knew about BJ within hours of her death. She must have caught a flight up immediately after she heard the news.

Meiling had known BJ for many years and introduced me to her. Meiling and I had a special relationship, but it was different from what developed between BJ and me. I often wondered why something didn't happen between us. I supposed it wasn't meant to be. That was our *karma*.

She was expecting my call. For the first few minutes neither of us spoke. I listened to her crying.

"I was going to call you, but I couldn't," she finally said. "I'm sorry."

"That's all right. I understand. I'm glad you were able to come to the funeral."

"How long will you stay?"

"I don't know. A day or so. Not much I can do here."

"I'm so sad about her. I'm also sorry for you. It was a perfect match."

"Bad *karma*," I said.

She didn't respond to my comment about "bad" *karma*. I knew why. She believed *karma* was neither good nor bad. It was just *karma*. Meant to be. Fate.

"It was just *karma*," she emphasized the word just.

I didn't want to debate the issue.

"Yes, it was."

She was silent and I could hear her sniffling. She blew her nose.

"When are you coming to Singapore?"

"I'm going to Vietnam next month and on my way back I can drop off in Singapore."

"Call me."

"I will. Take care, Meiling."

"I miss you."

"I miss you too."

Meiling, BJ, Roger, and Ahn were with me last December. They were very much involved when I was arrested after the Choi killing. Meiling was instrumental in obtaining my release and BJ provided my alibi for the night. Was that the reason BJ was killed? Would Meiling also be a target? Were others in danger? What about Ahn? I needed to talk to him about this.

I called Ahn and asked if he could meet me for dinner. We decided to go to the Kalbi House, a Korean restaurant where BJ and I had eaten several times. I first met Ahn there when BJ and I hired his taxi after our first dinner at the restaurant. The Kalbi House was also where I had a heated encounter with Choi that almost become physical. Good and bad memories.

The owner remembered me and greeted us with some fanfare.

"The community is very sorry about Ms. Ma's tragic death. We are very sorry for your loss."

"Thank you. She always enjoyed coming here, as I did and still do."

"We are pleased you are here now. I have a good table for you."

He led the way to a table in the center of the room and placed two menus before us. In a minute he returned with two glasses and a large bottle of Tsingtao beer.

"Compliments of the house," he said as he poured.

Ahn and I toasted him and drank. We gave him our orders and soon two large *kalbi* dinners were brought to the table with the usual dozen or so condiments. The aroma was wonderful. I was hungrier than I thought and devoured the two sections of beef short ribs, a bowl of rice, and *kimchi*. We concentrated on the food and ate in silence.

Another bottle of beer was brought to the table.

"How was the meeting with Hong?"

"Hong thinks another vehicle, probably a large truck, pushed her car off the road into that concrete wall."

"Does he say why?"

"He has no proof, but the only reason he can think why anyone would harm her is me. Some people connect me to Choi's death. So someone close to me could be thought to be also involved."

"Sounds reasonable. But, who?"

"Hong doesn't think someone connected to the government was involved."

"A local?"

"Are there locals who would hire out to do such work?"

"Not many Koreans have large trucks and people would know who they are. I have two and everyone knows my trucks."

"How about someone from another city?" I asked.

"More likely."

"Can we find someone who noticed something unusual that night? At a petro station or café where truckers stop to eat."

"This is a big city and all kinds of people and vehicles are on the road at all hours of the day and night."

"Hong says the police are looking but people might not be too eager to talk to them."

"I can start asking around."

"Tomorrow morning could we take a ride out there? I want to see the concrete wall she crashed into."

"Sure. About nine or ten okay?"

"Come about nine. We can go out there before going to the Ma home."

I drank some of my beer and looked at him.

"What is it?"

"Remember when I was taken to the police station the day after Choi was killed. BJ said she was with me all night. That was my alibi. The other woman who was here, the one who brought the Harbin Mayor to the police station, her name is Meiling. She was born here but now lives in Singapore. And my friend Roger, from Singapore, was also there."

"Yes. I remember. So?"

"Is someone avenging Choi by targeting the people who were involved with me?"

"Could be."

"BJ lived here and a convenient target."

"The others are not here, so they're safe."

"Well, there's one other person closely associated with me."

He thought a moment.

"You mean me?"

"You've been my main contact since I've been coming to Harbin. Maybe, you should think about putting some distance between us. I'll understand if you do. Your safety and your family's safety are primary concerns. And you have a business to run."

"This is family business. Your enemies are my enemies."

"Thank you. But, I don't want you to have trouble."

"Not to worry. There are people here who know what has happened and they give you their support. Like the owner of this Kalbi House. They know."

"I appreciate it, Ahn. More than I can say."

"Oh. Speaking of family, my wife wants you to come to dinner tomorrow night. Nothing special, but she wants to meet you. You can't refuse." He laughed.

"I'm honored."

"Good. You can have some real Korean food. Home cooked. This restaurant is okay, but it isn't home cooked food. At my home the food has a North Korean flavor."

"My mother was from Kim Hae, close to Pusan, and I grew up with South Korean food. But I'm always looking for different style Korean cooking."

"You'll like my wife's cooking."

"I'm sure I will."

"Even if you don't, you can tell her you like it." He laughed.

"I know better than to upset a Korean cook."

"Especially my wife." He was still laughing.

"She'll know how I feel without my saying anything."

"Yeah. I think so."

"I know so."

12

A HN DROPPED ME OFF at the hotel and said he would return about ten the next day. I went to my room, showered and tried to relax. I turned on the television and watched the news.

After a half hour of that, I went down to the bar. Paul, the bartender, remembered me and poured me a *Yoichi* scotch.

"First one's on the house." He smiled and set the drink in front of me. "We've heard who you are and know why you're here."

"Lots of rumors around."

"You have friends here."

"Thanks. I'm very fortunate."

"When you're ready for seconds, just let me know."

I waved the glass at Paul and took a sip, then a real swallow. It was as good as I remembered. I also remembered I had too much to drink the last time, so I concentrated on sipping.

In a city the size of Harbin, how could a driver of a large truck be found? If it was a Korean, it narrowed the odds, but not by much. How many Koreans were there in Harbin? Fifty or sixty thousand? How many in all of Heilongjiang province? A million? How many owned a truck? There had to be something different about this person.

And why would he kill BJ?

I saw her in the mirror behind the bar as she came into the lounge. She surveyed the room and immediately identified me as the only lone male in the place. A perfect mark. She came up to the bar, chose the second stool to my left, and ordered a glass of white wine.

As I ordered my second drink I turned and looked at her. She smiled and waved her drink at me. A very good looking hooker who was preparing to make her pitch. I smiled back at her. Of course I always smiled at good looking woman. Problem with hookers was they took it as a sign I was interested in their services.

She was dressed in an expensive black pantsuit. Under the jacket she wore a white silk blouse. She had just enough make up on to highlight her lovely face. A nice, not too red, lipstick and dark eye shadow gave her a glamorous look. Matching red fingernail polish brought one's eye to soft hands. No flashy jewelry. She wore what appeared to be diamond earrings and a pearl necklace. Both might be fakes, but they looked real. She had an apple green jade bracelet on her right wrist – no watch. A very nice diamond ring on her right hand. That could also have been zirconium. But fake or real, on her all her accessories looked good. Her ample breast pushed tightly against her blouse. She was an exceptionally good looking woman.

It was past ten. She didn't seem the kind who would be hustling at this hour in a hotel bar. I wondered why she was alone. Was there an earlier client was too quick and embarrassed because he was a poor performer? Maybe she'll surprise me and not be a whore. Yeah, sure.

She moved to the stool next to me. Paul looked at her and started to say something, but I waved him off. I shook my head and smiled. He shrugged okay.

"May I sit here?" she asked, smiling.

"I was saving the seat for you."

I was obviously not a local, which meant I would be a better than average score.

"Are you staying at this hotel?"

"Yes. Are you?"

"I could." She smiled.

"Ah, my love. I appreciate your attention, but not tonight. Sorry about that."

"You don't like me?" She pursed her lips.

"I think you're wonderful. But, this is not a good time."

"Business is bad?"

"Yeah, business is bad."

"I can help make you forget business."

"I'm sure you can, but not tonight."

She looked down at her wine glass and sighed. She was thirty, thirty-five at the most. Probably been working at this trade for at least ten years. She looked tired. My rejection was a disappointment.

"Been a tough night?" I asked.

"All nights are tough. This one is no different," she said in a resigned voice.

She was different from the younger ones who were flashy and pushed hard to score. If one was into paying for sex, she would be much better than most.

"Have you had dinner?"

She laughed. "Dinner was supposed to be part of the deal, along with other things. But, it didn't turn out that way."

"Would you like something to eat?"

She looked at me and smiled. "Are you treating?"

"That's our table right over there." I nodded toward a booth. "I think we can get something." I grinned and said, "I know the cook."

I asked Paul about some food and he said he would get her a bowl of noodles. I asked for another drink and ordered her a fresh glass of wine. She spun off the stool and walked to the booth. She carried herself with style.

I wondered why someone like her was in this business. Hell, maybe it was what she wanted to do. But why did her john dump her? Not the kind of woman one boots out, unless there's something wrong with her or the client was kinky. This was not my concern, I reminded myself.

She sat in the booth and looked at me for long moment without saying anything. Paul brought her a bowl of noodles, a side dish of *cha shu*, a glass of wine, and my scotch. She was hungry. Probably didn't have lunch. After she finished her noodles she lit a cigarette, took a deep drag, and sat back. She sipped her wine and put her left arm over her stomach and her right elbow in her left hand. She crooked her head and pointed her cigarette at me.

"You're from America, aren't you?"

"Am I that obvious?"

"You're also Korean."

"Wow! Is there a mark on my forehead?" I laughed. "Yes, I am."

"So am I," she said, with a smile.

"What's your name?"

"Rose."

"What's your Korean name?"

She didn't expect me to ask for her Korean name. She hesitated and finally decided to tell me.

"Jin Yong. My name is Jin Yong."

"I'll call you Jin. I like it better than Rose."

She shrugged and looked down into her wine glass. Then she raised her head and stared at me.

"Why are you sitting here with me, buying me a bowl of noodles and wine with no intention of taking me to bed?" she asked.

"You were hungry. Want another bowl?"

"No thanks. One bowl is enough."

"We can always get another."

"Why do you bother? I'm a whore and you don't want my services. So, why do you bother?"

"I think you're more than just a whore."

She started to say something, but didn't. She took another drag of her cigarette, blew out the smoke, sighed, and finished her wine.

"Want another one?"

"Yes."

I waved at Paul and pointed at her glass. He brought another glass and looked at me. I waved him off.

"What kind of business do you do?" she asked.

"A little of this, a little of that."

"Is that why you're here? To do a little of this and a little of that." She wagged her hand and smiled.

"Yeah." I smiled back at her. "Something like that."

"I hope your business is better than mine."

"Are you from Harbin?" I asked.

"No. I'm from Changchun. Down south of here. I came up here at the invitation of a client. As you can see, it didn't work out too well."

"Was he Chinese?"

"Yes. A government official with some rank. They're the worst kind. They have new money and some of them have power. They got the money and power very recently, so they don't really know what to do except hire whores like me. Goddamn bureaucrats."

"Did he leave you with anything? A place to stay?"

"He left me with two hundred RMB. He owed me almost three thousand."

Three thousand RMB would be about five hundred US dollars for the night. Her income that night was only about thirty US dollars.

"You want a place to stay tonight?"

"I thought you didn't want me."

"I don't mean with me. But we can get you a place here for the night."

"Why? You don't want sex but you will pay for a room. Why?"

"A friend of mine once said, there comes a time when everybody needs some help. Looks like you need some help."

"What are you? Some kind of do-good Christian."

I laughed at the thought of someone thinking I was a Christian.

"No. But I have a friend who calls me a monk." I thought of Kam Wah and what he would say about this. "Wait here. I'll be back in a minute."

I went to the reception desk and booked a room under my name and added it to my bill. I wanted to do something good. I was tired and pissed off, thinking about all the rotten things that had happened in the past few weeks. And she was a Korean down on her luck. She needed some help.

She looked surprised when I came back to the table. Did she think I would leave and stick her with the tab? I handed her the card key to the room.

"It's for one night. You have enough money for a train ticket?"

"Train tickets are cheap."

"Well, then, you're set for the night."

"Why are you doing this?"

"Because I want to."

"There has to be some reason."

"It's my own reason."

"Tell me."

71

"Nothing to tell. It's just something I want to do."

I waved at Paul and held up my glass. He nodded and brought me another scotch. She watched me take a good swallow.

"Seriously, why are you here in Harbin?"

"Someone very close to me died and I came to pay my respects."

"I see. Was it a business associate?"

"No."

"So, it was personal." She looked at me and then mouthed the word 'Ah.' "It was a woman."

"You know too much."

"I'm sorry for you."

I finished my drink and went to the bar and signed the bill and thanked Paul. When I came back she was standing next to the table. She pointed the card key at me.

"Whatever your reasons, I'm going to use this room tonight."

"That's why I got it for you. Be my guest and enjoy."

"Will you be coming to Changchun?"

"I don't think so."

"If you are, call me at this number. It's my cell phone."

She handed me a name card. I was impressed. A hooker with a name card. Hell, why not?

"I will. If I'm in Changchun."

"Now and then I come to Harbin, will you be here?"

"I don't think so."

"You have a name card?"

"No."

"What's your name? You asked for my name."

"That's because you're prettier than I am."

"Only fair I should know what to call you."

"People call me the Korean from America."

"Even if you told me, I know it wouldn't be your real name."

"Whatever you call me, it'll be real enough. Now, it's time for bed for me. Are you going to stay here?" I looked around the bar. "Some clients might come in."

"Now I don't feel like it."

"Good. You don't need them."

"You my big brother?"

"Everyone needs one. Come on I'll walk you to your room. Need anything? Toothbrush?"

"I came prepared." She held up her bag. "Have bag – will travel." She laughed.

I took her to her room and opened the door for her. She turned to me and sighed.

"It's not right. Food, drink, this room, and you ask for nothing."

"Tonight, this is what's right. Take care." I paused and said, "Why don't you think about another line of work."

She flashed an angry look and took in a deep breath.

"Go to Hell! I don't have to explain to you or anybody else why I do what I do."

"It makes no difference to me what you do. I just would be happier for you if you did something else."

Her lips closed tight and her eyes narrowed. She clenched her fist and shouted.

"Fuck you!"

I sighed and smiled.

"If you want breakfast, it's included with the room. Get a good breakfast before you leave. And here's a small token for your lovely company. I enjoyed it." I pushed a hundred-dollar bill into her hand.

"Wait. Don't leave."

"Good night, Jin."

She reached for me and grabbed my arm.

"I'm sorry I yelled at you."

"It's okay. No need to explain. I think I know why."

She put her arms around me and kissed me. Soft lips. Very nice.

"I won't forget you," she said.

"Yes, you will. But, that's all right."

"No. I'll remember you."

"Good night, Jin."

I left her standing in the doorway, watching me walk away.

Her john that night was one of those guys who have preconceived notions about women who are paid for sex. For some males, sex with a whore was not so much a sexual necessity as it was a psychological need to reaffirm their manhood and exercise male power. A whore wouldn't reject him as an ordinary woman might. It was a safe way to keep the male ego intact.

Sex was secondary for the bureaucrat who paid Jin for use of her body. A whore was the perfect way to validate his newly found status and power. He was a real jerk and cheated her out of what he promised to pay, proving he was inadequate in many ways. With losers like that, why didn't she get out of the life?

But, there was the female side to whoring. Separating whoring and the slave trade, some women liked the life and without being forced to do it, they wanted to sell their bodies. So, was Jin a victim or an entrepreneur who used her best assets to make a living? It had nothing to do with morals, it was a practical choice, and it was her choice.

What right did I have to say she should give up whoring? Who am I to pass judgment on her? She neither wanted nor needed my advice. Why was I worrying about this? Why did I get involved in these things? I could hear Kam Wah telling me to stop trying to save the world. The wayward monk he called me. Maybe that's what I was. Well, not so much a monk, but I was definitely wayward.

13

I WOKE LATER THAN usual but had time for an hour in the gym. After a shower and shave I called house keeping to pick up my laundry. Then I went down to the restaurant for breakfast. As I entered the room I saw her at a table in the center of the room. Two Japanese businessmen were standing at her table. So early in the morning? Why did that piss me off? Was this going to be one of those times?

I went to her table and smiled at her.

"I see you started without me. The workout was a little longer than I planned."

I looked at the two men and asked, "*Otetsudai shimashouka?*"

They hesitated until it was too late for them to make a response. They lost the edge. Without a word they went out to the lobby.

"What did you say to them?"

"I just asked if I could help them."

She laughed. "I think you've said that before. Always get that reaction?"

"Not always. Depends."

"You didn't have to do that," she said.

"I know. I just don't like them."

"Why? You don't know them."

"I don't know their names, but I know them."

"Well, now that you have run them off, are you going to sit down? I may need your help in case others come around."

"Since you've asked for my assistance, I will. Just in case they come back."

I waved at the waitress and sat down. She came with a coffee pot and poured me a cup. I ordered a continental breakfast.

"Have a good night?" I asked.

"Yes, I did. Did you?"

"I slept in this morning."

"You look better today," she said, smiling.

"Being with a good looking woman always helps."

"You like to flirt."

"Yeah, I do."

I grinned. She responded with a smile that said she knew all about me.

"I think you should to come to Changchun."

"I might."

"You have my number."

"Yes, I do. It's right on your card."

"I can stay for another day. Or two if you want."

"I would like that very much, but I have things to do."

"I thought this visit was not business."

"What I have to do is personal stuff."

"Does it have to do with the woman who died?"

"Sort of. It's just some obligations I have. What time is your train?"

"There's one that leaves in an hour."

"Okay. I'll give you a ride to the train station."

"It's okay. I can get a taxi."

"I have a taxi on call."

"I'm impressed."

"You should be. Now you know what an important man I am." I waved for the check.

"No need. Remember – breakfast comes with the room."

I laughed.

"That's right. But, I still have mine to pay for."

"You should get a room that includes breakfast. Next time I'll fix it up for you. I know a big time spender."

"I'm sure you do."

I signed the check for my breakfast.

She laughed, stood, took my hand, and pulled me out of my chair.

"Come on. Let's go catch a train."

The doorman smiled, opened the door, and touched the tip of his hat. As we went out the door I saw Ahn waiting on the street. I took her arm and we walked to the taxi. Ahn opened the door for her and she got in.

"Good morning."

"Good morning, Ahn. This lady needs a ride to the train station."

"The central station?"

I looked in the taxi. "Which station?"

"Central is fine," she said.

"The central station," I said to Ahn and got in the back with her.

When we arrived at the station, I got out and put out my hand. She grabbed my extended hand and gently pulled herself out of the taxi.

"You're a real gentleman. Thank you."

"I'll walk you to the gate." I looked at Ahn. "I'll be right back."

She put her arm into mine and we walked arm in arm into the station. She bought a ticket and held my hand as we leisurely walked to the gate.

"Have a good trip."

"I don't know what to say."

"No need to say anything."

"Will I see you again?"

"Never know. I might just show up one dark night."

"I want to see you again."

"One day you just might."

She put her arms around me and kissed me. I could taste her lipstick. It was sweet and light. Just like last night. She looked at me and held my hand.

"I'll be waiting."

She stared at me for a long moment, and then dropped my hand, turned and left. I watched her walk away and thought I would probably never see her again.

When I came out of the station I looked for Ahn. He had moved the taxi down the block. He waved at me.

"I had to move the car. Police don't want cars blocking the front entrance."

"No problem." I got into the front seat and put on the seat belt. "In case you want to know, that was a Korean lady I met in the bar last night. I didn't make use of her services, but she needed some help, so I helped her."

"You don't have to explain."

"I know, but just so it's clear."

"It's clear."

"Good. Now, I want to go to the accident site."

It took about thirty minutes to get out of the inner city and another twenty minutes to get to the spot where the accident occurred. On the way I looked for petro stations or cafes where a truck driver might stop. There was one petro station on the edge of the city and a couple of small restaurants were located every few miles. But they might not be open at night and if they were open, it probably wouldn't be later than eight.

She crashed on a broad two-lane stretch of open road. Farm land on both sides of the road. Some acres were planted, others were left fallow. No buildings for miles in both directions. Streetlights were spaced about three quarters of mile apart, so the road was well lit at night, as most of the modern highways were in China. It was a good road. No potholes or cracks in the pavement. There were wide shoulders on both sides of the road. Enough space for pedestrians, bicycles, and small carts. A ditch about two feet deep ran along the edge of the shoulder. It was dry, but would be full of water in the rainy season.

There was a wall on both sides of the road. The concrete wall she hit had a good size piece broken off where her car had crashed. The seven feet wall was made of nine by twelve inch concrete blocks and was around thirty-five inches high. The blocks were not just cemented together. Concrete in the empty blocks were reinforced with steel rods. It was a substantial structure, meant to last for many years. Probably a standard design used throughout the province. A three-foot wide tunnel ran under the road. A lot of water passed through the tunnel during the rainy season. A wall and tunnel were placed about a half a mile apart along that section of the highway.

Fifty feet before the concrete wall were tire marks made by a car that was apparently trying to brake. No other tire marks were evident. There were no bits and pieces of auto parts. The accident scene had been cleared. Obviously, the efficient work of Hong and his crew.

Ahn and I walked up and down the road a hundred feet before and after the concrete wall. I tried to imagine her car coming at a high speed toward the wall. She must have been traveling at sixty miles an hour or more when she crashed into the wall. If a truck struck her from behind and if the concrete wall had not been there, she could have flipped over into the ditch. If that happened, she might not have been killed. Lots of ifs.

After an hour of walking up and down the road and looking at the wall, I decided there was nothing more to learn there. We drove back to the hotel in silence.

Ahn parked the taxi and we went into the hotel coffee shop to have a cup of tea.

"I think her car was forced into that wall," Ahn said.

"Yes. I believe that and so does Hong. Someone murdered her."

Why did the word murder sound so ominous? Murder requires malicious forethought. It had to be planned and there had to be a reason for the planning. That someone planned the murder really bothered me. I thought of the terror she felt as she was being forced off the road. It was a thought I could never erase.

"Can Hong find the killer?" I wondered aloud. "If it's a known criminal he might. But I don't think it was. Someone out of the ordinary would be too obvious."

"It will take time."

"I know, Ahn. If you spend time with this, I'll pay for your time."

"I do what I do because it's what I want to do. No money is involved."

He sounded offended. I was sorry and embarrassed I mentioned money.

"I offer because I can't be here."

"You would be useless. You don't know who to talk to."

"You're right. I'm sorry that I'm dumping all this on you."

"Not a problem."

I could see he actually enjoyed doing this. Finding the killer was a challenge and he enjoyed a real challenge. Well, that's the help I needed. Someone who could do police work without the legal hang ups.

"Thanks, Ahn. I need all the help I can get."

"You have it."

"Let's go to her wake."

14

WE ARRIVED AT THE Ma home at about three o'clock. There were already a dozen people there and more were coming as we drove up to the house. Many of the visitors were relatives and some were parents of the students in BJ's class. Mrs. Ma met us at the opened door. She gave me a hug and shook hands with Ahn.

"Thank you for coming," she said.

Mr. Ma was greeting guests near the food table. He came to where we were standing with Mrs. Ma and shook my hand. He tapped Ahn on the arm and pointed toward the food table.

"Please have something to eat."

"Thank you," he said and went to get some food.

She came up behind me so I didn't see her. She grabbed my arm and turned me around. It was Mulan.

She put her arms around me. She didn't say anything, just hung on with her head on my shoulder and quietly cried. We stayed that way for several minutes. Mulan was not a shy one. Finally, she let go and stepped back.

"I knew you would come."

"If I had to walk all the way, I would be here."

"We all knew that. Your being here makes it complete. You can help bring closure to this terrible thing."

"I can't speak for others, but it's difficult for me to accept. May never happen."

"Come. I want you to meet the cousins and other friends of the family."

She pulled me toward the crowd. I smiled and made a helpless gesture at Mrs. Ma and let Mulan lead the way.

———————————

For the next half hour she introduced me to people who seemed to know who I was and most exclaimed "Oh, the Korean from America." A pleasant surprise was to see Mrs. Chung, a Korean from North Korea, whom I met last December. Mrs. Chung was the Associate Director at the Harbin mushroom beta glucan research institute. She had introduced me to the people who told me about Yong Suk's suicide in the North Korean prison.

Mrs. Chung then introduced me to Mr. Chang, the brother of Chang from Beijing, and his Korean wife. Among his many other contacts, the younger brother was probably a valuable source of information for Chang.

"I know your brother in Beijing."

"Yes. He has talked about you. You're involved with industrial diamonds, aren't you?"

"It's one of the items I deal in. Your brother has been a great help in a number of projects."

"He speaks highly of you."

"He's too kind."

"This unfortunate affair is very sad, but it did bring you to Harbin again. How long will you stay?"

"I'm leaving tomorrow."

"Tomorrow? So soon? Well, I hope you will not stay away too long."

"Yes. Come back soon," Mrs. Chung said.

"I will try."

Mulan bowed to them and said, "Excuse me, but my father just came."

We all shook hands and they said again they hoped I would come back. They were ideal examples of how the Chinese, Manchus, and Koreans all mixed in Harbin. Was this the mixing pot where I would be at home? Who was I kidding? I didn't believe I would be "at home" here or anywhere else for that matter.

Mr. and Mrs. Yuan were greeting people and working their way towards us.

"Hello, Mr. Yuan." I shook his hand and turned to his wife. "Mrs. Yuan, a pleasure." She held my hand and shook her head.

"Ah, such a terrible thing but I am glad to see you. Mulan said you would come."

"I was going to come to the farm, but when Mrs. Ma told me about this gathering, I knew you would be here."

"How long will you stay?"

"I leave tomorrow."

"You must return. She is no longer here, but we welcome you. Come back and visit the family," Mrs. Yuan said.

"Thank you. I will."

During the next hour or so, I met more cousins and friends of the family. They were a special group of people and I felt at ease with them.

I looked around the room and thought about the dinner I had with her family. We took several pictures that night and one I had taken of the family hung on the wall.

Too many memories. It was time to go. I caught Ahn's eye and motioned to the door. He nodded and went out. I said goodbye to Mr. and Mrs. Ma, but didn't seek the others out. Mulan put her arm in mine and walked me to the door.

"You know I was the last person to see her alive."

"Yes. She was coming from your house."

"She has driven that road many times. It doesn't make sense," she said. "What do you think?" she asked suddenly.

"About what?"

"Her accident."

"There are lots of questions."

"And?"

"There are just a lot of questions."

"What are you thinking?"

I looked at her and sighed. She was too smart. I put my arms around her.

"Take care of your mother and father. And take care of yourself."

"You take care too."

"I will. Good bye, Mulan."

As we were leaving I spotted two men walking around where the cars were parked. Two more were in the back yard. Hong had his crew at work. I wondered if they were following me.

Ahn dropped me off at the hotel and said he would be back at five-thirty. His wife had instructed him to have me at the house at six. Dinner would begin at six-thirty sharp. I had the feeling one didn't mess with her schedule.

I opened a bottle of Tsingtao and watched a soccer match between the Chinese national team and a team from Malaysia. A half an hour into the game my cell phone rang. It was Roger.

"I heard the news. I'm sorry."

"I guess you've talked to Meiling."

"She called me and gave me this cell number."

"Where are you?"

"In Surabaya. Working with Pak Dahlan on some things. So you're in Harbin."

"Yeah, be here for a day or two. Didn't make the funeral, but thought I would come and see her family."

"Have you been back to Harbin since we were there last December?"

"Yes. Came again last Spring. Was going to return in the Fall."

"So what are you doing? Still peddling that beta glucan?"

"Yeah. Have a few things to keep me occupied."

"Listen, why don't you come down to Surabaya? Pak Dahlan and everyone would be happy to see you. Spend a few days here in the tropical sunshine. Do you good."

"Well, don't know how much time I have. I'm planning on a trip to Vietnam as soon as I can get things arranged. I can meet up with you on my way back from Vietnam. Will you be in Singapore?"

"Don't know. Let me know what your schedule will be."

"I will."

"You sound down. I know this has been a shitty deal, but you have to get on with life. It's time to get on with it. Plenty to do and there are people waiting for you."

"Things change, Roger."

"Bullshit. Things are like they have always been. Some players are no longer there, but things are the same. You know that, so don't give me all that crap about how things are different. Things will always be down unless you pick it up."

"This some kind of pep talk?"

"Get your ass down here and quit this bullshit talk. We can make the rounds again in Jakarta."

"Jakarta? Thought you were in Surabaya."

"Fly into Jakarta and we can spend a couple of nights there. Remember how nice the nightclubs were. They're still there and lots of women waiting."

"Roger, a tour of the bars with you always takes several years off my life."

"True. But, what a way to go. Come on down."

"I will as soon as things work out in Vietnam."

"Everyone here will be waiting."

"Give Dorothy my love and hello to everybody in Surabaya."

"I expect you to be here, at least within a month."

"Take care, Roger."

"Remember what I said. Time to forget and move on. Don't go around with your head down – crying in your beer."

"Always good to hear your encouraging words."

"Listen to me. Or I'll sic Dorothy on to you and she won't mince words."

"I know."

"I'm sorry about her, but it's time to forget."

"See you soon, Roger."

"Don't make me come to find you. It's enough that I have to worry about you."

"Good bye, Roger. My love to Dorothy."

"Remember what I said."

"I'll remember."

85

Roger was an old and valuable friend. He introduced me to many good folks in Asia, including Meiling. We traveled together throughout Southeast Asia and he always made life enjoyable. He was one of those people who could get along with the Devil and St. Peter at the same time. He knew more heads of state and important officials in Asia than anyone I knew.

He made friends wherever he was, in any part of the world, even if he didn't speak their language. A half hour in a taxi and he would know where the "in" places were to eat and drink. He would also have the low down on politics and how the general citizenry felt about the government and life in general. Traveling with Roger was an exciting adventure with lots of perks along the way.

Roger was in Harbin when Choi was assassinated. He rushed down to the police station when I was arrested and with Meiling, who came with the Mayor of Harbin, demanded my release. Together they confronted the police officer in charge, who happened to have been Hong, and threatened to call the American embassy in Beijing and a host of other people. All of that became academic when BJ said she was with me all night. She wasn't, but she gave me my alibi for the night in question. I don't know if Roger or Meiling or Hong believed her, but Hong was obliged to release me.

Hearing from Roger was an emotional lift. He was gruff, but it was his way of voicing his support. He was one of the good guys.

15

I LOOKED FORWARD TO dinner with Ahn and his family, especially meeting his wife. Hopefully, it would get me out of my melancholy mood. Things brighten up quickly when we arrived at Ahn's home and sat down to a home cooked Korean dinner. His lovely wife, Kum Soon, called Soonie, made several special dishes that I ate with gusto, which was better than verbal compliments. She was pleased. His two sons sat quietly as long as they could and finally their father excused them. We had some Chinese wine and talked about Ahn's business and how things were looking up for the family.

After several pleasant hours I began to feel a bit tired. Ahn noticed this and suggested it was time for me to get some rest. I thanked Soonie for the great dinner and promised to come again on my next visit. It was after ten when we arrived at the hotel. I told him I would call tomorrow morning when I had a confirmed flight to Guangzhou.

Before going up to my room I dropped by the bar. By now I was well known to Paul, the bartender. He poured a healthy shot of *Yoichi* scotch without my ordering it.

"Thanks, Paul. Needed this."

"Long day?"

"Seems like it."

"Are you leaving tomorrow?"

"Yes."

Does everyone know my schedule?

"People feel bad about Ms. Ma and they wish you well."

"Thank you."

"The Korean community is pretty tight here. You have friends in Harbin."

"That's good to know."

Along with my travel schedule, everyone seemed to know about me and BJ. It was a comfort to know about my favorable status in the community, but I wondered about my affairs being an open book.

"Well, I'm going to have another one and then hit the sack."

"The drinks are on me."

I looked at him and wondered what stories he had heard. Well, I was never one to turn down a free drink, especially from a bartender.

"Thanks, Paul."

I finished the drink, bade Paul a good night, and went to my room. I took a long hot shower. Not a sauna, but was a passable substitute.

When I came out of the bathroom I noticed the red light flashing on the phone. I called the operator and she said I had three messages. One was from someone named Yasha, the second was from Police Superintendent Hong, and the third was from a woman named Jin Yong. That would be my new friend of last night from Changchun. All three messages said to call whatever hour I got in.

I called Hong on his cell phone number. I assumed he was at his home.

"Sorry to call at this hour, but your message said to call whatever hour I got in."

"Not a problem. I wanted to meet again before you left town. Can we meet for breakfast tomorrow morning?"

"Of course. When and where?"

"Say at nine o'clock. I'll pick you up at the hotel."

"Okay. Nine tomorrow morning."

What's this about? Has he found out something? If he did, why would he tell me? Pressure from Beijing?

Yasha was my banker, so any call from her was important.

"How did you know I was at this hotel?"

"I just called five star hotels until I found you. Found you on the second call."

"What's so important you want me to call at this hour?"

"I wanted to know where you're going from there."

"Guangzhou. I haven't made reservations yet, but will tomorrow."

"Never mind. I'll be in Guangzhou tomorrow at the White Swan and have a room reserved for you. We can finally have dinner."

"All this attention. Afraid I was going to slip out of China without telling you?"

"I'm just worried about you. I know you're having a difficult time."

"Not to worry. But, thanks, Yasha. I'll be at the White Swan about five or six."

"I'll see you then."

"Thanks again, Yasha."

I was becoming financially dependant on Yasha. It'll soon reach the point where I couldn't possibly pay her back – even if the job in Vietnam lasted a month.

———————————

Now, what does the lady in Changchun want? Do I want to be involved with this person? Well, I started the whole business, not her. Okay, one call.

"So I found you."

"How did you know my room number?"

"I told the operator I wanted to talk to the Korean from America. I think everyone knows who you are."

"I see. What can I do for you?"

"I just wanted to say thank you and ask you to come down to Changchun."

"Are you hustling me?" I laughed.

"No. This isn't a hustle. I'll never think of you as a client. I want you as a friend and I want to see you on my home ground. What you in America call turf."

"That's nice, but I'm leaving tomorrow. Sorry."

"I'm the one that's sorry."

"Is there any particular reason why do you want to see me?"

"My own reasons."

"Okay, one day we can talk about it."

"When?"

"One day."

"So, it's never." She heaved a sigh.

"I didn't say that."

"But, that's what it is."

"Maybe not."

"Come to see me."

"If I can, I will."

She wasn't soliciting – at least it didn't seem so. It was possible she really wanted to be friends. Well, I could do a whole lot worst.

16

I WOKE AT SEVEN and spent an hour in the gym. After a shower and a shave, I put my day together. My first priority was to find what airlines had direct flights to Guangzhou. I decided to use the hotel travel services.

I stopped at the reception desk and asked the young lady to prepare my bill for check out before noon. I went to the customer service desk and asked if she could get me a First Class seat on a flight to Guangzhou, leaving sometime in the early afternoon. She asked me to check back later.

I went into the restaurant and had a cup of coffee, then went back to the service desk. The clerk was one of those efficient people who made life easier for everyone, especially people like me.

"I was able to get you a First Class reservation on a Shenzhen Airline Flight to Guangzhou. It leaves at 2:10 PM and arrives at 6:30 PM."

She handed me a slip with the reservation number.

"Thank you. Can you put the plane charges on my hotel bill?"

"Yes sir, not a problem."

I called Ahn and asked him to pick me up about noon.

A few minutes before nine I walked out the front door and stood on the upper steps. Hong drove up in an unmarked car and waved at me to come to the car.

"Ready for breakfast?"

"Yes I am."

"Good. We can have a Chinese style breakfast."

We drove to a café about fifteen minutes away. It was busy, but not standing room only. Hong knew the owner who found us a table toward the rear of the room.

In China, *juk* was the common morning breakfast – a thick rice dish served steaming hot. You could add some spices or eat it plain. I put some small bits of bacon and spices in mine.

"I know you're leaving today. What time is your flight?"

"At two."

"Where are you going?"

"To Guangzhou."

"You have some strong ties there, don't you?"

"Yes, I do."

He chatted about his visits to Guangzhou and how south China was different from Harbin. I finished my bowl of juk and leaned back in my chair. Time we got to the purpose for this breakfast.

"It's always a pleasure to meet with you, but why did you want to meet me this morning?"

He spooned up the last of his *juk* and pushed his bowl aside.

"The reason I asked to meet is to inform you that we are officially treating Ms. Ma's death as a homicide. After thoroughly checking all the evidence we have concluded that it's reasonable to assume her car was forced into that concrete wall. I think it was a large truck, powerful enough to cause such a crash. The rear of her car clearly shows it was struck by another vehicle. The crash impact drove the steering wheel into her chest and was the cause of death. The autopsy verified this. We have not released any of this information and only the police have seen the car."

"When are you going to tell her parents?"

"I'll tell them later today or tomorrow. It won't be a pleasant chore." He looked out the window. "She was the least likely murder victim."

"I agree. So now, to find the killer."

"We are looking."

"What are the chances of finding him?"

"We will use all our resources, but as you know, Harbin is a very large city. There are five million people in the central urban area. In the greater metropolitan area there are over nine million people. And the killer may not be from Harbin."

"So, unless someone who knows something comes forward, chances of finding the killer are very slim."

"We have found people before."

"Well, I thank you for bringing me up to date. It's not very comforting to know she was murdered, but at least you confirmed my suspicions." I heaved a sigh and shook my head. "For some reason, she was murdered because of her relationship with me."

"We don't know that for certain. But there doesn't seem to any other reason someone would do this to her. If it is somehow tied to you, it is reasonable to assume that your involvement, or alleged involvement, with Choi's assassination has something to do with this."

He paused and looked at me. "Ms. Ma stated she was with you on that night. She was your alibi."

"You checked on that?"

"Yes. I asked her mother and she verified it."

"Then, is there any doubt?"

"If she and her mother both say she was with you, I have to accept their word."

"You don't think the North Koreans believe that."

"I don't know what they believe. But, she and you are integral parts of the whole incident. If someone believes you are the assassin, they may think she was involved and becomes a logical target."

"So, the killer is a North Korean agent."

"Not necessarily. North Koreans may be involved, but I do not believe they would directly hire someone to do the job. More likely a third party made the contract."

"You think the killer is a Korean."

"True. I still think that."

"Well, that might narrow the field some."

"It does. I'm counting on it."

"Thank you for the information. I appreciate it."

"By the way, if you have friends who find out anything, ask them to contact me."

"Friends?"

"Your friend, Ahn. He knows this city as well as anyone. Probably better than many policemen. He might learn something."

"I don't know how or why he would become involved. And I'll be out of China in a few days."

"Well, if he does tell you anything, I will appreciate knowing about it. Even a rumor will help."

"If I hear anything before I leave I'll call you."

I thanked him for the breakfast and looked at my watch.

"I guess I better get going. Haven't checked out of the hotel yet."

At the hotel, he got out of the car and came around to my side. I shook his extended hand.

"Thank your for sharing your findings."

"Please keep me informed if you hear anything."

"Yes. I will."

He gave me a doubtful look and nodded. He got into his car and waved as he drove off.

So, officially, BJ was murdered. How did things get to this point? It started when I came to Beijing last December to sell industrial diamonds to Chang. But Chang really didn't want to buy diamonds. He wanted me to help Bak and his sister defect from North Korea. That all ended badly. Choi put them in prison where Bak's sister killed herself. Then Choi was assassinated. The question was who killed BJ and why.

17

I PACKED MY ONE carryon bag and came down to the lobby to check out. After confirming my flight reservation with Shenzhen Airlines I called Kam Wah in Huangpo.

"I'm coming into Guangzhou on Shenzhen Airline. It gets in about six-thirty."

"I'll get a hotel room. What hotel you want?"

"I have a reservation at the White Swan hotel."

"Are matters there settled?"

"When are matters ever settled? As usual, there are many loose ends."

"Loose ends?"

"I'll tell you later."

"How long will you stay in Guangzhou?"

"Only a couple of days. I have to get back home to prepare for a trip to Vietnam."

"You are going to Vietnam?"

"Yes. I'm waiting for final word about meetings. That should be coming within a week. By the way, if possible, I would like to meet with Chief Wu. Give him a report on his daughter."

"A problem?"

"No. Everything is fine. But, Chief Wu spoke on my behalf to the police in Harbin, so I should take the time to tell him how his daughter is doing."

"That is a good idea. I will arrange a dinner."

"And, Kam Wah, ask him to bring his wife. I think she should hear directly from me how her daughter is doing."

"That is also a good idea."

"Can you have Wong pick me up at the airport?"

"No problem."

"Thanks, Kam Wah."

"We can have a real Chinese dinner tonight."

"Tonight is a problem. I promised to meet the Vietnam client tonight. She wants to have dinner."

"She? Are you taking a woman to Vietnam?"

"Her company is my client, not her. But, if you can arrange it, we can have dinner with Chief Wu and his wife tomorrow evening."

"Can do."

"How is Su Lin doing?"

"She is doing well. Her sister is studying computers and also works part-time at the massage parlor. Su Lin always asks about you."

"I'll try to see her. Maybe for lunch tomorrow."

"You have too many women. Now there is another woman you are taking to Vietnam."

"Kam Wah, that's business."

"You have not told me about that business."

"I will when I see you Guangzhou."

"You should tell me about these things."

"I haven't said anything because nothing is final yet. The trip to Vietnam depends on many things."

"Wong will pick you up."

"Thanks, Kam Wah."

"I can tell your health is not good."

"How can you tell over the phone?"

"You don't sound good."

"Well, when I get there your Chinese herbs will help me get better."

He paused for a moment while he lit a cigarette.

"I am sorry about the lady in Harbin."

"Thank you. That's a long, sad story and it's not ending soon."

"What do you mean?"

"I'll tell you when I see you."

"Always problems. You need to have a more quiet life."

"My life is very quiet."

"A good wife would help keep things more normal."

"Good bye, Kam Wah."

Ahn was waiting for me in the lobby. We went out to his taxi and settled in for the trip to the airport.

"The plane leaves at two. Will we be rushed?"

"No. Plenty of time."

"Hong called last night. We met this morning. He told me because of the physical evidence, which is primarily her car, he's treating her death as a homicide."

"So he's convinced someone killed her."

"Well, based on the evidence, he believes that someone jammed her car from behind and forced it into that concrete wall. The rear of her car was badly damaged and the trunk was caved in. The front end was crushed when the car hit that wall and the steering wheel was pushed up into her chest." I flinched when I thought about it. "They aren't releasing any information just yet. Hong will explain things to Mr. and Mrs. Ma today. He has a tough job."

I thought about how her parents would react to the news that the police believed that BJ was murdered. Mrs. Ma knew BJ lied to the police when she told them she was with me the night Choi was killed. She backed her story anyway. If Mrs. Ma connected her death and my problems with Choi, she may be sorry BJ ever met me.

"Hong believes the killer is a Korean who was hired to do the killing."

"Does he think the North Koreans are behind this?" Ahn asked.

"I think he does. It goes back to that son-of-bitch Choi. Hong thinks someone blames me for his death and this is pay back."

"I have thought that since the beginning."

"He's trying to narrow down the search. Might not be a local."

"I agree."

"Hong also asked that if you find out anything I should tell him."

"What do you want me to do?"

"If you can find out who did this, tell only me. This is the same as the Choi business. It has to be handled the same way."

"Yes. I agree."

What happened to Choi was a secret Ahn and I could never share with anyone. What happens after we find BJ's killer would be another one of those secrets.

"I'll give you cell phone numbers in the US, China, Singapore, and Vietnam. I will be in Guangzhou for a few days and then go to the US. In a week or so I'll go to Vietnam for about ten days. On the way back, I'll try to stop off in Singapore. At any time, if there is news, call those numbers until you find me. I will come directly here from wherever I am."

"It may take some time before I know anything."

"I understand. But finding the killer may be only half of the job. If someone gave orders to the killer, there's a third party in this murder. I want to find that person."

"It will be difficult to find that person."

"If I find the killer, he'll tell me."

He gave me a quick glance. I said that with too much emotion.

"You should get some rest. It's been a difficult time."

"I have things to do that will keep me busy for a while. And I'm committed to this trip to Vietnam."

"That's good. It will help take your mind off this business. Know that I will not jump to conclusions and will tell you only when I am certain about the facts. But it will take time. I know another trip back to Harbin will be difficult, so I'll be careful."

"I know you'll be thorough and I trust what you do."

18

THE SHENZHEN AIR FLIGHT to Guangzhou was uneventful and the one stopover in Tienjin was short. First Class was surprisingly very comfortable. I was in the second row, which was the last row in First Class. There was only one other passenger. Lunch was served by a lovely flight attendant and after lunch and a glass of wine, she sat in the empty seat next to me. She was from Tienjin and was enrolled at the university in Beijing. She wanted to practice her English with someone from America. It was a pleasant few hours.

Wong was waiting for me outside the terminal. He proudly showed me pictures of his new son and brought me up to date on how Su Lin and her sister were getting on. Everything was going well. After Harbin, it was a welcome relief.

Yasha made reservations at the White Swan and I had a good room on the ninth floor. There was a well stocked mini-bar and a king sized bed. I took off my shoes, turned on the television, and opened a Heineken beer. I was finishing my beer when my phone rang. It could only be Yasha.

"Hello."

"Hi. I hope the room is okay."

"The room is fine. How long have you been here?"

"Got in about noon. I'm two doors down from you. Room 912."

"You probably have a suite."

"Want to share my room?"

"Behave, Yasha."

"You notice I haven't come to your room."

"I wondered about that."

"I can be there in a second."

"Not now. I have to get ready for this big dinner you're taking me to."

"What time do you want to go?"

"Whenever you're ready."

"How about seven?"

"Seven sounds good. I'll come by your room."

"Okay." She paused a moment. "I'm glad you're here."

"So am I."

I was really pleased about Yasha. I needed her company. The coming trip to Vietnam was going to be much more enjoyable than other trips to Nam because she was coming along.

I had another beer and called Kam Wah.

"Thanks for having Wong pick me up. I'm here at the White Swan. Can Wong pick me up tomorrow morning?"

"What time?"

"About ten or eleven. I'll call."

"No problem."

"I would like to have lunch with Su Lin and Amanda if that's alright with you."

"You have to ask Amanda. She's the boss of Su Lin."

"Okay. I'll call and ask. Are we set for dinner tomorrow with Chief Wu?"

"Yes. His wife is also coming. But must be an early dinner."

"Any time is good with me. I'm pleased she's coming."

"We can get a massage in the afternoon and go directly from there."

"Sounds even better. I'm leaving day after tomorrow, Kam Wah."

"Are you leaving from Hong Kong?"

"I think I'll try to fly to Shanghai and get a direct flight from there."

"Maybe that's easier than the train to Hong Kong."

"It will also give me some time with my client."

"How is that?"

"The client's headquarters is in Shanghai."

"I see. Where will you eat tonight?"

"I don't know. She'll pick a place."

"Does she know anything about Guangzhou food?"

"I don't know. She's from Shanghai."

"Shanghai people know nothing about good food."

"Kam Wah, it's only one dinner."

"She should have asked me."

"Next time I'll tell her to."

"Dinner is important, you know."

"I know, Kam Wah. I'm sure it will be a good restaurant."

"Shanghai people don't know about food. You remember how terrible the food was when we were in Shanghai."

"You can pick a good restaurant for my lunch with Su Lin tomorrow."

"It won't be Shanghai food."

"I'll see you tomorrow, Kam Wah."

I really missed Kam Wah's tirades against things like Shanghai food. He always made my day.

After a shower and shave I put on a clean shirt and decided to wear my one and only tie. I went to Room 912 and rang the door bell. She peered through the peephole in the door and unlocked the door.

"Ready?"

"Yes."

"Okay, let's go?"

"Want to see my room?"

"No."

"If you want, you can check it out."

"Let's go, Yasha."

As she often did, she surprised me again. She was wearing a light brown silk pants suit. The jacket was short and had nice rounded edges, pleated in back. Under the jacket she had on a light green silk blouse with an open collar. A very light beige scarf was tied around her neck and tucked into her shirt. Her earrings were small pearl shaped jade balls. The bracelet on her right wrist matched the apple green color of the earrings. A jade ring was on her left middle finger. Nicely made up eye shadow and rose colored lipstick. Her nail polish matched the color of her lipstick. Her hair was flowing around her shoulders. She was really quite beautiful. I always thought she was very good looking, but seeing her dressed up certainly up graded that assessment.

"You look lovely, Yasha."

"You finally noticed."

"Pretty as you are, you're hard to miss."

She was not prepared for the compliment. I noticed her blushing. She looked down and smiled.

"I picked a special restaurant for our dinner. You'll like it."

The restaurant Yasha picked was a unique restaurant that specialized in seafood. I was there once a few years ago. It was on an island in the middle of a large lake and was accessible only by a boat that ferried diners to and from the island. She made reservations with special instructions so we had a table next to the window with a nice view of the lake. The special on the menu that night was a fresh water fish, similar to the American trout. It was all very nice. Kam Wah would have approved.

"This is very special, Yasha. I'm impressed."

"I thought it would be nice to have something special. It's our first dinner together."

"I'm sure we'll have more."

"That's what I have planned."

I stopped and stared at her. That's what BJ would say and she would use those exact words. I blinked and shook my head. I turned and looked out at the lake. I couldn't mask my feelings.

"What is it? What did I say?"

I turned back and looked at her. She was confused. I took a deep breath and gave her a weak smile.

"Nothing. Really. It's just me."

"Some memories?"

"Yeah. Something like that. But, it's okay."

"I'm sorry."

"Don't be sorry. You never have to be sorry. Remember that."

She hesitated and changed the subject.

"I didn't tell you. The application form and other materials were sent from our Hamburg office and the proposal was printed up as you said. I think the cover looks great. Lot of people worked on this. I'll have a copy of everything for you."

"Look forward to seeing it."

"When do you think we'll hear?"

"I'll ask Kevin to check it out."

"I'll have to get a visa. I think I can get one in Shanghai. But, if not, I can have an agency take care of it in Beijing."

"By the way, Kevin should be paid for his time and expertise."

"How much?"

"If we get to the second stage and they're serious, I think five thousand US is about right. Also, his expenses. It won't cost anything if your proposal is rejected."

"Five thousand plus expenses? That's almost as much as you're being paid."

"Kevin is worth as much if not more than I'm paid. And you'll want to use him later if the proposal is accepted."

"What about you? I'll need you."

"Yasha, remember what I said. I won't always be around. I have other business to take care of."

"I know." She looked out the window and bit her lower lip. She looked back at me and said, "I also know this is a big project. I admit I need as much help as I can get."

"You'll do just fine. But, what you're proposing will take at least three to five years to complete. If there are problems with the government it could take longer. Remember, Vietnam can be a swamp that devours foreign companies along with millions of dollars."

"I just need to know you'll be there if I need you."

"You can always count on me."

"I knew that." She smiled. "I should tell you, I told my mother about you. She wants to meet you."

"Your mother will think I'm much too old for you."

"That's what you always say. Do you really know how old I am?"

"I guess you're somewhere just under thirty."

She laughed and shook her head.

"You really don't know. You think of me as being a young girl. That's flattering, but that's not the way it is. We're the ideal age for each other."

"Really? Well, are you going to tell me?"

"Will it make a difference?"

"No, but since you brought it up, just how old are you?"

She laughed. "Now you're really curious. I'll keep it a secret until you agree to my plan."

"Your plan? What's that?"

"You'll know when it happens."

"Okay. Does my age make a difference?"

"No. I like you just the way you are. Has nothing to do with age."

"Guess I'll have to live with that."

"You're perfect for me. And my mother agrees."

"Well, your mother and father might think different if they want grandchildren."

"I want you to be the father of my children."

"Wait a minute. Children? I have four children now. And when did you decide I was going to sire your children?"

"It's all part of the plan."

"Your plan again."

"I'll tell you in time. You don't talk about your children or your wife."

"My ex-wife. I'm divorced."

"Was she Korean?"

"No. She was a White American."

"So your children are half Korean."

"Yes."

"Was her being White the reason it didn't work out?"

"Most of the problem was me and how I was. How I am."

"You blame yourself."

"Yes."

"Were you going to marry the woman in Harbin?"

"No. I don't intend to marry again."

"That's alright. You don't have to marry me. That's not a condition."

"Condition? What is this? Why are we talking about marriage and children?"

She smiled and looked out the window.

"My mother and I talk about this a lot. We talk about you and about grandchildren and such. And I'm getting older. That's one reason she wants to meet you."

"Having children is not going to happen. Your parents are gonna have to look elsewhere. You never told me, but do you have brothers and sisters? Are there others who can provide your parents with grandchildren?"

"Nope. I have an older sister who was crippled with polio. She has worn a leg brace since she was twelve years old. She was married but couldn't have children because she had vaginal cancer and had surgery to remove it. So there won't be any grandchildren from her. Unfortunately, her husband wanted a son and after a time he divorced her."

"Where is she now?"

"She lives with my parents. She's forty-two years old and not much hope for a husband at this late date."

"I'm sorry. It must be difficult for her."

"She helps my parents on the farm. She has a good attitude and she's tough."

"From what I see in you, toughness runs in the family."

"It's how we survive. But, there's lots of love too."

"That's wonderful."

"I talk to my parents and my sister at least twice a week."

"I didn't know that. I envy your good fortune to have such a family."

"I also had a brother. He was five years older than me."

"Oh? Had a brother?"

"He died five years ago."

"I'm sorry. How did he die?"

"He was killed in a helicopter crash. He was in the army at the time. He could have given my parents grandchildren."

"So now there is only you."

"All the more reason to live a full life."

"You're closer to your family than I am to my own children. I haven't been an ideal father."

"Why do you say that?"

"I don't know. There was always something that kept me from settling down as a school teacher and raising children. I never had all the qualities of a solid middle class citizen. I love my four children, but I haven't been as committed as a father should be. It's the one thing I regret. I'm a failure as a father."

"I don't believe you're a failure as a father or anything else."

"Contrary to your opinion, I'm a disaster. It would be unwise to be tied to me."

"You're not a failure. Whatever you think, it doesn't make any difference to me. I'm not without faults and serious failings. I did what I did because I thought it was best for me. You did the same. But this doesn't mean you and I lack the ability to love."

"True. But, what we think is best may not be the best. I have doubts everyday."

"The doubts make you real. Others are too sure of themselves. And you've had many successes you don't give yourself credit for. I know about you. Remember, I've check you out."

"You know, I really don't know much about you. Tell me about yourself."

"Really not much to tell. I grew up on my parent's farm and went to common school. I watched my parents, sister, and brother work so hard and there were some very difficult times. While he was alive my brother couldn't attend college because he stayed on the farm to help my parents. Then the army called him up. I decided I wanted something different. I wanted to help my family by being something different, not to be just an extra farm worker. So I began my plan to change myself and my life."

She paused and turned her eyes out the window, wondering how to tell me the rest of her story. She looked back at me and wet her lips.

"After I finished common school, I worked for a while in a branch office of the company I work for now. I met the owner who I thought owned all of China. He thought I was bright enough to go to college and he sent me to George Washington University. You probably know why he did that."

"Not important to know."

"It lasted for a little over two years. It was before I went to the

US. He had others before and after me. But, he was a kind man. He gave me an executive job after I finished my MBA at the University of Washington. He treats me pretty much like family and has been good to me. At the time, it was my way out. I was willing to pay the price."

"You don't have to explain."

"I want you to know. You probably heard some stories about me, but I wanted to tell you myself. What do you think of me? Am I some kind of whore? You want, I can tell you more details."

Unconsciously, she became defensive. She wasn't ashamed of how she got to college and her job, but saying it aloud to me made it seem sordid.

"I don't need details. It happened – it's past. You never have to explain yourself to me or anyone else. Remember that. I only care about you as you are now. Nothing else matters."

Her eyes moistened and she looked out the window. It was something she had to live with for the rest of her life. She thought she had to tell me, but she felt guilty about her "way out." I doubt she ever spoke of it to her parents and sister. They all knew, but didn't blame her. I certainly didn't.

I put my hand over hers and smiled. I realized I didn't really know about Yasha as a person. This was the first personal and meaningful talk we had.

"I'm sorry. I just felt I had to say something. I've never told anyone about this. You're the first. You probably guessed part of it, but I wanted to tell you myself."

"Thank you, Yasha. It means a great deal to me that you would tell me. Now, you never have to mention it again."

She wiped the tears and sighed. It was something that weighted on her and she was relieved she told me. She sipped her tea and looked at me, searching for signs of disapproval in my face. She found none and gave me a pleased grin.

"You've talked about your sister and brother, but what about your parents? What about them?" I asked, changing the subject.

"My parents and my grandparents before them were farmers. They raise cotton and food crops. It hasn't been an easy life for them, but they kept the family together. There were three of us, not like a lot of families with the one child policy. I think the government let them have my brother because of my sister's health problems and a son was needed on the farm. I was allowed to be because the party leader in the area was my uncle and my parents wanted another child."

"Whatever. Your parents provided a good stable home for you. It has affected the way you are today and will be in the future. You are an exceptional woman."

"My father and mother would be pleased to hear you say that."

She put her folded arms on the table and leaned toward me. Her confident self was back and things were almost normal again.

"Now, what about your family? I know something about you, but nothing about your family background."

She was quite frank in revealing her story and I felt I should tell her a bit about my family and my life.

"My father left his home in Seoul when he was fifteen. He traveled for about ten years, learning about life in Okinawa, Hawaii, and America. While in America he saw a photo of my mother and decided she was the one. She was sixteen. He went back to Korea and over the objections of her brothers, took her as his bride. He didn't have to force her because she wanted to come to America. It was her chance to live the greatest adventure of her life. My mother and father were truly pioneers and they risked everything to go to America.

"My mother attended elementary school, but my father never went to school. Still, he could speak three languages. He was a migrant laborer and followed the harvest from Montana to Mexico. He organized his fellow Korean immigrants into a labor organization and later formed an association similar to a retirement group.

"Because they traveled so much, the five children in our family were born in three different states. My oldest sister and I were born in Montana, my brother in Utah, and two sisters in California.

"When I was four, we settled in a tiny town called Parlier in the central valley of California. That's where I grew up. I wasn't a model Korean son and was corrupted with the American way of life by the time I was ten years old. I graduated from high school when I was sixteen, joined the army when I was seventeen, and after my discharge went to college on the GI Bill. After the BA I got a graduate scholarship for the MA. One thing led to another and I ended up with a doctorate.

"I was a teacher for a while. Not too successful. I was fired from most of my jobs in education, for one reason or another. I was fired from my first job because I was married to a White woman.

"My mother wasn't too happy when I married a White woman. My father had passed away before I got married, but I don't think interracial marriages concerned him. He would have been pleased with the four grandchildren.

"After a time I left education and got into this business. Maybe it wasn't a good decision. I haven't made much money and my personal life hasn't been that good."

I sighed and looked out the window.

"That's about it. Nothing spectacular."

"Where are your brother and sisters?"

"My brother and his wife live in Hawaii. My oldest sister passed away. The other older sister never married and is living in Central California. She arranged parties and things for movie and television stars. The youngest sister married a White guy and is living in the central valley close to where we all grew up. She has four children."

"I knew your life and family would be different. You're not the typical Asian. You're part western, but you have many real Asian values."

"You're right. Most of my personal values are based on Asian values. I can thank my mother for that."

"I think I'm sorta part Asian and western too. Going to school in the US helped. My father thinks I'm too western, but my mother doesn't think that. That's why she thinks you would be right for me."

"Yasha, beware. I'm not a knight in shinning armor. I carry a lot of hard luck baggage and I'm reaching a point of no return."

"Whatever you say, still doesn't change things for me."

I talked about myself more with her than I had with anyone else. Reminiscing seems to have become a thing with me. Was this a middle age peculiarity?

We fell silent for a time, lost in our thoughts about our families. We looked out the window and watched two boys paddling a small rowboat across the lake. A lantern hug from a pole tied to the bow of their boat. They were out night fishing. They knew how to live the good life.

I wondered about Yasha and myself. She was so certain how our relationship should be. Why is that?

"So, you decided about me?

She tilted her head and smiled at me.

"Of course. It's our *karma*."

"When did this happen?"

"It started when we became best friends. Everything after that is our *karma* and that's where we are now."

Did she believe that or was this just rationalizing what she wanted? I would never know, because I didn't completely and absolutely believe about *karma*. But, as BJ believed, so Yasha believed. Actually, it was kinda scary.

"You want dessert?" she asked.

"No. I've had too much to eat. You can have a dessert if you want."

"I've had enough too."

"Why don't we finish our perfect dinner with a drink at the hotel?"

She waved at the waiter. She paid with a Chinese credit card and left the tip in cash. We were given a royal send off as half dozen waiters lined the way to the exit where a boat was waiting for us. At the landing, we took the first taxi in the queue.

She snuggled up to me in the taxi and put her arms through mine. Yasha was pleased with the way things went. So was I.

It was a light crowd in the lounge and we took a booth facing the bar. The bar maid came over and took our order. Yasha had a glass of white wine and I had a drambuie.

"It's been a delightful evening, but time to get on to reality. I'm going to be tied up all day tomorrow and have a dinner engagement tomorrow night."

"When are you leaving?" she asked.

"Day after tomorrow. I need your help again. Can you get me to Shanghai and a flight direct to San Francisco?"

"Okay. We'll fly up together. You can get a connection to San

Francisco from Shanghai. If not, you might have to spend a night in Shanghai."

"I rather not if I can avoid it."

"You can spend the night with me."

"I could do that tonight."

"That's right. You could. I have a king size bed here."

"Yasha, you have to behave."

"It's a thought."

"Yasha."

"Think of all those nights in Vietnam."

"Not going to happen."

"You don't know. Things happen."

I shook my head and sighed.

"Oh, Yasha."

"Where are you going tomorrow?"

"Just some personal things I have to take care of. Nothing to do with business."

"Does it have to do with Harbin?"

"No."

"Are you going to tell me about Harbin?"

"Someday."

"You used to say you would tell me things when I'm old enough."

"Yeah. When you're old enough."

"You've changed."

"I'm the one that's getting older."

"These past few weeks have changed you. I can feel it. You're sad inside."

I looked at her for a moment. How was she so attuned to my feelings? She was probably smarter than me. That was also kinda scary.

"Do you want another drink?" I asked.

"No. This one is enough for me."

I waved at the barmaid, held up one finger, and pointed to my drink.

"I'm going to have one more drink and then I'm going up to bed."

"It's okay." She put her hand over mine. "I know you have some personal problems. I'm here if you need me. Remember you said we were friends."

"You're right, Yasha. You're one of my best friends."

"You are my best friend. I'm glad we talked about things."

"So am I. I think we know each other better now."

"That's one major step in our relationship."

"There are more?"

"Several. They'll be easier now that we're past this."

"You're getting kinda spooky, Yasha."

"You'll get use to it." She laughed.

We finished our drinks and went out to the elevators. I walked her to her room.

"Yasha, thank you for a wonderful dinner. It was really grand."

"Finally. We finally had a real dinner."

"Yes we did." I smiled. "One I won't forget."

She put her arms around my neck and kissed me. It was a long kiss with a lot of feeling.

"I'm waiting," she whispered.

"Yasha. You know ..."

"Good night, best friend," she said and closed the door.

I stood staring at the closed door. How did things change so suddenly? Why did I have the feeling I had lost control of the situation?

19

T HE NEXT MORNING I went through my usual routine – an hour in the gym, showered, shaved, called house keeping for laundry pickup, and watched the news. Had my life become routine? Kam Wah told me to get a "normal" life. Was normal just routine?

It was eight o'clock when I called Amanda at the Huangpo office.

"Hello Amanda."

"Hello. Kam Wah said you were back."

"I was coming into the office today and wondered if you and Su Lin could have lunch with me."

"I won't be able to, but Su Lin can."

"Are you sure? It's only an hour lunch."

"Thanks, but I have to be at a meeting at city hall at noon. Crazy time for a meeting, but that's what they wanted."

"Kam Wah says things are going well with Su Lin. Thank you for helping her."

"She is learning very quickly. A smart girl. Wait a minute and I'll switch you over to her phone."

Su Lin came on the line. She was excited.

"You're here! Amanda says you're coming for lunch."

"Yes. I'll be there about noon."

"I'll be waiting. I have so much to tell you."

"Good. See you in a couple of hours."

She sounded wonderful. Almost a full recovery from a life of misery and bad experiences. There was an escape from a vicious moneylender, her mother passing away, her father abandoning the family, and suddenly becoming responsible for her younger sister. Hadn't been an easy time for her, but she was getting it together.

"Can Wong come to pick me up at eleven-thirty?"

"Not a problem. I have scheduled a dinner with police Chief Wu and his wife at six tonight. We can go to the massage parlor before dinner."

"That's great. I need a massage."

"Yes. That and Chinese herbs."

"Today, I really need the massage. Even more than the herbs," I said.

"That is a problem with you. Herbs are important. You are well today because of Chinese herbs."

"I was only joking. Of course, the herbs are more important."

I reminded myself - again - to not joke about those things.

"Don't forget that."

"I won't."

"I will remind you."

"I know you will."

I called Yasha and asked if she wanted to meet for breakfast in a half an hour. She said yes. I went down and found a table overlooking the Pearl River.

One wall of the restaurant at the White Swan was a series of floor to ceiling glass panels. It was a good seat to watch the river junks and rafts carrying cargo up and down the river. Just below and directly across from the hotel, river ferries brought workers from one side of the river to the other. All positive signs of a busy and growing society. China, a state controlled economy, would soon become the world's largest economy. When that happened, would I be around?

"Good morning."

"Good morning, Yasha."

"Did you have your morning workout?" she asked.

"Yes, I did. Did you?"

"No. Since I'm going to be alone, I might go sometime later today."

She decided to have the buffet breakfast and I had the continental.

I picked at my croissant and drank part of the orange juice. I was losing my appetite. I was sure Kam Wah would have something to say about that. Among other things, it was the lack of herbs, he would say.

"My dinner engagement tonight is an early one. If I get back early we can have a drink. Okay?"

"Sure. Oh, I'm checking on the plane reservations for tomorrow. It'll be an early morning flight to Shanghai and hopefully there'll be a flight to the US before midnight. I'll know for sure later."

"Thanks, Yasha. As always, you're a great help."

"I'll also have my office staff bring a copy of the Vietnam proposal to the airport. You can see how the finished copy looks."

"Sounds good. What are you going to do today?"

"I have to find a freight forwarder for goods shipped from the factory in Hunan. We need to bring them to Huangpo for shipment to Japan. Using Shanghai is difficult because it's such a busy port."

"What kind of goods?"

"Some auto parts. Plastic dashboard facings and other similar items."

"So you'll be busy."

"Yes. I think there's a lunch involved, so I won't need much of a dinner."

"It was a great dinner last night, Yasha."

"Yes it was. The one we will have in Shanghai will be even better."

I thought about Kam Wah's comments about Shanghai cuisine. It really wasn't as bad as he says it was. Of course, nothing was as good as Guangzhou food. Was I as bad as Kam Wah? Yeah, I was.

Yasha talked about her tasks for the day, but I only half listened. I watched her with a bemused smile. I thought about our dinner last night and how lovely she looked. Seven months ago I didn't really know who Yasha was. It was fitting that she was from Shanghai, the original and now renewed, exotic commercial center of China. It was the modern China and people like Yasha were the new generation.

Her company bosses were from the older generation who made fortunes when China adopted new quasi-capitalist economic ways. But, now they relied on the western educated ones. I was actually in the upper age group of the younger generation, but was more mentally attuned with the older generation. I would be obsolete before too long, if I wasn't already.

I admired the new ones, but also resented them. They asked for advice, but once they had learned the way, they no longer needed mentors. I was fast becoming out of date. The Internet and computers eliminated the world I knew.

My real value was making people contact, but most of the people I knew were older than me and some had already died off. Soon they'll be gone, which didn't matter because the younger ones will have their own contacts.

So why was Yasha attracted to me? And why was I attracted to her? I thought we were from different generations, but we were actually in the same general age group. So, why do I think she's too young? Hell, she's just a few years younger than I am. Have I mentally and emotionally aged before my time?

"Are you listening to me?" she asked suddenly.

"Of course. I always listen to you."

"You look as if your mind is off somewhere. Is it the Harbin business again?"

"No. But, you should know us older folks' minds wanders sometime."

"Sure, like when you're planning something you don't want me to know about."

"Running out of things to plan, Yasha."

"Well, I need you to help me plan."

"Even that will end soon."

"What's the matter? Is something wrong?"

"Lots of things happened this past week. So many things so quick.

The sand in the hourglass is draining. Can't stop it or even slow it down."

"That Harbin business is wearing you down. Is there something I can do?"

"You already have. We had a great dinner last night. It made my day and I don't think I'll have too many more like that."

"Yes, we will. I've planned for many more."

"Don't I get a say in this?"

"Of course. You can pick one of the restaurants."

"Just one?"

"Well, depends on the quality of the food in the one you pick."

"It's a losing battle."

"You can change all that."

"Oh? How?"

"Just go with the plan."

"What plan?"

"My plan."

20

IT WAS A PLEASANT sunny morning, but would warm up by mid afternoon. Maybe the warm summer would bring better times. Anything would be better than the events of the past spring.

At eleven-thirty Wong drove into the hotel driveway and parked next to the taxi queue. He saw me standing at the door and waved. Since Kam Wah was not there, I rode in front.

We arrived at the Huangpo office as the office staff was leaving for lunch. Su Lin came out, anxiously looking for me. I think she wanted to rush up to me but demurely stood to one side. I went up to her and gave her a hug. She wasn't embarrassed and hugged me back. She kept her arms around me for a long moment.

"You're here," she whispered.

"How are you, Su Lin?"

"Much better since you're here."

I smiled and held her at arms length and looked at her.

"You're getting more beautiful every time I see you."

She blushed and looked down. I laughed and hugged her again.

Kam Wah came out and watched us. He thought I should take Su Lin as a wife. But, he thought that about Amanda also, as well as every Chinese woman I met.

"I called for a taxi. I will tell the driver where to take you for *dim sum* lunch. I need Wong here."

"Thank you, Kam Wah."

It was a nice restaurant and crowded, as all *dim sum* restaurants are at noon. Kam Wah had called ahead and we were seated in one of the semi-private rooms. There were three other customers in the room. As soon as tea was served, the waitresses wheeled their carts with *dim sum* into the room and I had several of my favorites.

"You've done a great job in getting things in order. How is your sister doing?"

"She's a part time student. Studying computer science. And working part time at the massage parlor where I used to work. Oh, and she's learning to speak English."

"Great."

"You think it's okay that she works at the massage parlor?"

"If she had a job at a factory or office she wouldn't have time for school. And the pay is good at the massage parlor."

"It's just that some people look down on women who work there."

"Never mind. What they think is not important. I think it is a very good situation for her, as it was for you."

"Your saying that makes me feel better."

"Believe it – because it's true."

We talked about her new apartment and the things she was learning at the office. It was a few minutes past the hour she had for lunch when we returned to the office. She was worried she would be late.

"Thank you for lunch."

"You're really a success, Su Lin. I'm very proud of you."

She didn't cry this time but her eyes became moist. She hugged me.

"Thank you again for my life," she whispered.

I thought about Su Lin and Yasha. Yasha was a few years older and both had difficult times, but Yasha lucked out and found a way to escape a dead end life.

Su Lin's road was rougher and she needed a different kind of help. But, she was making it. One day she'll get married and have children to worry about. Her story was one of those happenings that took place in between the businesses I was involved with. The in-betweens, like Su Lin, were what made my life worthwhile.

21

I WAS ADDICTED TO spas and massages and made use of them whenever I was in Huangpo or Hong Kong. The massage and spa in Huangpo was a favorite hangout and the staff knew Kam Wah and me well. It was there that I met Su Lin.

After sweating a couple of gallons of booze and other poisons in the sauna we relaxed in the lounge and had some fruit juice.

I brought him up to date on Harbin and recounted what had happened there since last December. I told him about the hunt for the killer being carried on by the police and hinted that others were also looking. He wanted to know about all the people involved, including BJ's family. We rehashed our encounter with Choi at the White Swan Hotel in Guangzhou last December. He reminded me about Bak and his sister and how vicious the North Koreans were. He had his own opinions about Choi's assassination and probably discussed this with Chief Wu. I knew he would ask Chief Wu about BJ's death. He definitely didn't want me to go back to Harbin.

He was more positive about Yasha's resort project and was impressed that there was an entity that would put up so much capital for the enterprise. As most businessmen in China, he knew of the Li Wah company's resources and its Chairman, T.S. Tsai. He was not certain about my munitions plant proposal. He didn't trust the Vietnamese military. He didn't say why, he just mistrusted them.

After our discussion and much criticism about my motives in Harbin, we let the subject drop. I usually listened carefully to Kam Wah's opinions, but I knew I wouldn't change my mind.

After a while, I dozed off. Twenty minutes later, he shook me and said it was time to go to the massage rooms.

———————————

Wendy was the masseuse I used most often and she was waiting for me. She gave me a warm welcome and padded the mat, motioning me to lie down.

"How are you, Wendy?"

"I'm fine. So happy you have returned."

"Ah yes. It has been too long since I've had a good massage."

"I have been waiting for you."

"I'm here, so do your best."

The hot tub and sauna made me a little light headed and Wendy's strong fingers made my body's aches and pains disappear.

"You were tense at your earlier visit, but, much more relaxed today."

"Your magic fingers help."

"Have you seen Sophie?"

"You mean Su Lin?"

"Oh, you know her Chinese name. Good. She is happy and even happier now that her sister is with her. Do you know her sister works here part time?"

"Yes, I know."

"She's not here now, but next time you can have her."

"You do just fine."

"We have all heard what you did for her. That was very heroic."

"Heroic?" I laughed. "I'm not a hero."

"I mean it was a good thing and few men would do what you did. That was her *karma*."

Karma again. I supposed it was what Su Lin and Wendy believed and things did turn out in a positive way for her. So I was given the title of savior. Quite different from the results of my relationship with BJ. I thought about the events, actions, and decisions I made that placed her in a position to be murdered. That was her *karma*. I didn't do much for her.

"You are getting tense. Is something wrong?" Wendy was very good at her craft. She knew immediately that I had tensed up.

"Ah, Wendy. Nothing's wrong. You're doing what is best for me."

"You are thinking of something that has happened. Is it something I said?"

"No. Not to worry. You're doing just fine."

In spite of my sudden troubled state of mind the massage ended well. Kam Wah paid for the massages, but I gave Wendy an extra tip. The manager, who also knew about Su Lin and the moneylender, was pleased to see me again. He and several of the women came out to say good bye.

Back at the office Kam Wah called the restaurant to confirm our dinner reservations. We had a cup of tea and talked some more about Harbin and Vietnam. He expressed real concerns again about Harbin and repeated that I should not go back. He suggested that I should at least wait for awhile.

After the tea break, I said my good byes again to Amanda and Su Lin. Amanda was very attentive, as she always was, and she and Su Lin walked me to the door. They were very special ladies. Kam Wah was right, both would be good wives.

Wong was waiting to take us to the restaurant. As usual, I sat in back and Kam Wah sat in front next to Wong with the window rolled down so the cigarette smoke was sucked out. When not discussing business affairs or the family, Kam Wah's favorite topic was my marital status. He didn't let this opportunity pass.

"You should think about Amanda as a wife."

"Kam Wah, let's not start that again."

Wong grinned and shook his head.

"If the Manchu lady is gone and you do not intend to consider Su Lin, Amanda is a very good choice. She likes you very much."

"And I like her. But, it's not going to happen."

"This is what keeps you from becoming truly Chinese."

"Then, so be it."

"The family will be disappointed."

"I'm sorry."

"You have come very close to being Chinese." He sighed and lit another cigarette. "Well, we have to find some way. It is for your own good."

"I know."

"Pay attention to what I say."

"I will."

"So you say."

Wong was laughing.

Dinner with the Chief and his wife was at a new restaurant in the Tienhe district. As usual, Kam Wah had reserved a private room. We arrived a few minutes early, which gave Kam Wah time to check on the dishes he ordered. Our early arrival also made certain the Chief and his wife would not have to wait without a host. That would have been most embarrassing.

A few minutes after six they arrived. Kam Wah greeted them at the door and bowed to Mrs. Wu. I stepped up and shook the Chief's hand. He turned to his wife.

"This is Meilan's mother."

I bowed and extended my hand.

"Mrs. Wu, it is a pleasure to meet Meilan's mother."

"She has spoken of you often."

"I'm pleased she has taken note of me."

She smiled and nodded. Kam Wah beamed at my good manners and very polite words. If I kept this up I might even be allowed to become a Chinese without a wife.

She was probably about fifteen years older than me. Her charm and grace were the traits that Meilan had inherited. Her lovely face was clear and smooth, without a wrinkle or line anywhere. Except for some very light powder, she didn't wear much makeup, a light ruby color on her lips, and her hair was cut short. There were a few gray strands in her very black hair.

She wore a blue ankle length *cheongsam* with a flower pattern. It was a modern cut, a small slit on the side, with enough room to walk comfortably. She had a pink silk shawl over her shoulders. Most women wore a shawl to ward off the cold created by the air conditioners. At good restaurants, if a guest did not have a shawl, one was provided.

Kam Wah and the Chief stood to one side and chatted about the news of the day. Mrs. Wu gently pulled me toward the table.

"She told me about the dinner. She was very pleased."

"It was my pleasure. She was beautifully dressed. The *cheongsam* was perfect for the evening."

"She also told us about the bicycle. That was very good of you. We must make arrangements to pay for it."

"Please. There is no need. It is my way of helping Meilan to adjust to college life. It should not be mentioned again. Please." I didn't want to get into a discussion over this.

She nodded an okay and we didn't mention it again. She understood how I felt and she accepted my wishes.

Two waiters came into the room with damp hand towels for everyone. Several condiments were placed on the table. One of my favorites was slices of *cha shu* and Kam Wah never forgot.

Kam Wah directed us to our designated seats. Mrs. Wu was seated facing the door. I sat next to her and Kam Wah and the Chief sat across from us. A waiter came in and poured tea for everyone. Thereafter, Kam Wah, as host monitored the tea pot and poured. While we sipped the *bolai* tea, a large bottle of Tsingtao beer was brought in and everyone had a glass, even Mrs. Wu.

Mrs. Wu asked what I did in China and I talked about this and that without getting into any details. I asked her about her second daughter and what her plans were for the future. She said she would finish common school next year and probably join her sister at Mills College.

After a bit, the Chief joined our conversation.

"Well, what do you think of her academic progress?" he asked.

"As you know, her grades for the last quarter were excellent. She achieved a four-point grade average. That's as good as one can do. I think she is doing very well."

"Have you seen her dormitory?"

"Yes. I have been to the dorm. I haven't been in her room but the living quarters are reported to be very good. I also met her roommate."

"She told us about her. Meilan says they get on well."

"Yes, they do. Schoolgirls know how to handle these relationships.

Of course, they aren't girls. They're young adults. Meilan knows what to do. She has adapted well."

"Do you see her often?"

He asked, but knew exactly how many times I had seen her, including the times we had dinner. Probably knew what we had to eat.

"I have seen her twice since January. I don't want to take up too much of her time because she needs the time for her studies. But, I will see her again after this trip. She knows to contact me if she needs help."

"Help? What kind of help?"

"Whatever she thinks she needs help with. But I'll drop in on her now and then to let her know I'm around."

"That's good."

The Chief would like it if I saw her every week. But that wasn't going to happen.

"Thank you for the bicycle. We will attend to that matter later."

"As I mentioned to Mrs. Wu that is not necessary."

She gave the Chief a stern look and very slight shake of her head. It was a matter of face with me and she understood. I was certain she would mention it to the Chief later tonight. He stopped talking about repayment for the bicycle. I was relieved.

As the eight course dinner was coming to an end, the Chief brought up a sensitive subject. He stammered a bit and glanced anxiously at his wife. Then finally said what he wanted to say.

"We, Mrs. Wu and I, greatly appreciate what you are doing for our daughter. It gives us comfort and we feel more confident in sending our second daughter to America."

"It is my pleasure."

"For your time and efforts, and later when our second daughter goes, we feel we must provide some kind of compensation."

So, he wanted to pay me to babysit Meilan and later his second daughter. This conversation would freak Meilan out. But, it was reasonable for him to make such an offer. He and I didn't have any family or business ties and we had known each other for less than a year. He did me a favor with getting my visa after the incident in Harbin and he took an interest in my problems with the North Koreans. So my keeping tabs on Meilan was *quid pro quo*. But to be certain that I would be there for his daughter, paying me was better than depending on my good intentions. However, a paid babysitter I was not. Time to get this all straighten out.

I stared at him for a long moment and then turned to Mrs. Wu. She looked down at her tea cup. This was also a matter of face. Kam Wah was watching me carefully.

"Chief Wu, please hear me on this. Under no circumstances, never, ever, offer me any money or other compensation for anything I do for Meilan. I do what I do for Meilan because I think of her as my own. Even if you and I had strong differences, I will continue to be her friend and look out for her well being. I will appreciate it if we never discuss this subject again."

He was surprised. Kam Wah beamed. I was almost totally Chinese. It would have been acceptable if I had said I would be grateful for anything, but nothing was necessary. That would have been very businesslike. But it was not how I felt.

I think everyone in the room was pleased with what I said. The Chief smiled and put out his hand. I took it. He put his other hand over mine.

"Thank you," he said.

Mrs. Wu reached over and placed her hand on my arm.

"I told you he would say that," she said to her husband but looked at me.

I understood his motive and reasoning and the Chief felt he had to say what he said. No harm done. The moment came and vanished without issue.

A signal that the dinner was coming to an end was when the waiters – there were two and a third helped when the meal was served – came with some fruit. There were slices of watermelon, mangos, cantaloupe, and oranges. Another bottle of beer was served.

The Chief stood and waved his glass of beer at me and made a toast.

"My wife and I are thankful for your kindness. We treasure your friendship. Thank you."

It was a reaffirmation of the bond we had just formed. We all clinked glasses.

It was a good dinner and an important issue had been made clear. The Chief and his wife felt better about their daughter's well being and about me. Kam Wah was happy that I was almost Chinese. I needed a real drink.

As we were leaving, Mrs. Wu put her hand on my arm and gently pulled me toward her.

She leaned over and whispered, "Meilan calls you *shu fu* and considers you a family member. So do I."

"Thank you."

———————

We said our goodbyes and walked out to the entrance where Wong was waiting. Kam Wah sat in the designated smoking area in the front seat and I sat in the back seat.

"That all went well," Kam Wah said, obviously very pleased, as he blew smoke out the open window.

"Mrs. Wu is a very nice lady."

"She was pleased. You handled the matter of money the correct way. If I didn't know better I would have thought you were Chinese."

"But not totally."

"I will tell you honestly. It is very close."

"I suppose a Chinese wife would cinch it."

"Almost a hundred percent certain."

I couldn't help but laugh and soon all three of us were laughing.

After we quieted down, I thought about this in a more serious manner. Kam Wah wants me to be Chinese, but I'm Korean and was born in America. Most referred to me just as the Korean from America. Who was I, really?

"Being Chinese is fine with you, but what would my parents say? They wanted me to be Korean. In fact, I disappointed them when I didn't take a Korean wife."

He became serious. To him, there was much more to taking a wife than living with a woman. Taking a wife was completion of self. It was not only his way, it was the Chinese way.

"When you're in Korea, you should be Korean. If you take a Korean wife, I would accept that. You took a White wife and that did not work out. You came to China because it was more natural to be here. You are more Chinese than you are Korean. You have some bad habits that are American, but you are least of all American."

"I carry an American passport. So I'm identified as an American."

"Only on paper. I have a Hong Kong ID and can be considered a British subject, but, that is only for show. I am Chinese. You can be Chinese and Korean. That is good, because both are better than being an American. "

These were issues of identity I had struggled with for years. Kam Wah was serious about identity and being identified as Chinese was essential in his life. All his values, concept of self, and relationship with others were what he believed to be the Chinese *tao*. He wanted me to share that with him. It was acceptable for me to be Korean, but when I was in his environment, I should be Chinese.

Kam Wah often joked about taking a wife, but it was very serious matter. I was part of his family and he wanted me to be a whole person. A wife, especially a Chinese wife, would complete my being.

"I must admit, I have been struggling with who I am for most of my life."

"I know. That is why you are in China. You have not completed your true self in America. You can do that here."

"I have children in America. There is an important part of me there."

"They are American. Unfortunately, they do not have the advantages of growing up in a Chinese or Korean family. You have an opportunity to return to your real roots. You can always have more children."

Kam Wah knew me better than anyone and appreciated my problems of identity. I was wearing down and was in danger of heeding his advice to take a Chinese wife. Maybe I would – in another life.

We rode a while in silence. Time to change the subject.

"I'm leaving tomorrow."

"You are going to Shanghai and then home?"

"Yes."

"When will you be back?"

"When I'm finished in Vietnam, I'll connect with a flight from there to Hong Kong."

"I know the business in Harbin weighs on you. You must get on with life."

"I'll try."

"You must do, not just try," he was adamant.

"I suppose if I was Chinese I could forget," I grinned.

"Maybe not forget, but learn to live with it."

It was what Roger said. They thought alike and they were reasonable men who had my best interest in mind. But, there were unusual circumstances connected with this and I felt I had to do my thing. Was I just being obstinate? Harbin and identity. Several vital issues I have to deal with. Not an especially good note to end a pleasant evening.

"Give my best to the family."

"You could tell them yourself if you lived here. You should consider it."

"I will."

"So you say."

22

IT WAS TEN O'CLOCK when I got back to the hotel. Might be too late for Yasha, but I told her I would check with her. I went to the house phones in the lobby and called.

"I didn't know if you were still awake."

"Where are you?"

"I'm down here in the lobby. I'm going to the bar and get a drink."

"I'll be down in a minute."

"Okay."

I sat at the end of the bar and asked the bartender if he had single malt scotch. He said he did and I ordered one, neat.

Yasha came to the bar as I was being served.

"Want a drink?"

"I'll have a glass of white wine."

I motioned to the bartender and ordered her a glass of white wine.

"So, how did your business go with the freight forwarder?'

"All set. Got some very good prices."

I knew she would find a freight forwarder and also get bargain prices. She was pretty good at taking care of business.

"Were you able to get plane reservations to Shanghai and San Francisco?"

"Need you ask? Of course. We leave tomorrow at 9 AM and get to Shanghai at 11:15AM. Your United flight leaves at 1:45 PM and arrives in SFO at 8:08 AM the next day. All Business Class."

"That's great. Thanks, Yasha."

"So how was your day?"

"Pretty good. Got to see everyone I had to see. Sweated for awhile in a hot sauna, and had a great massage."

"Massage?"

"Yes. Next time I go for a massage you can come with me."

"I don't know. I haven't had a massage before."

"Time you started." I smiled. "I think you would like it."

"We'll see. By the way, so you know, your hotel is taken care of."

"Thanks. Guess my Vietnam consultant fee is pretty much used up."

"Well, your time hasn't really started yet."

"Whatever. I'll depend on you to keep track. I'm sure you'll cut me off when it runs out."

"You sound tired. You can get some rest when you get home. I mean really get some rest. It'll be a busy time in Vietnam."

"Well, most of the paperwork is done and Kevin will set up the meetings. So I'm hoping that it won't be that bad."

"Are you going to tell me what your business is in Vietnam?"

"Okay. I guess you're old enough."

"I'm old enough for a lot of things."

"Yeah, I noticed."

"Time for you to take advantage of that."

"I don't know if you're really old enough."

"You'll never know until you've tried."

"Yasha."

"I'll be patient."

"Good."

I finished my drink and waved at the bartender and pointed at my glass.

"Do you want another?"

"No thanks."

The bartender gave me another scotch and put a bowl of popcorn on the bar.

"You know in Hawaii they give drinkers *kimchi* instead of peanuts or popcorn."

"Don't change the subject. You were going to tell me about your business in Vietnam."

"Okay. There's a munitions plant in Vietnam that is in disrepair. They can't produce quality goods or in any quantity to make it profitable. I work with an arms company in the Philippines and we can refurbish the plant, make it efficient, and produce enough for domestic use as well as export. We've submitted a proposal to do that."

"Is this part of your gas mask business?"

"Yes and no. The gas masks were a different kind of deal."

"One day you'll tell me everything, won't you?"

"Yeah. One day I'll tell you everything."

"Gas masks and ammunition. What else?"

"Yasha, I don't really deal in goods. I really deal in people. I put deals together because that's what people want. What the deal involves in terms of goods is not important. It's getting the fucking people together that's important!"

Why was I getting worked up? Yasha frowned and grabbed my arm. I looked around. A few people were giving me curious looks. Even the bartender looked at me with a questioning eye. Was I shouting? Guess I was.

"I'm sorry. It's been a long day, Yasha."

"Not to worry. I know you're going through a tough time. I'm sorry I ask so many questions."

"Don't be sorry. There isn't anything you can't ask me. I may not give you an answer, but you can ask." I took a long sip of scotch. "Maybe I'm not the person to help with your business."

"Yes, you are. At your worse, you're better than everyone else. I trust you. A lot is at stake for me and I need your support."

"How do you know I won't just quit? We haven't signed a contract."

"We don't need a contract. You gave me your word."

"You know me too well."

"You're easy to know."

"Oh?"

"Your word is everything to you. I expect others to keep their word in the same way. But, not everyone does. You do and that's why I trust you."

"Yeah. My word. Well, what else do I have? Nothing, really. Just my word. I don't have any money or political power. I only have my word to offer. And I don't know how much that's worth on today's market."

"For me that's more important than anything else. You also know people and you know how things come together. Those are things I need. And," she grinned, "I have a mad crush on you."

"What am I going to do with you?"

"I've made several suggestions."

"Yasha, you're incorrigible." I had to laugh. "Well, I'm going to bed. A nine o'clock flight? Is the gym open at 5:30?"

"I'll tell the manager I want to use the gym at 5:30."

"Oh? You'll tell the manager?"

"His brother works in our company branch office here in Guangzhou. Why do you think I stay here whenever I'm in Guangzhou?"

"Well, that's better than knowing the bartender."

We went up to the ninth floor and walked arm in arm to her to her room.

"I'm sorry about tonight. I usually don't shout and swear aloud."

"You needed to do that. Not because that's the way you are, but because you had something bad happen. I know that."

"Good night, Yasha."

She grabbed my hand and stood against me. She kissed me.

"Behave, Yasha."

"I'm not old enough to behave."

"Yasha."

"Remember, five-thirty tomorrow morning."

23

WHEN YASHA SAID THE gym would be opened at 5:30, I knew the gym would be opened at 5:30. We met at the gym and worked out for about forty minutes and then went to our rooms to clean up and pack.

The plane left at nine, so we were cutting it close. I paid the taxi driver an extra twenty-five RMB to get us there on time. We were the last ones to board. Yasha used her special company card and we were bumped up to First Class. She had all the right credentials. It was a commuter flight and most of the Business Class and Economy seats were taken.

Breakfast was served as soon as we were airborne. I passed on the hot breakfast and had a Danish instead. Yasha had eggs, potatoes, and a roll. After breakfast, I dozed and Yasha read some magazines and chatted with the flight attendant.

When we landed we went to immigration and I filed my exit form. From there we went to the departure area. Yasha showed her identification and was allowed into the areas restricted to passengers only. It pays to be a member of the elite, at least an employee of an elite organization.

She steered me toward the VIP lounge. Her company maintained a membership and it was an ideal place to wait for my flight to San Francisco. Drinks and snacks were also available.

As she had planned, a copy of her Vietnam proposal was waiting at the reception desk. We found a quiet corner and settled in.

"You don't have to wait around here, Yasha. My flight isn't for a couple hours. I'm sure you have things to do."

"I have you to take care of." she said.

"I can take care of myself."

"Now you have me to do that. Get used to it." She laughed and handed me a package. "Here's the finished Vietnam proposal. You like the cover?"

The cover and everything else was in perfect order. I was impressed with the presentation.

"Yes. Looks great, Yasha. They'll be impressed."

"I put it together as you suggested. Except it's longer than you said it should be. About fifty pages not counting the graphs and design drawings. Hope that's okay. I'm taking an English copy and a Vietnamese copy with me. I've already sent five copies to Hanoi. Oh, before I forget. Here are the name cards you asked for. I had them delivered with the proposal."

"More of your efficiency."

"You're pleased. I can tell." She was grinning at me.

"Yes. I'm very pleased. You do an excellent job with everything."

"I'm glad you noticed."

She was proud of her work. This was the real Yasha – very intelligent and fiercely determined to accomplish her objectives. If I thought she would be an innocent when dealing with the Vietnamese, I was mistaken. It was they who would be on the defensive. I felt better about her every day.

She wanted to show off her work. She put the booklet on my lap and flipped through the pages, commenting on the drawings and photos. It was extremely well done.

Suddenly I heard a cell phone ring. The chime sounded distant and I thought it was her phone. I looked at Yasha and gave her a quizzical look. She shook her head and waved her silent phone. I realized it was my cell phone. Was it Ahn? I reached into my coat pocket and pulled out the chiming, vibrating instrument. The number lit up on the small screen had a Beijing area code. I clicked the talk button.

"Hello."

"Ah, I found you at last. This is Chang."

"Mr. Chang. This is a pleasant surprise."

"I rang your US number several times and when there was no answer I assumed you were still in China."

"You knew I was in China?"

"Yes. I talked to my brother in Harbin and he told me you were at a gathering honoring the lady who was killed." He was silent a moment. "I'm sorry for your loss."

"Thank you."

Obviously, he knew about BJ. He said the lady who was killed, not the lady who died. Was this call about that?

"What can I do for you, Mr. Chang?"

"I need your help on a very confidential matter."

Ah, yes. It was time to repay the help he provided me with the gas masks and dealing with the American CIA agent in Harbin.

"If I can, I'm happy to help."

"Thank you. I knew I could count on you. This problem has to do with a young man who is in America. In the city of Chicago. He is the son of a well-known party official in China. The young man's name is Ho Man Pei. He calls himself Tony in America. He is in his third year at the University of Chicago. Unfortunately, he has fallen on bad times. This is of his own doing. He was arrested for being in possession of drugs. According to our sources he can be convicted and sentenced to a year or more in prison."

"Does he have an attorney?"

"We would prefer to settle this without an attorney or going to court. It is our wish to keep all of this as confidential as possible."

"What do you have in mind?"

"I want to have the charges dropped."

"I don't know, Mr. Chang. The American courts don't appreciate foreigners who deal in drugs. Do you know if he was using or selling? He's a student and if it was a small amount it might be classed as recreational use and not be a serious crime."

"It was said to be a significant amount. And he is accused of using and selling."

So, he was a dealer as well as a user. I sighed. Nothing was ever easy.

"I can look into it."

"Time is important. The news has not yet reached these shores, but if there is a trial and a jail sentence is imposed, it will certainly become known. It would be most embarrassing and will have a very negative effect on certain officials. Not only his father but others as well."

"I see."

"I know this will require expenses. I will deposit twenty-five thousand US dollars in your account immediately. More if you need it. Can you give me an account number?"

I owed him and he was counting on that. There really wasn't any question that I would help. I gave him my bank account and routing numbers at Citibank.

"If I can get him out of this situation, what do you want me to do with him?"

"Send him back to Beijing immediately."

"Immediately?"

"Yes. Immediately."

"I don't know what the situation is so it may take some doing."

"I'm confident you will find a way. Are you on your way back to the US now?"

"My plane leaves in an hour. I will be in San Francisco tomorrow. I will try to get a flight to Chicago the same day. Please understand, I don't know if I'll be able to do anything."

"It is imperative to do something immediately. That is why I hoped to find you in the US. We need to have this matter settled as soon as possible."

"I'll certainly try, but I cannot promise I can make anything happen. I don't have any influence over the legal system in Chicago, or anywhere else, for that matter."

"I am confident you will find a way. I will deposit the money now. It will be in your account within the hour."

As far as Chang was concerned, I was already committed. Well, so be it. The next favor I ask from him will be a big one.

"I'll call you as soon as I know anything. What number shall I use?"

"Use this cell phone number. It is on the card you have. I look forward to hearing your good news."

"Good bye, Mr. Chang."

"Good bye. Have a good trip."

What the hell was this all about? A wayward son of a high ranking official who was into drugs? It must be important to Chang. I assumed no Chinese, official or unofficial, was involved in this attempt to spring the young man from jail. Just me. Someone who owed him a favor. Well, I did owe him. And so now, he owed me.

———————————

"Is there a problem?" Yasha asked.

"Something I have to deal with."

"Do you need help?"

"On this one, you can't help."

"Are you going to tell me what it's about?"

"I will, but not now. I have to get to Chicago as soon as possible. Can we work out a plane schedule? I want this ticket on this credit card." I gave her my card.

"Okay. We can ask the reception desk."

We went to the front desk and Yasha spoke to the woman who worked the computer. She explained that I had a family emergency and had to get to Chicago as soon as possible. It took about thirty minutes of checking airline schedules.

There were no direct flights to Chicago, but that was okay. Non-stop to San Francisco was long enough to sit in an airplane. We were able to schedule American Airlines leaving San Francisco at 11:55 AM, arriving at O'Hare airport at 6:10 PM. It was also nonstop.

The SFO-Chicago ticket was charged to my card and would be covered with money deposited in my account by Chang. The age of computers worked wonders.

"Well, we don't have to rush. You have an hour before you have to go. Shall we go back in the lounge?"

"Why don't we go to the United Red Carpet lounge? I have a membership. And even without it, the Business Class ticket gives us access."

"Okay. We have to find it where it is." She went back to the reservations clerk. "Where is the United Red Carpet lounge?"

"They don't have one here. But, we honor Red Carpet members. Several airlines do. ANA, Singapore Air, Air Canada."

"Well, we might as well just stay here." Yasha shrugged.

"Wait. Let's check which departure gate." I looked at the departure screen. "It's on the other side of this terminal. We can take our time and walk."

We thanked the people at the front desk and left. It was a good opportunity to stretch my legs. We walked leisurely to the United departure gate and took a seat.

"Yasha, this thing I have to do will take several days and I'll be in Chicago. But, I can get Email or phone calls. If you hear from the Vietnamese government call me. Then get your visa and plane reservations from Hong Kong to Ho Chi Minh City for you and me. And I'll need plane reservations from San Francisco to Hong Kong. I hope all of this can be Business Class."

"Not a problem." She hesitated, "This thing in Chicago is important?"

"Yes. The person for whom I'm doing this is as important to me as you are."

"That important, huh?"

"Yeah. Maybe not as important you, but very important."

"That was a nice save."

She looked at the schedule monitor and stood.

"It's time."

"Thank you, Yasha, for all you've done."

"Will I be talking to you soon?" she asked.

"Within a week."

"Not before?"

"If there is a need, of course."

"There's always a need. At least, for me."

"Yasha."

"Okay. But, I have needs too, you know."

"I'll keep that in mind."

The passengers were lining up at the gate. The Business Class queue was separate from the Economy line and would board first.

She was holding my hand. She kissed me. It was a nice long kiss.

"You didn't scold me, so I guess I'm winning."

"You're always winning."

"Take care, best friend."

"You too."

She turned and walked away. She went a few yards and stopped. She smiled and waved. I waved back. Yeah, things were happening.

24

I PAUSED AT THE Business Class entrance and looked out the window. They were loading the last of the baggage and getting ready to shut the bay doors.

Megan was my one hope of finding someone to help with this problem. She was the only one I knew in Chicago who might have the right connections.

She wasn't part of any business I was involved with, she was just a friend. Was I ripping her off for my own purposes? What could I give in return for her help? Why didn't I ask myself these things when I asked Yasha for help? Well, I really didn't have a choice, I said to myself. It was the same excuse used when there was no reasonable explanation for many of my decisions.

I had about ten minutes before I had to board. Just enough time to call her. It was almost two in the afternoon in Shanghai so it would be after one in the morning in Chicago. After nine rings she answered.

"Hello."

"Hey, Megan. It's me."

"My God, it is you. Jesus, what time is it? Wait a minute."

I could hear her turning on the bedside light.

"It's after one. Where are you? I suppose you're right outside my door and you called just in case I had company. Right?"

"Not quite. I'm in Shanghai, getting ready to board a plane."

"And you missed me and thought you would call."

"Yeah. Something like that."

"I knew you couldn't hold out for long."

"Can't fight all that Irish beauty and charm."

"How are you?"

"Okay. And you?"

"As always." She paused. "A call at this time in the morning must be something important. Other than your passion for me."

"There's always that, but I do need help with something."

"Okay. What is it?"

"Your father has been an attorney in Chicago for a while, hasn't he?"

"Over thirty years."

"If he's as successful as I think he is, he would know a lot of people in the system."

"Yeah. He's pretty well connected. You need a lawyer?"

"Not for me. There's a young Chinese student attending the University of Chicago who's in trouble and it involves drugs. I don't know how bad it is. Obviously, he isn't going win the foreign student of the year award. Anyway, he faces a year or more in prison. I need to get him off."

"There are lots of attorneys and Public Defenders for that kind of work."

"I know, but I need someone with lots of muscle who can do this quietly and quickly."

"Why?"

"The young man's father is well known in China. Certain people in the party and in the government want to avoid any adverse publicity. It's critical."

"And you think my father can help."

"If he knows the right people, I'm hoping he can have all charges dropped and the young man released. I will guarantee that he'll disappear."

"Disappear?"

"He'll go back to China and never dirty American bath towels again."

"Why would the court do this?"

"If your father can use his influence to convince the court that it will greatly help diplomatic relations it might make a difference. Has a lot to do with foreign good will and all that crap. We'll pay whatever fines the court imposes."

"This is important to you?"

"Very."

"I'll see what I can do. Are you coming to Chicago?"

"I get in to SFO about eight-thirty tomorrow morning. I booked a flight on American Air that leaves SFO just before noon. It gets into O'Hare at 6:10 PM."

"I'll pick you up. And you'll stay with me, of course."

"Well, that depends on the room charge."

"There's special on this week. Very reasonable prices."

"Is breakfast included?"

"Ordinarily that would be extra, but we can work something out."

"I'll call when I get to San Francisco."

"Take care."

"You too."

"I've missed you," she said.

"All good things come to those who are patient."

"I've been more than patient."

"Yeah, you have. See you tomorrow."

"I'll be the one holding the sign with your name on it."

"Make sure you spell my name right."

"What was your name again?"

"How soon they forget."

"Oh, yeah. Now I remember." I could hear her laughing.

"Have a plane to catch. See ya."

"Bye."

I was the last passenger to board. The flight attendant offered me a glass of Champagne as I strapped myself in. Later she brought a hot damp towel and a menu. Dinner was the typical choice of steak, chicken, or fish entree. A California wine, Stag's Leap cabernet sauvignon was also available. I chose the chicken. Part of my campaign to eat less beef. I looked at the fish that the person across the aisle had. I should have had that. A mini-bottle of scotch after the Champagne made all that moot.

There were six Business Class passengers other than myself. Four men and two women. One woman and one man were Chinese. They were business people, going home or going to America for business. I was going to Chicago to try to get a stupid punk out of jail because he had become an embarrassment to his father and others in the Chinese government.

Whatever, it was going to be a long night and an even longer day tomorrow. I didn't have time to go home, so I had to find a shower at the airport. I had a clean shirt but little else to wear as a quasi representative of a foreign government. I would have to buy some clothes when I got to Chicago.

I decided to spend the time reading Yasha's proposal. She introduced the project with a brief, but insightful, evaluation of the trend in resorts and cited successful ones in various resort locations in Asia. Her rationale for building a major resort was supported with costs and income data from a number of existing Asian sites. Macao was the best-known gambling center, but was also becoming a resort type of destination. The income there was extremely good, as was the income in Las Vegas resorts. She also included information about the new casino resort being built in Singapore.

She presented the building costs and explained each construction phase in simple direct terms. The financial support needed was carefully outlined and provisions were provided to include a Vietnamese joint venture partner. All the hard cash would be provided by her company.

Staff training programs and personnel cost were also presented. Profits for the resort were anticipated to begin within three years and if a casino were added, net profits could be realized in two years. All the figures were shown in graphs and charts. The architects did an excellent job with the preliminary design of the resort, both inside and out. Drawings and photos were attached. The graphics were in color and very well done.

An important suggestion was to revamp the tourist structure in Vietnam. She did her homework with this and proposed a revised organization with branches in major cities in Asia and a few in the US.

It was a great piece of work. My admiration for Yasha grew. The Vietnamese would be fools not to leap at the project. Hopefully, not all fools were also stupid.

25 ———————————————————

TWELVE HOURS OF FLYING were enough to give me a sore back, and if not fortified with drink, I would have been in a very bad mood. I went through the SFO immigration and headed to the Red Carpet lounge. I took advantage of their shower facilities and changed into clean clothes. I shaved, using my dull electric shaver. I usually bought a razor at the hotels I stayed at, but found none in the airport. A fall out from security measures. The shower and clean clothes helped me to feel better. Breakfast was available in the lounge and I had juice, coffee, and two slices of toast. About two and a half hours to kill before my flight at noon.

I found the computers United made available for Business and First Class passengers. I was hoping for some news from Ahn, but there was nothing. I really didn't expect him to Email me. He would call.

There was a message from Chang, telling me the money had been deposited. He said he was looking forward to an early conclusion to this affair. He didn't seem to have any doubts I would settle things. I wasn't as confident as he was and helping a drug dealer stay out of jail was a violation of my values. But, because of my debt to Chang, I was on my way to Chicago.

———————————————————

Jia Bao Pei was an important party official who was faced with a serious situation created by his son. Pei had worked his way up the party hierarchy the hard way and in time achieved an important position in the government. He also participated in lucrative business ventures, especially with Japanese companies.

Pei had a son who was the apple of his eye and he gave him those material things he never had. That was his first major mistake. But, he was a good father who loved his son. The Pei family had a prestigious status in China and the young son's future was bright with many possibilities.

The subject of all of this attention was Ho Man Pei, AKA Tony in America, who would be twenty-two years old in two months. He was bright enough and easily qualified and accepted at the University of Chicago. He had been in America for over two years and had a reasonably acceptable academic record at the university. His college major was business administration.

In China, Ho Man was as spoiled as many first born sons were in affluent and politically connected families, as they were in any society. Growing up in a special class in the "classless communist system," he had everything going for him,

In America, Tony Pei proved how easy it was for a foreign student with money to become an American playboy. He was free to be himself – without the constraints of traditional and institutional customs. Not only was he free, he had money. He quickly became intoxicated with his freedom and new way of life.

America was the Land of Opportunity and before long he was living life in the fast lane. In a very short period, from being a son of Han he metamorphosed into a punk drug dealer.

The drug business was not only to make money, but was a way he could demonstrate how clever he was. It was cool to be a Chinese drug dealer. Shades of Fu Man Chu.

All this abruptly ended with his arrest and he had to pay for his stupid behavior. The drug arrest seriously damaged any chances he had for a career in government or any government sanctioned business in China. The good life in China and America had come to an end.

Thousands of Chinese came to study in America and most returned to China and did something of value. Yasha was one of those. Not many had a father with rank and power.

I couldn't muster an ounce of sympathy for Tony Pei. I believed all drug dealers should be killed on the spot and normally I would have nothing to do with people involved with drugs.

Was this another moral dilemma? Was my word to Chang to save a drug dealer greater than my moral beliefs? Why am I worried now? I made my choice and gave my word to Chang.

I was going to be very tired when I arrived in Chicago and thinking about drug dealer Tony Pei pissed me off. The thought of having to involve Megan and her father in this untidy affair pissed me off even more.

I looked at my watch. Should get over to the American Airline departure gate. Plane leaves in thirty minutes. On the way over to the departure gate I called Megan, telling her the plane was on time.

"I'll be there," she said. "If there's problem finding me, look for the sign with your name on it. It'll be me that's holding it."

"Forgotten what I look like?"

"No. Just wanted others to know who you belong to."

"I don't think you'll have any competition."

"Better not be. I can get nasty if there is."

"See you in about four hours."

"Don't eat anything on the plane. I have a dinner planned."

"Sounds good. But, mostly, I'm going to need sleep."

"You'll get that too."

"It's a deal."

"And don't flirt with the stewardesses."

"I'll try to behave."

"See ya."

———

Megan was willing to help me because I helped her in Guangzhou. Yasha helped me in exchange for helping her in Vietnam, but I was being paid for that. I owed her. I meant them no harm, but I used them, just as Chang used me and I used him. Everybody was using everybody. We all ended up owing something to someone. Was anybody keeping score? Did it matter?

———

Business Class didn't exist on domestic flights, so I flew First Class.

I had one drink and fell asleep after an hour or so into the flight. Before I knew it, the flight attendant was gently shaking me and asking me to put my seat back to its upright position. There had been a summer rain earlier in the day in Chicago and that cooled things off.

I had one small carry on bag that contained everything I needed on my trip overseas, but the trip had turned into a real trek. I had to buy some clothes. And I really needed a razor. The electric shaver was never really satisfying. Problems of a weary traveler.

She was standing where passengers exited from the tunneled ramp. As usual, she was the best looking woman in the place. She gave me an affectionate kiss and held on to me for a long moment.

"I can't believe you've finally come to see me."

"Gotta have faith. Look at you. As beautiful as ever."

"I have to confess. You haven't noticed, but I gained a pound," she laughed.

"Oh? I'll have to find where."

"I'll help."

"May take a while."

"No hurry. Want to make sure you find it."

"I'll look til I do."

"It could take time," she gave me a grin.

"I have time."

"Do we have time now?"

"You know, I think you would."

She laughed and grabbed my hand.

"You have any bags checked?"

"No. This is it. As a friend said, have bag, will travel." I held up my carry on.

"Okay. Let's go."

She didn't park her car in the parking lot. Instead, she left her car with a valet curb side parking service. The valet delivered a white BMW M3 coupe to the curb. Why did I know she would have at least a BMW? Could have just as easily been a Mercedes or Jaguar. She paid the valet and gave a good tip.

"I didn't have a chance to go home, so I'm going to have to buy some clothes."

"Okay."

"I don't need to be too formally dressed do I? I mean with your father, and dinner tonight."

"No. Contrary to the propaganda, we easterners are not as formal as you westerners think."

She found a Macys that was still open. I bought two white shirts, a tie, and a pair of dress trousers because I thought my jeans might be out of place. It was warm so I threw in a lightweight cotton two button seersucker jacket. We stopped at a neighborhood market and I got a razor and shaving cream.

The drive to her apartment was exciting. She drove beyond the speed limit and ignored most of the yellow lights as well as some yellow lights that had turned red. It was how she was and how she lived her life. A totally emancipated woman who had a real feel for independence and freedom. Keeping up with her was a challenge.

Her apartment was not the penthouse in the building, but close. Two bedrooms, each with its own bath, a half bath for guests, a modern stainless steel kitchen, a large living room-dining area, a den that doubled as an office, and a balcony overlooking the street. Hardwood floors. Lots of plants scattered about and everything neatly in its place. Impressive paintings and pictures hung in every room. Some might have been originals. Expensive furniture and Persian rugs in the living room and bedrooms. A forty-two inch television set in both bedrooms and a fifty inch set in the living room. Very big and fancy and very Megan.

She led me to the second bedroom.

"This bed is all yours." She smiled, "I'm in the bedroom down the hall. You're welcome to visit."

"I'll have to check my schedule."

"I've made up your schedule. You're fully booked."

"I never get to decide anything."

"Not on this trip."

"I'm just putty in your hands."

She laughed and she gave me a quick kiss.

"Get yourself together and we'll go have dinner."

"Okay. Won't be long."

"I can't believe I've got ya here."

"I left a trail of crackers so people can find me."

"Oh those. I have a trained flock of birds to get rid of them."

"You mean I'm not gonna be rescued?"

"Nope. You're a slave in my clutches."

She laughed and closed the door as she went out.

I showered and finally got to shave with a razor. I wore my jeans and one of the new shirts. Saving my new clothes for lunch with her parents. I decided to wear the tie. What the hell, why not? Probably eat in a classy restaurant, pretty much like her.

Actually, it was a neighborhood Italian restaurant and they served real Italian style food. Well, maybe real Italian food Chicago style. It was a quiet family type restaurant. I had a very standard pasta dish, linguini with clam sauce. She had the chef salad. The bread was warm and fresh. We had a non-descript Italian red wine with dinner. The manager, who was probably the owner, came to the table and asked how we enjoyed the dinner. Obviously, he knew Megan.

"I guess you want to know what my father has been doing about your problem."

"Good news is always welcome."

"I told him what you needed and he said he would look into it. He didn't think it would be a problem. We're gonna meet him tomorrow for lunch. He'll tell you what he's been able to do."

"Okay."

"My mother wants to come to lunch."

"A real family affair."

"Both my parents are curious about you. I told them about you the same time I told them I was divorcing my husband. They probably think the two things are tied together."

"And?"

"And nothing. They haven't been that interested in the men I've been with before. It all has to do with my going to China, starting this business, and then dumping my husband. Maybe it was a bit much for them. I haven't done anything like that before."

"All of that should have happened years ago. They'll have to learn to live with it."

"You're probably right. Do you mind? I mean my parents and their curiousness about you."

"Not at all. We celebrities get use to things like that."

"Well, I don't think they're going to ask for your autograph or a signed picture. But, they'll ask questions."

"You mean like an interview?"

"Sorta. I told them your intentions were honorable."

"They know I'm staying with you."

"I always took in stay cats and dogs."

"Ah, Megan. My kind of woman. Do they serve real liquor in this place?"

"Sure."

"Let's get that waiter over here."

I waved to the waiter, who hurriedly came to the table.

"What'll you have?" I asked her.

"I'll have a brandy," she said.

I ordered a brandy for her and a single malt scotch for myself. I sighed and reached over and took her hand.

"I truly appreciate your help. Don't know how I can repay you."

"Well, you haven't heard what I intend to charge you." She was grinning.

"Seriously, I needed help with this business and you came through."

"You helped me when I needed help. It's the same thing."

"You're a very special woman, Megan O'Connor."

"That's the rumor I been spreading."

"I believe it."

I finished my drink and looked around at the other tables.

"Want coffee? Or another brandy? Or desert?"

"No. This one's enough. And I've given up on deserts. That's how I got that extra pound."

"I'll pass too."

She looked at me and frowned.

"I guess it's been a bad time for you. You look tired."

"Been a long day and I'm feeling it."

"You can get some rest tonight. Sleep in. The meeting with Dad is at twelve. It's at his club."

"His club?"

"Actually, it's a private place where lawyers and their clients meet. It's fancy and impressive so the clients won't complain when they pay the exorbitant attorney fees. They plot and plan all kind of things there."

"Sounds about what I thought it would be. That's okay. As long as things can be worked out, I don't care where we meet."

"Well, shall we get going?"

I signaled for the check.

"No. I'm buying dinner. You can buy the next one. This way, you'll feel obligated to take me to dinner." She smiled and put her credit card on the table.

———————

It was about eleven when we got back to her apartment. I loosen my tie, took off my jacket, and sank into the soft sofa. I closed my eyes and started to drift off. She grabbed my hand, pulled me up, and led me into my bedroom.

"You're dead on your feet. If you can't get undressed, I'll do it for you."

"We Space Aliens tend to fall asleep when we're exhausted. It's flaw in the genes."

"That's okay. You're exciting enough when you're awake."

She kissed me good night. It was a long and warm kiss. If I hadn't been so tired. She went to the door and turned.

"You get a pass tonight, but I won't promise anything tomorrow."

"I'll try to be prepared."

"Good, cuz I am."

She waved as she closed the door.

I got undressed, got in bed and in a few minutes was asleep.

26

I OFTEN HAD DREAMS and never knew what they meant. In the dream I had that morning I saw BJ as I remembered her the last time I saw her. She was standing in the doorway at her school and her first grade students were laughing and dancing around her. She was smiling and waving to me.

Then suddenly the scene changed. I was standing in the middle of a crowd of my friends. Andre, Kam Wah, Chick, Ahn, Kevin, Gary were all there. They were asking each other "Where is he? Have you seen him?" I shouted, "Here I am. I'm here." They look through me. I tried to get their attention, but they didn't see me.

Finally, I screamed, "Hey, I'm here!"

My scream woke me and I bolted upright. I looked around and then remembered where I was. I looked at the clock on the bed stand. It was nearly ten-thirty. I had been asleep for ten hours. It was a few seconds before I realized someone was knocking on the door. Megan opened the door and stood with her hands on her hips. She stared at me for a few minutes, wondering if I had dropped off into never-never land.

"You called?"

I looked around me, feeling a bit foolish. I fell back on the pillow and heaved a sigh.

"Yes, I did. You said breakfast was included in the price of the room."

She came to the bed, sat on the edge of the bed, and put her hand on my face. She looked concerned.

"You okay? You feel sweaty."

"I'm fine. Just my usual morning routine. Wake up yelling."

"You've been asleep for a while. At least your body is rested. Don't know about your psyche. Do you want a real breakfast?"

"No. Juice and coffee will do. I have lunch to consider."

"That's in a couple of hours. Plenty of time."

"Well, unless you're going to scrub my back, you can fix the juice and coffee while I shower and shave."

"I do backs," she said with a straight face.

"That's what the girl at the Huangpo massage parlor said."

"All this foreign competition and at cheaper wages. How can I compete?"

"You'll do just fine." I looked at the clock on the night stand. "Ten-thirty. Don't know when that's happened before."

I kissed her lightly and gave her a gentle push off the bed. "Scoot!"

After a long shower I shaved with a real razor again. I stared into the mirror and noticed redness in my eyes. I rubbed them and splashed water on my face. I peered into the face in the mirror. Eyes were still red and a bit puffy under the lower lids. Looking closer I noticed lines along the sides of my eyes. My cheeks looked hollow. Have I lost weight or gained weight? I was growing older every second I stood there.

I was without hotel laundry service so I hand washed my underwear and socks and hung them on the shower door. I suppose Megan had a washer and dryer, but this was simpler.

I put on the new shirt, tie, pants, and jacket. I looked like a worn out teacher on the way to class – the way I looked a thousand years ago.

Megan had a glass of orange juice and a cup of coffee waiting for me.

"You were having a nightmare. Want to talk about Harbin?"

"Not right now."

"Okay. When you want to, you'll tell me."

"Tell me about your father."

"Okay." She sighed and began. "He's a very successful attorney and very rich. Been wheeling and dealing in the city all of his life. He's a tough Irishman, oozing charm, and very clever. Some say he has a heart of stone. Whether it's a bet or a court case, he wins almost all the time. Knows lots of people, especially people who are in the right places –

both good and bad. He's provided for his family in grand fashion for as long as I can remember. Gave me everything I wanted and has been faithful to my mother, except for two occasions about seven years ago. Who, by the way, also has a law degree. My mother, not the women with whom he had these indiscretions.

"Neither my mother nor father expected me to do anything, which was kind of a slap in the face. Why shouldn't I do something? They expected me to get married and provide them with grandchildren. They're very Catholic and very Irish.

"I may not be all they wished for, but I haven't gone off the deep end either. Some I know have. My only real sins are not producing grandchildren and getting a divorce."

"Why is he willing to help me?"

"Because I asked. And both he and my mother know how I feel about you."

"So, it's really a favor to you."

"I suppose it is. But, does it make a difference if you get what you want?"

"No. I'll take what I can get any way I can." I looked at her over the rim of my coffee cup. "Getting your help is really special. And you're good looking on top of everything else."

"Nice of you to notice." She smiled, reached over, and put her hand on mine. "How long are you going to stay?"

"If this works out, I'll have to get back home and began preparations for the trip to Vietnam. So I won't be here too long."

"Will you be at the Canton fair in October? I have a large group this time – could be as many as thirty people."

"If I can I will be. But, after Vietnam I may have some things to do. I won't know where I'll be."

"Will I see you after?"

"Yes. Unless I get tied up. But, you're first on my list."

"List? I'm on a list?"

"You're the only person thing on the list. That's not like thing things to do."

"Person thing? I'm a thing?"

"Actually, a very special person thing."

"Oh, you sly dog, you."

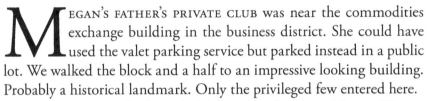

27

EGAN'S FATHER'S PRIVATE CLUB was near the commodities exchange building in the business district. She could have used the valet parking service but parked instead in a public lot. We walked the block and a half to an impressive looking building. Probably a historical landmark. Only the privileged few entered here.

We were met at the front desk by a man who knew Megan. He was dressed in a black suit, white shirt, and black tie. You would expect someone dressed as he was to greet you at a funeral parlor. He greeted her by name and a nod of his head. A more formal bow was probably reserved for club members. He was expecting her and a guest.

"Please, this way." He pointed with his open hand and led the way into the dining room.

A soft carpet covered the floor leading to the dinning room. The carpet, I was certain, was a hundred percent wool. The dining room was spacious and impressive. The room had a very high ceiling and sun rays beamed through arched stained glass windows. You could fire a cannon in the room and only a muffled sound would be heard. Royal red velvet drapes hung on the walls. Diners sat in armed chairs with curved backs, made of cherry or similar hardwood. The upholstery on the seat and back of the chairs was silk. Everything was real, not an ounce of synthetic material in sight.

The tables were set in what appeared to be a random configuration, but were actually carefully placed so conversations were not easily overheard. A half a dozen tables were occupied by men. Megan and her mother were the only women there.

Mr. and Mrs. Timothy O'Connor were seated at a table near the center of the room. No doubt it was a permanently reserved table for the right honorable Mr. O'Connor. His chair was facing the entrance and his wife sat to his left.

He rose and greeted us with a cheery, "Well, here they are."

She remained seated. Megan gave them each a buss. I shook his hand and bowed my head to Mrs. O'Connor. She extended her hand, palm side down. I held her soft and warm hand, not in a hand shake grip. I suppose some would have kissed her hand in real continental style. I didn't. I don't know if she was disappointed or not.

He pointed me to the seat directly across from him. I pulled her chair out and Megan sat to my left.

Timothy O'Connor was a tall man, six feet plus. I guessed his age to be sixty-five, give or take a year. His hair was mostly gray and neatly trimmed. The eye glasses sitting on the table were probably for reading only. He had a handsome face, without age wrinkles. His gray eyes were clear and alert – and when needed, used to stare down at and intimidate people. He appeared to be in excellent physical shape, the result of regular visits to the gym. The suit he wore was made of very light weight wool material – light gray with pin stripes. Perfect for Chicago summers. He had on a red power tie. The only jewelry he wore was a wedding band and what looked like a class ring. It might have been a religious/social fraternity ring. Knights of Columbus? On his left wrist was the standard status symbol, the Rolex watch.

I was grossly underdressed compared to him. I imagined my rather drab attire would be a topic of discussion later. Was this a sign of my meager financial state or evidence of my lingering academic liberalism?

Mrs. Fiona O'Connor was a lovely upper class society figure. Probably sixty years old. Her light red hair had a few gray strands, but they were not really noticeable. Her eyes were green, as were Megan's. She had a sensuous mouth, lips were tinted light red. Her complexion was clear and a bit paler than Megan's. Finger nails were nicely manicured and her hair was obviously fashioned by a professional. She wore a summer outfit, light and silky, with faint green flower prints on the dress. She was probably as beautiful as Megan when she was her age, but more subdued. In contrast, Megan emitted a strong sexual aura.

A waiter dressed in a black suit and bow tie, placed menus before us. He asked if we cared for cocktails. I ordered a single malt scotch – neat. O'Connor had a Bushmills Black Bush Irish whiskey – a real Irish drink. The ladies passed.

There was a choice of various cuts of beef and seafood on the menu. I chose the Atlantic salmon and a Caesar salad. The ladies had the mahi mahi. He had a sirloin steak, medium rare. In earlier years I would guess he had his steak rare, but he was more health conscious in his older years. A bottle of chardonnay was ordered for me and the ladies and a glass of Cabernet Sauvignon for himself.

The conversation centered on some personal data Megan had told them about me. As expected, her mother asked about my children and my years as a college president. The ninety-eight percent Black student body in a make shift college in the ghettos of Oakland was an interesting topic. Similar to Chicago's south side. Not what a Yale or Harvard grad would be into, but, a UCLA doctorate would do that sort of thing in a heartbeat.

Both said they appreciated the help I had given Megan in her new business venture in exotic China. We chatted casually about nothing important throughout the lunch and after the waiter cleared the dishes, coffee was ordered. I declined dessert, as did the others. No mention was made of why we were meeting.

———————————————

At the appropriate moment, Mrs. O'Connor suggested that she and Megan adjourn to the powder room. I rose and pulled Megan's chair back and he did the same for his wife. We remained standing until the ladies were gone. Then, with a sigh, he sat down, as did I.

"Do you smoke?" he asked.

"No. Gave it up some years ago."

"I'd love to have my cigar. But, keeping with the times, they banned smoking in here." He shook his head. Obviously, he did not favor the ban.

"Some years ago, I smoked Churchills," I said. "I admit I miss them."

"That's a Jamaican cigar isn't it? Named after Churchill."

"Yes."

"Can always tell a man by the cigar he smokes." He laughed.

I nodded and smiled. "That's one way."

The time to talk about the reason we were having this lunch had arrived.

"Well, now. This problem you have. I think something can be done about that. I spoke to Judge Higgins who is familiar with the case. The person handling the case is Assistant District Attorney Claire Kowalski. She's not happy about the judge getting involved and certainly not happy about turning the young man loose. Your man was charged with possession with the intent to sell. He had a kilo of heroin, enough drugs to be considered a major offense. I was told he is also a user. As you may know, Chicago is not a friendly town for drug dealers."

"I realize that. I can't say that there is any reason why he shouldn't be punished. I can only argue that in this case the results of a conviction would have greater consequences than the crime itself."

"I understand that. But, the courts demand their pound of flesh."

"How can we solve this problem?"

"You say he will leave the country."

"Immediately. And never return."

"How can you guarantee that?"

"He'll leave immediately because I will personally put him on a plane. As to his non-return, his government will make that guarantee."

"There's a fine to be paid. That would ordinarily be in addition to the jail sentence."

"Whatever the amount, the fine will be paid."

"You, personally, will take responsibility for this person?"

"Yes."

"The fine is five thousand dollars. Could be much higher."

"Not a problem. How shall I arrange payment?"

"You'll have to take care of that at the municipal courthouse. You can make arrangements for payment there. Kowalski will have other papers for you to sign."

"I'm sorry about overriding Kowalski's feelings about all this."

"That's not a problem. The judge's position is what's important. He understands this involves an official in a foreign government and there are extenuating circumstances. Kowalski, on the other hand, is an avid prosecutor of drug dealers. She's not involved with international politics."

"So, the matter is settled?"

"Yes." He was matter of fact about it. Something he did every day.

I watched him sip his coffee. It probably didn't take more than one or two phone calls and the matter was settled. A piece of cake. What will this cost?

"My client greatly appreciates your efforts and has asks how he might compensate you for your time and efforts."

"That's appreciated, but there is no payment for this. I'm doing this because Megan asked me to help you and you're special to her. You've helped her through a very rough time in her life."

"I'm very happy to help Megan, at any time, but please understand, all of this is not for my benefit. The father of this wayward young man is the one you're helping. There is also the matter of maintaining good diplomatic relations with an important country."

"Yes, I understand. But, those considerations are not my primary concern."

He really didn't care about the international repercussions or how it affected Tony Pei's father or the communist party superstructure in China. Those issues were not important to him. Why should he be concerned with those things? No reason.

"After you see Kowalski you can pick up the young man at this police station. Ask for a Captain Finn. He'll know what to do. Kowalski's office number is on there too." He handed me a slip of paper with names, phone numbers, and addresses.

"The people I represent will be eternally grateful." I bowed my head toward him.

"Spoken like a true Oriental."

He gave me a condescending smile. I was an Oriental, not Asian, or Korean. It was an interesting choice of racial identification. I knew how he thought about this and how he felt about me, Tony Pei, and the whole Chinese government.

"It's important to play the part well." I said. "Otherwise, you might learn who we really are." I gave him a tight smile.

He fixed his gaze on me for a long moment. My comment was not

Young Park

expected. He may wonder if he had underestimated me. He knew little about Asians, AKA Orientals. He would be more certain of me if I were Black or even Hispanic – people he dealt with on a daily basis.

I wondered if I could ever like this man. I really didn't want to spend the energy to find out. Still, he came through on this matter. It was easy for him. He had more power than I thought. Was it too much power for one individual to have? How much of this power extended over Megan?

"Ah, the ladies are returning," he said, pointing in the direction of Megan and her mother.

We both stood and held the chairs for the ladies. They looked properly refreshed. A second cup of coffee was served. Mrs. O'Connor carried on and did most of the talking. Actually, not talking but asking more questions. She asked when I would be leaving. So soon? When will you be returning? Will you be in China in October when Megan goes back? Do your children travel with you? Do you have people in China or is it South Korea? Oh, yes, I remember Megan said Korea. You're going to Vietnam aren't you? That must be interesting, with the war and all.

It went on this way for another thirty minutes or so. I was patient and said what was expected of me. Kam Wah would have been proud of how respectful I was to people I didn't particularly like. It was, after all, the way of Asians, AKA Orientals.

The lunch finally came to an end. The waiter presented the bill and O'Connor initialed it. We pull the chairs for the ladies and all walked to the front of the building. I shook hands with him and his wife. Megan gave them a peck on the cheek and we left.

I was grateful that O'Connor helped with getting Tony Pei out of jail, but I didn't think it was the beginning of a long and lasting friendship. They were rich upper class White Americans. I didn't particularly like them. Could I be superimposing my own prejudices on them because they had everything and I had nothing? Was I being as closed minded as I thought they were?

28

WE DROVE BACK TO her apartment without much talk. Maybe she sensed how I felt about her parents. I wondered if it would become an issue. I hoped not.

When we arrived at her apartment, I took off my coat and tie and headed for the refrigerator.

"I could do with a beer."

"I'll get one for you."

"You have a computer handy?"

"Yes I do."

She brought me a bottle of Heineken and led me by the hand into the den. A laptop was sitting on the desk. She opened it and signed in.

"All yours."

"Thanks, Love."

I logged into my Email and looked for a message from Ahn. None from him, but, there was one from Kevin. It was encouraging news. A meeting could be setup for both my project and Yasha's as soon as we could arrange to be in Vietnam. Coincidentally, there was a message from Yasha, asking about news from Vietnam. A note from Chick telling me that he had an inquiry about Vietnam rice. One from Andre asking where I was and when I was coming back. Other messages included two from people in Pakistan asking about gas masks and two that wanted data on 9 *mm* ammunition and sniper bullets. Pretty normal fare.

A welcome note was from Carolyn who asked where I was and when we could meet for lunch. Carolyn was a lovely lady who always made my day. I replied with a promise I would be in touch very soon.

My first task was to get plane reservations from Chicago to Beijing for Tony Pei. United Airlines had a direct non-stop flight leaving at 1:01 PM. If I got to the police station around nine, I would have about four hours to get Pei out of jail and to the airport. It'll be close, but I didn't want to be saddled with him overnight. I booked him a seat on Flight 851. The short notice cost extra, but that was expected. Actually, the airline sold me an Economy seat that was empty, that I could have purchased at a discount price if I had bought it two weeks ago. It was the same seat whether I booked it two weeks ago or today. Slick business is alive and well in the airline industry. At least there wasn't any baggage fee to pay. I hoped I cheated them out of something, but it was a losing battle.

The flight would arrive in Beijing at 3:40 PM the next day. I wanted a non-stop flight because I didn't want to risk the chance he might get off at a stopover. Would he try to get off the plane to avoid facing his father? Whatever, it was easier this way. I paid with my debit/credit card and requested confirmation and seat assignment be sent to Megan's Email address.

Next, I Emailed Yasha telling her we would leave for Vietnam in a week and she should get a visa now. Also that she would be receiving an official invitation from the Vietnamese at her company offices in Hamburg. I replied to Kevin, thanking him for his work and keeping the pressure on the people involved. I would let him know what my plane schedule was within a couple of days. Things were coming together nicely for Vietnam.

I called the number O'Connor gave for Assistant District Attorney Claire Kowalski. She answered on the third ring. No secretary. I introduced myself and explained my business involved a person called Tony Pei.

"Yes. I was told about you." She was terse and direct.

"Well, then, if it is convenient for you, may I come in to take care of the paperwork?"

"I'll be free for a meeting if you can make it in an hour."

"I'll be there. Thank you Ms. Kowalski" I tried to sound grateful for the appointment.

"Fine." She hung up.

Obviously, she was not happy about all of this. Can't say I blame her. If it was up to me, I'd throw the bastard in jail and let him rot there. But, ours is not to reason why.

Next I called the police station where Pei was being held.

"Hello. Seventy-third precinct."

"May I speak to Captain Finn?"

"What's this about?"

"It concerns a young man you're holding on a drug charge. Judge Higgins asked that I call."

There was a moment of silence.

"Hang on. I'll see if he's in."

It was several minutes before he came on the line.

"Finn here."

"I believe Judge Higgins spoke to you about the matter of a young man named Ho Man Pei, AKA Tony, who is being held at your station."

"Oh, yeah. Are you coming down to get him?"

"Well, I have to meet with the district attorney office this afternoon. I can come to get the young man tomorrow morning. I have plane reservations for him on a plane that leaves O'Hare at 1:01 PM tomorrow. Can we make that flight?"

"Well, the judge said this was important. Can you be here before by ten?"

"Yes, I can. How long will it take to get to the airport?"

"Is this punk that important?"

"As a person he's a worthless prick. But the situation he represents is very important. It involves the Chinese government." I lied, but in a way it was true.

"I'll see if we can arrange for a car to take you there."

"That would be most appreciated, Captain."

"Okay. You can get the release forms from the DA's office. The other papers here are all in order."

"Very good. I'll be there around ten tomorrow. Thank you for your assistance. It's much appreciated."

"Not a problem."

At least Finn was more agreeable than Kowalski. Maybe he was just happy to be rid of a punk drug dealer. And a foreigner to boot. Or maybe Judge Higgins suggested he cooperate. That was more likely the case.

Whatever, a solution had been arranged. People who made the decisions were properly contacted and everyone was in agreement. I reminded myself, "It's not what you know, but who you know." In China or in America, it was the same. Ain't life grand?

I'll tell Chang that O'Connor refused any money payment, which meant that Pei would send some token of appreciation. A Ming or Ch'ing Dynasty vase would be appropriate. Mrs. O'Connor probably appreciated that sort of thing. I assumed she would know what the value of a Ming or Ch'ing Dynasty vase was. That was a condescending thought. Sounds racist.

I finished the beer and sat back, feeling satisfied with the day's work. Megan had been watching me. She came over and sat beside me and held my hand.

"Megan, I have to go down to city hall and see an Assistant District Attorney, sign some papers and pay a fine. I'll have to stop at a Citibank and get some money."

"I'll drive you."

"No. I'll take a cab."

"I don't mind, really."

"I know. But, I'll deal with this. I'm sure you have things to do and you can plan what we're going to do about dinner tonight. By the way, I have to leave here by nine-thirty tomorrow morning"

"Okay. Not a problem."

"Thanks, Megan. You're spoiling me."

"Just remember that."

"How could I forget?"

City halls in most major American cities always made me feel uncomfortable. I thought of them as the citadels of the ruling class and I distrusted any kind of government. I wasn't an anarchist and understood the need for governments, but I believed the people who held the power were corrupt. Maybe not all were financially corrupt, but I thought many were morally corrupt. Government officials had power – the essential force that fueled corruption. That was the American way. Actually, it was the same in all countries. There were very few "untouchables" in any government. Maybe I should have tried to get some of that power and money, but then I would be one those people I disliked.

I checked the directory in the entrance hall and found Claire Kowalski listed under "District Attorney office and staff." Her name and office number 2550 were listed on the giant directory hanging on the wall to the right of the entry way.

Second floors in city halls in all the major cities in the nation seem to be at least twenty feet above the ground floor. I walked up the broad stairway and followed the arrow with the numbers 2000-3000 under it. Her office was one of a dozen or so along a long corridor. I found number 2550 with her name on the door half way down the hallway.

I knocked and heard a loud "Come in."

I went in and introduced myself. She didn't smile, but she stood and shook my hand. A good firm grip.

"Please have a seat."

She motioned me to the chair in front of her desk that was piled high with papers. No ash tray. But I thought I saw a no smoking sign in the hallway.

I took a seat and gave her my best "get 'em every time" smile. No response. It was not a warm welcome, but not really cold either. Kind of indifferent. She hadn't totally written me off, yet. Maybe it was because I didn't wear a two thousand dollar suit, no diamond rings on my fingers, and no Rolex watch on my wrist. I didn't appear to be a high priced attorney bought and paid for by Chicago crooks – public or private. I looked pretty much like a lower middle class plodder. An academic misfit who was muddling through a bureaucratic maze.

She was probably thirty-two, maybe a year or two older. Not older than thirty-five. Not plain looking by any means. With a different hairdo and some make up she would be much more attractive. Her light brown hair was cut short. Her face was nicely shaped, with high cheek bones, and smooth complexion. Some rouge on her cheeks would have added highlights to her pretty face. A straight nose and nice full mouth, faint red color on her lips.

Real natural pearl earrings were inserted in her pierced ears. She had a gold cross on a gold chain around her neck. Nice hands, slender long fingers. No polish on her nails and no ring on her left hand. Probably too busy with her career to get involved with a man. The desk hid her lower half, but her upper body was nicely filled out.

She had large beautiful eyes. They spoke volumes about her intelligence and strength. She was the woman for whom the song "I Am Woman" was written.

She stared at me, trying to decide who I was and why I wanted to get a drug dealer out of jail. She knew I was not an attorney and certainly not a local city hall insider.

"You apparently have friends who can move judges."

"Not really. Some people helped, but I think it's more a matter of circumstances working out in my favor."

"Whatever." She flipped her hand in the air. "You're taking custody of one Ho Man Pei, AKA Tony, a Chinese national here on a student visa." She picked up several sheets. "There are a few forms for you to sign and a fine of five thousand dollars to pay."

"I know you disagree with this course of action and I'm sorry."

I wanted to let her know I was not in favor of freeing Pei. I was really on her side.

She probably argued long and hard with her superiors about this case. She started to say something and stopped. She looked down at the papers before her and then abruptly looked up at me. I imagined her saying to herself, "the hell with it," and deciding to say her piece.

"I prosecute hundreds of drug cases that involve human misery that is indescribably bad. Kids ten years old are hooked and sell their bodies to get dope. People sell their souls for shit they shoot into their veins, inhale into their lungs, snort into their noses, and ingest in a dozen other ways. It's the bottomless pit of wretchedness.

"Your guy was supposed to be here for a college education. Apparently his parents are able to afford his tuition and provide more than average living expenses. Instead of taking advantage of this opportunity, he became part of the White upper middle class user group. Then he starts to sell to his fellow users and was on the verge of becoming a hard nosed pusher. In a year he would be a big time dealer. I want to put him in jail just as I put the scum dealers from the ghetto in jail. I see no distinction between them."

"I agree."

"Then why are you here?"

"It's an obligation I have assumed. Because of special circumstances, a Chinese official has asked me to get this jerk out of jail and send him home. I promised I would."

"So he gets a 'get out of jail card' because his father is some big shot."

"Yeah. Pretty much as it is here and everywhere else."

"It stinks."

"Yes, it does." I heaved a sigh. "I would deal with drug dealers in a much more direct fashion, as I would with child molesters and rapists, but I don't make the rules. And doing it this way is supposed to serve the greater good, meaning the government wants it that way."

"You don't like doing this, do you?"

"Not my favorite thing."

"Then why do it?"

"Because I gave my word."

"Well, that's something."

"It's all I have." I sighed. "Why do you do it?"

"It's my job."

"There are other jobs."

"Yes. There are. There are also other jobs you can do."

"So we both end up doing some things we would rather not do. Maybe we both need career counseling," I said.

I smiled and she smiled back. She was less angry now. I hoped she felt better because she decided I was not a defender of drug dealer's civil rights. I was just a hired hand doing a distasteful job. Just as she was doing her job.

"Maybe we do this work because it's what we do best," I said.

"For better or worse, that's probably true."

She took a large brown envelope from her desk and handed it to me.

"These are his personal things."

"You have his passport?" I asked.

"Yes. It's in there. We found it when we searched his dorm room. There was quite a bit of junk there as well. Over a kilo. His roommate was in this with him, but we don't have the goods on him – yet. We scared him into backing off. At least for now. He was ready to testify against this Pei. A real pal. But, he'll be back in it before too long. Then, we'll nail him."

"There's a wallet here with about fifteen hundred bucks. Part of his drug profits?"

"I would guess so."

"I'll send the wallet and cash on to his father. He can explain to him where the money came from."

"You have to sign these forms. One is your promise to be responsible for Mr. Pei. The second one is that you agree to pay his fine of five thousand dollars."

I glanced at the forms and signed and dated them. She turned to a copy machine on the credenza behind her and made copies of each. She put them into an envelope and handed them to me. I handed her five thousand dollars.

"My understanding is that he will leave the country. Will he try to come back?"

"A part of the deal is that he won't. Of course, the US can refuse to give him a visa – of any kind. But the US government gives visas to all kinds of people, including terrorists, and people can easily slip into this country, with or without a visa. I don't know if he'll try. I doubt it. But I will convince him that if he does come back, I will find him and he'll be sorry for the rest of his life. I want him to be more fearful of me than he is of his father."

"Well, that sounds ominous." She paused. "You're different from what I expected."

"So are you."

"Guess we have some things in common."

"I'm sure we do. It's Claire, isn't it?"

"It's Claire."

"Okay. Claire." I smiled. "I like that."

She responded with a grin. She reached up to her cross and held it between her thumb and forefinger. She rubbed it and stared at me.

"You have what looks like two surnames. What do I call you?"

"People who know me well call me Precious."

She laughed and continued to rub her cross.

"Okay, Precious. You're obviously not from China."

"San Francisco. The city by the bay."

"Come here often?"

"First time in several years."

"You want to try some good Polish food?"

"You have no idea how much I would love to, but have a commitment tonight."

"Well, maybe next time you're in the neighborhood."

"That's a promise."

We stood and shook hands across the desk. She was much prettier when she was relaxed and smiling. I picked up the envelope, smiled some more, and said good-bye. She came around the desk and opened the door. I got a chance to see her full view. Very nice looking legs. Tall and well proportioned. In high heels she would be a fraction of an inch taller than me. She was a winner and I was glad I took the time to be polite. I was certain I had won her over. It must have been my charm and good looks. I know it wasn't money or power, because I had neither. Actually, I was short on real good looks too, but had just enough charm to get by.

29

MEGAN MET ME AT the door with a glass of scotch, which I paid for with a kiss. One thing led to another and I almost forgot about the drink. I had to shake myself loose and take care of business.

"I have to call United and see about a plane reservation for tomorrow. Okay?"

"I can wait."

"We all make sacrifices."

"I've made my share."

"I know. I've kept score, Megan."

"I expect a reward."

"Very soon."

"Tick tock."

I called United and the best I could do was a non-stop flight that left Chicago at 4:49 PM and arrived at SFO at 7:48 PM. Tony's plane left at 1:01 PM. I resigned myself to waiting at the airport for three hours and booked a First Class ticket. My life had become dominated by plane schedules. Hopefully, this was the last trip until the long haul to Vietnam.

I dropped onto the sofa and took a large swallow of scotch. Megan offered me a chip loaded with avocado dip. It was very good. She set the bowl of dip on the coffee table and sat next to me.

"How'd it go?

"Very well."

"So, you did what you came to do."

"I didn't do much. Your father did what had to be done."

She sipped her wine and frowned.

"You don't like him, do you?"

"Megan, I don't know him well enough to like or not like him. I certainly appreciate the fact that he has muscle in this town and feel fortunate that I'm a beneficiary of that power."

"He comes from another era. He won't be able to function as he does too much longer. That time is coming soon."

"I'm sure he has enough money to last several life times."

"It's not so much the money. It's the power he'll miss."

"Power is intoxicating. For some people it gives a high like nothing else."

"You have a similar kind of power."

"Oh, no. I have no power. I barely have control over myself."

"You have a different kind of power. But, you don't like his kind of power."

"He's from a special class of people and that distinguishes him from me. He and I live in two different worlds and we each have a different set of values."

"Where does that put me?"

"You're in a class all by yourself."

"Seriously. Do you think I'm part of his world?"

"You are and you aren't. You're from that world but not necessarily a part of it. As I said, you're different. It's not easy to join another world. We're all pretty much captives of the world in which we were born."

"You mean I'm racially and socially excluded from your world?"

"No, not at all. And race doesn't have anything to do with it. We all inherit genes from our parents, but there are other things, like customs and values. In time we become individuals with distinct values and perceptions, but those values and perceptions are generally based on what our parents taught us. We can change some of those values, but it's not often that a person develops totally different values. But, your personal values are certainly compatible with those in my world."

"I'm not like my parents."

"To an extent, externally you are. Like having this apartment and driving a BMW. But, internally you're different. You have different values and perceptions."

"Like what?"

"Like choosing me to be your friend. I think your parents were more comfortable with your soon to be ex-husband."

"He's a bastard and my parents agree. At least my mother does."

"Yes. He's a bastard, but he's their bastard."

She blinked and frowned. She thought about this and heaved a sigh.

"Do you think my parents are racists?"

"They're not KKK members or vocal segregationists, but they have ingrained feelings about race that go back a ways. Subconsciously I think they have some racist beliefs."

"How do you know?"

"People from my side of the street know. If one is born non-White in this country one learns about racism quickly. It's a defense mechanism. First, it's to avoid having your feelings hurt and for some, fighting for their lives. Later, it becomes a means of identifying the enemy and deciding how to defend yourself. And if necessary, how to fight back."

"You think I'm a racist?"

"Hardly. You're the perfect innocent. You only dislike people who are jerks, regardless of their skin color. It's not a secret that you're different from your parents."

"I've never thought about this."

"There was never a need. Not to worry."

"I really can't do anything about how my parents think. I'm more concerned with what you think about me."

"You know how I feel about you. Nothing can change that."

"You mean that?"

"Yes."

"Seeing you and my parents together gave me another perspective on things."

"Not to worry." I leaned forward and kissed her on the forehead. "Now, what's for dinner?"

"I took out a couple of T-bone steaks and defrosted them. Also have some stuff for salad and two potatoes to bake. I have a broiler on the top of my stove. You can do the steaks while I make the salad. How's that for a love fest?"

"Sounds like a deal."

She was determined to enjoy the time we had and so was I. She talked about her new group she was taking to the October fair. She was excited about her growing business and was planning to take a course in Chinese. She was really into her new life and I was happy for her.

I wondered how she would balance that new world with her world here. It could be difficult for her. It was difficult for me. Was I out of place here in her luxury apartment, cooking a two inch T-bone steak on a very fancy stove? Could I live in this world? This was miles away from the one I was used to.

It was also a world in which I was identified in a particular way.

"Megan is with that guy from the west coast. You know that Oriental fellow," her father would say. I would never be a just a guy – an American – to him.

I'll never get used to it. Sorry about that, Megan. Was this the way it was meant to be? Was that our *karma*?

Well, the hell with it all. I wanted to forget about the negatives and enjoy what was here. For the moment, life was good. I had a great T-bone steak, single malt scotch whiskey, and a dynamite woman in a plush apartment. Can't beat that.

We cleaned the table, loaded the dish washer, and settled down to wine for her and more scotch for me.

"Okay. Want to hear about my business?"

"Yes. I want to know all about your growing empire."

"I know you don't, but I'll tell you anyway."

One of the nice things about Megan was she made no demands. It made our relationship simple. Why was I hesitating?

"Want another drink? I bought this eighteen year single malt scotch just for you, so you have to finish it."

"I will. It'll help me relax after a long day."

"Relax? Maybe I should put the bottle away."

I laughed. "Aha. So you have devious plans."

"I've been planning this for over six months. I have you here in my apartment and seduction is part of my plan."

"Seduction? Didn't something like that happen in Guangzhou?"

"Yeah, it did. I remember it all very clearly."

"As I recall, I seduced you after plying you with a bottle of Champagne."

"Actually, I brought the Champagne and seduced you."

"Really? I thought it was the other way round."

"I can refresh your memory with instant playback."

"I did promise to find that extra pound."

"I certainly hope you do."

"The last time was back in December. Once every six months. This must be some kind of record."

"It is for me," she was grinning.

"Well, I'm always ready and willing to help break records."

"Your bed or mine?"

30

I WOKE WITH A start and looked at the clock. It was six o'clock. I heard the water running in her shower. I got up and went to my assigned bedroom and showered and shaved. I haven't had a workout for almost a week and was feeling fat. I had to cut down on my food intake. Am I getting older and fatter? Yeah, looks that way.

We met in the kitchen, both of us wrapped in giant towels. Coffee was perking. She poured me a glass of orange juice, buttered my toast, and gave me a kiss. If there was nothing else in the world to deal with, I could get use to this.

"Aren't you having breakfast?"

"No. Trying to lose that extra pound."

"You know, I looked for that extra pound last night. I couldn't find it."

"Maybe you didn't look in the right places."

"I thought I covered most of the places it might be."

"Well, you can try again."

"You know how I hate to not carry out my responsibilities."

"You're such a perfectionist."

"Family trait."

"You mean there are more like you?"

"Actually, they're similar, but not really like me."

"I didn't think there would be another you."

"You know there is a place or two I might look."

"I'll help."

"I need all the help I can get."

"Not really. You do alright on your own."

"Shall we?"

"Why not?"

"I have to call someone in China."

"Use the phone here."

"I'll use my cell phone while I finish dressing."

"Okay. As long it isn't a woman."

"Not to worry. I've been spoiled."

"Success at last."

"Hold that thought."

I went to my bedroom, laid out my clothes, and called Chang. It was about nine in the evening in Beijing.

"Mr. Chang? Hello."

"Ah, I was looking for a call from you."

"I hope this late call is not too great an inconvenience."

"Not at all. What news have you?"

"I'm pleased to report that the young man will be released today. I'll put him on a non-stop flight to Beijing. United Air Flight 851 arriving in Beijing at 3:40 PM tomorrow."

"That's good news. How are you? I know it's been a hectic few days. I hope you are getting some rest."

"I'm fine."

"Where will you be, now that this matter is finished?"

"I'll leave Chicago today and be at home for a few days. Then I'll leave for business in Vietnam and will be there for about a week to ten days."

"I see. Do you plan to come to Beijing soon?"

"I don't know. If I do I will certainly call you. By the way, there are funds left over. I'll send it to you when I get back to San Francisco."

"I want you to keep it. It is small payment for what you have done."

"I didn't do this for payment."

"I know, but I insist."

"I'm sorry, Mr. Chang, but I cannot accept any payment. I did not do this for money. Please understand."

He was silent for a few minutes.

"You are a moral man. Very Confucian. I am pleased you are my friend. Take care and come to Beijing as soon as you can."

"I will."

I suppose it would have been all right to accept the money. There was about fifteen thousand left. But, money has never been a part of my dealings with Chang. With the end of the Pei business Chang was obligated to me big time and I didn't want his debt to be measured in terms of dollars. Was I being practical rather than being moral? Yeah, I was. I could pass up a few dollars to obligate Chang to me in other more important ways. Did Chang know what I was doing? Yeah, he did.

I finished dressing and packed. It was nine o'clock when I came out to the den. She was sitting at the desk working on her laptop.

"Was that the young man's father?"

"No. It was the person who asked me to do this for the father."

"He must be a good friend."

"Yes, he is."

"Is he in Guangzhou?"

"No. He's in Beijing."

"You don't want to talk about this?"

"Not much to talk about. He's just a friend. We've been involved in couple of things. Nothing important."

"Was he part of your business with the gas masks?"

"Not directly. But he helped when I needed some assistance."

"Are you ever going to tell me about your business?"

"Really nothing much to tell. I help out with things people need."

"Things?"

"Yeah. I'm a handy man that works puzzles. I help put the pieces together."

"Like you helped me."

"Not exactly. You're different."

"Whatever, it worked for me."

"You don't need my help. You'll do well all by yourself."

She looked at the clock on the desk.

"I guess it's time."

"Yep. I'll call a cab."

"Let me drive you."

"No. I'll say goodbye here, not at a police station."

She started to say something, but stopped. Her eyes began to water.

"Okay," she said.

I called a cab, gathered my things, and went to the door. She held my hand and tears formed. I kissed her and held her close.

"Call me when you get home."

"I will."

"I'm so glad we had our time. It's a thank you for saving my life."

"Don't say that."

"Don't say what?"

"I didn't save your life. I can't save lives."

"What I mean is that you helped to change my life. Remember we talked about this in Guangzhou. I was lost until I found you. When I was in Guangzhou trying to get a handle on this China business, there were lots of guys hovering around. None of those jerks really wanted to help me and some didn't know as much as I did. Most of them just wanted to jump my bones. Then I found you. You were willing to help without any strings. Whatever it was and whatever you said, it was right for me. It might have been accidental, but you changed my life."

"For all you know, my helping you might have just been a whim."

"You don't do things on a whim. That's the way you are. Some of us will take advantage of you whenever we can. Get used to it. It was and is special for me."

I took in a deep breath and thought about BJ. I didn't save her life.

"Sometimes knowing me can be deadly."

"I can't imagine knowing you can cause someone harm."

"It's happened."

"Does this have to do with the lady in Harbin?"

"It does."

"Whatever that was, I'm sorry, but I'm lucky to have you."

"You're really special, Megan. Very special."

"I hoped you would notice. I've prancing around for months, waiting." She laughed and I laughed with her. She was okay again.

"Time to go. Thank you for everything. I couldn't have done this without you."

"I'm so glad I could help. Think about me. Don't forget me."

"Couldn't if I tried."

"Call me."

"I will. Take care, Megan."

I arrived at the police station a few minutes after ten. Captain Finn was in his office, waiting for me.

"You got the papers from the ADA?"

"Yep. All signed and sealed. You want to make copies?"

"Okay."

He took the papers and gave them to a civilian clerk to make copies.

"Your guy is kinda jumpy. Been in here with the drunks and overnighters for about a week. He hasn't been bothered too much, if you know what I mean. But the thugs in there made him nervous."

"Good. He can get an idea how much worse it can get."

"You want him cleaned up? He smells a little."

"That would help. He's going to be on a plane for thirteen hours. Don't suppose there's any extra clothes he can change into."

"Yeah. We can get a clean shirt and a windbreaker jacket. Might even find a pair of jeans somewhere."

"That's great."

"I'll tell them to scrub him down and bring him out."

Thirty minutes later Finn came back to the office.

"I put him in an interrogation room. He doesn't know what's going to happen. Plenty scared. Does he know you?"

"Never laid eyes on him."

"Well, he had breakfast about six this morning. He's cleaned up and doesn't smell any more. But, he's still a bit shaky."

"That's the way I want him."

Finn led me down the hall to a series of rooms marked as Interview rooms. He stopped at the second door and looked at me. I nodded and he opened the door.

"Push that button if you need anything. We have a time limit if you're going to make your schedule."

"I won't be long."

Finn nodded and closed the door.

Tony Pei was sitting in a chair drying his hair with some paper towels. The cops must have stripped him and threw him into a shower and told him to soap himself down. At least he smelled clean.

I walked around behind him and put my hands on the back of his chair. He was nervous. He twisted in his chair and looked at me and back toward the door. He may have thought I was Chinese, putting me in a particular subservient class in relationship to him. He thought he had a glimmer of hope.

"What's going on here?" he demanded. "Who are you? Do you know who I am? Do you know who my father is? I demand to see an attorney. I know my rights."

I grabbed the front of his shirt with my left hand and turned him so he was facing me. I punched him hard with my right fist on the left side of his face. I caught part of his nose. Blood started to flow from his nose and a small cut appeared on his cheek. I didn't want to break his nose. That would create a medical problem. The cut and nose bleed was enough. He let out a cry. I caught him just as he started to fall off his chair. Not too much blood, but enough. It was a good solid punch. No one had ever hit him before. The initial shock was greater than the pain.

It took several minutes before he was able to focus. He stared at me, confused and afraid – wondering who I was.

I grabbed him under his neck and put up a finger to his face.

"Do not say a word. Not one word."

I pushed the paper towel at him and he wiped the blood on his face.

"You will listen to what I say and do not say another word. Do you understand?"

The week in the jail cell had put him on edge. The blow to his face caused pain and increased his fears of physical harm. While in the cell the threat was only potential. I made the threat real. He knew I was not a policeman but was someone with power to do what I wanted. He understood about power.

"Look at me."

I grabbed him under his chin and turned his face toward me.

"I said look at me!"

He blinked and looked up at me. I could see fear in his eyes.

"Listen very carefully to what I have to say."

I leaned in close, until my face was about ten inches from his. He was breathing heavily, eyes wide open.

"There are two things that can happen to you. One, I can turn you back to the police to be tried in a summary court – no jury trial. You will be found guilty of selling drugs and sentenced to two years in prison. I can arrange for this to happen. This will be a real prison, not like the holding cell you've been in. In prison you will be raped every day by some animal that needs a special kind of love. Do you understand me?"

I paused for a few minutes while he thought about prison. The goons he met in the holding cell were boy scouts compared to what he would meet in prison. I hoped he realized this.

Finally, he nodded and said, "Yes."

"That's one thing that can happen to you. The other is this. You do exactly what I tell you and I will put you on a plane that will take you to Beijing. You will keep your mouth shut and not talk to anyone until you arrive in Beijing. Do you understand?"

I waited a minute. "Well? What's it going to be? Say now. You will not get another chance to decide anything."

"I'll do what you say," he said quickly.

"You make one mistake – step out line one inch – and you'll be back in jail without any hope of salvation. You understand?"

"Yes."

"Speak up!"

"Yes. I understand," he said aloud.

"Okay. We're going to go out of this room and get into a police car. It will take us to the airport and you will board a plane. Some one will meet you at the Beijing airport and you will do what that person tells you to do.

"You will give up your right forever to attend school in the US. You will never come back to this country. If you come back, I will find you. Believe me, I can find you wherever you are. And when I find you, you will regret it for the rest of your life. Do you understand what I said?"

"Yes."

"I can't hear you. Louder."

"Yes," he shouted.

"Okay. Get up and follow me."

———————————————

"We're ready, Captain Finn. Can he use the restroom first?"

"Sure. Second door on your left." He pointed down the hall.

"Go use the toilet and wash your face. Be quick about it."

He nodded and went to the restroom. Finn looked after him.

"How'd he get a nose bleed?"

"Anxiety attack."

"I see."

"Think I'm pushing too hard?"

"He's a dope dealer. How hard is hard? You been on the force?"

"No. Actually, I was a school teacher."

"Oh, yeah? Imagine that."

"How's our time, Captain?"

"The squad car can make it without a problem. I told the two patrolmen to escort you to the boarding gate. I'll call ahead and alert the people out there."

"This is all greatly appreciated."

"Well, can't do too much for dope peddlers."

Tony Pei came out of the restroom and stood with his head down and his hands in his pants pockets. He had washed his face and stopped the bleeding. Finn led us out to the area where the patrol cars were parked. He pointed at two police officers.

"This is Garcia and Simpson. They know what to do. You got a little under two hours."

I shook their hands, then turned to Finn and extended my hand.

"Thanks again, Captain."

"It's been a pleasure to see an educator at work."

He nodded at the two policemen and walked away.

Noon traffic was heavy and when needed, they used the siren. The patrol car and siren assured us we would be there with a few minutes to spare. They parked the squad car at the curb and the four of us went directly to the passenger scanner. It was fifteen minutes to one when we arrived at the departure gate. I showed the clerk at the desk the confirmation slip. She punched some keys and the computer spit out the boarding pass.

I walked Pei to the gate and turned him to face me.

"Here is your passport and boarding pass. Hear me well. You were given an opportunity of a lifetime when you came to this country, but you fucked it all up by getting involved with drugs. That was most stupid thing you will ever do in your entire life. Be grateful that you're not going to prison where you could be killed."

He'll analyze all of this later and realize I had no legal authority. But for the time being I was a person with a great deal of power. He truly feared me, which is what I wanted him to feel.

"Now get on the plane. I never, ever, want to see you again."

He looked down at his passport and ticket. He was trembling.

"Get on the plane," I said, pointing toward the plane.

He hesitated and then turned and walked to the flight attendant collecting boarding passes and handed her his boarding pass. She tore off one part and gave him the rest. He looked back at me with a confused look, hesitated, and unconsciously waved at me. I didn't return the farewell gesture. He put his hand down, turned, and walked into the plane. That was the last I saw of him.

The flight attendant saw the police officers and came to me.

"Is there a problem with this passenger? Is he someone important?"

"No. He's just a wayward son on his way home."

"He looked sad. I guess leaving here was difficult for him."

"Not as difficult as his homecoming will be."

I thanked Garcia and Simpson for their help. I invited them to lunch but they declined the offer. They had to get back to work. I stayed at the departure gate until I saw the plane taxi out and down to the runway. It was twenty minutes before it was air borne.

Three hours before my plane was scheduled to leave. I went to the Red Carpet lounge and had a Coors, a deviled egg sandwich, and a small bag of chips. It was a pretty good sandwich and the beer was really cold.

I was relieved this was over. I thought about Claire Kowalski. She was the only one who wanted to do what she believed to be right. She was a real winner. I wanted to meet her again.

The others involved didn't spend too much time worrying about what was the right thing to do. What was legal and what was right didn't matter to them. Appropriately applied political pressure bent the law so a foreign student was freed of a drug charge. It was the expedient thing to do. Was this a great county or what?

Going through my bag I found the papers I had signed for Pei's release and was reminded to fax them to Chang. I wondered around looking for a fax machine. One was available at the United reception desk. The clerk saw the Beijing number and hesitated. She finally decided because I was a First Class passenger and a Red Carpet member, it was okay to fax the two sheets to Chang's number without charge. I'll send the wallet with the drug money by UPS when I got home.

After a half an hour wait I got a turn at a computer and checked my Email. Nothing from Ahn. There was a long message from Yasha. She had received the invitation. I knew she would call me later so I didn't reply to her message. I went back to the main lounge and thought about another beer, then decided to pass on it.

My cell phone chimed and Megan's name and number came up on the screen.

"Did I forget something?"

"No. Just called to tell you everything was perfect."

"I agree. Couldn't have asked for more."

"I've been thinking about things."

"Things?"

"Things we talked about."

"We talked about a lot of things."

"I'm concerned about how my parents affect things between us."

"Are they involved?"

"No. I want you to know they are not a part of you and me."

"Then there's no problem."

"I think I understand what you mean about how they are about things."

"Things again."

"About race and things."

"How they think about such matters is their business. It's not the way you think. That's all that matters."

"No, it isn't how I think. I wanted you to know that."

"I got that impression last night when we decided which bed to use."

"Actually, the beds are identical. Mine just has better linen."

"You mean the bed I slept in had inferior linen?"

"Well, you only slept in it one night."

"I didn't know exactly what it was, but I felt there was a difference."

"Hereafter, you can sleep in my bed with the better linen."

"Will we share the bed?"

"Of course. I want to make certain you have the best."

"Can't argue with that."

"I had a great two days."

"So did I." I really meant it.

"Have a safe trip."

"Bye."

"Bye."

31

T HERE WERE ONLY TWO other First Class passengers on the flight. The one flight attendant was a middle aged woman who was probably not too many years from retirement. She served Champagne and handed out dinner menus. I declined dinner and had some cookies instead. The wine on the dinner menu was a California Pinot Noir and I had several glasses.

Everything in Chicago went better than expected. So, why was I feeling down? Was I on edge because I hadn't heard from Ahn? I'll call him when I get home.

It was nine o'clock when I arrived at my apartment. I threw the clothes into the washer and showered. I had a drink and watched television for an hour. It was one in the afternoon in Harbin. I called Ahn.

"I'm sorry I don't have any news yet. But, I'm talking to a lot of people and through a process of elimination, getting an idea of what to look for."

"I know it will take time and you don't have any help. I just called to lend some moral support."

"Thanks for the thought."

"Don't let this mess up your life and business."

"Not a problem."

"I'll leave for Vietnam in a few days and will be there for about a week. You have my Vietnam number?"

"Yes."

"Take care, Ahn. And thanks."

"I'll call as soon as I know anything."

It was a tedious and tiring task for Ahn. Pretty much what the police did in murder cases. Asking questions and hoping someone would provide a clue that would lead to something. Ahn had taken on a monumental task. Without him I would be lost.

I didn't hear the phone ringing until the fifth or sixth ring. It was the landline phone, not my cell phone. I thought it might be Yasha. It was.

"I tried your cell phone earlier and left a message. You didn't call so I called your home number."

"Sorry."

"You've been traveling? How are you?"

"I'm fine. So, you received the invitation."

"Yes. And I have my visa. There are two invitations. One is from someone in Nha Trang and the other is from Hanoi. The first meeting is in Ho Chi Minh City then I guess we go to Hanoi. Why not just meet in Hanoi?"

"The first meeting is with a local, probably from a possible site for the project, but you'll meet with decision makers in Hanoi. Anyway, not to worry. Kevin will have more definite news about meetings. Meanwhile, get hotel reservations in Saigon. There are a couple of hotels I've used that are pretty good. One is the New World and the other is the Caravelle. But, there are other five star hotels you can pick from. I'll get my visa tomorrow. It takes a day here. Why don't we plan on meeting in Hong Kong in three days?"

"Okay. I'll have your ticket from San Francisco to Hong Kong arranged tomorrow. I'll Email you the time of your flight. Singapore Air okay?"

"Of course. But any airline will do if it's Business Class."

"It will be. Did you read my proposal?"

"Yes, I did. It was excellent. You did a remarkable job."

"Thanks. Let's hope the Vietnamese think so."

"They will."

"Talk to you soon, best friend."

"Take care, Yasha."

"You too."

With matters coming together in Vietnam, it was time to call Kevin. He moved around a lot and some days it was difficult to locate him. The best time was about noon when he was awake and available. He used three cell phones and with luck I could get him on one of them. I finally found him when I called the second cell phone number.

"Kevin. How are you?"

"Fine. Looking forward to seeing you."

"How's the family? I got the pictures of the new boy. Now you have a boy and a girl. Family's growing."

"Yes. I want as many as I can get. How are things with you?"

"Getting old, but getting by. My Shanghai associate got her invitation. It said to meet in Ho Chi Minh City. Is this the same go around?"

"Yes. A local official is given a chance to make a few dollars. He's from the area where a resort might be built. Hanoi wants to keep good relations with locals. If things go right, he'll recommend your lady and project to more important people in Hanoi."

"You have to tell her how much to put in the red envelope. But, I don't want it to be out of sight."

"I'll bargain."

"Good. Now. What about our ammunition project?"

"That meeting is in Hanoi. A date and time will be set today or tomorrow."

"Any problems?" I asked.

"I don't think so. The proposal is a good one and Vietnam needs a good producing ammunition plant."

"I hope they really read the proposal. It states plainly that the army stands to make millions."

"I know, but not all of the old party comrades have died off yet. Sometimes they make strange demands that make no sense. Some old timers are still fighting the revolution. They haven't been told that they won the war."

"Well, we'll have to deal with it. I'm also very interested in the resort proposal. With the casino, the income can be in the millions of dollars. I've read the proposal and it is excellent."

"This woman. How well do you know her? She is Chinese?"

"Yes. She's Chinese and I know her very well. Her name is Yasha Hsiao. On the outside she uses the name Alice. A very intelligent woman. Has a MBA from the University of Washington and studied law at George Washington University."

"Is it a personal thing with you?"

"She's very special to me."

"I see. What about her company?"

"She works for a giant company, probably worth billions. Maybe you've heard of them. Li Wah out of Shanghai."

"Oh, yeah. That's big time. Do you work for them now?"

"No. I'm only a consultant on this project. It's the same with you. You'll be paid as a consultant."

"Not necessary."

"I know, but you'll be paid. The company can certainly afford it and you've been a great help. Might need more help if this gets going and you can hire on fulltime or whatever you want."

"We'll see. You have a hotel."

"She'll handle that. I assume this first go around will be only one day in Ho Chi Minh City," I said.

"Yes. At least I hope so. After the envelope is passed, she shouldn't have any problems going on to the next level in Hanoi."

"I don't have too much time this go around, Kevin. I would like to see this ammunition proposal finished in two days."

"Possible. They've had plenty of time to look at the written proposal. Enough time to decide if they really want to do something."

"Sounds good. I'll Email you the flight schedule."

"I'll pick you up at the airport."

"Okay. By the way, how's Charlie Oh doing?"

"Doing good. Still works for that French shipping company. Want to see him?"

"Well, if he has time. How's married life going for him? I haven't met his wife yet. How long has she been in Vietnam?"

"She's been here for a couple of years. Works for the South Korean embassy."

"I'm sorry I missed the wedding. They have a family started?"

"No baby yet."

"Well, we'll have to give him a 'how to' manual."

"Korean women are good at having babies. My wife does okay."

"And we need more."

"I keep trying."

"I know you will."

32

THE NEXT MORNING I went to the Vietnamese consulate and applied for a visa. For an extra sixty dollars the visa was available the next day. I paid the sixty dollars.

I called my children and explained why I would be leaving the country again. It wasn't much of an explanation, but they were polite and pretended it was okay. I was glad I had the four children, but I had been less than an ideal father. They were fortunate their mother made up for my shortcomings. Whatever successes they have will be because of Catheryn's efforts, not mine. As I told Yasha, it was my greatest failing and I didn't know how to make up for it.

I called Andre and caught him as he was getting ready to board a plane to Panama.

"I'll be in Nam day after tomorrow. Meetings with the army have been set, so things are coming together."

"Sounds good."

"I hope all this will be finished in a couple of days. I'll let you know how things go as soon as I know."

"How are you feeling?"

"Me? I'm okay."

"You were down a little last time we met."

"Not a problem. Are you coming back home after Panama?" I asked.

"No. Quick trip to Paris and then to Miami to see my mother, then home."

"I don't know exactly when I'll be home. Have some things to finish up in China."

"In China? Is there a problem?"

"No. Just some personal things to attend to."

"Is this something I should know about?"

"Nothing that important, Andre. Have a good trip and I'll be talking to you soon."

"If you need help, you should say."

"I know. If I need help I'll holler."

"Take care my friend."

"You too."

"*Adieu.*"

I wondered what Andre would say about my quest to find BJ's killer. I was sure he would side with Kam Wah and counsel me against going back to Harbin.

My computer chimed, indicating the arrival of Email. There were several messages. One was from Yasha. I was booked Business Class on Singapore Flight SQ1, leaving San Francisco day after tomorrow at 1:05 AM arriving in Hong Kong at 6:35 AM the following day. I was to meet her in the Cathay Pacific VIP lounge. Our flight to Ho Chi Minh City was on Cathay Pacific, leaving at 2:45 PM and arriving at 4:10 PM. I had several hours to kill, but Cathay's VIP lounge was as comfortable as any in Hong Kong.

There was also a message from Gary suggesting lunch this week. I wrote back and suggested a date two weeks hence. That reminded me to send a note to Carolyn about lunch. I sent a note suggesting a date in a week. I probably wouldn't be able to keep either date. But, I always promised I would try.

Chick sent a note reminding me about Vietnamese rice. I answered, telling him I was going to Vietnam especially to find his rice. There was a message from Mark, asked about an investment casting in China. My contact for the casting business was Mary in Dongying. I wouldn't have time for that until I got back, so I sent a reply telling him I'd be in touch. Other messages from Cyd and Corky were several days old.

A surprise was a message from Big Man. He was the only contact I still had of the people who were at Grove. Another lifetime ago. He was married to a lovely lady, Carole, and lived in Forestville, close to Santa Rosa. He spent his time as a disc jockey on the local radio station, spinning jazz records with a running commentary on the artists. He was still fighting the good fight and active in community organizations. I sent a reply, suggesting a meeting in a month.

The lack of exercise in the last two weeks resulted in certain proof of my declining physical condition. I felt flabby. So I gathered my gear and went to the gym and used all the torture devices there for two hours. I was exhausted but felt better.

My dinner was take-out Chinese food from a restaurant several blocks from my apartment. I knew the owner-chef and he gave me lots of specials. I finished it off with the second scotch and settled down to watch television.

"*Ni hao ma?* How about that? Been practicing."

"Sounds like an old China hand."

"I called because I was feeling kinda lonely. We could solve this loneliness problem by moving in together."

"Yeah, I suppose so. But, your idea of an apartment is far above my pay grade."

"We could make some kind of arrangement."

"Lots of complications."

"Nothing that can't be solved and I'm the best deal in town," Megan said. I could see her pointing her thumb at herself.

"Can't argue with that."

"Are you leaving soon?"

"I leave tomorrow – a few minutes after midnight."

"Send me an Email now and then. Just so I'll know not to sell the farm and come looking for you."

"I will. Take care."

"Bye."

I wondered where this was all going. Whatever. I knew things weren't gonna happen as Megan might want. How was I going to handle that?

The thought of the long transpacific flight didn't improve my state of mind. It was going to be difficult enough without trying to make decisions about things that were impossible to decide.

I missed the spa and massage in Huangpo. I also missed Kam Wah's herbs and banquet style dinners. I missed all the people in Hong Kong, Huangpo, Harbin, and Singapore. I missed my kids and felt guilty about that. I missed a lot of things. I was pretty lonely. But, it was the life I had chosen. Too late to bitch. As so many lost souls, I was looking for answers. I knew I would never find them, but I kept telling myself a rewarding life was just over the hill. Pretty sad state of affairs.

Harbin, Guangzhou, Vietnam, and places like Chicago in between were supposed to be my thing. Being lonely didn't help fight off depression. Should I be looking for someone to give me comfort and loving care? On numerous occasions Kam Wah has suggested several names and they were more than willing. So why am I still alone? My *karma*?

I gave up worrying about these things, had another drink, and went to bed.

I woke early and decided to go the gym. After a two-hour workout I felt better. I came back and had breakfast – finishing what was left of the orange juice. I didn't know exactly how long I would be gone, so the refrigerator and pantry were bare again.

I put my traveling clothes on the bed to decide what I would take. That didn't take long. My travel wardrobe consisted of two pair of denim jeans, three T-shirts, a pair of gym shorts, a pair of light canvas walking shoes, two dress shirt, two sports shirts, five pairs of shorts, three pairs of socks, and a summer jacket. Everything was washable and hotels provided six hour laundry service. And if necessary, I could buy whatever I needed cheap. Except the cold plane cabin, it was summer and the weather would be warm to hot, so didn't need a sweater. I debated whether I should take a tie and decided I would.

My small personal bag was empty except for a toothbrush. Tubes of toothpaste and razors were not allowed on airplanes. I always wondered what terrorists could do with toothpaste. Do people really feel safer if they can't take a tube of toothpaste? Was airport security great or what? It took about five minutes to pack.

At noon I went to the Vietnamese consulate and picked up my passport. I called Singapore Air to confirm my reservation and checked my Email. A message from Andre, who was worried about my emotional state and my cryptic reference to having things to do in China. Chang sent a brief note saying Ho Man Pei, AKA Tony, had arrived in Beijing. He thanked me and asked when I would be coming to Beijing. I Emailed the plane schedule to Kevin and a message to Yasha to tell her I was on my way.

I phoned the kids and left a message for them on their mother's answering machine. UPS came to pick up Tony Pei's personal belongings I was sending to Chang. I spent the rest of the afternoon going over the ammunition proposal and had another look at Yasha's proposal. About eight o'clock I got my things together and closed up the apartment.

I took a taxi to the Korea House on Post Street and had a bowl of *bibimbop* and bottle of Hite beer. At nine-thirty I walked to the Japantown Bart station and rode the train to the Daly City station. This was where travelers to the airport changed trains. It disembarked in the domestic terminal, so I had a bit of a walk to the international terminal.

My boarding pass was waiting for me at the check in counter. The Singapore Silver Kris lounge was available for Business Class passengers and I spent the final time before boarding there. It was a new lounge, very comfortable and not crowded.

A computer was available for Business and First Class passengers and I made a last minute check of my Email. There was one from Yasha telling me, again, to wait in the Cathay lounge. She was coming in on a mid-morning flight.

I sent a message to Chang telling him I received his note and that I didn't know exactly when I was coming back to Beijing. No word from Ahn. At this point, even if he had news, I wouldn't leave Yasha until matters were settled in Vietnam.

Flying Singapore Air was one of the great experiences in traveling.

The food was very good and they had scotch whiskey. The world renowned beautiful stewardesses did wonders for tired people like me. I watched a movie and read the latest Jack Higgins and Elmore Leonard novels I bought at a bookstore in the airport. Then I slept for a couple of hours and woke in time for breakfast. We landed in Chek Lap Kok Airport a few minutes ahead of schedule.

I went through the transit gate and walked to the section of the terminal where the airline lounges were located. The Cathay Pacific lounge was one of the better ones in the Hong Kong International. I identified myself to the lady at the reception desk and she confirmed my reservation on the Vietnam flight. Boarding passes would be issued later, she said. I went in and found a sofa seat next to the window. It was eight in the morning and Yasha was scheduled to arrive at ten-thirty. I looked forward to seeing her.

33

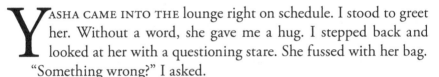

YASHA CAME INTO THE lounge right on schedule. I stood to greet her. Without a word, she gave me a hug. I stepped back and looked at her with a questioning stare. She fussed with her bag. "Something wrong?" I asked.

"No."

"Are you alright, Yasha?"

"Yes."

"Okay. What is it?"

"Had a long meeting with the company heads, last night."

"They worried?"

"No. Well, yes, they're concerned. Lots of money at stake. But, they haven't said anything negative, yet."

"So? They have doubts?"

"Well, this is the biggest deal I've been involved with. They wanted to make sure I knew what I was doing."

"Have they read the proposal? It's as well constructed as anything I've seen. If Vietnam approves it can't miss."

"They've read it. They think it's good, but I've never honchoed something this big before."

"They want to send in some back up?"

"No. If this fails it'll be all on me."

"It'll be just fine, Yasha."

"You're the one who says it isn't done until the fat lady sings. I'm counting on you to help bring the fat lady in."

"Your bosses must know this depends on approval by the Vietnam government. Until then it won't cost them much money."

"They know that."

"So what's the problem?"

"I don't want to blow this."

"You won't. I won't let you."

"I really need your help."

"That's why I'm here."

"You won't leave me, will you?"

"No. I will not leave you."

"I know that. I'm just talking."

This was unlike her usual self. She was feeling anxious about Vietnam and needed to be reassured she was not alone. It was one of the few times she displayed a bit of insecurity. But I knew that would pass.

"You're gonna do just fine. Okay." I smiled and held her hand. "Do you want something to drink or eat?"

"Maybe some tea."

"I'll get it."

I went to the food and drink bar and fixed her a cup of tea. I opened a bottle of Tiger beer and grabbed two biscuits and a bag of chips. I watched her as she sipped her tea. She looked up at me and gave me a weak smile.

"I've set up banking arrangements with Deutsche Bank so we can withdraw cash when we need it. Oh, I made a copy of the invitation letter."

She opened her brief case, fished around, and pulled out the copy.

"Also, here's a copy of the fax about the meeting in Ho Chi Minh City."

The invitation from a Deputy Prime Minister was a formal letter inviting Ms. Alice Hsiao to meet and discuss the proposal she had submitted. It was called Project Resort #6. Did that mean there had been five other resorts proposals before Yasha's?

The fax was from a Mr. Nguyen Tham from Nha Trang City. His title was Director, Economic Development, Nha Trang City. He asked that Yasha inform him where she was staying and time and day for a meeting. A second fax was sent from Hanoi saying a meeting would be held per time and date arranged by Mr. Le Bui Lan, who was my contact, AKA Kevin.

"Well, unless there's a problem with Nguyen, you will meet with the Deputy Prime Minister's people in Hanoi in a couple of days. Did you decide on a hotel in Ho Chi Minh City?"

"We're staying at the New World. I sent a message to Nguyen to meet us there tomorrow morning at eleven. He verified the date and time by return fax. I don't know why he doesn't use Email. Faxing is so out of date and cumbersome."

"Not everyone is into high tech in Nam. Most are, like Kevin, but some, like local politicos, are not. You have to adjust."

"I know. I'm just bitching." She sighed and frown at me. "You look tired. I know you've been traveling."

"Had that other thing to take care of in the states."

"Oh yes, the business in Chicago."

"All done with that now. Kevin said he'll meet us at the airport."

"You think this Nguyen is important?"

"Yes and no. He's the local guy. If the powers decide Nha Trang is the location they want, you will have to deal with him again. The party counts on him in that part of Vietnam."

"Does he have a say whether the proposal is accepted."

"Well, not directly. But he can express an opinion and the decision makers will consider his opinion of you. That's what the red envelope is for. Help convince him to like you. You can get some US dollars tomorrow morning and Kevin will give him the envelope before we meet."

"How much?"

"We can ask Kevin but I think three thousand should do it. That buys a lot of good will for what he has to do at this stage."

"Does Nguyen have a copy of the proposal?"

"No. At this point, he really doesn't have to know all the details. If he's satisfied that you're really interested in Nha Trang and easy to work with, he'll pass on a favorable report. If not, he'll say another meeting is necessary, which means another red envelope."

I sighed and drank the rest of my beer.

"I'm worried about you. You really do look tired," she said, frowning.

"Looking tired can be mistaken for old age."

"Well, it's not a long flight to Ho Chi Minh City and you can get some rest tonight. Sleep in tomorrow. Meeting isn't till eleven."

"I'll be okay."

"I'll make sure you are."

"Oh?"

"For once, you can do as I say."

"You won't get much argument from me. I am tired."

"Be warned. I'll take advantage of your weaken state."

"Oh. How?"

"That's for me to know. But, don't worry. I'll be gentle."

She laughed and gave me a poke on my arm. She was feeling her old self again. It was important that she was okay because I wasn't too certain about myself.

The HCMC flight left a few minutes after the scheduled departure time, but the pilot pushed it and we landed right on time. After going through immigration and customs, we walked past the corridor of people lined up waiting for arriving passengers. Since we didn't have to wait for bags we went directly outside.

Yasha had one large carry on bag, which she fortunately didn't have to check, and a large handbag, containing her laptop among other things. I had my usual one small carryon bag, so I carried her large briefcase as one of my bags. It weighed a ton because the bag contained written material. The papers would be left in Vietnam and she would fill the empty bags with clothes and other things she would buy.

As soon as we walked through the doors the very hot and humid heat hit me full on. June and July were the hottest months of the year and the wettest. Temperature in Saigon averaged 28 C, a bit hotter in Hanoi that averaged 30 C.

We were met by a dozen or more taxi drivers and private cars who offered us special deals on transportation into the city.

Kevin was standing at the edge of the crowd. He waved as we came past the transportation vendors. He looked the same as when I first met him years ago. He was dressed in his usual white dress shirt, with the sleeves rolled up to his elbow. I have never seen him wear a coat or a tie.

As most Vietnamese his age, he looked younger than this years. He was about thirty-five. I never really knew his real age. His hairline was beginning to recede and his thin triangular face looked a bit shallow. The thinness of his face was further accentuated by his horn rimed glasses. The only jewelry was a digital watch and a wedding ring. He smoked continuously – reminding me of Kam Wah.

"Kevin, this is Yasha. Yasha, Kevin."

"Nice to meet you, Kevin."

"My pleasure." He shook her hand, grabbed her bag, and led us to his car.

"We're booked at the New World," I said.

"You should have told me. I can get a discount."

"Well, you can mention that to them when we check in," Yasha said.

———

Ho Chi Minh City was the living example of the rapid growth and development of the country in the past five years. It was formerly known as Saigon and many still referred to the city by that name.

Nine million plus was the latest population count in metropolitan area, the city, and surrounding towns. The city proper had a population of about six and a half million people and a large number of these were in the under thirty-five age group. They were bright and ambitious – budding capitalists in the making. Very aggressive in everything they did.

As they were in all Asian cities, the roads were congested with trucks, cars, bicycles, motorbikes, and pedestrians. The motor bikes and bicycles took up most of the street on both sides, so the cars and trucks were squeezed in the middle two lanes. The noise and fumes were overwhelming.

There was always a never ending string of construction projects in HCMC, as there was in all Asian cities. New buildings and partially completed ones were seen all the way into the city. Most of the new buildings were apartment complexes with small shops, cafes, and businesses housed in twenty by twenty feet spaces on the ground floor. Some spaces were much smaller. Pull down doors, similar to garage doors, closed the spaces at night.

Kevin dropped us off at the hotel and we agreed to meet in an hour. The New World was a relatively new hotel with all the modern amenities. After registering we went up to our rooms to freshen up. I needed a shower. In the humid climate two showers a day was average. If I was out and about during the day, three and sometimes four showers were needed.

Yasha arranged for us to have adjoining rooms on the ninth floor. A door separated our rooms. She opened the door and walked in.

She waved a key at me.

"This will save going out to the hall. So I can come in here or you can come into my room without going out to the hallway. See?" She swung the door back and forth.

"Yeah, I see. Now you have to excuse me. I'm going to take a shower."

"Me too. See ya."

After the shower I checked the bar. There was cold Tiger beer in the refrigerator and mini bottles of gin and wine available on the bar. A card on top of the television announced that a gym on the top floor opened at six o'clock in the morning. Massages were also available from four in the afternoon until midnight. Good news.

Yasha suddenly came into the room and stood with one hand on her hip and the other on the door knob.

"Ready?"

"You should knock before you open the door. I might be naked."

"Well, I don't want to miss anything."

"You have to behave, Yasha."

"I don't promise anything."

I sighed and shook my head.

"Let's go."

Kevin took us to a very nice Vietnamese restaurant. It was properly air-conditioned – not too cold as many places were – and the food was excellent. Most of our discussion centered on Yasha's meeting tomorrow.

"Do you know this Nguyen Tham?" Yasha asked.

"I've met him once. He's a good party member and has been in control of things in the Nha Trang region for about five years. It's a growing city in central Vietnam and an important part of the national economic development program. Has a beautiful coast line. Population is about 300,000 and growing. It's hot there – averages about 28 to 30 C. It would be ideal for your resort. I think the central government likes it."

"How important is he to our project?"

"If he thinks you are a friend he can be a very big help. And if your project is built there, he will be your main contact. All labor, utilities, and all licenses, are in his hands."

"How much do we pay him?"

"I think three thousand US is a good number."

"I'll go to the bank tomorrow morning so you'll have the money before we meet. Will that be acceptable?"

"Okay. I'll know how it is with him when I talk to him. Get a feel of how he is reacting to this deal."

"Whatever you think is fine." She paused for a moment. "I want you to know my company will compensate you for your time and assistance. I can pay you part now and the rest when we finish. Or all at the end. However, you want."

"It is not necessary. Help with expenses is all I need for now."

"The company will pay you for your time."

"We shall see."

After dinner, we came back to the hotel and Yasha excused herself and went to her room. She knew Kevin and I had to talk about my proposal.

"She seems to be well prepared."

"Yes, she is. I think she'll handle Nguyen."

"Nguyen is shrewd and a survivor. But, he can be bought. He didn't have much chance to make anything until this proposal came along."

"Okay, sounds good. Now what about my proposal?"

"As always, there's a committee and they'll decide how to proceed. We'll meet them at army headquarters in Hanoi. I was told it will be a small group. Early word is that there'll be five people representing the army. Four are military professionals. One is a party man. My contact, Dinh, will be the sixth person.

"Dinh thinks the army is interested because of the potential profits from sale of ammunition in the world market. According to him, there aren't too many problems. The army didn't appoint a heavy business type to handle this. They gave the job to an old soldier. Name is Pham. He's about seventy-five years old and a war hero. Most people know his name. He's tough. I was told he doesn't like Americans or Chinese."

"Well, the company I represent isn't American. It's a Filipino company."

"Whatever. It has a good chance to get accepted."

"Is there talk about up front money?"

"Not from the government side. Don't know about the army. But, a long term profit sharing plan should work."

"Well, the army can end up with millions. It's a good proposal. If this works out, you'll get the usual three percent and all expenses. If there are other things related to this project, especially domestic business, you'll get an extra fee."

"I'm good with all that."

"I'll prepare a contract and we can sign it when and if this goes through."

"Okay."

"You should take the fee from Yasha. You can also work something out when the project gets underway."

"I'll see how it goes. No need to rush."

"I can work out a contract with her company for you. Will there be a conflict in meeting times?"

"Depends. Our meeting is set for day after tomorrow. Early in the morning. Eight o'clock."

"That means we have to leave here latest tomorrow night."

"Yes. So she has to settle matters with Nguyen at that meeting. If it goes well, she'll have the Hanoi meeting with the people handling her project in two days."

"You know who this will be?" I asked.

"It'll be another committee. Most likely from the Deputy Prime Minister's office. There's been a big push to modernize the government in the Public Administration Reform program. The Reform program is, quote, 'to create an economy that meets requirements for managing a developing economy with a socialist orientation,' unquote. I don't know what all that means and most of the people in government know even less. They'll look at the resort proposal and try to decide if it's compatible with what they think is socialism."

"Does it make a difference if Vietnam makes money?"

"Yes and no. Purists want communism-socialism, but they don't know what that is. But, that's the party line. Others know that to make money a certain amount of capitalism is necessary. This is what happened in China and they're doing pretty good. And a resort is very good because it doesn't involve a manufactured product that has to be marketed."

"So it depends on who's in that group."

"Yes. For both your proposal and hers."

"Well, let's hope we both get a good draw."

"The red envelop for Nguyen is the only up front money needed."

"Good. She has to get to the bank in the morning."

"I think the Deutsche bank opens at nine."

"So, there's no problem. And thanks for picking us up at the airport and for the great dinner. I haven't asked, but how's the family?"

"Everything is fine."

"Give my best to the wife."

"Will do. Thank you."

"See you tomorrow."

I went up to my room, took off my shoes, put on the hotel slippers, and opened a mini-bottle of gin. I heard a tap on the adjoining door. I yelled "come in." Yasha came in wearing a giant size terry bathrobe. She probably didn't have anything on under it. It was what she would do – it added to her unpretentious sexual aura. I don't think she was aware of this and she didn't make a concerted attempt to be sexually attractive. She just was who she was.

She didn't lead an austere life, but she was busy with her career and appeared not to pay much attention to the opposite sex. At least, that I knew. Was I the exception? This made me wonder how serious her feelings for me were. Whatever, as with so many things in her life, she had decided what to do and that was it.

"I remembered to knock."

"Good. Shows you're paying attention to what I say. Want something to drink? There's wine or beer."

"No. But can you heat water for tea?"

"Sure."

I got water from the wash basin tap and plugged in the pot. Tea bags were available. In a minute the water was boiling and I poured some into a cup.

"No tea leaves. Just tea bags."

"That's all right." She let the tea bag soak a while. "Business go okay with Kevin?"

"Yeah. But, we'll have a tight schedule. It'll be important to get finished with Nguyen tomorrow. If everything goes well, we'll fly out of here to Hanoi tomorrow night. My meeting is set for eight in the morning, day after tomorrow. Your meeting will be the next day."

"So, it depends on Nguyen."

"Yes it does. But, however that goes, I have to be in Hanoi for my meeting."

"I know. If it comes to that, we'll just have to figure something out."

"That's about it."

"It'll work out," she said.

"I'm sure you'll be able to handle Nguyen."

"I'll try."

"I know you will," I said.

"You'll be with me, so I'm not worried."

I smiled and she grinned back at me.

"Well, Yasha, there's you and me. We should be able to take on the Vietnamese government."

"They don't stand a chance."

"You damn right." I gave her thumbs up.

"I'm really glad you're here."

"I can't think of any other place I'd rather be."

She came to me, put her arms around my neck, and kissed me. Not a long kiss, but a warm soft kiss.

"This is getting to be habit."

"It's a habit I can't break. I'm hooked." She smiled.

"May have to look for a cure."

"Nothing will work."

"Yasha …"

"It's alright. I can live with things as they are for now."

She went to the door, turned, and pointed her finger at me.

"You're my guy."

34

A T SIX I WENT up to the gym for a workout. I was on a treadmill
farthest from the door with my head down, walking a good pace,
not running. It was a minute before I looked up to see Yasha on
the machine next to mine. She smiled and gave me thumbs up.

It was a delightful hour, spent with someone as bright and cheerful
as Yasha. She was becoming an important part of my life.

After the workout I went to my room and showered, shaved, and
called housekeeping to pick up my laundry. I was thinking about
brewing a cup of coffee when Yasha rapped on the door.

"Ready?"

"As ever I will be."

"Let's go get a cup of coffee."

After a cup of coffee in the restaurant, Yasha and I went to the
Deutsche bank and she cashed part of an open letter of credit. The
bank manager counted out five thousand US dollars in one hundred
dollar bills.

We booked a private conference room and put in an order for
refreshments with room service.

Kevin came in and reported that he had checked Vietnam Airlines
flight schedules to Hanoi. A non-stop flight left at 5:15 PM. He would
book seats on that flight if matters went well with Nguyen. Yasha gave
him three thousand dollars for Nguyen's red envelop.

A large coffee urn and hot water for tea were brought into the conference room. A plate of fruits and biscuits were set on the table. Only a tiny bit of the food would be touched, but good impressions were important. Some employees of the hotel would have a lot of left overs to take home.

Kevin met Nguyen in the lobby and had a short private conversation. After ten minutes of negotiations, he handed the envelope to Nguyen and shook his hand. Kevin probably started at two thousand dollars and Nguyen began at four thousand. Without too much haggling, he accepted the compromised figure of three thousand dollars, a small fortune for him. He was already in a good mood because he probably thought he would have to settle for less. They came to the conference room where Yasha and I were waiting.

Nguyen was in his late forties or early fifties. He was taller than the average Vietnamese, about five feet seven, slender, and probably never weighed more than a hundred and forty pounds. He was a wiry looking guy, balding on top, with thinning hair over each ear. He wore the ubiquitous white shirt with the sleeves rolled up to his elbows, black trousers, and open toed sandals. He was a smoker.

Yasha walked around the table to shake his hand. She bowed slightly.

"*Chao mung ban, thay* Nguyen," she said in Vietnamese.

I was as surprised as Nguyen when she greeted him in Vietnamese. She had done her homework and it was a good first impression. She motioned him to a chair on one side of the table and presented her name card, offering it with both hands. She introduced me and I handed him my company name card. He gave each of us his name card.

Although Nguyen's spoken English was not fluent, he could make himself understood without too much difficulty. He understood English without any problems. Kevin interpreted only when needed.

She asked if he wanted coffee or tea. He chose coffee. It was not Vietnamese style, dark and strong, but it was passable hotel coffee.

"Thank you for taking the time to visit with us today. It is greatly appreciated," she smiled and pushed the fruit and biscuits towards him. "Please." He took a biscuit.

"I am always interested in meeting new people and discussing business opportunities." He gave the standard communist-socialist greeting used at business meetings.

"Is Nha Trang very far from here?" she asked. "I hope the trip was not too tiring."

"No. I make this trip often. Sometimes twice a week."

"I certainly hope to visit your city soon."

"You are most welcome," he said.

"As you may know, our company is very interested in establishing a resort in Vietnam and Nha Trang was suggested as an ideal place."

"Yes, authorities in Hanoi have alerted me about your project."

"We are anxious to begin discussions with the government in Hanoi, but I'm pleased you have agreed to meet with us before our meeting with them. Since Nha Trang is a prime location, we believe it is important to be in touch with local officials, such as yourself."

"I'm always interested in business proposals, but I'm not familiar with all the details of your plans."

As we thought, he had not been given a copy of the proposal. Hanoi would not inform him of the project's details until the project had been approved. Hanoi operated as a need to know hierarchy.

"The plan is to build a very expansive complex consisting of a seven to eight hundred room hotel, a golf course, and family recreation park. Of course, if permitted, a casino would also be added."

"That's a big project."

"Yes, it is. That's why we will need local assistance with the entire project. There are many details involving licenses and permits, finding semi-skilled and skilled labor, and, of course, management personnel. You can help us in all those areas," Yasha said with a smile as she sipped her tea.

"I should let you know, several other locales have been suggested." She paused for a moment. "Including places, such as Can Tho, Da Nang, Hue, and even here in Ho Chi Minh City."

I looked at Nguyen. His eyes blinked. He had not thought seriously about possible competition from other cities. Had Hanoi asked others to meet with her?

Yasha produced five printed sheets, written in Vietnamese, with an outline of the project with target dates, costs figures, and the financial investment involved.

"This is a brief recap of the project. After our meeting in Hanoi we can have a complete copy of the proposal sent to you."

Nguyen examined the five pages, carefully studying the sections with costs and investments figures. It was greater than he first thought. The creation of hundreds of jobs and a leading role for him was a once in a life time opportunity.

If the project was approved and built in Nha Trang it would be a vital source of income for years to come. He could devote the rest of his life to this project. In time, it was something even his children could become involved with. He was thinking of how to get a copy of the proposal.

It was no longer a matter of his accepting Yasha's company, but the other way around. Would Yasha accept Nha Trang? Yasha was the money source and she would have a voice in picking the site. He was thinking how to convince Hanoi that Nha Trang was the ideal place for this project.

"This project is perfectly suited for Nha Trang. The other cities are good locales, but Nha Trang is the best." He hesitated then asked, "Are you meeting with people from other places?"

She gave me a quick glance. I looked at Kevin and both of us thought, you're hooked, Nguyen.

"We have a busy schedule and may not be able to meet with everyone on this trip. But, we certainly want to take the opportunity to meet with as many people as possible." She hesitated a moment. "As you know, we will be meeting with officials from the Deputy Prime Minister's office the day after tomorrow."

"Yes. I will advise them of our meeting today."

Meaning he would give Hanoi a favorable report and describe how he was able to handle this woman. But, will Hanoi ask her to meet with other cities?

"Wonderful. I was hoping you would favor such a project for Nha

213

Trang. You should know, we think Nha Trang would be an ideal location," she said.

Nguyen was smiling. He nodded and put his hands together, as in prayer – touching his lips with his fingers.

"I believe we can both benefit from this venture," Nguyen said.

Kevin looked at me and turned his eyes up.

"The pre-construction phase will require several months and the construction of the resort will take several years to complete. Obviously, it will bring a great deal of economic development to the area," Yasha said.

"We are prepared for this at Nha Trang."

"I hope so." Yasha smiled again and tilted her head.

"When you visit our city you will see."

"I look forward to coming to Nha Trang after our meetings in Hanoi."

"I can make arrangements for your visit as soon as your Hanoi meetings are concluded. I will inform the directors in Hanoi tonight."

"That would be greatly appreciated." Yasha smiled and closed her notebook. "Now, will you honor us by joining us for lunch?"

Lunch? He had wondered if he had to buy lunch. But, she offered first. Another indication Yasha and her millions were coming to his town.

"I will be very pleased," he said, smiling.

So, I said to myself, this part of the negotiations was finished.

Nguyen wanted to eat at the hotel restaurant. Western food was a treat for him and the buffet luncheon was an elaborate spread. He rarely had the opportunity to eat at the hotel.

Kevin excused himself and went to the travel agency in the hotel to make reservations for the three of us on the late afternoon flight.

Yasha was a charming hostess and outdid herself chatting with Nguyen. She asked about his family and learned he had three children, two girls and a son. Teen aged students. In addition to their normal studies they were learning English. Yasha promised to come to Nha Trang to meet the family. I imagined Nguyen would plan an elaborate reception for her.

"I think he's bought and paid for," Kevin said.

"I agree," I said. "You did very well, Yasha."

"It didn't take very long, did it?"

"Well, the money Kevin passed to him, and his dreams of much more, all helped. And he likes you."

Kevin laughed. "He's worried about Hanoi contacting other cities."

"What do you think he will say to the people in Hanoi?" Yasha asked.

"Hanoi wants to know how Nguyen reacts to you. With his favorable report of this meeting, Hanoi will be satisfied you can get along with the locals," Kevin said. "Of course, Hanoi could have other places in mind."

I was getting tired of trying to out guess Hanoi. Playing games was a way of life for them. They never seem to tire of this routine.

"Whatever. They'll have a favorable assessment from a local party member and that's what we were looking for," I said as I got up from the chair. "What time is our flight?"

"Vietnam Air departs 5:15 and arrives 7:25. I reserved Business Class seats for you two."

"Aren't you going?" she asked, puzzled.

"Oh yes. But, I travel Economy."

"Why?"

"I travel Economy." He smiled and looked away.

She looked at me with a surprised look on her face. I waved her off.

"That gives us about two and half hours to get checked out and to the airport. I guess you'll want to go home first."

"Yes. I'll meet you at the airport. Remember it's the domestic terminal. You can pick up the confirmation in the hotel business center."

"Okay. And thanks, Kevin."

He waved and was gone. Yasha grabbed my arm as I started out of the room.

"Wait a minute. What was that about? He can't fly Business Class?"

"That's his way, Yasha. Don't worry about it."

"I don't understand."

"Don't worry about it. We move along if we're going to make the flight."

She pursed her lips and had a frown on her forehead.

"Yasha. I said to forget it."

"You'll have to explain this to me."

"Not now. Later."

"Everything is later."

"Yeah. I'll tell you when you've had too much to drink."

"I can drink you under the table any day of the week."

"I'm talking about real booze – not soft drinks."

"So was I."

"Yasha, I'm going up to my room and pack. You coming?"

"I've been drunk plenty times."

"Sure you have. Let's go."

I finally pulled Yasha out of the conference room and we went to our rooms and packed.

At the check out desk Yasha paid for the rooms and the plane tickets. She asked the clerk if she could make hotel reservations for us in Hanoi.

The clerk suggested several hotels and Yasha picked the Hilton Hanoi Opera House Hotel. I stayed there once. It was a five star hotel. Plush Vietnamese style, with some French influences, and it overlooked the Opera House. It was named the Hilton Hanoi Opera House Hotel to distance itself from the movie title "Hanoi Hilton," which was a Vietnamese prison, Hao Lo Prison, where American prisoners were held.

"Did you book a room for Kevin?" I asked.

"Of course. He might not want to fly with us but he can stay at the same hotel."

"Cancel his reservation."

"Why?"

"He has his own place to stay."

"Oh. Does he have a place in Hanoi?"

"Yeah. Sort of."

"What does 'sort of' mean?"

"He has a friend there."

"A friend?"

"Yes."

"Is that what I think it means?"

"Yes."

"Oh." She shrugged. "Okay."

After checking out and paying for the airline tickets we went to the taxi queue. The first taxi in line didn't want to drive out to the airport, so we asked the next taxi in the queue. I offered him a hundred thousand *dong* extra, which was about $5.00 US dollars. He asked for a hundred and fifty thousand. I said okay. It was too hot to haggle. He pressed the button and the rear door swung open.

Thankfully the taxi had air conditioning. There was a no smoking sign hanging on the plastic divider, which was paradoxical in a country where everyone smoked. A cold beer would hit the spot. I couldn't remember if the airline served beer. I think they did the last time I flew Vietnam Air. It was Business Class, so there was hope.

Yasha and I went to the Business Class counter and Kevin picked up his boarding pass at the Economy check in counter. We went through the security scanner and rode the escalator up to the departure area, which didn't make much sense because we had to walk back down the stairs to a bus that took us to the plane.

"I still wonder about Kevin flying Economy."

"You worry about too many unimportant things."

"Didn't you wonder about it the first time it happened?"

"Not really. If that's his thing, it's his business."

"You never tell me anything."

"I've told you more than I tell other people because we're friends."

"But not close enough friends to tell me about Kevin and Economy Class."

"Okay. I'll tell you when we get to Hanoi."

"Think I'll forget you said that, don't you?"

"No. I know you won't. Ah, the stewardess. Miss, do you have beer?"

"Yes, we serve beer."

"Do you have Tiger beer?"

"No sir. We have Hue or Halida."

"Okay. I'll have a Halida. Want something Yasha?"

"A cup of tea."

The flight attendant brought me a beer and Yasha a cup of tea. The beer was one of Vietnam's own brew and tasted a bit like Coors. The refreshments stopped her from pestering about Kevin's refusal to fly in Business Class.

It was a pleasant flight and we landed on time. We met up with Kevin, hired a taxi, and rode into the center of the city where the Hanoi Hilton was located. The general landscape from the airport to the city was much as it was from the Saigon airport into central HCMC. But, once inside Hanoi, although the buildings were similar, there was a different feel to the city. There was more of the traditional Vietnam with qualities of the old colonial culture. Some foods and customs had a certain French flavor. Hanoi's French style pastry was the best in Asia.

Hanoi was smaller and had not been as damaged as Ho Chi Minh City was during the war. Much of HCMC had been rebuilt and became the new business center of postwar Vietnam. But Hanoi stayed pretty much as it had always been and remained the hub of political power.

"I talked to my contact and this is the latest. I don't know everyone who will be there by name but I know General Pham will be there. There will be a party member, his name is Lam. He's ambitious. The others will be military aides. And finally, Dinh, my contact. His job is as a liaison between the army and the Deputy Prime Minister's office."

"Who will do the talking? The General?"

"I think the party representative will do the talking. But, the General will have the final say."

"Okay. We'll play it as it comes."

"I'll be here at seven-thirty. The army offices are near by so we won't have far to travel."

"See you then."

"She's wondering about things, isn't she?" He nodded toward Yasha standing at the reception desk.

"She's a very bright woman and has to have answers. She wants to know everything."

"I see. You like her? I mean outside of business."

"Yes, I do. Very much."

"I think she would do you fine."

"Maybe she's more than I can handle."

"From what I saw earlier, she may be more than most can handle."

"I agree."

"Tomorrow?"

"Tomorrow."

35

THE HOTEL EXECUTIVE ROOMS were the size of a small apartment. The Internet site advertised executive room as being over 350 square feet and they were not exaggerating. The room had a giant king sized bed, marbled bathroom, three phones – on the desk, next to the bed and in the bathroom – a well stocked mini-bar, large luxurious bathrobes and slippers, a 40" television, Internet connections, and a view of the French Quarters. Very plush and complete.

Yasha had arranged for adjoining rooms again. There were two doors separating the rooms, one in each room. Of course she had the keys that unlocked the two doors. She was at home with all of this and enjoying herself. She unlocked the door on her side then came to my front door and rang the doorbell. I looked through the peephole and saw her standing outside holding a key. I opened the door.

"There are two doors over there between your room and mine." She pointed to wall between our rooms. "One on my side and one on your side. I opened my side and now I'm opening your side."

She unlocked the door.

"See. You can walk right into my room."

"Rooms look alike. I supposed I have everything in my room that you have in your room."

"Except me."

"Guess I'll have to learn to live with that."

"I just wanted you to know that we can use this door and not have to go out in the hall to go from room to room. Same as in the New World."

"I see. Well, this room is pretty complete. I have everything I need."

"As I said, you have everything except me."

She laughed and stepped across the threshold into my room.

"What are we going to eat tonight? Vietnamese, Chinese? The reception desk clerk said there is an excellent Chinese restaurant close by. Or western food here in the hotel. I think they have Italian food. They also have a buffet."

"I don't care. Whatever you decide is okay by me."

"You haven't eaten much on this trip. You pick at your food. You should eat better."

"Oh, I eat enough. You know they have a first class gym here. I'll have to get up very early if I'm going to use it tomorrow. Wonder if they're open at five-thirty."

"I'll tell them to open at five-thirty."

"This isn't the White Swan in Guangzhou where the manager's brother-in-law works for your company."

"We'll see."

"Whatever. I'm going to shower."

"Me too. In my shower of course." She was grinning. "Can I come back for a drink?"

"You certainly can."

"I'll be back."

"Okay. Oh, can you leave your laptop?"

"Yes. I'll get it."

She went to her room and brought the laptop and placed it on my desk.

"See you in a half an hour. Maybe forty-five minutes."

I got into the shower and stood under the hot water for fifteen minutes. I missed the spa and massage in Huangpo. I noticed the sign on the television inviting guests to the spa and massage in the hotel. Wonder if I had time tonight. We'll see.

I opened a can of Heineken beer and turn the computer on to check on my Email. No message from Ahn, but a dozen or more from others. Chang's note was another invitation to come to Beijing. There was a surprise message from Mulan asking how I was and when I would come back to Harbin. Quick hellos from Gary and Andre. One from Chick, asking about rice and canned mackerel in tomato sauce. He also had pecans for sale. Two messages from the kids. Megan sent a message reminding me to call her.

Things were going well. No disasters pending. There were two good business proposals to think about and there was Yasha, who made this trip even more up beat. Lots of good things were happening, but looming over everything was Harbin. I thought about it all the time and I knew that once I heard from Ahn, everything else would become secondary.

I didn't hear Yasha's knock on the door. She opened the door and stood with her hand on her hip.

"Didn't you hear me knock?"

"I was preoccupied with the computer. Sorry."

She started to say something but stopped.

"Is something wrong?" she asked.

"No."

"Your mind seems to be somewhere else."

"I'm fine."

"Is it the business with the woman in Harbin?"

"Well, it's been on my mind."

"Want to tell me about it?"

"Nothing to tell. She was killed. That's about it."

"Killed?"

"Did I say killed?"

"How was she killed?"

"In an automobile accident."

"In Harbin?"

"It was outside the city. In the countryside."

She came to where I was sitting and stood by me. She put her hand on my shoulder. I reached up and put my hand over hers. Neither of us spoke for several minutes. I stared down at the laptop, and then looked up at her. She smiled, leaned down, and kissed me on the forehead.

"You ready for dinner?"

"You said you wanted a drink."

"I thought I did, but, I can get one at dinner or after."

"Okay." I closed the laptop. She reached for my hand. Holding her hand was nice.

"There's Vietnamese place down the street the reception clerk told me about. Want to try that?"

"Why not? When in Rome."

We went down to the lobby and Yasha stopped at the reception desk and asked to speak to the manager on duty. He came out and listened to her for several minutes. She nodded and shook his hand.

"The hotel gym will be open at five-thirty tomorrow morning. But only for tomorrow. After that you have to wait until six o'clock."

"You're full of surprises."

"More than you know," she said.

"Lot of things I don't know."

"You should make an effort to find out."

"One of these days I just might. Then what will you say?"

"Ask what took you so long."

I laughed and she smiled as she put her arm into mine.

───────────

We walked the two blocks to the restaurant. It was a very nice place and the service was tailored for foreign tourists. We didn't talk about business. Instead we chatted about her family and mine and forgot about problems. After dinner we walked around the block holding hands and ended up in the hotel bar for an after dinner drink.

"Are you feeling better?"

"Yeah. Much better."

"I would like to hear more about Harbin. I want to know."

"Why do you want to know?"

"So I can know you better."

"There are some things not worth knowing."

"You know, there are things about me I don't talk to anyone. I've told you so you'll know who I am." She focused on me with a serious look.

"I will listen if you want to tell me, but it's not necessary."

"I know that. When you and I really become something, we will share secrets."

"That may not happen, Yasha."

"You don't know that. You know how it is with me."

She was very serious. I reached for her hand and smiled.

"What am I going to do with you, Yasha?"

"I've made several suggestions."

"I remember one or two of them."

"Offer is still open."

"No expiration date?"

"Standing offer. Open ended."

"I'll have to remember that."

"I'm here to remind you."

"I knew you would be."

After my second scotch, we went back to her room. I walked to the adjoining door, stopped and looked back at her.

"It's been a very nice evening, Yasha. Thanks for everything."

"I would like you to stay, but for now, I'll be content with a goodnight kiss."

She came up to me and kissed me. She kept her arms around my neck and smiled.

"Real progress. You even helped."

She kissed me again.

"That was even better."

"Good night, Yasha."

"Good night, very best friend."

36

I WOKE AT FIVE and at five-thirty went to the gym. I was truly impressed that Yasha convinced the hotel manager to have the gym open at five-thirty. After an hour on the treadmill I went back to my room, showered, shaved with a razor I bought at the hotel, called house keeping about my laundry, and got dressed. My morning routine.

I wore the new gray shirt without a tie. At seven I went down to the coffee shop for breakfast.

A few minutes after I sat down, Yasha came into the café.

"Thought I would have an early breakfast."

She took a seat next to me.

"What are you gonna do today?" I asked.

"Well, later I thought I would go to the gym and work out. Then go shopping."

"If my meeting ends early I'll call you. You have your Vietnam cell phone?"

"Yes. Oh. Here's Kevin. Good morning, Kevin."

"Good morning."

"Have you had breakfast?" she asked.

"Yes, thank you." He looked at me. "We have to get going."

"I'll see you later."

"Take care."

She touched my hand and smiled at me. Kevin took it all in and looked away. He was smiling.

The army headquarters was an impressive building that stood apart from the other buildings in the quad. As we entered the building a guard standing just inside the door directed us to the reception desk. I told the clerk who we were and he found our names on a list of visitors expected that morning. He pointed toward folding chairs placed along the wall and asked us to take a seat. It was a few minutes before eight.

A number of visitors came up to the desk. Some were sent off in various directions and others sat with us and waited. At eight-thirty-five, an army officer came to the desk and called my name. Three stars with a stripe were on his sleeve, a Senior Lieutenant. He was probably thirty years old. He was dressed in a well tailored uniform. He did not have a military hair cut, but his very black hair was correctly trimmed. His face had a ruddy complexion, evidence of time spent in the field. His demeanor was polite with a distinct military touch. I rose, shook his hand, and introduced Kevin. He asked us to come with him.

We followed him up the stairs to the second floor. He stopped at a door mid-way down the hall and rapped on the door. Someone in uniform opened the door, stepped aside, and waved us in.

The wall facing the door had eight large windows panes about six feet wide and five feet high. The window wall was on the east side, so the morning sun lit up the room. Metal folding shutters were folded against the walls. These would be closed in case of an attack on the building. Venetian blinds were used to defuse the morning sunlight. A high cabinet counter ran the length of the room under the window.

In the center of the room, two rows of two six foot tables were placed end to end. The tables were three feet wide. At each end another six foot table was placed perpendicular to the two rows. It created a ninety square foot space. Ideal for a war room where maps and miniature combat scenes could be spread out for planning. Seven armed chairs on rollers were on each side of the giant table.

There were five people in the room. Stars and stripes on their uniforms indicated what rank they held. In addition to the Senior Lieutenant there was a Major, one star with two stripes. The third officer was a Colonel, four stars and two stripes. The highest rank in the room was the Major General, who had one gold star on his shoulder. The fifth person was a civilian. Obviously, the party representative.

Kevin and I looked for Dinh. He was not present. So we were

without a friend in court. The situation was totally different from what we expected. Not a good sign.

Three generations were represented by the officer ranks. The Major was older than the Senior Lieutenant and the Colonel was not much more than a year to two older than the Major. The Colonel and Major were old enough to have served during the war. They were probably in their early teens then, which was normal because most of the Viet Cong fighters were very young. The General was from the generation who was part of the revolution before open rebellion broke out against the French. They all looked as though they could handle themselves in combat.

The group of five was on the side of the table facing the wall. They did not sit and remained standing. The civilian was to the General's right and the officers were to the left, lined according to rank.

The civilian pulled his chair out and stood with his hands on the table.

"We welcome you to Vietnam. My name is Lam." No other name was given.

Thanh Lam joined the Party as a youth organizer. He earned his BA at Can Tho University with a major in Information and Communications Technology. When he graduated he was fluent in English.

He spent most of his early professional career designing propaganda pamphlets and educational brochures. Contrary to his hopes, his job was not the stepping stone to greater things. After five years, he felt his career was at a dead end.

Lam's life became further complicated when he married Cao Mai. Mai was the second daughter of a college instructor at Vietnam National University. Mai's parents often compared her to her sister, who had married a rising star in the Ministry of Finance. Lam was constantly reminded of his menial job and having to get by on his meager civil service salary. His future seemed hopeless.

Things changed dramatically one night when he accidentally found himself in the right place at the right time.

It was over an hour after the usual quitting time and Lam was trying to finish a project with an early morning deadline. His wife would be upset, again. Absorbed in his thoughts, he almost didn't hear his name being whispered as he passed the small supply room. He stopped and cautiously went to the slightly opened door. Standing behind the door was the supervisor of his division, waving frantically at him.

Lam peered into the darken room and saw the woman on the floor. He drew back but the supervisor grabbed his coat and pulled him into the room.

"What do you want?" He was frightened.

"Be quiet. I have a problem here and I need your help."

"My help?"

"I'm your supervisor and I'm ordering you to help me."

"Who is that?" Lam pointed at the body on the floor. "Does she work here?"

"It doesn't matter who she is. I need help to get her out of here."

"Is she dead?"

"No. She had some drugs and took several pills. She just passed out. I have to get her out of the building. Is anyone still here in the building?"

"I don't know. I was working late. I might be the only one here."

"Good. Help me carry her to the elevator and down to the street."

"Who is she?"

"Just someone who provides a service."

"A service?"

"Don't be stupid. She's a whore."

Lam finally understood the fix his supervisor was in. He was fucking this whore and now she might be dead. He looks desperate and he's in deep trouble. If I help him, what can he do for me?

"Are you going to help me?"

"I can't risk getting into trouble."

"You won't get into trouble. Listen to me Lam. Help me with this and I promise I'll take care of you."

He's panicking. He needs me. Can he really do something for me? He's never liked me, but now he needs me. What can he do for me?

"Come on, Lam. Grab her feet and help me get her to the elevator."

They half carried and half dragged her from the supply room to the elevator. They pulled her into the elevator and pushed the down button. In two minutes they were on the ground floor. The door opened and the supervisor cautiously stepped out and looked around the lobby. A security guard was at the reception counter.

"I'll get the security guard to come upstairs with me. You take the woman out of the building."

"What will I do with her?"

"Find some place to put her."

"Where?"

"Find a place."

"You're asking me to risk my life."

"Do this for me and I will take care of you."

How will he take care of me?

"Okay."

Lam nodded and the supervisor tidied himself up and went out to the lobby. The security guard knew who he was and there wasn't any problem getting him to accompany him upstairs. Lam put his hands under her arms and started to drag her out to the lobby. Suddenly the woman let out a grunt and tried to sit up. Her sudden movement startled him and he dropped her.

"Where am I?"

"You're in an office building and you have to leave immediately."

She was just barely aware of what was happening and allowed herself to be pushed toward the lobby. After a few steps she fell. Lam grabbed her under her arms and dragged her to the front door. He had to turn the lock before he could open the door. She fell again. Finally, he opened the door and dragged her out to the street. He propped her against the wall and looked up and down the street. No one was about. He could leave her there, but she could try to reenter the building. He called a taxi on his cell phone.

After an agonizing ten minutes a taxi appeared. She was more alert now and could stand without help. He led her to the taxi and told the driver to take her to central Hanoi. He helped her into the taxi and gave the driver four hundred thousand dong. He watched the taxi drive away and smiled as he thought about his supervisor. Tomorrow he would collect his reward.

Within a week Lam was assigned to special projects in the Ministry of Defense. One of his first major assignments was to translate a proposal to remodel an ammunition plant in Vietnam. His job was to assess the proposal and make recommendations to the army. He was to provide assistance when a meeting was arranged with the company proposing the project. The person in charge was an army General named Pham.

Lam wore the common white dress shirt and black trousers. But his sleeves were not rolled up and unlike most, he buttoned the top button of the shirt, closing the shirt collar around his neck. He had a slight built, average height and weight. Full head of unruly black hair with strands of white. A Seiko digital watch was on his right wrist. A wedding ring on his left hand ring finger. He was about thirty-five years old.

Before he began speaking he took a pair of steel rimed glasses from his shirt pocket and put them on. Lam was the official translator for the group. The General understood English and probably could speak a broken version.

Lam turned toward the General, bowing his head slightly.

"May I introduce Major General Pham, the chairman of this group?"

General Pham nodded. The others were not introduced. The General was not tall, about five feet five or six inches, rotund and heavy set. He seemed to be in good health. He took off his hat after being introduced, showing a receding hairline, and thinning gray hair, cut short. His hands were stubby and his fingers gnarled. Eyes were alert and fixed on me. Spread across his chest were a number of medals, including the metal showing he had been wounded, the Armed Forces Honor medal, the Liberation War Order, the Victory Declaration, and Civil Action medal.

No one offered to shake hands.

"Please be seated." Lam waved at the chairs across from him. The officers waited until the General sat and then took their seats.

The Senior Lieutenant moved his chair so it was directly behind the General. He was his personal interpreter and the one the General depended on for an honest translation.

Kevin and I remained standing across from the group. I bowed slightly.

"Thank you, Mr. Lam."

I leaned across the table and handed my name card to the General, holding it with both hands. The General placed the card in front of him.

After looking down at it, he picked it up and turned it over. One side was printed in Vietnamese and the other side was in English. He kept the Vietnamese side up.

I handed a card to Lam. He looked at both sides of the card and held it for a moment. He rubbed the surface. The printing was raised. It was an expensive card. Lam made a mental note of that.

"May I present Le Bui Lan, my close Vietnamese associate of many years."

Kevin nodded and Lam and the General nodded in return.

"I am grateful for this opportunity to come to Vietnam and to meet with your group and most grateful that someone as important as the General has taken the time to be here."

I nodded toward the General and sat down in the chair directly across from him. Kevin took the chair to my right.

Three bottles of water and two ash trays were on the table in front of us. There were five bottles and four ash trays on the other side of the table. The General opened a bottle and took a swallow.

Lam offered me a cigarette.

"Have you tried our Vietnamese cigarettes?"

"Thank you, but I do not smoke."

He lit one for himself. The General had already lit a cigarette. Lam waved at Kevin.

"Please, smoke if you wish."

Kevin took out a pack of American cigarettes and offered the pack to the others sitting across from him. After a nod from the General, the Colonel took the pack and extracted a cigarette. He then passed it on to the Major, who took a one and handed the pack to the Senior Lieutenant. They all lit up. The room was soon filled with smoke.

Lam opened his yellow note pad and laid a ball point pen next to it. A copy of my proposal was under the pad.

"We have considered your proposal to remodel an ammunition plant here in Vietnam," Lam said and smiled. "It is an interesting proposal."

In truth, remodel was a misleading verb. The small plant on the outskirts of Hanoi was hardly worth saving. A new plant would have to be built from the ground up and all new equipment installed.

"I think it has great potential for Vietnam," I said.

"Is Squires Corporation totally owned by Filipinos? Or are there other owners, from America or Europe?" Lam asked.

"It is totally owned by the Tuson family, a Filipino family, and has been for two generations. The company was started as a general merchandising business and after World War II was converted to arms manufacturing."

"I see. What is your position in the company? Your name card indicates you are involved with project development."

"I work with the Vice President of the company in marketing and project development. This proposal is part of that function."

"Why did you decide to present this proposal to us?"

"Vietnam is a developing country and you have a fine military organization, but foreigners have supplied much of your military needs during and since the last war. We seek to assist you in rebuilding your own arms industry."

"Why have you chosen ammunition production and not weapons?"

"Ammunition, especially 9 mm ammunition, is in great demand throughout the world. Ammunition is relatively inexpensive to manufacture in large quantities, compared to design and production of weapons. Once the refurbished plant is operational, you will have a standard product to sell on the international market."

"Does Squires manufacture ammunition?"

"Yes. It's one of the world's leading producers."

"Has the company established similar joint ventures in other countries?"

"No, this will be the first. The company has been asked to consider joint ventures but have not accepted those offers."

"Why not?"

"The timing wasn't right for the company and the offers were not from an Asian country."

"Can you explain how the joint venture responsibilities are to be shared?"

The proposal detailed how everyone would participate. He knew this but wanted me to give a verbal account. Was this to see if I was willing to compromise?

"As the proposal states, we propose that Vietnam provide all the licenses and permits required, the existing physical plant, labor, utilities for operation, and assistance in all legal matters. Squires will provide all the capital, technology, materials, and state of the art production equipment. Also, we will handle all marketing on a world wide basis."

"Do you consider this a fifty percent shared financial commitment by both joint venture partners?"

"Well, it's difficult to say what the actual value of labor and licenses is in terms of dollars. It is also difficult to put an exact dollar value on skills and technology. It's really a merger of needs and capabilities."

Lam opened the proposal. He turned to a page he had ear marked.

"There have been some questions raised about the division of proceeds. You propose Vietnam receive fifteen percent of the production for domestic use and the proceeds from the remaining eight-five percent be a twenty-five and seventy-five percent division. Squires retaining seventy-five percent. We do not think this is a fair distribution of returns."

"Well, if you include the fifteen percent for domestic use, Vietnam will receive a total of thirty-six percent of the production. Moreover, Squires will assist in world marketing for Vietnam."

In truth, all the international marketing would be handled by Squires. Vietnam would receive the proceeds from twenty-one percent of the goods sold without contributing a cent or any marketing personnel. Additionally, they would receive fifteen percent of all production for domestic use, free of charge. I assumed that some of that fifteen percent would be secretly sold by them to foreign buyers.

"But, it's not truly forty percent, since the twenty-five percent is taken from the eighty-five percent, not from a hundred percent."

"True. The percentages are not based on a hundred percent. However, the entire capital required is over twenty million US dollars, all of which will be provided by Squires. The first four to five months of operations will not produce a net profit. Hence, the financial risk is far greater for Squires than for Vietnam. Actually, Vietnam does not have any capital outlay obligations."

The Senior Lieutenant gave a running translation for the General of my comments. Every now and then, the General asked the Senior Lieutenant for clarification of a word or phrase.

No one commented on my explanations.

Soon everyone, except the General, paged through the proposal and asked questions about sections they had earmarked. They asked for clarification on certain provisions, explanation of technical terms, world marketing strategy, and world prices. After several hours of questions and answers and what seemed like a bon fire of hundreds of cigarettes, Lam held up his hand.

"I suggest we take a lunch break. The General invites you to join us in the general mess hall and share our modest fare."

"Thank you. We will be pleased to join you."

We all adjourned to the large hall where everyone in the building ate. A separate table was set aside at one side of the hall for our group. The food was plain – the typical soldier's meal of rice, some vegetables, and fried fish. A treat for visitors was a soft drink, in addition to hot tea.

No business matters were discussed during the meal. We talked about the weather and the flight from HCMC last night.

After lunch, Kevin and I were invited to relax in the inner courtyard. We agreed to meet in a half an hour. The group stood and remained standing until Kevin and I left the room.

"They spent a lot of time just talking," Kevin said.

"Yes. I think they're getting ready to ask for up front cash."

"I agree."

"How do you think that subject will be approached?"

"Not all of the people in there may be included in any side benefits."

"You think the General has a plan?"

"He hasn't said anything – hard to tell what he's about."

"Could be he wants to have something more than medals to retire on."

"It's too bad Dinh isn't here. He would know how things are going."

"Is Lam a bigger cheese than Dinh?"

"No, but I think the General didn't want anyone other than his people here. Especially not someone from the Deputy Prime Minister's office."

"There's a reason for that and I have a feeling we'll find out soon. Well, Kevin, we may be pounding sand. The proposal is pretty clear cut and they're nit picking about nothing. This morning was a waste of time."

"Maybe they're ready to say what they really want."

"If not, I'm going to walk."

The Senior Lieutenant came out to the courtyard and announced the group was ready to resume talks. We came back into the conference room and took our seats. Everyone who smoked, which meant everyone but me, lit up again. I felt my lungs filling up with smoke.

Lam began by summarizing key points from our prior discussions, which was really a rehash of the written proposal. He then asked if I had any questions or something to add. Maybe it was the smoke or maybe I was just tired, but I thought it was time to get matters settled.

"I appreciate the General's time and all of your considerations. I believe our proposal is fair and will provide a very good product source and income for the Vietnamese army. This income will continue to grow and by the end of the first year could amount to over a half a million US dollars a month. An eighteen hour production schedule will multiply the income three fold. I also believe the proposal's plan on how to divide the proceeds is fair and equitable.

"However, I propose that the joint venture responsibilities remain as written, but that the proceeds are divided on a sixty-forty percent basis. Sixty percent for Squires and forty percent for Vietnam. The forty percent will include the fifteen percent originally set aside for domestic use. This is an increase of five percent over the original proposal.

"Please bear in mind, Vietnam does not have any financial obligations and Squires will provide all technical expertise as well as all world marketing. Additionally, the army will have a newly built plant."

I made the proposed compromise in a tone that indicated it was my best/last offer. It was a prime deal for the Vietnamese. No one else would offer as much and the sale of ammunition was reaching record numbers in the world market. Our offer was an excellent opportunity to created millions for the Vietnamese army.

Everyone looked to the General. He lit another cigarette and stared stoically at the wall. Then he turned and stared at me. Finally, he waved his hand at the officers. The three officers rose and left the room.

The General turned his piercing eyes toward me and motioned to Lam. Lam leaned over and the General whispered in his ear. Lam sat up and looked at me with a smug look on his face.

"The General asks what you offer as incentive."

So, we reached the heart of the matter.

The General was sitting hunched over, smoking his cigarette. He was out of his element. A proud soldier who was reduced to asking for a bribe. His heart wasn't in it. He was not destitute and his pension would give him and his wife a home and a monthly stipend for the rest of their lives. Properly structured, this project could provide a very ample addition to his retirement. Was this not enough?

But, he had other personal problems that had nothing to do with money. He had not been promoted beyond the rank of Major General because he was not political enough. Others from his generation were two and three star generals. Some still had major combat commands.

No one fought harder than he had. He led thousands into battle, many to their deaths. Even Ho Chi Minh, the leader himself, said he was a true patriot.

He didn't want the materials things, such as money or a villa, as some had. He only wanted to be recognized and allowed to continue his work as a patriot. They had not permitted him to retain combat status after the fighting stopped. He no longer commanded combat troops, as a true solder should. They didn't know what to do with him. He was reduced to attending to what seemed to be meaningless chores. He thought this meeting was one of those chores.

He spent the morning thinking to himself about his predicament. He did not listen to the discussion about the proposal; he only heard his own thoughts.

"Why must I talk to this person about Vietnam's military needs? Who

is this foreigner who wants to use the Vietnamese army to make money? He is a Korean from America who speaks for a Philippine business. All foreigners. He talks about percentages. Money is what matters to him. After a lifetime of fighting for my country I am reduced to asking for money from a foreigner. Better to die a soldier's death.

"Now I must rely on a civilian. A party official, who has not served a day in the military and yet, here he is, speaking for the army. My army."

The General didn't know who to blame or to hold accountable for this state of affairs. No one believed in the true cause any longer.

Lam had convinced him there was another cause to fight for.

"We have to make them pay. You must take care of yourself because the army is no longer the army you knew. Things have changed and it's every man for himself. Look about you. Others are reaping the harvest of victory and they have given you nothing of real value.

"The time of fighting is over. Now the new Vietnam patriot is a businessman. The new hero is a man who creates fortunes by using the foreigner and his wealth. The foreigners are no longer national enemies, but tools to be used for the benefit of Vietnam. That is the new patriotism. It is the way of the new Vietnam."

Lam repeated these new truths over and over again.

The General didn't understand all of this, but it seemed to be a reasonable explanation of what was happening to him in postwar Vietnam.

"Let me help you become a hero again. A new patriotic hero. I will help you," Lam had convinced him to take another path.

"Incentive?" I drew back, feigning surprise.

Lam quickly interjected, "There are many needs to be taken care of. It will cost a great deal to set this project in motion."

"What are these needs?"

"There are many needs," the General spoke in a soft quiet voice, as if he were talking to himself. It was an answer he had learned to say as rationale for his actions.

"What is the cost of these needs?" I asked.

"Five hundred thousand US dollars," Lam said quickly.

He did not consult with the General. They had already agreed on the amount of the bribe. He had been waiting to spit out the sum since the meeting began. He had to say it aloud before it felt real.

A half million dollars. I looked at the General. He turned away and stared down at his cigarette.

Well, they weren't starting out as petty crooks.

"What the General wants to say is that certain changes in organization must be made and the plant in question must be put under different management. There is much to prepare," Lam said.

"To whom is this payment to be made?"

"An account will be created to receive these funds."

"In what bank is this account located and who will administer it?"

"You will be notified."

Obviously not an army account. It would be a separate private account. What the hell did this guy think he was doing? Lam was an amateur. Bribes were asked for and given every day, but most were sophisticated and the clever ones used creative ways that required organization and planning. Those programs provided a continuous source of income for those who were knowledgeable about such matters. This was a direct cash bribe and Lam made no effort to hide it. It was obviously his first shot at big money. He had a lot to learn about the refined forms of corruption.

I felt pity for the General. He played it straight all of his life and never learned how to be a clever crook. He was pathetic.

"This is an unexpected development," I said. "I will have to confer with the company before any action can be taken."

I looked at the General. He continued to stare down at his cigarette. Whatever his image was during the war, he had become a broken down soldier with his hand out begging for money. He was at the end of the road.

"I will notify you of the company's decision within a week."

Lam was surprised that I didn't negotiate the bribe. I'm sure he thought he could get at least a quarter of a million with some haggling. Still, I didn't say no outright. He might have thought there was a chance. Sure, when pigs fly.

I closed my notebook and rose.

"Thank you, General." I extended my hand.

He stood awkwardly and shook my hand but avoided direct eye contact. I turned and looked at Lam for a moment. He had an uncertain look.

"And thank you, Mr. Lam," I said and held out my hand.

He stood and gave me a handshake. He looked at me with a feeble smile. I didn't say anything more and kept an expressionless face. I nodded at Kevin. They looked away as we left the room.

When I chose not to negotiate, the General and Lam knew I wasn't going to consider any kind of "incentive" payment. They may learn how to do these things after a few more failures, but by then the General would be either dead or put permanently out to pasture. No way to know what would happen to Lam. Something bad, I hoped.

"I wonder exactly how much the army brass knows about this. Someone in power felt the project was worthwhile enough to have the General meet with me. You know, the General could've ended up a hero by bringing home a very profitable business. Even Lam would've looked good. "

"This was very stupid. It would be simple to create a process that would pay a good percentage every month to everyone." Kevin shook his head and made a face. "They could have asked for fifty thousand. Would have been more reasonable."

"Even if I agreed to pay up front money there is no way it could be kept a secret. Even a smaller amount. If the army brass is not included in this bribe, they will find out. Then I would be accused of giving a bribe and the project would be shut down. It's a loser.

"The General doesn't know what he asked for or why. Does he even know what a half a million dollars is? What the hell would he do with that money? He wouldn't know how to spend it. You might talk to your contact and ask what happened. It's plain to see why the General didn't want him at the meeting. But, for now, as far as I'm concerned, this deal is dead. A long trip for nothing. And used up a lot of your time. Sorry about that."

"You lost more than I did."

"Contact Dinh and explain what happened. Find out if the Deputy Prime Minister's office agrees with what went down. If not, see if Dinh can arrange another meeting with the army or whoever. Someone who understands business and who knows how to create a long term source of income. I'll come back with the same proposal if they're interested."

"Could take time. If the higher ups didn't know about this bribe, they might want to punish the General and take care of Lam. To do this without too much publicity will require some behind the scene deals. Could be the end of the two of them."

"Well, so be it. But, if it can be worked out, I'll come back."

"I'll let you know how it goes down."

"Good. And thanks."

I was very tired. The proposal was a very good one with no great risk for either side and extremely profitable for all concerned. I was irritated and pissed off. The deal was doomed because of two very stupid people.

"We'll see you about seven-thirty in the morning. Unless you want to have dinner tonight."

"Would like to, but have this lady to deal with. She is complaining about the early hours," he smiled.

"Tell her that's how it is with big time dealers."

"She still complains."

"Buy her something."

"I already have."

"Buy her something that's more expensive."

"That will spoil her."

"You'll have to find another friend."

"Have another one in mind," he was smiling.

"I'm glad I don't have those problems."

"You have a different kind of problem. Or is she's the one who has the problem?"

"If so, she'll have to solve it."

"I think she will."

"Oh?"

"She's a very smart lady."

"Yes, she is."

"She's very smart and much prettier than most. You should think about it."

"No time for that."

"Forgive me for saying, but you should take time," he said. "I can tell, you have other things on your mind. Not business. Too much of that is not healthy."

"You a doctor now?"

"Since you've been here you have been preoccupied. You have big problems?"

"I always have problems."

"Something has happened?"

I guess my emotional state was showing. Was I so transparent? But Kevin was a good friend and I felt comfortable sharing my problem with him.

"A lady very close to me was killed several weeks ago."

"In the states?"

"No. In Harbin."

"Was she family?"

"No. But, very close to me. She had a five year old son. No husband."

"How was she killed?"

"Her car was forced into a concrete wall."

"Forced? So, somebody killed her."

"Yes."

"You know why?"

"Someone wanted to get at me by killing her."

"You know who did it?"

"Looking now."

"Police involved?"

"They're looking also, but I don't think they'll find him."

"When you find this person, then what?"

"I'll have to take care of business."

"It's that way?"

"Yes, it is."

"I see. Need help? I can go to Harbin."

"No. But thanks for the offer."

37

I WAS FEELING DOWN when I got back to the hotel, so I decided to revive my spirits with a massage. The hotel massage service was available until midnight and was on the same floor as the gym. It cost thirty-five US dollars for the customary fifty-minute hour. Unfortunately, a sauna was not available. I thought the young Vietnamese girl was almost as good as Wanda in Huangpo. I gave her a good tip and went back to my room for a long hot shower.

After my revival ritual I went to Yasha's room to get her laptop. I tapped on her door. She opened the door and grinned at me.

"So, you've decided to give up and come to my room."

I went in and glanced around the room and looked out the window down at the French Quarter below. Checked the mini-bar and took a peek into the bathroom. She smiled as I went through my room inspection.

"I think I like my room better."

"Okay. We can make do in your room." She was laughing.

"Make do?"

"Why don't you let me show you?"

I had to laugh and she laughed with me.

"What I really need is your laptop. Is it handy?"

"Sure. Wait, I'll get it."

She brought out the laptop and a large bag.

"What's that?"

"Just some things I bought. Want to see them?"

"Sure. What are they? More clothes?"

"No. Just some stuff for my parents, sister, and friends at the office."

"You remembered your family. That's good. I'm proud of you."

"I knew you'd say that."

She showed me a set of pearl earrings for her mother, a bracelet for her sister, and a hand carved pipe for her father. There were hand sewn purses and silk scarves for people in her office.

She hesitated and then said, "I got something for you."

She handed me a small box and stood back with her arms straight at her sides. She appeared awkward and embarrassed, which was out of character for Yasha, who was always pretty sure of herself.

I turned the box over, examining all sides of it. It was wrapped in gold paper. This was not just a souvenir to be discarded after a few days. It was an important gift. She seemed unsure how I would receive it.

I opened the small box. Buried in soft tissue paper was a round jade medallion with a small diamond stone in the middle. It was attached to a gold necklace. I took it out and examined the medallion in the light. It was a beautiful piece. I had not worn any jewelry since I took off my wedding ring some years ago.

"It's beautiful, Yasha. I don't know what to say."

"Let me help put it on." She put it around my neck and snapped the lock. "It looks just right. Come look in the mirror." She pulled me out of the chair and stood me in front of the mirror."

It was a beautiful gift. I looked in the mirror and rubbed the medallion between my thumb and forefinger. It reminded me of the jade medallion I had given to BJ. That medallion and the jade ring were buried with her in a grave in Harbin. Yasha's present brought back a sudden rush of memories. Instead of joy, my face reflected sorrow.

She stepped back, embarrassed.

"You don't have to wear it."

I turned and grabbed her, pulled her to me, and held her. She was confused. I had never embraced her in this way.

"Thank you, Yasha. I'll wear it because it's my reminder of someone who has become very dear to me."

She hugged me tighter and I thought I heard her sniffle. I started to pull back. She tighten her hug and held on to me.

"I don't want you to see me crying."

We stood locked in a tight embrace for several minutes. She finally released me and went in search of a tissue. She blotted her eyes and blew her nose. Things were back to normal, I hoped.

"We're getting to be more than just best friends, aren't we?" she asked.

"I don't know what more we can be."

"I've made suggestions about that."

"Ah, Yasha," I let out a sigh.

"Seriously, you're important to me."

"And you are to me. I'm sorry I don't have a gift for you"

"That's all right. You will."

"I will? How do you know that?"

"I know."

"Okay." I rubbed the medallion and smiled. "Now, I have to get ready for dinner."

"In an hour. Okay?"

I took the laptop and went to the door. I turned and smiled.

"This is a very special gift, Yasha. Thank you."

"It tells you how I feel."

"I know. I'm sorry I have nothing for you."

"You will soon."

"May not be as precious as this."

"It will be. I know it will be."

"How do you know all these things?"

"It's my *karma* to know."

I opened the laptop and checked my Email. Nothing from Ahn. A note from Andre asking about the ammunition proposal. I'll tell him about the deal's demise later. Bad news can wait.

Gary and Carolyn replied to my note and asked for date, time, and place. I'll have to find a way to get back for those lunch dates.

Chick was asking again about rice. I'll have to remember to mention this to Kevin. Sonny from Georgia asked if anyone in China wanted to buy refined peanut oil. Finding a buyer would take time and I didn't have the energy for this. A new inquiry about copper ore sounded more promising. My contact in the UK had copper ore. I'll have to contact him. I wasn't pushing these items. Why not? Wasn't this my business?

I really wanted to see a note from Ahn. It's been almost a month since she was killed. I was not as morose as I was the first week, but my anger was still intact. I thought I should be in Harbin helping Ahn. Instead I was here in Vietnam and the ammunition project just went into the tank.

My salvation was Yasha. I rubbed the medallion and thought about her. Things were changing with her and I certainly wasn't fighting it. Was this different from Megan? Yeah, it was different. In many ways, it was different.

Yasha and I had dinner at the Chez Manon restaurant in the hotel. I had a special shrimp casserole dish with a delicious sauce. She had the mahi mahi. The seafood was fresh and the service was excellent.

We talked about the meeting tomorrow and made guesses of what to expect. Unfortunately, meetings of this kind were always a mystery. One never knew if they were serious or simply going through the motions. Some turned into real fiascos, as my munitions project.

After dinner we adjourned to the bar and had Napoleon cognac. It was quiet and the serious drinkers and tourists had not yet come in. We left before the night crowd took over.

She made tea for us in her room. I sat on the sofa, feeling weary. It had not been a good day.

"You haven't said, but I can tell things didn't go well with your meeting."

"Things blew up."

"Is there a way to make it work?"

"I don't think so."

"Why?"

"The people only wanted to milk some money from me."

"How much?"

"They wanted five hundred thousand US dollars up front."

"Five hundred thousand? Wow! I wouldn't have expected that."

"A different kind of bribe I can understand. Something more sophisticated. But, they wanted a quick and dirty deal. The General was somehow convinced this was the way to go."

"Who convinced him?"

"A party hack who had dreams of making a fortune."

"So the General is corrupt."

"Yes and no. Maybe he doesn't think of this as a bribe, but payment rightfully due him. He spent his entire life fighting for the revolution, so he believes someone owes him. But, I don't owe him a damn thing."

"You're disappointed in him, aren't you?"

"Yes. I also feel sorry for him. The glory days are over and he has nothing to do. No one to fight. His world is gone."

"I'm sorry it didn't work out."

"You're going to find out that most of these deals don't work out. You have a better chance with your resort proposal. The people who you'll meet are different. They'll be people who understand about business."

"I hope so."

"I think they'll be more sophisticated."

"Are you going to stay?"

"Of course. Why do you ask?"

"Well, your proposal didn't work out – and you seem to have other things on your mind."

"I always have other things on my mind. Do you think you might have a better chance with your proposal without me? I'll understand if you do."

"Never. I just know when the time comes – you'll leave."

"Well, I don't plan to leave right now."

"Your leaving will be tied to what happened in Harbin, won't it? You changed after that trip. You've been preoccupied with that."

"It's a very personal thing. I told you that."

"I know. Is there something I can do?"

"Thanks, but there's nothing anyone can do."

"People who care want to help," she said.

"I appreciate that."

"I guess she was really very special."

"She was."

"Will you tell me about her?"

"Not now."

"That's okay. One day you will."

"Let's not talk about this, Yasha. It does no good."

"I guess you think I'm prying, but I want to know about you. I've told you this before. Before this Harbin thing happened."

"This is not for you, Yasha."

"I can handle it."

"I'm sure you can, but for now, let's let it go."

"Okay. You can tell me about it later."

She sat next to me and held my hand. After a while she gave me a kiss on the cheek and got up.

"Well, I'm going to get myself ready for tomorrow."

"Good. Breakfast at a quarter to seven."

"We have time for breakfast?"

"Yes. I think the offices are only fifteen minutes from here. Kevin will be here at seven-thirty."

"I'll be up before that."

I went to the door and turned toward her.

"Thanks again for the medallion. It's a very precious gift."

She came to me and kissed me. I looked into her eyes and kissed her.

"It's going to happen," she whispered.

"Yasha. I ..."

"It's okay. Not right now, but soon."

She gave me a peck on the cheek and smiled.

"Breakfast at seven?"

"Yes."

38

A T SEVEN O'CLOCK WE met in the restaurant and Yasha had her usual breakfast, which was twice what I ate. Kevin came in for a quick cup of coffee.

"I hope we won't have to wait as we did at army headquarters."

"I don't think so," Kevin said. "These people are more business like. It should be much better."

"Let's go," Yasha said as she closed her briefcase. She was getting impatient.

We rode a taxi to one of the office buildings that housed the many bureaus and departments of the Prime Minister's office. Thankfully, Kevin knew in which building we were having the meeting. We checked in at the reception desk and were asked to wait. In a few minutes a young woman came out and asked us to follow her.

Unlike other government buildings, this one had an elevator that we took to the third floor. Our guide directed us to a large conference room. In the center of the room were two tables, placed end to end. Each was about six feet long and four feet wide. A dozen or more chairs were set around the tables.

"Some one would be coming soon. Please make yourselves comfortable," she said and closed the door.

We didn't sit because we didn't know which side of the room we were assigned. We walked around the tables and looked out the window. There were ashtrays on the tables and a bottle of water was placed before each chair.

About five minutes later there was a knock on the door. The door opened and a group of seven people came in, led by a woman who was obviously the leader.

———————————

"Good morning. I am Ngo Thanh Linh."
Yasha stepped forward and shook her hand.
"Good morning, Ms. Ngo. My name is Yasha Hsiao and these are my associates."
She introduced Kevin and me.

Ms. Ngo gave us a warm handshake, then pointed toward the others and introduced each of them by name. They nodded and stood at attention as their names were spoken.

Ms. Ngo was probably in her mid forties. She looked plain because she didn't wear make up. But this didn't detract from her bright and alert eyes. Her facial features were sharp and clear. There was a sprinkle of freckles below her eyes, giving her a youthful look. Her hair had a few strands of gray and pulled back and tied in a ball. She was a striking woman who had maintained much of the fragile beauty of her youth. Unlike other women officials, who wore pants, she wore a traditional Vietnamese jacket over a skirt that came to her ankles. Was she a good party member? One thing for certain, not all party members looked this good.

Yasha presented her name card to all seven people. I followed and gave them my name card. My card was used only in Vietnam and had a Vietnamese cell phone number. Ms. Ngo handed her name card to Yasha and me, but not to Kevin. The others didn't offer name cards.

"Please, be seated." Ms. Ngo directed us to the chairs facing the window. Fortunately, venetian blinds defused the sunlight. The seven of them sat facing the wall.

"Ms. Ngo, I have a request." Yasha asked.
"What is it?"
"I have some drawings and photos I would like to share with you. I was wondering if an overhead projector and a side projector are available."

Ms. Ngo looked at her group. One young man put up his hand and said he thought he knew where he could find them. She nodded an okay and he left on his errand.

"I'm sure we can find something," Ms. Ngo said.

"Thank you."

The group members each had a copy of Yasha's proposal. Ms. Ngo opened a folder and looked at us, smiling. Very nice smile. I wondered if she was married. No ring on the left ring finger, but one was on her right hand middle finger. Her fingers were well manicured, no nail polish. Her only jewelry was a small digital watch and a thin jade bracelet on her right wrist.

"I welcome you to Vietnam. Thank you for your proposal, Ms. Hsiao. Our government has asked us to explore the possibilities of implementing the plan. As a start, could you give us some information about your company?"

"I'll be happy to. The Hamburg branch of our company is taking the lead in the proposal and worked with me in designing the project. We are strongly supported by the parent company, the Li Wah Trust and Holding Company, headquartered in Shanghai. We also have branches in Tokyo, New York, San Francisco, Hamburg, London, and Dubai. The Chairman of the Board, T.S. Tsai, is a well-known financier.

"Li Wah is a diversified organization and we are involved in several business fields – including finance and banking. We own and operate fourteen plants that produce electronics and many other products, including parts used in the automobile and computer industries. We have three computer research and development firms, and five other light industrial manufacturing facilities. Our company has joint ventures in Japan, the US, and Germany. I believe a brochure was included with the proposal. Did you receive these?"

"Yes. Your name card states you are the Vice President and Director of Development and New Projects. Are you the one responsible for this proposal?"

"Yes, I am." Yasha said with authority.

She pointed at me. "I notice your name is listed as an advisor in the proposal."

I looked at Yasha and asked, "May I interrupt?" She nodded her assent. "I am an international business consultant who has been engaged to assist Ms. Hsiao in an advisor capacity only. I am not involved in the design or implementation of the project. Ms. Hsiao is the originator and author of the proposal. My primary role is to assist in considering international implications of such a project."

"I see." She nodded and looked at my card.

"Mr. Le," I said, nodding toward Kevin, "is assisting us in finding our way around Vietnam. He is a longtime business associate who has assisted me on a number of occasions."

"Yes. I know of Mr. Le's background."

She turned to Yasha.

"Have you visited any of the potential sites?"

"Not yet. We did meet with a representative from Nha Trang. However, I plan to stay in Vietnam for a few days and visit several cities. Nha Trang, Cao Tho, and Da Nang were suggested as possible sites. If there are others you can suggest, I will also visit those."

"I see."

"I brought our annual fiscal report for your review. It is the latest report and was published just this last week. Too late to send with the proposal."

She opened her brief case and brought out the report. I had not seen it before.

Ms. Ngo accepted it without comment. She leafed through the report, nodded to the woman to her left, and handed her the report. She glanced at it briefly and whispered to Ms. Ngo, who nodded and looked at Yasha.

"We would like to review this fiscal report. If you will excuse us, we will take the time now. Meanwhile, someone will give you a brief tour of our facilities."

Yasha, Kevin, and I stepped out of the room and one of the young men went to fetch a young woman who was to be our escort on a tour of the grounds. Her name was Nguyen Lan. Nguyen was a common name and probably over half of the people in Vietnam had that surname. Lan wanted to practice English and was happy to have the opportunity to converse in English. We went through the building and out to the garden area on the ground floor. She gave a well rehearsed narrative describing the functions of the Deputy Prime Minister's office.

It was almost twelve when Ms. Ngo called us back to the conference room. She apologized for the delay and asked us to join the staff for lunch in the cafeteria. We accepted and trooped off with the group to a company style lunch. Having had the military lunch yesterday, I would have preferred to take the entire group for *pho* noodles.

After lunch the members of the group went off to attend to personal matters. Ms. Ngo, Yasha, Kevin, and I walked back to the conference room.

"I hope you have enjoyed your visit to Hanoi," Ms. Ngo said. "Along with being a historic city it has a wide variety of Vietnamese food as well as French cuisine. You might take advantage of your time here and sample the different foods of Hanoi. I can give you the names of some very nice places."

I looked at Kevin, who immediately picked up on it. Yasha did also, but continued to chat about visiting Nha Trang. As we came to the conference room, Kevin went into the room, leaving Yasha and me with Ms. Ngo in the hallway.

"I've never been to Hanoi before and I was wondering if you could join us for dinner tonight at a place you recommend," Yasha asked.

Ms. Ngo smiled and looked around. We were alone.

"I would be delighted. Shall I come by your hotel about seven?"

"That would be perfect."

If Yasha had not taken the initiative would Ms. Ngo have made the invitation to dinner? Unusual. Very interesting and very unusual.

When we came into the conference room, Yasha was pleased to find an overhead projector and a slide projector on the table. They were pointed toward the wall behind the chairs the three of us occupied. Yasha thanked the young man who went for the equipment.

Yasha opened her briefcase and produced a folder containing architectural drawings and artist rendering of the proposed hotel and adjoining buildings. These were shown on the wall with the overhead projector. The details showed up very clearly against the pale vanilla colored wall. She used a red light pointer to identify places she described in her narrative.

I was even more impressed when she took out the slides. These were graphs and figures that detailed construction timelines and costs.

She also presented projected earnings over a ten-year period. Her presentation was very well done.

During the rest of the afternoon the group asked questions about details in her presentation. We took two ten minute breaks. A few minutes after five o'clock Ms. Ngo brought the meeting to a close and suggested we meet again at one tomorrow afternoon. By then, the group will have spent the evening and the next morning analyzing the data presented by Yasha.

We all shook hands and thanked each other for a glorious meeting and how much we looked forward to a successful outcome. Ms. Ngo shook my hand and held it for a moment while she looked into my face. She had something in mind. I didn't think she was into bribes, but I could be wrong. I hoped she was not, because I liked her.

It had been a good day and Yasha had distinguished herself. It was a happy ride back to the hotel, quite unlike my post-meeting yesterday.

"You were just great, Yasha," I said.

"Thank you," she beamed with pleasure.

"I didn't expect the drawings and slides. You didn't tell me about that. It was exceptionally well done."

"Yes, it was," Kevin said. "They were very impressed. I was impressed."

"Thank you. It went well, didn't it?"

"Couldn't have been better."

"What do you think about Ms. Ngo?" she asked.

I looked at Kevin.

"Kevin?"

"She's an important person. She doesn't have to prove how important to us or to anyone else. But, there's something else going on with her."

"She wanted to meet alone. For dinner. I wonder why."

"You think she wants a red envelope?" Yasha asked. "I can get money tomorrow morning. You said there might be a second pay off. Is she the one?"

"I didn't think so, but why else ask for a side meeting, alone?"

Kevin shook his head. "Not the way it's done. If she wanted an envelope she would not do it personally. Someone else would do that."

"Maybe we'll find out tonight."

"Whatever it is, she doesn't wants me to be there. She talked to you two. She never looked at me."

"But if there is to be a pay off, you'll do it, not us," Yasha said.

"If it comes to that, I can do it. But, I think it best to wait and see."

"Okay, Kevin. Meet you in the hotel restaurant for lunch tomorrow at noon."

"See you then." He looked at Yasha. "That was a good show today."

"Thanks."

She was pleased and I was happy for her. She took my arm and led me to the elevator.

"You see, everyone is impressed. You're a woman of many talents."

"So, I'm finally a woman."

"And then some."

"Well, then you should treat me like one."

"You're right. I'll do better from now on."

"You know women have needs."

"So I've heard."

"Like lots of attention."

"I give you tons of attention."

"Well, not exactly tons."

"I don't want to spoil you."

"I need to be spoiled."

"I suppose you'll get your way whether I agree or not."

"Part of my plan."

"Not all plans succeed you know."

"I have a no fail plan."

"Okay, in self defense, I'm gonna get a drink."

"I'll have one too."

"Wow! It's not even dark yet. Drinking kinda early, aren't you?"

"Remember, I'm a woman, so I'll drink when I want to."

39

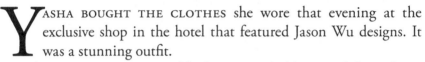

Y ASHA BOUGHT THE CLOTHES she wore that evening at the exclusive shop in the hotel that featured Jason Wu designs. It was a stunning outfit.

The cotton top was ivory, had a scoop neckline, and fringed cap sleeves. The silk skirt was black, with red, purple, blue-tiered colorblock, gathered in a band at high waist. She wore black glossy high heels. The skirt and heels drew attention to her well formed legs. The outfit made me more aware of her trim waist and ample bust line. She looked tall and shapely.

Her face was very nicely made up. Darken eye shadow and lashes with some color on her cheeks. A light red lipstick color and matching nail polish provided color highlights. She was beautiful. Did she have a professional help her or did she do this all by herself? Another talent I didn't know she had.

I wore a white shirt and a grey cotton two button blazer. I was only adequately dressed.

"If I knew you were going to be a fashion statement, I would have worn a tie."

"Something I got yesterday. Like it?"

"Yes, I do. I'm sure everyone will be impressed."

"I want you to be impressed."

"I am. Very impressed."

"Just so you know what you're missing."

"I'm beginning to see that."

"You are?"

"Well, it's really too early to tell."

"What do I have to do?"

"Nothing. You're doing everything just right. Come on, Ms. Ngo will be waiting."

As we came out of the elevator, Ms. Ngo was coming through the front door. She saw us and waved.

Ms. Ngo wore a simple modern version of the *ao dai* Vietnamese dress. It was light blue, a color suited for a woman of her age, with a mandarin collar and long sleeves. The skirt part of the Vietnamese dress was cut into two parts, which formed front and back flaps that came to her ankles. Under the dress she had on white pants. She wore white heels. Tonight her face showed a touch of make up, eye liner that outlining her eyes and a slight tinge of color on her cheeks – a soft rose color on her lips. Her hair was still in a ball at the back of her head. Jade earrings and golden hair clip were added for the evening.

I was beginning to feel self conscious, standing beside these two beautiful women. People around us stared. I supposed they wondered who the guy with them was. Probably thought I was one of the Korean gangsters who had invaded Vietnam in recent years.

"I plan to treat you to a special dinner tonight," Ms. Ngo said.

"It was our invitation. We can't impose on you."

"Nonsense. It's my pleasure. The restaurant is a favorite of mine and I want to share it with you."

She took us to a very classy French restaurant on the top floor of an office building in downtown Hanoi. The management and staff knew her, not as a government official, but as a valued and special guest. We were seated next to a window with a great view of Hanoi's city lights.

She ordered *hors'd orderves* for us. Roasted apricot brie with Chambord glaze and escargot stuffed mushrooms. For dinner she had cognac shrimp with beurre blanc sauce. Yasha had wine poached salmon with black truffles. I had the *coq au vin*, rooster in red wine. It was a special grommet stew. The chicken didn't have to be a rooster, a chicken of either sex would do. I wondered if my chicken was a rooster or a hen. Whatever, it was delicious. We had a nice New Zealand Chardonnay with the dinner. The ladies passed on dessert but I had the chocolate grand Marnier crepes.

———————————

During dinner Ms. Ngo told us about attending a Catholic school where she had learned to speak, read, and write French. While there she converted to the Catholic faith. It was not unusual for some Vietnamese to speak French and English, as she did. That was about all she said about herself and didn't reveal any thing about her life's history.

After asking about Yasha's family in China, she queried me about my prior visits to Vietnam.

"Did you have an opportunity to meet Dr. Nguyen Xuan Oanh? As you know he was a former Prime Minister of the South Vietnam government in the mid-1960s."

"Yes. I knew him."

"How well did you know him?"

"We met on numerous occasions, and worked on several projects before his death. We travel together from Ho Chi Minh City to Hanoi a number of times to meet with government officials here."

"I see."

Dr. Oanh? What did he have to do with anything? Where was this going?

"You also have a doctorate, do you not?"

"Yes I do."

"I believe you received it at the University of California at Los Angeles. You were also a president of a college."

"That was all some years ago."

"Well, you would understand the needs of students and how education is important to them."

She obviously had the resources to obtain these bits of information about me. But I was only listed as a consultant in the proposal. Not really important. What did this personal data have to do with a resort/casino in Nha Trang? Education and needs of students? Was it just polite conversation? I didn't think so.

She turned to Yasha. "I believe you also have several degrees."

"My BA is from George Washington University and my MBA is

from the University of Washington. That's in the state of Washington, not Washington DC."

"Both of you are certainly well prepared for your work."

"Do you have a family, Ms. Ngo?" I hoped to turn the talk to her background.

"No I don't. They're all gone." She was abrupt and short. Obviously, not a topic she wanted to chat about. She glanced at her watch.

"It's after nine," she smiled. "It's been a wonderful visit, but I've taken up too much of your precious time this evening."

"Not at all. It's our pleasure." Yasha smiled.

The dinner was over.

She waved at the waiter and asked for the check. She paid with a Hong Kong credit card. Many restaurants in Vietnam accepted US dollars as well as international credit cards that were much more convenient than the millions of Vietnamese *dong* needed to pay for such a dinner.

We walked to the elevator, past the manager and staff who stood in line to bid us farewell. At the curb, she insisted we take the first taxi.

"Thank you for the wonderful dinner," both of us said, several times.

She stood on the curb and waved goodbye as we drove away.

"I liked the French cooking," Yasha said, "but, she wasn't the warmest person to spend an evening with."

"Obviously she knew the answers to the questions she asked."

"She didn't talk about the proposal."

"This was a different kind of working dinner. I think she's positive about the proposal."

"Really? Why?"

"I don't know. Good sign is she wanted to have dinner with us."

"She was well dressed. A very good looking woman."

"Yes, she is. But, she couldn't match you. You're very special tonight, Yasha."

"I'm really special every night," she said with a grin. "But, I'm pleased you noticed."

"I enjoyed the evening because dinner with you is always special."

"Now and then you say some nice things."

"I have a book full of nice things I say on special occasions. This is one of those times."

She put her arms in mine and leaned her head against me.

"You're going to leave me, aren't you?"

"You know when this is done, I'll leave. You make it sound as if I'm leaving forever. But, I've no reason to stay and I have to take care of other business."

"I'll be here. Isn't that reason enough to stay?"

"Things are not that way, Yasha."

"Things can change."

"Not right now."

"Some things might change, but how I feel doesn't change."

"You're right. I'll always be getting older and better looking."

"Then you should think about things while you're still young enough. Looks won't help if you're too old."

"You suppose there's pill I can take?"

"No. But, you'll be missing out if you don't try."

I laughed and gave her a hug.

We stopped at the hotel bar and settled in a booth. It was quiet and peaceful. I had a single malt scotch. She had a *crème de mint*.

"Who is this Dr. Nguyen she asked about? Was he important?"

"His name was Nguyen Xuan Oanh, popularly known as Dr. Oanh, educated at Harvard University. In the 1960's he worked for the International Monetary Fund and World Bank. He was an economist who wasn't a communist or capitalist.

"He served as Prime Minister in 64 and 65, when the US was trying to prop up the Vietnamese government. After the fall of Saigon he could have fled to the US, instead he stayed to help rebuild Vietnam. He was maligned by the Vietnamese in the US as a traitor because he remained in Vietnam.

"The communist government placed him under house arrest, but needed his expertise as an economist. He was the architect of *doi moi* that served as the backbone of the Vietnamese economic system.

"I met Dr. Oanh because of life insurance. A member of the

American Insurance Group contacted me about establishing a life insurance program in Vietnam. Vietnam didn't have a life insurance program then. I discussed this proposal with Roger, my friend from Singapore, and he introduced me to Dr. Oanh, who was interested in the program. We spent some time on that project and a few other things. We met a number of times here and in Ho Chi Minh City and when he came to the US.

"But, that was some time ago. He died a year ago. Maybe Ms. Ngo agrees that he was a hero or maybe she thinks Dr. Oanh was a CIA agent. I don't know what the party line is on him now. I do know many people, young and old, think highly of him."

"She might be testing you."

"Maybe, but I don't know why."

"Will any of this have an effect on my proposal?"

"I don't see how."

"A lot of strange things here."

"Most things are strange here. Get use to it."

My cell phone suddenly chimed. I looked at the small screen, thinking it might be from Ahn. It was a local number.

"Hello."

"This is Ms. Ngo. Forgive me for this late night call, but I have a special request. I will be grateful if you will meet with me. Alone. Can you come now?"

"Now?"

"Yes."

"Alone?"

"It's not about the proposal. This is personal."

Personal? Could it have an effect on Yasha's proposal?

"Okay. I guess I can."

"Please meet me at this address. Do you have a pen and paper?"

"Wait." I waved at the bartender. "I need a pen." He handed me one from the cup next to the cash register. "Okay, what is it?"

She spelled out an address that I wrote on a napkin.

"It's a café. The place is closed, but someone will let you in when you knock. It shouldn't take more than twenty minutes from your hotel."

"I'll see you there."

"Thank you."

This was a surprise. Why did she want to meet? To ask for a bribe? If so, why ask for me and not Yasha?

"Yasha, I have something to deal with. I have to leave now."

"Right now?"

"I'm going to take you up to your room first."

"Are you going to tell me what this is about?"

"Later."

I signed for the tab and we went up to our rooms. I felt uneasy about a secret meeting with a government official I didn't know well. Was something up? I went into Yasha's room first and looked around. I unscrewed the telephone attachments. No bugs. I looked under the desk, behind the pictures on the wall, and the clock on the night stand. Nothing. I checked my room as well.

"What's up?" she asked.

"Just checking."

"Do you think somebody bugged our rooms?"

"Just checking. Don't go out."

"Are you trying to spook me?"

"Tonight is a bit strange. Probably nothing. I'll be back in an hour."

"Don't be too long."

"I won't be."

"I worry, especially when you don't tell me what's happening."

"No need. You trust me, remember?"

"When are you going to trust me and tell me things?"

"I trust you, Yasha. I won't be long."

I suppose I was being overly secretive and my room check didn't help to ease her concerns. But, the call from Ms. Ngo was unusual. Was I being paranoid? Was she on my side or was she the enemy?

I gave Yasha a peck on her forehead and left her frowning.

40

I TOOK THE FIRST taxi in the queue and showed the driver the address written on the napkin. He thought a moment and then nodded his head. He must have wondered why I wanted to go to a restaurant that was closed. It took less than twenty minutes. The address was a small restaurant wedged in between a grocery shop and a bakery. The same family probably owned all three businesses. Budding capitalism sprouting its wings.

I paid the driver and went to the front of the restaurant. I tried the darken glass door of the restaurant. It was locked. I peered inside and saw a light in the back. I rapped on the door. A woman came out from a room in back and looked at me through the glass door. She unlatched the lock and opened the door. She didn't speak. She waved her hand, palm down, to follow her. I followed her through a swinging door that led to the food preparation area. She stopped and pointed into the kitchen.

At one end of the kitchen, away from the stoves and sink, there was a table and two chairs. Ms. Ngo was sitting there. She rose when she saw me and put out her hand. I remembered her hands were soft and smooth. They were not as warm this time. She smiled and motioned to the other chair. There were two cups and a pot of tea on the table. She poured me a cup.

"Thank you for coming. I realize this is a bit strange but I needed to meet with you alone."

"Well, I'm here. What is it?"

"It's a personal problem I have."

"What kind of personal problem?"

"You don't remember me from five years ago?"

I cocked my head and squinted at her.

"Have we met?"

"We didn't formally meet, but I was there when you came to see Dr. Oanh. I was assigned to him."

"What do you mean assigned to him?"

"When I was with Dr. Oanh I was really working for national security. When the war ended there were many who were eliminated because they were accused of treason. Dr. Oanh was internationally well known and placed under house arrest. But, he did not work for the Americans. And he did not defect to America as so many others did."

"Yes. I know. But, most of those who got out would have been killed if they had stayed. So there was no right or wrong with leaving Vietnam at that time."

"I agree. It was my good fortunate he decided to stay. When he needed a person with my language skills, the government sent him a list of approved personnel. He hired me from that list. I was assigned to keep track of him and report who he saw, what he did. That's how I know about you."

"Did we actually meet? I mean, were we introduced?"

"No. But I served you tea at his house that day."

"Did he know why you were there? As an agent of national security."

"Yes. But he also knew I didn't want to spy on him and he knew about my problems. I was with him for two years. He told me toward the end of my time with him that if I ever needed help from the outside to try to contact you. He thought highly of you and said I could trust you."

I tried to remember the times I was at his home. It was a while ago and it was a hectic time. I didn't recall seeing her. How could I not notice her? I must have been really preoccupied. That preoccupied?

"How did you get involved in all of this?"

"It's all tied up with my personal history." She sighed and took a deep breath and began her story.

"Both of my parents were killed in a bombing raid outside of Da Nang when I was ten years old. I had no family so I was alone, as were hundreds of others. Some of us made it to Saigon and I lived on the streets for almost a year. Then the nuns found me. I became a part of a group of orphans who lived at the Catholic school, where I converted and became a Catholic. I stayed at the school for the next twelve years. That's where I learned French and English.

"When I finished school I went to back to Da Nang, hoping to find relatives who might still be alive. That was when I met a man who had just finished studies to become an engineer. We lived together in a village outside of Da Nang and were planning to marry and move to Saigon. Then I became pregnant. In my third month of pregnancy my man became very ill. He had liver cancer. The doctors said his cancer was caused by Agent Orange. He suffered a great deal and died in my eighth month. Six weeks later, I gave birth to a son.

"My family was all gone. I had no means of support and no hope of establishing a normal life there. Life for an unmarried mother is always difficult. I went back to Saigon and got a job with the government. They had need of my language skills and, of course, they wanted to use me as an informant.

"I contacted a woman I knew when I was at the school and she cared for the baby. I gave her money when I could. When he was about nine years old the nuns took him in and raised him as a Catholic.

"Not many people know about this boy. Well, he's not a boy any more. He's a young man who needs help to go to college. The nuns had him tested and his IQ is 150. They were so impressed they urged him to apply at Cal Tech."

"Cal Tech? That is impressive. Have they accepted him?"

"Yes."

"Then, what's the problem?"

"He has to have an American patron. The nuns and I will support him financially in school, but someone has to guarantee his financial support. It has to be someone in the US. When I saw your name on Ms. Hsiao's proposal I thought it was an opportunity sent by heaven.

"If the Vietnam government realizes he is very intelligent they will make him a government man. I want him to get away and be educated in America. Then he could be free of this country's government."

"Ms. Ngo, you know if I were to do this, it will be considered a bribe. That would put this project, Ms. Hsiao, and you in great jeopardy. The government knows who I am and my name is on that resort proposal. If my name shows up on your son's application they will know. They always do. And I will not allow anything to happen to Ms. Hsiao. I'm sorry, Ms. Ngo, I can do nothing."

Did they know about Ms. Ngo's "secret son"? Hell, they know everything about everybody, especially everybody working in the government and those who knew foreign businessmen. It was a no win situation.

"How old is your son?"

"He'll be eighteen next month."

"What's his name?"

"The nuns gave him his name. He's called Robert in English. Bao in Vietnamese. I have a picture of him. It was taken last year. The nuns sent it to me."

She took a photo from her purse and handed it to me, with a pleased look on her face. A mother's pride and joy. He was a good-looking young lad, standing straight with his arms held against his sides. A mop of unkempt hair on his head and a boyish grin on his face.

"Can he speak English?"

"Yes. The nuns taught him to speak English and French. So he is trilingual, as I am. He passed the Tofel test without any problems."

"If his father died as a result of Agent Orange there is probably a record someplace. Was he in the army?"

"Yes."

"So they have records. Who are listed as his parents in the college and visa applications?"

"His parents are listed as dead."

"The nuns know."

"They will not say anything."

"The woman who took care of him knows."

"She is dead."

She answered too quickly. She had asked herself these same questions and came up with pat answers.

"The woman sitting out there is the one who took care of him, isn't she?"

"No one knows."

"Ms. Ngo, they know everything."

"Are you saying this is impossible to do?"

"No. It can be done, but not by me. I'm already identified in a proposal you have the authority to recommend or reject. Simply put, if, in exchange for helping your son you gave a flavorful endorsement of this resort project, it would be a bribe."

"Yes, I know that's how it can be interpreted. I'm sorry. But at this point I have nothing to lose. I favor Ms. Hsiao's proposal and I don't want to put it in jeopardy, but I don't know what else to do. Asking for your help has nothing to do with Ms. Hsiao's proposal. You are my last hope for my son."

"If I help you, Ms. Hsiao will risk her career. Why should she risk her career for your son?"

"There is no reason. Except to help someone who is not to blame for how his life is and who has no other way to make it better."

"I understand your problem, but there's nothing I can do."

She pursed her lips and sighed. Her shoulders sagged and she looked down at her hands. She sat silently with a dejected look about her.

"What is the name of this Catholic school?"

She turned to me with a surprised look on her face. I had a blank expression. She recovered from her initial shock and pulled a folder from her purse.

"I have his folder here. It has all the information about him including a copy of his application and test scores."

She held out a large envelope. I didn't take it. She laid it on the table.

"Will you help him?"

"No, I will not. And I told you why."

She was confused. I got up and walked out of the kitchen. I found the woman who opened the door for me in a small office. I asked her to call me a taxi.

I went back to the kitchen to where Ms. Ngo was sitting. She looked up at me. She was quietly crying.

I could hear Kam Wah telling me to not become involved. But, what the hell, this young man's father died because of Agent Orange. Agent Orange was a poisonous chemical – a real weapon of mass destruction. It was supposedly used to kill vegetation, but instead it killed people and it will go on killing and babies will be born deformed for generations to come. Hell, it even killed American soldiers. That was what America did for this kid. Maybe it was time America made up for that.

I sighed and looked passively at her. She started to say something, but I put up my hand and shook my head.

"Dr. Oanh was a good man. There are too few like him. Agent Orange was a crime against humanity and people will suffer because of it for generations to come. No matter how small, something good must come out of that."

I picked up the folder and left. The woman was waiting at the door. She unlocked the door and let me out. I went to the curb and waited for the taxi. As I got in the taxi I looked back at the glass door. The woman was watching me. She put her hands together, touched her forehead, and bowed.

It was almost eleven when I got back to the hotel. I went into the lounge and took a stool at the far end of the bar. The bartender remembered me and asked if I wanted a single malt scotch. I smiled and nodded. He poured me a good shot.

I looked at the manila envelope. It was a lot to ask - financial guarantee for a young man they've never met. Well, I couldn't do it, but someone else might. Maybe a corporate donor.

An IQ of 150 was far out. A whole helleva lot better than most people on earth. I opened the envelope and took out the papers. His IQ was actually 156. Test scores were excellent and his essay explaining why he wanted to attend Cal Tech was well written. I guessed the nuns helped with that.

Always good to have nuns on your side. I remembered the Sisters at St. Joseph College didn't care that I wasn't a Catholic or even a practicing Christian. They lit a candle for me anyway.

"I knew this was where you would be."

"Ah, Yasha. I was thinking about calling you to join me."

"Sure you were."

I waved to the bartender. "You want something?"

"No thanks. Had enough for tonight."

I ordered another scotch.

"So where did you go?"

"It was an emergency that wasn't an emergency."

"Something else you're not going to tell me."

"If I told you everything there would no longer be any secrets."

"Why is it important to have secrets?"

"Because secrets are a source of power. It's necessary to have power to make things happen."

"Like Ms. Ngo. She has the power to make or break my project."

"She's a power on one level. There are others who have more power."

"I'm beginning to wonder if she will kill my proposal."

"Ms. Ngo will support your proposal."

"She didn't sound that way."

"Things aren't always the way they appear to be."

"Why are you so confident?"

"Just a feeling I have."

"Why don't I get that feeling?"

"Yasha. If your proposal is rejected it will be because someone higher up the ladder decides. Not because of Ms. Ngo."

"Do you know something you're not telling me? Is that what this mysterious trip tonight was about?"

"Is your laptop in your room or mine?"

"I left it in your room. Why aren't you going to tell me about tonight?"

"I need the computer. Let's go."

I signaled the bartender for the bill and signed it.

"Come on. You can walk across the room in that sexy outfit and give all these guys a thrill."

"At least with them I have better a chance than with you."

"How do you know that?"

"Well, I've been striking out pretty consistently."

"That's no reason to quit trying."
"I haven't had too much encouragement."
"Things can change."
"I'll be the first to know," she said.
"Not before me."

Yasha went to her room to change. I took off my coat and shoes. I opened the curtains and stared out the window. The city lights spread out as far as the eye could see. Night lights were always a beautiful sight. It was otherworldly. The floating lights that dotted the dark night hid all the unsightly and damaged parts of the city. One didn't see the people in the dark, some in their homes, some living on the streets, many existing on the edge of poverty.

A far cry from the time when no lights were on because American bombers came to bomb the city. I guess it was the same for Berlin, London, Tokyo, Shanghai, and all the other cities that were blown to hell. I wondered how many Americans know they were spared that ordeal. Ain't war grand?

Well, at least the Americans didn't use Agent Orange in Hanoi, but a lot of folks carried other kinds of scars, emotional as well as physical.

Things had changed, I've been told. Changed enough to propose building resorts and gaming casinos in a country America bombed to bits and used poisonous chemicals that were still killing men, women, and children. We've come a long way, they say. Or have we? I just proposed building an ammunition plant to produce bullets used to kill people. The holier than thou argument was that the gun didn't kill – the shooter did. Pretty stupid argument. But, it was better to keep the real world out of sight – in the dark – so we can lie to ourselves about how righteous we are.

I turned on the computer and took a sip from a mini-bottle of gin. I stared at the computer screen. Would Ms. Ngo put the curse on Yasha's proposal if I didn't help her? I didn't think so. I believed she would make the right choice regardless of what I did. Ms. Ngo's son deserved the help, but I was committed to Yasha and her resort proposal. Another one of those decisions. How was my moral fiber holding up?

41

YASHA CAME BACK TO my room wrapped in her giant terry robe. She opened a mini-bottle of wine and poured some into a water glass. She pulled back the bed cover, stacked the pillows, propped herself up against the head board, and settled in. She turned on the television and sipped her wine. She smiled at me and waved her glass of wine. She did this as if she did it every night. I watched her with a bemused smile and without comment.

I went back to the computer and checked my Email messages. A note from Chang, still asking when I was coming to Beijing. There was no message from Ahn. I thought I might call him tomorrow. There were messages from my children and friends who wondered why I didn't answer them. Megan's message was a short one that simply said "Call me, damn it." I was negligent and told myself to answer the messages.

I sent Andre a message that I would call him tomorrow about six or seven in the evening, his time. I didn't say why, just that it was important.

About midnight I finished my gin drink and took a shower. I came out to find Yasha asleep. I suppose I could go to her room and sleep in her bed. I said the hell with it and got into the bed. I reached over and turned off the lamp.

"Did you think I would sleep through all of this?"

"So, you're awake. Faking it, huh?"

"Well, I did doze for a minute."
I turned and reached for the lamp.
"Don't turn the light on."
"Are you going to sleep here?"
"Do you mind?"
"No. You're welcome anytime."
"I was hoping so."
"But, is this a good idea?"
"What idea?"
"This."
She sighed and propped herself up with her head on her hand.
"You've had your way about this for as long as I've known you."
"For your own good."
"You're always deciding what's good for me. What you think is good for me is not always right or what I want."
"Maybe I'm not only thinking what's good for you. I could be thinking about myself. This may not be good for either one of us."
"It will be good for you and me. I decided a long time ago," she said.
"You decided?"
"Right after we met."
"Really?"
"I know you were trying to be honorable and not take advantage of me. I know all that stuff. What makes you think you're my guardian? I'm a grown woman. I'm not a child. I can decide what I want."
"Maybe I'm just trying to avoid getting involved. For your sake as well as mine."
"You know how I am about you and I know you have feelings for me. You just try not to show it."
"Yasha ..."
"Listen to me. If you don't want me, I understand. But, I know you have feelings for me."
"Yes, I do."
"I know you have other women in your life. I don't make any real demands on you. I don't expect you to be mine exclusively. Just sometime. Well, more than that. I would like it to be most of the time."

"Yasha, I don't consider what you ask to be a demand. Actually, I'm pleased that you've picked me to be your very best friend."

She grew silent and reached for my hand under the covers. Her head lay on my shoulder.

"You know I'm more than a best friend."

"Yasha, I would be lost without you."

"That was part of my plan."

"A part of your plan? What was the other part?"

"You'll have to find out."

"I guess getting you in bed is a start."

"I've already done that part for you."

"I guess it's time to do my part."

"I've been waiting."

"I won't keep you waiting any longer."

I slept longer than usual. I looked over to the other side of the bed. It was empty. Why do women always wake up before me after a night of intimacy?

Whatever, I decided to go to the gym. For the next hour I sweated and strained with the torture machines. A poster was pinned to the bulletin board that sauna and massage service were available in the hotel. I made a mental note of that and thought about using it tonight. I went back to my room and had a long hot shower. I looked at my jeans and decided it was time to send them with shirt and underwear to the laundry. Should also dry clean the jacket. I called house keeping for a pick up.

Yasha rapped on the adjoining door. She came into the room, looking fresh and smiling. She leaned on the door, crossed her feet, and put her hand on her hip.

"Do I have to keep on with this business of knocking?"

"I guess not."

"Good. Ready for breakfast?" she asked.

"Yes."

"You went to the gym?"

"Haven't been as often as I should. Getting out of shape."

"Oh, I think you're in good shape."

"I don't know about that."

"But, I do," she said with a sly grin. She gave me a quick kiss.

"Yeah, I guess you would know."

"Actually, you're probably in better shape than I am."

"Have to be, so I can keep up."

"You do just fine. Last night was just the beginning," she laughed.

"I might not be able to last."

"Oh. I think you will."

"I'm sure you'll make certain I do,"

"I plan to."

"I give up. Let's go get some breakfast. Then I have some phone calls to make."

"Our meeting with Ngo is at one."

"We have time for us now."

"Yasha."

"Okay. I can wait. When is Kevin coming?"

"About lunch time."

"Let's go. I'm hungry."

"You're always hungry."

"Just a growing girl."

"I can see that."

"I hoped you would notice."

There was a new intimacy between us and it felt good. It was a comfortable state of mind and it made all that chatter about sex easy and fun. I forgot about my concerns about getting involved. I didn't know why it had been a problem before. But I was unsure of sustaining a relationship because I hadn't been that successful in the past.

After breakfast Yasha announced she was going shopping and would be back in time for lunch. I went back to my room and checked the Email again. Andre answered my message and said he would be expecting my call.

I should call Megan. Why was I hesitating? I wasn't being honest with the women in my life. I wasn't really committed to anyone.

I met Yasha before I met BJ. In fact, I met Megan before I met BJ. The three women were different but alike in some ways. Kam Wah would be pleased if Yasha became a real part of my life. He would say she would be a true mate – something Kam Wah believed Megan could never be. He could always point to my divorce from my first wife, who was not an Asian. He believed that an Asian wife was better for me, especially a Chinese wife. Was this a bit of racism?

The interracial thing wasn't really a problem with my first wife and I wondered if it would be with someone like Megan. My feelings for Megan were not the same as my feelings for Yasha. How I felt about BJ was unlike my feelings about Yasha or Megan. Why am I going over all of this stuff? I gave up analyzing and called Megan.

"Hello."

"Is it too late to call?" I asked.

"Well, finally."

"Been busy. Sorry."

"It's okay. I've been busy too. Getting people together for October."

Megan was excited about the success she was enjoying. The number of people who wanted to get on her Canton Fair express train was growing. We talked for ten minutes – or rather she talked for ten minutes. She was busy with her new company and happy with her life.

I didn't feel any strings tugging at me and that was the way I wanted it to be. Ironically, things didn't happen between Megan and me last December because I met BJ. And now there's Yasha. Was I keeping score? Why was I getting hung up on these issues?

A few minutes after seven, California time, I called Andre. He answered on the second ring – he was anxious to get the call.

"Hello, my friend. How are things in Vietnam?"

"Things are not as good as I would like them to be."

"The deal went sour?"

"The people I talked to wanted a half a million dollars to continue with the deal. This isn't official. I doubt the army even knows. Just two greedy guys looking for a way to make big bucks."

"Fuck 'em."

"I agree. I understand about bribes and have no problem with paying, but this was crass and very dirty. It wasn't right. A very hungry party cadre took over. He and an old veteran general were the ones I met. It's an old story you've heard before. They pissed me off because it was so stupid. Everybody could have made lots of money with this deal."

"The only ones who make money are those who understand how to make money. Everyone else only pretend they know and they fuck up everything for everybody else."

"I've asked my contact here to get with his man in the Deputy Prime Minister's office and see if people there know about the General and his partner. Bribes are common, but this one could be unacceptable to the powers that be. If so, I'll see about another meeting with people who know how to do business. With people other than the army."

"If you think it's worthwhile, give it a go."

"Sorry about this."

"Don't feel bad about this. It's a good proposal and if there are people with some sense, it can happen."

"We're always looking for people with sense, Andre. Why is so difficult to find them?"

"I read a quote the other day. It said genius has its limitations, but stupidity is not so handicapped. We have to live with it. But, give it another go. You have my support, a hundred percent."

"Okay. Listen, Andre, I need help with something – again."

"Yes?"

"There's a young Vietnamese lad who needs help. He's a certified genius and Cal Tech has accepted him. His expenses are all taken care of, but there's need for an American to guarantee he won't steal the family jewels. Essentially, it's a guarantee for bills he might incur and can't pay. And, as a last resort, a plane ticket home if all goes to hell. But, with this young man, that won't happen."

"This person is special?"

"Yes. To give you a clue, he has an IQ of 156."

"156? That's genius class."

"Yeah. It's a long and complicated story. I would do this but my name cannot appear on anything connected with this young man."

"Political?"

"Yes. Very. And, it's personal."

"Do you want me to provide this?"

"No. Not you personally. I thought you might use your own corporation. It would look good for the company and won't cost anything. And, you have my personal guarantee if anything goes wrong."

"It's important to you?"

"Yes. It's a commitment."

He was silent for a minute. I could hear him sipping his wine.

"Okay. What do I have to do?"

"I'll fax you his records and application. It'll have all the information and instructions in the package. Not much to do, just a letter on company letterhead stating it will guarantee his financial support. I'll include a sample letter."

"Consider it done. When are you coming home?"

"Don't know exactly when, but should be in a couple of days."

"What about the business you said you had to attend to?"

"That's up in the air at the moment."

"Will I have to come to China to bail you out?"

"No. Not to worry, Andre. Things are okay."

"Call me when you get back."

"I will. The papers will be faxed within the hour."

"Take care, my friend."

"Thanks, Andre. Again, you saved my life and helped some very good people."

"Saving your life is always a pleasure, my friend."

42

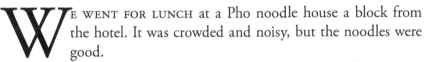

W**E WENT FOR LUNCH** at a Pho noodle house a block from the hotel. It was crowded and noisy, but the noodles were good.

At twelve-thirty we arrived at the meeting room, a half hour early. I was surprised to see everyone was there, waiting. Ms. Ngo greeted us and asked if we could start right away. Yasha said yes and we all trooped into the conference room.

Tea was served, which was more than the usual bottled water. Was it a special day? Ms. Ngo rose and looked around at everyone.

"May I have your attention please?" All eyes turned to her.

"First, we wish to thank you," she looked at Yasha, "Ms. Hsiao, for coming to Vietnam. Your presentations were excellent and clear as to purpose and design. Our committee members met last night and again this morning to consider your proposal."

She paused and looked around the room. A bit theatrical, but it was okay.

"We have decided to submit a recommendation to the Deputy Prime Minister to begin serious planning immediately for its implementation."

It was a grand surprise. Yasha was overjoyed. She had expected further discussions and thought recommendations would be put off for a future time. She smiled broadly and looked at me. She walked around the table, and shook Ms. Ngo's hand.

"Thank you Ms. Ngo. And thanks to all of you on the committee.

You have taken a giant step toward creating something of great value for Vietnam."

The committee members rose and applauded. Yasha went around the table and shook everyone's hand. She was very pleased and the committee members were pleased that she was pleased. Good feelings from everyone.

She came to me, pulled me out of my chair, and gave me a hug, which prompted another round of applause from the committee.

Yasha turned to Ms. Ngo and asked, "Will all of you be my guest at a celebration dinner tonight?"

Ms. Ngo looked at the committee members. They obviously wanted to celebrate with Yasha.

"Of course. We will be delighted to accept your invitation."

"Wonderful."

"I will come to the hotel at six to pick you up. We can celebrate at a very popular Vietnamese restaurant I have in mind that will be just right for this group."

After another round of applause from the group, we all shook hands and promised to celebrate that night.

Kevin said he would meet us later and went off to attend to his lady companion's feelings of being neglected. Yasha and I went back to the hotel and I suggested a Champagne toast. We went into the bar and ordered Champagne.

"Everything is working out, Yasha. I'm very proud of you." I toasted her. "To you, Yasha."

"We're winning, aren't we?" she asked.

"You're winning. That's for sure."

"You knew what she was going to say, didn't you?"

"I wasn't that surprised, but I didn't know for certain."

"You can tell me about it one day."

"It'll be one of a million things I have to tell you."

"I want to hear them all."

The restaurant Ms. Ngo chose had a private dining room large enough for the group. The Vietnamese cuisine was excellent. It also had a swinging bar and up to date *karaoke* system. Even Kevin was impressed. The group enjoyed themselves, breaking out in song and even an impromptu dance.

Ms. Ngo introduced a young lady at the party who was not a committee member. Ms. Lo was a member of the department that dealt with tourist programs, or so we were told. She was a graduate from the Vietnam National University, College of Foreign Languages and International School, in Hanoi. She spoke English with a slight accent – just enough to make her all the more attractive. She was a bright and charming young talent who would soon have serious responsibilities.

She was about twenty-five, a pretty young lady with lovely jet black hair, much longer than the style worn by older women. She wore glasses, but removed them when the party got underway. Without them, her bright eyes were more noticeable. Quick to smile and friendly, she was a delight.

Ms. Ngo suggested that Ms. Lo accompany Yasha on her fact-finding tour to three cities that might be considered as sites for the resort. Yasha was delighted to have a personal guide.

Kevin and I exchanged glances. We knew she was a plant to watch over Yasha. The idea of having a watchdog might not sit well with some, but as long as she was safe, I didn't care.

As the evening wore on, per my habit at these gatherings, I slowly withdrew from the group. Standing to one side, I watched the revelers and sipped my drink. Ms. Ngo came across the room and stood next to me, looking at the group.

"Will you be leaving soon?"

"Yes."

"When will you return?"

"I don't know. Ms. Hsiao has matters well in hand and I don't think she will need my help."

"How can I get in touch with you?"

"The number and Email address are all on my name card."

"Do you have other numbers?"

"Do you?" I asked.

"Yes."

"Why don't you give me the number?"

She handed me a card with a number written on the back.

"You have another number?" she asked.

"I don't think it's wise for you to contact me."

"But ..."

"I want to see this project succeed. Once this program is underway, we may have occasion to meet again."

She smiled and nodded.

"I understand. Thank you." She put her hand on my arm and gave me a light squeeze. Then she drifted away.

Ms. Ngo thought Yasha's proposal was excellent and gave it her highest recommendation. She would follow up and work to have it approved by the final decision makers. Through Andre's company, I helped her son so she had it all. It was a win-win for her, her son, and Yasha. They all came out winners. Was this a moral victory or a slick business deal? Whatever, I felt good about it.

Yasha came up to me and looked after Ms. Ngo.

"How long will this party last?"

"It can go on all night. Everyone decides for themselves when to leave."

"Are you ready to leave?"

"Yes."

"So am I. What about Kevin?"

"He'll find his own way."

"I guess I better pay for this bash."

"I'll meet you outside."

I got Kevin's attention and waved at him. He gave me a thumbs up signal. He was busy singing a *karaoke* duet with Ms. Lo. His lady friend will be sorry she complained about the early hours.

Yasha paid the bill and we caught a taxi back to the hotel. It had become a habit for us to stop off at the hotel bar and we did again. The bartender recognized us and poured me a single malt scotch drink. Yasha had a brandy. She clicked my glass with hers.

"It was fun."

"Yes. It was."

"Did you make some kind of deal with Ms. Ngo?"

"No."

"I think you did. But, it's okay. You can tell me about it someday. I don't know if I should be upset that she was coming on to you."

"Coming on to me?" I laughed.

"I saw her siding up to you at the party."

"Siding up?"

"I notice these things. What do you think about this Ms. Lo?"

"Pretty young lady."

"You would notice, but I'm not talking about that."

"She should be a great help when you visit these cities."

"She's there to watch me, isn't she?"

"You're learning. But, it's okay. She'll protect you. And she'll keep you out of mischief."

"Kevin was hitting on her."

"Good for him. Hope he scores."

I heard my cell phone chime and before I turned it on, I knew it was Ahn. I looked at Yasha and put up my hand and shook my head. I walked out of the bar.

"Ahn?"

"I have some news."

"Yes?"

"I'm certain I found the people."

"Okay. I'll call as soon as I can arrange things."

"I'll wait for your call."

So the time had come. He said the people. Were there more than one? Well, one or a dozen, it was the same. There were things to do. First, I had to get some money. Yasha again.

"What was that?"

"Let's go up to the room."

"Will this lead to something?"

"Not now, Love."

She frowned. "You're leaving."

"Yes." I looked away. "Let's go."

I signed for the bill and we went up to her room. She knew whatever it was, it was serious.

"How much money do I have coming?"

"How much do you want?"

"I need about seven or eight thousand."

"Okay."

"Can you get this in cash tomorrow?"

"Yes. Credit line at Deutsche bank is not a problem."

"I need a flight out of here tomorrow to Hong Kong. And then to Beijing?"

"Just to Beijing?"

"Actually, I have to get to Harbin."

"I knew it was Harbin," she said dejectedly. "Okay. I'll get you a flight to Harbin from Beijing."

"I don't know what my schedule will be in Beijing. One night will be about right."

"You want late or early."

"Late is better."

"What about a return?"

"Haven't gotten that far yet."

"I guess I'll never know what this is about."

"You don't want to know."

"Yes I do. But, I guess I'll have to wait." She sighed. She wrote on the pad next to the telephone. "Hanoi to Hong Kong to Beijing to Harbin. Return open." She looked at me with a serious face. "Does this mean I won't see you again?"

"Yasha, you'll see me as much as you want. But, right now I have some things I must attend to. It has nothing to do with us."

"Everything you do has an effect on us."

She looked at me for a long moment. Then, with a resigned look she left.

In thirty minutes she came back to my room. She rapidly read off the schedule.

"Tomorrow, Cathay Air 11:05 AM – arrives Hong Kong 1:55 PM. Same day, Air China 5 PM – arrives Beijing 8:15 PM. The next day, Air China at 8:35 PM – arrives Harbin at 10:15 PM. If you want you can probably get an earlier flight to Harbin."

"No. This schedule works out just fine."

"It'll be tight in the morning. I'll try to get the bank to open up for me at eight. I have the manager's cell phone number."

"Thanks, Yasha. This is a great help."

"I'm helping you to leave me."

"It won't be for very long."

"Why do I think it will be?"

"Yasha, you have a new world opening up here in Vietnam. I'm really not that important to the new project."

"You're important to me."

"And you are to me, Yasha."

"Then why are you leaving me?"

"There are some things I have to do."

"Are you leaving me as you have others? Am I just like the others?"

"You have nothing to prove."

"Tell me true, will I see you again?"

"Yasha, unless I'm dead, I promise we will meet as soon as this business is finished. And I have this to remind me." I rubbed the medallion.

"I want tonight to be special."

"There's no one else I'd rather be with. Especially tonight."

"You make it sound like its our last night."

"What happened to the Yasha of yesterday? You're going to have to be more positive about us."

"I know about me. It's what you're involved with that I'm not always sure of."

"This Harbin business will be coming to an end soon."

"Right now I want you to hold me."

"I'm getting used to holding you."

"That's how I planned it to be."

"So, I fell right into your net."

"Just hold me."

"I can do more than that."

"I hoped you would."

43

THE NEXT MORNING WE rose early and Yasha and I showered together. In a very short time, togetherness had become a thing with us. After our shower and while we were getting dressed she didn't say much and avoided looking me. She wasn't happy that I was leaving and she didn't pretend it wasn't an issue. This was different from my earlier departures. I finally had responded to her and become a real part of her life. Now I was leaving. She felt abandoned. That wasn't true, but that's how she felt.

At eight she went to the bank to withdraw the money for me.

I called Kam Wah to meet in Hong Kong, my first stopover.

"I'll be at the Hong Kong airport at two this afternoon. I have a couple of hours lay over."

"I will come to the airport. We can have lunch at the *cha shu* shop on the main floor. You know where that is? It's close to the airport express ticket counter."

"Yes, I know."

"Where are you going from here?"

"To Beijing and then to Harbin."

"Harbin again?"

"Yes."

"I am concerned about this."

"No need."

284

"We must talk."

"See you soon, Kam Wah."

I didn't know how I was going to explain this trip to Kam Wah. He would be very opposed to what I had in mind.

I called Kevin and told him I was leaving. He said he would meet me in the coffee shop in a half an hour.

"Are you going to Hong Kong?"

"Yes, and points north."

"To Harbin?"

"Yes."

"Sometimes things happen. Is this going to be one of those times?"

"I'll have to see how it goes."

"When are you coming back?"

"Don't know. But if she's here I'll come back."

"That Lo lady is okay and she'll be a good watchdog."

"Still, I would appreciate it if you can keep an eye out for Yasha."

"Will do."

"Too bad about the army. But, let me know if Dinh can work something out. Thanks for your help, Kevin. Maybe next time."

"Always a next time."

"Well, here's Yasha. Need to get a taxi."

"I'll get one."

He nodded to Yasha and went out to get a taxi.

"Here's ten thousand dollars. Plane tickets are all electronic so you can get a boarding pass at the check in gate."

"Are you going to say good bye or are you going to ignore me?"

"I don't know why you're leaving and I don't like it."

"Yasha, there are things I have to do."

"This isn't business as usual. This is something else."

"Please, Yasha. Let's not argue."

She came to me and put her arms around my neck. She held me tight and cried.

"I don't want to go to the airport."

"No need Yasha."

"I love you. Very much."

She put her hands to my lips.

"Don't say anything. Just so you know."

She hugged me and cried some more. She stepped back, dropped her arms, and quickly walked away. I didn't want to lose her.

Kevin and I rode most of the way to the airport in silence. We got out in front of the international terminal and Kevin told the taxi to wait.

"Let me know how it goes," Kevin said.

"I will. Take care and thanks for helping Yasha."

"No problem."

"I'll try to keep in touch."

"If you need help, call me."

"Thanks. Take care, Kevin."

Getting through Vietnamese immigrations and customs was getting much simpler than when I first came to Vietnam, but there were still forms to fill out. There were also more tourists and this made leaving Vietnam much more time consuming than arriving. Patience was an absolute necessity. I haven't mastered this virtue. Maybe in another life.

Business Class on Cathay was as good as Singapore Air and much better than United. The short flight to Hong Kong was very pleasant. I had several cups of coffee and a croissant. The coffee was hot. Things might be looking up.

Yasha's last words lingered on my mind. My relationship with her had become special. She was sure about us – it was our *karma*, she would say.

Hong Kong immigration always took time because of the usual heavy passenger traffic, but on that day it was relatively easy. At the exit doors I saw Kam Wah standing in the back of the crowd. Always a comfort to know he was there. He smiled and waved.

He stood with his hands behind his back and was fidgeting because he couldn't smoke. There was a smoking ban in public places that included the airport terminal, but smoking rooms were available. I didn't give him any sympathy because I thought he should quit smoking or at least cut back.

We went to the *cha shu* eatery. He pointed at an empty table and told me to sit. He went to the counter and brought back two orders of *cha shu* and rice. He set them on the table and he went back to get two paper cups of tea.

We talked about family matters and the apartment/commercial complex he was building in Huangpo. After we finished eating we took the escalator to the upper deck and found a smoking room.

I waited outside and used the time to call Chang in Beijing, my second stopover.

"I was hoping you would be coming to Beijing."

"I'll be there for a night and a day. I have a flight out at eight PM tomorrow night."

"Ah, then we have plenty of time to meet for lunch. Where are you staying?"

"I haven't made any reservations yet."

"I believe you stayed at the Beijing Palace the last time."

"Yes."

"I can arrange that for you."

"I don't want to put you to any trouble."

"No trouble at all. It will be arranged."

He never said things would be done or be taken care of. Things were always arranged. As always, it would be Liu who would make the arrangements.

"Thank you, sir."

"Not at all. I can come to pick you up at eleven tomorrow at the hotel. Is that convenient?"

"Yes. I'll meet you in the lobby."

"See you there."

"Good bye, Mr. Chang."

"Good bye."

It was time to bring closure to the Pei affair. Chang owed me and I was counting on that. I might need his help if things went wrong in Harbin.

Kam Wah came out of the smoking room and we walked toward the terminal where my flight to Beijing boarded. He brought me up to date on Su Lin and her sister. Both were doing very well and under the tutelage of Amanda, Su Lin had become a computer whiz. He told the office staff I was in transit and that he was meeting me at the airport. They all sent their good wishes. Amanda had sent a special greeting – at least that's what Kam Wah said.

"Both Su Lin and Amanda would make very good wives," he said, commenting causally, as if it were a part of the conversation.

"Kam Wah, not again."

"They are both Chinese and perfect for you."

"They're both wonderful women, but I'm not in need of a wife."

"I have spoken to you about this matter before."

"Yes. About a thousand times. Kam Wah, I don't need a wife."

"You do. Not only a wife, but a Chinese wife. If not Su Lin or Amanda, what about this woman from Shanghai?"

"Enough, Kam Wah."

"Why are you going back to Harbin? You said the Manchu lady was dead. You have no business there. Is there any reason to go there?"

"Just things to wrap up."

He reached for his cigarettes and remembered the smoking ban. He looked for a sign. There was a smoking room down past several boarding gates. We walked down to the room.

"I need to have a cigarette."

"It's only been twenty minutes since your last smoke. You really should cut down."

He ignored me and took out his cigarettes.

I sighed. "Okay. I'll wait here."

"I want to know why you're going to Harbin," he said as he turned and went into the smoking room. I wondered what I could tell him. This was not just another trip to Harbin. This trip was different. I was different.

I called Ahn, my last stop.

"I'll arrive tomorrow night from Beijing at 10:55 PM."

"I'll be there."

"I'm not anxious to have too many people know I'm coming. Hong will know because he checks all foreigners coming into Harbin. But, others don't need to know."

"What hotel do you want?"

"Is there a good hotel near the train station?"

"Several. Four or five star?"

"I'm supposed to be a tourist, so makes sense to be a five star."

"Anything else?"

"Yes, but we can talk when I get there. You know, I need a reason to be coming back to Harbin."

"The Ma family is putting a gravestone on her grave. Not a big celebration, but it's a reason."

"When is this?"

"In a couple of days I think. I'll find out."

"Okay. And, thanks, Ahn. For all the help."

"You got it."

Kam Wah came out of the smoking room and pointed down the walk way.

"I checked and your flight leaves at Gate 68. It's this way."

"This airport is so damn big it should have shuttle buses."

"These moving walks are good enough. You haven't said what your business is in Harbin."

"The family is putting a gravestone on her grave. I wanted to be there for that."

It was a lame explanation, but the only one I had.

"That's long way to go for a gravestone ceremony."

"It's something I have to do."

"Something you have to do? Are you going to tell me the real reason you are going to Harbin?"

"It's not something I want to talk about."

"Is it going to be the same as the affair with the Korean girl and her brother? Will this be a problem with the North Koreans, as it was with that Choi?"

"I don't know, Kam Wah. It seems that everything in the past year started with that girl and her brother. I'm hoping this trip will bring all of that to a close."

"I know it has to do with the Manchu woman who was killed. You must remember, this is China. It is a big thing to take matters into your own hands."

"I know."

"As I have told you, our influence does not go too far beyond Beijing. I do not know what it is like in Harbin. I only have business contacts there – with the yarn people. I don't think they are that powerful, but I can contact them if necessary. Do you have connections there?"

"I have several very good personal contacts."

"I know I cannot stop you from doing what is on your mind and I know you believe it is something you must do. I can only caution you to take care. You must keep in close contact with me. It is important."

"I will. Not to worry."

"Are you coming back here or Guangzhou?"

"If I can I'll come to Guangzhou. I'll call and let you know."

He walked with his head down and hands behind his back.

"When you come back, we can talk about a change in your life."

"Kam Wah, I don't need a wife."

"I am serious now. This is not just passing conversation. Your life is rootless at the moment. You need a solid foundation."

"A solid foundation?"

"It is a natural need that must be filled. It is the *Yin* and *Yang* of nature. All things follow this principle. You've been alone too long."

I had to agree. The past year had not been good times and BJ's death could have triggered some of these unstable feelings – but it was more than that. Was it because I was getting to that age when I felt I didn't have much to show for my life. Other than my four children, that I could be accused of abandoning, there really wasn't too much of value in my life. Kam Wah was probably right. I should think about changes.

"I understand. When this matter is finished, we can talk."

"I worry about this business in Harbin."

Kam Wah, Roger, and Andre all would think what I was planning to be foolish. Should I listen to old friends who had my best interest at heart? Ahn and Kevin were more than willing to help, even though they knew what I had in mind was reckless. They also were good friends and willing to give me all their support. Different perspectives. Different values. Whatever. I was committed and determined to do this.

"I know and I appreciate your concerns."

We walked in silence. There was nothing more to say.

"Well, here's the gate. Thank you for coming out here."

"Not a problem."

"Tell everyone hello."

"They expect you to come and tell them yourself."

"I will."

He stood with his hands behind his back. He was as serious as I have ever seen him. Not angry, but very concerned. He knew about Harbin and the search for BJ's killer. Without my telling him, he also knew that somehow I had found the killer. He guessed what I was planning to do. He waited a moment, wanting to be certain I was listening.

"There is a Chinese saying. Before you began a journey of vengeance, dig two graves."

44

Yasha booked me in First Class, which should have made the trip easier, but I was on edge. I tried to sleep, but couldn't. The plane was almost full, so it took about a half an hour to clear immigration and customs at the Beijing airport. I waited in the taxi queue for fifteen minutes and the ride into the city took longer than usual, making me impatient. It started to rain. I was not dressed for rain. These insignificant things began to aggravate me. Obviously, I was anxious about Harbin.

When I registered at the hotel, I noticed my reservation was starred. I learned this meant I had a room up grade. The clerk informed me that I was assigned an executive room. It had a king sized bed and a giant bathroom. All the plush extras were included and the mini-bar was well stocked. I was very appreciative of Chang's influence, but didn't look forward to paying the bill. It was a very expensive room.

After a shower I decided to go to the bar. I was impressed that the bartender remembered me from my last visit. Bartenders are unique people with prodigious memories. I was even more amazed when he asked if I wanted a single malt scotch drink. I said I did.

Sipping the scotch, I knew that the closer I got to Harbin the more anxious I would be. I no longer had to ask who killed BJ. I would actually meet the person responsible for her death. He was no longer a vague image without form. This person was real and I wanted to kill him.

After two more drinks I signed the tab and went up to bed. I was tired and fell asleep while watching the news on television. I had another dream just before I woke. In it I saw my father and mother. They were on their way to some place, maybe to church. My mother was a good Presbyterian, but my father was not a tried and true follower of the Christian faith. They were getting into the blue four-door Nash sedan I remembered so well. My sisters and brother were playing in the large bare yard where the cars and trucks parked. I called out to my parents, as they drove away. Then I shouted at my sisters and brother. No one heard me. I yelled again and that woke me.

The television was still on. I was in the floating world – nothing seemed to be real. It was seven o'clock in the morning and I was in the Beijing Palace Hotel. Tonight I would be in Harbin.

Two hours in the gym helped ease my tensions and a long shower restored some of my emotional stability. I went down to the coffee shop. At the entrance I found a stack of the Asian edition of the Wall Street Journal and took a copy to read. I ordered a cup of coffee and some toast. I had read through most of the paper when my cell phone chimed.

I didn't recognize the number on the small screen, but it was a Beijing prefix.

"Hello."

"Hello. This is Lai. Mr. Chang said you were at the Palace Hotel."

"Well, good morning, sir."

"Are you staying in Beijing long?"

"No. Just on my way through."

"When are you leaving?"

"I leave tonight."

"What time?"

"Flight leaves at 8:35."

"That gives us time to have an early dinner."

"Sounds fine."

"I'll come to your hotel about five. We can have a bite and I'll drive you to the airport. Would that be convenient?"

"Yes. That would be fine."

"Good. I'll see you at five."

"At five."

There was obviously a close tie between Chang and Lai. Did they belong to the same government agency? An intelligence agency or a security group? Whatever it was, they had considerable power. Was Lai meeting with me because he knew why I was going to Harbin? Whatever Chang knew, Lai knew. But, what, exactly, did they know?

Per his word, Chang came into the hotel lobby at eleven. He gave me a warm welcome and led the way to the car waiting outside. Liu was standing next to the car with the rear door open. He greeted me with a word of welcome and a handshake. As before, Chang and I rode in the back seat.

"I thought you might like to have Peking duck today," he said.

"Sounds wonderful. It's been several years since I've had Peking duck."

The restaurant was world famous and had been serving Peking duck for a hundred years. The last time Kam Wah and I had eaten there was two years ago. The manager met us at the entrance and led us to a private room. This was unusual. Chang and I had always eaten in the regular dinning areas at our prior meetings. It was normal for Kam Wah to have a private room, but not Chang.

"You've been traveling a good deal this past month."

"Yes. I was in Vietnam assisting a company with a project."

"Did it work out?"

"A great deal of progress was made."

"And now you're off to Harbin?"

How did he know I was going to Harbin? I didn't tell him. I told him my plane leaves tonight, but not where I was going. Yasha made the reservations only yesterday. How much more did he know?

"Yes, I am."

"You know my brother lives in Harbin."

"Yes. I've met him at the funeral wake for the woman who was killed."

"I believe the family name is Ma."

I was certain he knew all about BJ's death. For all I knew, Superintendent Hong reported directly to him.

"Yes, it is. The family is erecting a gravestone at her grave. I plan to attend."

"Good. Your presence will be a comfort to her parents."

"It will also help me."

"I understand."

"By the way, Mr. Lai called today," I said.

"Ah, yes. I told him you were in Beijing. Will you have time to meet with him?"

Obviously, he and Lai were in continuous communication as I only told Chang yesterday that I was coming to Beijing. I had never seen them together, but they must talk often. Everyday? More than once a day?

"Yes. He has offered to drive me to the airport."

"Very good."

I gave him an update of the Pei affair and told him about O'Connor's role in the release of Ho Man Pei. I also explained how the Chicago Assistant District Attorney and the police helped. Names I mentioned, plus my comments about each of them, were duly noted by Liu in his blue notebook.

———

Towards the end of the lunch, Chang glanced at Liu. He rose and silently left the room. I thought the lunch was over and Liu had gone to take care of the bill. I was in for a surprise. About fifteen minutes after he left the room, Liu returned with a distinguished looking gentleman.

He looked to be about fifty years old and had a polished appearance. He wore a gray pin striped suit and a red tie. His hair was neatly combed and didn't show any gray. Was his black hair dyed? He wore rimless glasses. A ring was on his left hand ring finger and he had a Rolex watch on his wrist. I would imagine he had a Mont Blanc pen in his inside coat pocket. The unofficial uniform and accessories of a high ranking Chinese government official. Very neat and up to date.

As he approached the table, Chang rose to greet him. I automatically stood. They shook hands. Chang motioned toward the man, looking at me.

"This is Mr. Pei," he said. "I believe you know his son."

So this was the father of the wayward son whose face I had smashed, put on a plane, and told never return to America.

"Mr. Pei. A pleasure." I extended my hand.

"The pleasure is all mine." He looked directly at me and held my hand with both of his. "You have done me a great personal favor. I will not forget it."

"I'm pleased I could help."

Chang motioned to all and said, "Please, sit."

We sat down and Liu poured tea.

"Are you in Beijing for business?"

"No. I'm in transit, but stopped to have lunch with Mr. Chang. I'll be leaving tonight."

"That's unfortunate. When you visit Beijing again please set aside an evening so we can have dinner."

"Thank you. I will."

"Mr. Chang has told me you come to China often."

"Yes. In fact, this is my third trip this year."

"I hope your trips have been profitable."

"Only moderately so."

Except for his earlier comment about being in my debt, he never mentioned his son. He wanted to meet me to show his gratitude, but he was embarrassed because the reason he was in my debt was the shameful behavior of his son. He could only hope that sometime in the future I would need his help. There was no other way to repay me. In fact, he may never be able to repay me.

After thirty minutes of shop talk, Chang commented that he appreciated Pei taking the time to drop by to say hello. It was a signal to end the meeting. Pei looked at his Rolex watch and said he was late for an appointment.

We all rose and shook hands. Pei looked at me and held my hand with both of his.

"Thank you."

He released my hand, stepped back, and bowed. I returned his gesture with a bow. He nodded to Chang and Liu, turned, and left.

"He wanted to meet you and say thank you for what you did."

"He should know that there were others who were involved and without their help I couldn't have done much."

"He knows. But it was you who set it all in motion."

"I'm glad I could be of help."

It was almost two when we left the restaurant. When we reached the hotel, Chang and Liu both got out of the car to shake my hand. Liu went quickly back to the car and held the door for Chang. Chang stopped before he got in the car and turned to me.

"I hope your business in Harbin goes well. If for any reason you need any help, please call me."

He looked at me for a long moment before entering the car. I wondered if Chang knew what my business in Harbin really was. Why not? He knew everything else.

45

THE MEETING WITH LAI would take up the rest of the afternoon, so I decided to check out. I packed my bag and went down to the reception desk. It was four-thirty when I asked the clerk for my bill. I thought I would have a problem because it was two hours past the regular check out time.

"Your bill has been taken care of, sir."

"What?"

"Your bill has been paid."

"Paid? By whom?"

"It was prepaid when the reservation was made yesterday."

Chang booked the room, or as he put it, had it arranged. Did he pay for the room? It was more likely Pei who paid the bill. Whoever paid, it was appreciated. The cost of the suite was more than five hundred US dollars a day. But, with a discount for the right people, the price could be as low as two hundred fifty. I'll never know because I wasn't given a receipt. I went out to the lobby and found a seat on a sofa facing the entrance.

A good time for people watching. One of my favorite pastimes. There were many foreign business men and women who were finishing a day of meetings. In the late afternoon, they were looking forward to cocktails and time to relax. A few ladies of the evening were getting an early start, hoping to latch on to a foreigner who was tired and needed cheering up. A willowy lady caught my attention and started toward me. I smiled and shook my head no. She smiled back, waved with a flicker of her fingers, and went into the bar to continue her hunt.

Lai arrived a few minutes before five. He was dressed in his normal white shirt and black trousers with his sleeves rolled up to his elbows. He wore dark glasses, not ultra stylish, but up to date modern. He spotted me at once and came over with his outstretched hand.

"Welcome to Beijing."

"Hello, Mr. Lai."

"Have you checked out?"

"Yes, I have."

"It's a bit early for a full dinner and you probably had a good lunch with Mr. Chang. So, why don't we have afternoon tea?"

"That sounds fine."

"Come. My car is parked right outside."

He led the way out of the lobby to a white Geely four-door sedan. I assumed it was an agency car. We drove for a half an hour to a neighborhood teahouse that served the Beijing version of Guangzhou *dim sum*. We were probably thirty minutes from the airport. It was quiet and not crowded. He was a smoker and places such as these were convenient for him because major hotels and many restaurants in China had banned smoking.

We talked about Yao Ming and American basketball and soccer matches being played in Kuala Lumpur, Malaysia. After a few tasty dishes and several cups of tea, the topic shifted to other business.

"Are you still involved with military equipment?"

"Yes."

"Here in China?"

"No."

"Have you been in contact with the person who wanted to buy the gas masks?"

"No. Is he involved in another project?"

"Not that I know. But whatever he does will be carefully monitored."

"I see."

"You're going to Harbin, Mr. Chang said."

"Yes."

"He said it was a personal matter."

"Yes, it is."

"Is there anything I can be assistance with?" he asked.

"Thank you, but it's not that important."

"There has been some trouble in Harbin and I was told you might be connected with it somehow."

"Trouble?"

"A woman with whom you had a close relationship was killed. The police think she was murdered."

"Yes. According to Hong, evidence seems to indicate that."

"Some think it was related to the death of a North Korean secret policeman who you had a run in with."

"Well, the Harbin police said there might be a connection."

"What do you think happened?" he asked.

"I only know what the police have told me about the incident."

"I've read Superintendent Hong's report."

"Well then, you know what I know."

"The Superintendent is a very competent police officer. He will find the killer."

"I hope so."

"You can rely on the police doing their job and finding the guilty party."

"Yes," I said half heartedly.

He looked at me and smiled.

"I don't think you are totally satisfied with what the police can do. Are you thinking of some individual American style vigilante action?"

He was very direct. But, I expected that from Lai.

I voiced a loud "Hah," and laughed.

"I'm surprised you think I can or would do anything of the sort."

"I think you can try and maybe do some damage. Whether you will or not remains to be seen. I know your relationship with the woman was serious."

"You need not be concerned about me. I will pay my respects at her grave site and depart a much sadder man."

"I'm sorry for your loss. I'm confident that Hong will find whoever is responsible."

I looked at my watch. It was seven o'clock. "I'm sorry, but I think I better get going. My plane leaves in little over an hour."

"Not to worry. You'll not miss your flight. We have time." He looked around for the waiter. "They have a special dish here you must try."

He signaled the waiter and held up two fingers. The waiter brought another dish.

The dish was a meat and vegetable filled fried dumpling.

"In America we call this a pot sticker. It's a very popular dish."

"Really?"

We ate the pot stickers and sipped more tea. I was getting anxious about the time and looked at my watch. He noticed my nervousness and smiled.

"I believe your plane leaves at 8:35 PM."

"Yes."

"Trust me. You have plenty of time. "

After another cup of tea, he waved at the waiter to bring the bill. He paid and when we left the restaurant it was a quarter to eight. I checked my watch again and estimated the time I had left. After the drive to the airport, which could take up to thirty minutes, there was customs and immigration to go through. I was certain I was going to miss my flight.

Lai came out of the restaurant, looked around, and spotted the uniformed officer who was parked across the street. He called him over and apparently gave him his orders.

I didn't think it was pure chance that a patrolman would be there at that precise moment. So, was this all planned? With the police car leading the way, we arrived at the airport at ten minutes after eight.

The patrolman parked at the curb and Lai pulled up behind him. Over my objections, he took my bag and led the way to the boarding entrance. We didn't go through the screening process or immigration. We went directly to the boarding gate.

The passengers had already boarded the plane and an attendant was putting tickets and boarding passes away. She looked up when Lai came to the boarding gate. It was eight-thirty.

Lai showed his identification card again and explained to the attendant that my name was on the passenger list. The attendant checked the list and found my name. She gave me a boarding pass with my name and seat number on it.

"I hope you have a pleasant flight."

"I didn't think I would make it," I grinned.

He put out his hand and then put his other hand over mine, and smiled.

"Please let me know if I can be of any assistance. You have my number. Do not hesitate to use it."

"Thank you."

I picked up my bag and walked to the cabin door. I turned and saw him standing with his hands behind his back. He smiled and waved. I waved back.

Both Lai and Chang were the ultimate mystery men. The inscrutable ones who knew a million secrets I would never know.

46

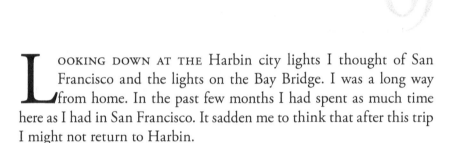

Looking down at the Harbin city lights I thought of San Francisco and the lights on the Bay Bridge. I was a long way from home. In the past few months I had spent as much time here as I had in San Francisco. It sadden me to think that after this trip I might not return to Harbin.

It was the rainy season and that helped to keep the weather cool. It had been raining steadily that day.

Ahn was standing at the edge of the crowd that had gathered to meet arriving passengers. He waved as I walked through the crowd.

"I booked a room at the Fortune Hotel. It's a five star hotel. Close to the train station and an easy drive to the airport."

"Good. How's the family?"

"Everybody is doing fine. Soonie asked if you'll come to dinner again."

"I would like to. We'll see."

"I know you'll be busy. Told her maybe."

"There are many things I need to know. We can talk more when I get checked in, but, I want to know now, who is the killer?"

"There are two brothers. Names are Jung Hee and Jung Sam. Jung Hee is the oldest. Last name is Shin. They have a business in Changchun but they live with their families in Jilin City. Their parents and sisters live in Musan, across the border in North Korea."

"They have trucking business similar to mine. Changchun manufacturers make auto parts and the Shin brothers make deliveries of these parts and other items to Harbin about twice a month. I checked their schedule and they were making deliveries on the day before she was killed. The delivery route that day was the same route they always use. They made six stops. Usually they finished their deliveries by four in the afternoon and are gone after that. Two of the customers said they saw the truck again the next day. They thought it strange that they were in Harbin on a Saturday. They were sure it was them because the truck had a Jilin license plate. The character for Jilin province and the letter A is for Changchun vehicles. So, people know that truck.

"Customers here know their business address and phone number because they order products by phone. The receipt for cash payments has a company address in Changchun. I went down to Changchun to check out their business place. From Harbin it takes about an hour and forty-five minutes by train.

"I told them I was in the market for a used truck and asked if they wanted to sell theirs. They were interested. I checked out the truck and found dents and paint on the front fender and on the grill. I asked them about that. They said they had an accident a couple of days ago.

"I asked if the accident was in Harbin, because there has been quite a few lately. They said no. They backed off and didn't want to talk about it any more."

"You're sure about the truck?"

"Yes. The paint on the bent fender and grill was the same color as her car. I went to the Harbin police garage where they keep vehicles they've impounded and double-checked the rear damage and paint. It was the same."

"How did you get into the police garage?"

"Told them I was looking for truck parts. They have trucks and cars that were impounded several years ago. They really didn't care."

We drove into a broad driveway leading to the front of the Fortune Hotel. Ahn parked his taxi in a space set aside for not-in-service taxis. When I had finished registering, we rode the elevator to my room on the eleventh floor.

It was touted as a five star hotel and proved to be just that. A large king sized bed, spacious bathroom, television, Internet, two phones in the bedroom and one in the bathroom, and a well stocked mini-bar. It was an expensive room.

––––––––––––––––––

"A fancy room. Much fancier than the Victory or Shangri-La."

"I got a twenty percent discount," Ahn said.

"That's good news. How about a beer?"

"Okay."

I got two Sapporo beers from the refrigerator and opened a bag of chips.

"What do you know about these brothers?"

"Jung Hee is the oldest. About forty-one or forty-two years old. The younger brother, Jung Sam, is four or five years younger. Both are married and have children. Jung Hee's wife is Korean, but Jung Sam's wife is Chinese. They've lived in Jilin for over fifteen years. They set up a business in Changchun about ten years ago. They have one truck and haul freight from Changchun to Jilin and other towns near the border. They've been delivering auto parts and other goods to Harbin for about two years now."

"Is their business big?"

"About average for a one truck business. From what I saw at their office, it was not too busy. They handle everything themselves. They don't have any clerical help or a mechanic to help maintain the truck."

"Why would they do this?"

"Might be several reasons. I got information on them from people I know in the taxi business in Changchun. They have family in Musan. Parents are still alive and they have two sisters. One is married. They also have an uncle who works for the North Korean government. I don't know as what. Only that the brothers talk about a relative on a high level of government. I don't know if this is true, but they have close family ties in North Korea."

"Could be a threat against their family. Maybe the uncle put pressure on them."

"Possible. There is talk that they are looking to buy a new truck and expanding their business to Harbin. Also develop new business in Shenyang. They talked about going as far south as Dalian. So there may have been promises made for new business."

"Would they kill an innocent woman for a chance to expand their business?"

"New opportunities to expand their business along with political and physical threats to their family in Jilin and Musan might be more than enough. They're not nice guys. When I was there, they weren't friendly. I was told they're drinkers and do some whoring. They had a low income business for a long time and are just now getting ahead. I don't think the family in Musan has ever had anything, so it hasn't been an easy life. Might be simple to manipulate them."

"So they're the ones."

"Yes, I'm sure they are."

I finished my beer and went to the refrigerator.

"Another beer?"

Ahn shook his head no. I opened one for myself.

"Okay. Now there are some details to take care of. I need a gun. Can you find a dealer who sells guns? The Russians, Japanese, and Chinese warlords have been here for over hundred years. There has to be a dealer left over from the old days."

"I know someone who might know someone."

"Good. I'll pay whatever it takes. But, I want to personally make the buy. No middle man."

"Okay."

"I want to be low key for the next few days. The reason I'm here is to attend the gravestone ceremony so other than that, I'm just looking for some business opportunities. By the way, when is the ceremony?"

"In three days. But, may be postponed if there's a heavy rain. This is the rainy season in Harbin and sometimes it can come down pretty hard."

"I'm sure Hong will know about the gravestone ceremony."

"He keeps track of these things."

"Well, it's getting late. Sorry about taking all your time."

"Not a problem. I'll be back tomorrow morning about nine."

"I'll be in the lobby or restaurant. Come on. I'll go down with you. I'm going to get a drink in the bar."

I walked Ahn to the hotel entrance and came back to the bar.

There were two men sitting at a booth with two ladies who were being paid for their time and services. The men were Japanese. The women were either Chinese or Korean. They were not boisterous, but laughing, as most businessmen do when they're out drinking and paying for the company of women. At least they weren't singing with a *karaoke* mike.

The bar stools were empty. Not a lot of late night drinkers. I took a stool towards the end of the bar where I could see behind me and to my right in the giant mirror.

"Just check in?" the bartender asked.

"Yes."

"First one's on the house. What'll you have?"

"You have *Yoichi* scotch?"

"Yes, we do. So, you know your scotch."

"I'll have the first one neat."

He poured me a good shot and put a bowl of nuts on the bar. His name tag said his name was Henry.

"Are you Korean, Henry?"

"Yes, I am."

Were all the bartenders in Harbin hotels Korean? Why not?

"So am I. Here's to all the good guys, Henry."

I waved my glass at him and took a swallow. Just as I remembered, it was an excellent scotch.

"Business looks kinda slow tonight," I said as I looked around the lounge.

"That time of the week. And hotel bars are not as popular as the nightclubs."

"Not too many guest this time of year, I guess," I said.

"It's not as good as in the winter when we have the ice shows, but it's not too bad. This is the rainy season and it's warmer. Are you staying long?"

"No. Just a couple of days." I finished the scotch and pushed the glass toward him. "I'll have another."

I glanced up at my image in the mirror and thought how old I looked. I certainly felt old. Is this how old people look and feel? Am I up for what I had in mind? Whatever, it was time to get some sleep.

I finished my drink, signed the tab, and started out of the lounge.

One of the women in the booth looked at me and smiled. She raised an eyebrow. Probably drew a loser from the client pool and hoped to score with someone else. A good-looking lady. Not too flashy. Nicely dressed. A seasoned pro. I winked at her. She smiled.

47

IT WAS AFTER SEVEN when I woke. I put on a T-shirt, gym shorts, and sneakers, and went up to the gym. A woman and a man were working out. The woman was Japanese and the man was a European. Probably German. Both were serious gymnasts and worked diligently on the machines. I got on a treadmill and walked steadily for an hour. I spent another half hour on the stepper. It was a good workout.

A long hot shower and shave helped me feel fresh and clean. I called house keeping to pick up my laundry and made myself a cup of coffee. I turned on the television news. I went to the window and looked down at the city below. The weather was clearing and partly sunny. But that could change at any time because, as the weatherman said, July was the rainy season.

I thought about how Ahn found the Shin brothers. He did a great job. Still, I had to prove the Shin brothers were really the ones who killed BJ. And finding the person who put out the contract was as important as finding the killers. Was it a North Korean agent? Didn't seem likely. The most reasonable answer was that it was someone who was a part of the Korean community. A North Korean mole?

If BJ was murdered because of her ties to me, I assumed that I was also a target. I wondered if they knew I was back in Harbin.

A few minutes after ten I went down to the restaurant and waited for Ahn. The restaurant was only partially full. I got a seat over looking the street. The hotel was only a few miles from the train station and some of the people rushing about were probably headed there. Most either carried umbrellas or wore plastic rain covers. Rainy days were always a favorite time for me, especially if I was sitting in a nice dry place where I could watch the street scene.

Ahn was right on time.

"Want some breakfast?"

"No thanks. Had breakfast at home."

"If you don't mind I'll get something to eat."

"Of course. You want to go out or eat here."

"Here is fine. I don't want much."

I ordered a continental breakfast and Ahn had a cup of coffee.

"Did you get a good nights rest?"

"Yes. The room is very comfortable. I also used the gym this morning. This is a real five star hotel."

"There are two five star hotels near by, but this one gave the biggest discount."

"Every bit helps."

The waiter brought my breakfast. The croissant was flaky and very nice. I ate it with butter and honey.

"I talked to a friend who knew how to get in touch with someone who might provide what you want."

"You know the person who deals in this?"

"No. I only know this friend who might know."

"Might know?"

"Everything is maybe. No one says it's this or that. Only maybe. But maybe usually means it can be done."

"Of course there's always a price for the connection."

"Money was not mentioned, but my guy has to be paid."

"How much?"

"For this kind of contact could be up to five hundred US. But, this is an old friend, so I think three hundred is okay. I've done favors for him."

"Done."

"I told my friend I would call if you wanted to deal. He'll get in touch with the source and let me know where to go."

"Make the call."

"Okay."

Ahn got up and walked to the lobby, dialing his cell phone. He walked back and forth and stopped when the call was answered. He turned to the wall and spoke into his cell phone. He came back and waved at the waiter for more coffee.

"He'll call me."

"Okay. We wait."

"Will you tell the Ma family you're here?"

"Not yet. I'm waiting to see what Hong will do."

"He may not think it's important that you're here."

"Oh, I think he does. I don't want him to come looking for me if I'm in Changchun. So, I'll call him today and set up a meeting."

Ahn's cell phone rang. He flipped the lid and nodded at me. He didn't speak, only listened. He took out his pen and wrote on his palm, snapped the lid shut, and checked his watch.

"I have an address. It'll cost two hundred dollars just to meet the dealer. I don't know what the piece will cost. I was warned. He will shoot you if he thinks you are not on the up and up. No explanation or reason given. He'll kill you on the spot."

"Sounds fair. When do we meet this dealer?"

"In one hour. If you are not there in exactly one hour, you get nothing." He looked at this watch. "It was eleven-thirty when I hung up. You have to be there exactly at twelve-thirty."

"You have the address?"

He showed me his hand. The address was written on his palm.

"I have to go up to my room and get some money. It'll take a few minutes."

I waved at the waiter and signaled for the check.

"Go. I'll get this." Ahn waved me off.

I went to the lobby and waited impatiently for the elevator car. The ride to the eleventh floor seem to take forever. I rushed into the room and opened the room safe. I took out two thousand dollars. It took another six or seven minutes to get down to the lobby.

Ahn was waiting by the front entrance. We went down the steps and out to the street where he had parked the taxi. We were cutting this close. If we missed the time deadline, we would have to ask for another meeting time. Maybe the dealer wouldn't meet again.

At exactly twelve-twenty-nine Ahn double parked in front of a two story building and pointed to a door.

"That's it."

"Okay."

"I'll be parked across the street."

I opened the door and heard a bell tinkle. As I walked through the door a clock chimed. It was twelve-thirty.

It was not a large store. There were three counters that formed a U, with the sides extending to the left and right as one entered the store. A curtain hid an entry to the back. The counters were glass and contained all kinds of odds and ends. Antique dealers would love this place. There were toasters, hand held mixers, an old electric coffee maker, an electric can opener, an old radio next to a more up to date one, an electric razor, several different brands of fountain pens, and dozens of other personal items, many over twenty-five years old. Some of the items, like the cuff links and pocket watches, were probably made before the Japanese invasion.

A variety of clocks hung on the wall – some were electric and others were battery powered. A few were manually wound. They all showed a different time. Only one large clock's hands were at twelve-thirty. It was the one that chimed.

48

HE CAME THROUGH THE doorway, brushing aside the curtain. He placed his hands on the counter and looked at me. There was no doubt that he was a Russian. About sixty years old, he was a mountain of a man. At least six feet four inches tall and weighted in the neighborhood of three hundred plus pounds. He presented an intimidating figure.

His face was framed by wind blown white hair, bushy eyebrows, and a heavy gray beard on his cheeks, chin, and neck connected to the flowing moustache that covered his upper lip. His clear blue eyes stared intently into people's faces. He wore faded blue overalls over a blue, long sleeve denim shirt. He looked as if a Hollywood make up artist had created him.

Dense hair covered the back of his large hands and I imagine the rest of his body as well. He was smoking a cigarette that almost disappeared in his hairy face. I wondered if he had ever set fire to his beard when lighting a cigarette.

He looked out the window to be certain that no one was with me. "What you want?" he finally asked.

"I was told you might have a special item I need."

"Special item?"

"I was told if I came to this place exactly at twelve-thirty I could buy a hand gun."

He put out his cigarette in the large glass tray on the counter and brushed some ashes off the counter. He looked intently at me and stroked his beard. He was making an assessment. A Korean from America who wants to buy a gun, he was told. Why does a Korean from America in Harbin want a gun? Was he going to kill somebody? Very dangerous business for Americans to have a gun in China. Was okay, the contact had said. Well, he came on time. Does he have the up front money?

"You pay two hundred US dollar, now."

I took the money from my coat pocket and took two hundred dollar bills from the roll. I held the money and looked at him.

"Are we going to do business?"

"Depends."

"No. I don't want to hear depends. Yes or no. I don't want any bullshit. I want to buy a gun. Do you have one?"

He looked at the money and back at me. He decided to do business.

"*Da*." He nodded.

I pushed the two hundred dollar bills toward him. He picked up the money and put the bills in his shirt pocket.

"What kind you want?"

"An automatic. If you don't have one, I'll take a revolver. I will test it to make sure it is working properly. And fifty rounds of ammunition."

"Make?"

"Does not matter if the piece is in excellent working order and ammunition is available. Also, I want a silencer."

"Have three automatics. One, Browning Hi-power 9mm. Is made in Belgian. Has thirteen round magazine. Second, Russian Markarov PM. Problem with Markarov PM. Use special cartridge. 9.3mm. Designed this way so if enemy captured can not use. For you, best is Type 67 silencer made by Chinese. Type 67 use 7.65mm caliber cartridge in nine round clip. Weight two thirds less than original Type 64. Have only one model silencer. Fits Browning. With the Chinese 67 don't need silencer."

The Browning was the best weapon of the three. More dependable and used a 9mm cartridge. But the silencer would extend the barrel at least six inches and was an extra item to carry. The Russian Markarov PM was unusual because of the special caliber cartridge it used. There were hundreds of these on the market in Eastern Europe. But, no silencer. The Chinese 67 was a unique piece. I had heard about the built in silencer but never fired one. For my needs, it was the best bet.

"I'll try the Type 67."
He came around the counter, looked out the window, and locked the front door.
"Come."

He led the way through the curtains into the back room. There was a stairway that went up to the second floor. Probably led to his living quarters. A large closet was against the far wall. He opened the doors of the closet and removed the back panel, revealing a five by four foot opening. He motioned me to enter. I stepped into the opening and he squeezed in after me and closed the closet doors.

A stairway led down to a dug out basement. He switched on the lights, revealing a space about fifteen by ten feet. A corridor about fifteen feet long extended out from the space. It smelled musty. There was also a lingering smell of gunpowder. He went to an old metal safe, about two feet square, and turned the combination. The lock clicked and he opened the door. There were several weapons inside the safe. He picked one up and handed it to me.

"You know this pistol?"
"I have not used it."
"Listen closely. I say only once. Type 67 is new version of Type 64. Semiautomatic or manual single shot. Is silencer use for assassination work. Is original silenced weapon, not adaptation of non-silenced design. Use 7.65mm Type 64 ammunition developed for Type 64. Ammunition is low power, so little noise. Range point blank to fifteen meters. Used for very close work.

"Barrel is different. Silencer barrel is thin steel case. Inside is a steel mesh and baffles. Slows down and cools muzzle blast. You see how barrel made. This design have blowback mechanism. When the lock mechanism engaged becomes manual operated magazine fed weapon, so no sound of recoiling slide. No case ejection. Cartridges feed from single stack. Magazine holds nine rounds. You want you can try."

He handed me a magazine. I put the magazine in, pulled the bolt back, and released it, putting a cartridge into the chamber. There was no target at the end of the corridor so I fired at the dirt wall. I fired three rapid rounds and then three more. Even in the tightly enclosed area, the sound was muffled.

"Wait." He engaged the lock mechanism. "Now you fire one at a time."

It became a manually operated weapon, very much as a revolver. I fired the remaining three shots one at a time. Manually ejecting the shell each time. Not the smoothest piece made but it certainly suited my purposes.

"You have ammunition?"

"Yes, but in short supply. Can give you thirty-five rounds."

"Okay."

"We go up." He pointed to the stairs.

He picked up the gun and a box of ammunition and pointed me to the stairs. I went through the closet and into the room. He followed and put the closet back in place. He closed the doors to the closet and motioned me into the store. He directed me to the other side of the glass counter and placed the gun and ammunition on the counter top.

"Gun price one thousand US dollar. Include ammunition."

The average price for a gun in the Chinese black market was about three hundred US dollars. Since I was an American the price would be higher. Still, a thousand dollars was exorbitant.

"I know the price of black market guns in China. I'll pay three hundred US dollars."

He stared at me and pulled on his beard.

"You know? How you know?"

"On the outside, I deal in weapons."

"This is China, not like outside."

True. This was China and it was illegal to possess any kind of firearm. Only authorized individuals holding hunting permits are allowed to purchase firearms. Illegal possession or sale of firearms meant a minimum of three years in prison. Use of guns in any crime was punished by execution. Even a replica is outlawed and sentences of up to twenty years are given for use of a gun replica in a crime.

"I don't have time to haggle. You want to do business? Say now."

"Five hundred and ammunition is free."

"Four hundred and ammunition is free. My last offer."

He pulled on his beard some more. With the two hundred up front the total would be six hundred dollars. Normally, he would sell it for three hundred and charge for the ammunition. Six hundred was a good day's work for him.

It was worth the money for me because finding a gun dealer who had reliable goods was difficult. But it was as difficult and dangerous for the Russian. He had to pay someone in the government to continue his arms business and that payment would be a regular one, over a long period of time.

"You accept? Say now or I'm leaving."

He looked at me and raised one eyebrow. Was I really was an arms dealer on the outside? Whatever, I had the cash and it would be a simple transaction.

"*Da.*"

With the three hundred for Ahn's contact I paid a total of nine hundred dollars for a piece that was probably really worth about two hundred and fifty dollars.

I counted out the four hundred dollars. He reached under the counter and brought out a small oblong shaped canvas bag. He placed the gun and cartridges in it, zipped it up, and handed it to me. He gathered up the money and put the bills into his overall pants pocket.

I picked up the bag and went to the front door. He came around the counter and unlocked the door, opened it, and stood aside. I walked across the street to where Ahn was parked and got in the car. It started to rain. As we pulled away from the curb I looked back at the store front door. He was standing there, hands in his pockets, staring after me.

49

IT WAS ABOUT ONE-THIRTY when we returned to the hotel. We went up to my room and I put the small bag in the room safe. Ahn waved off my offer of a beer. I opened a bottle of Tsingtao beer.

"I'm going to call Hong. Ask him to meet with me this afternoon. See if he's found out something since we last met."

"He may want to trade for information you might have."

"Are the Shin brothers well known here in Harbin?"

"Only people who have them deliver goods know them, but not well. No family ties or friends so they don't spend a lot of time in Harbin."

"Hong must have figured out the killer was from some other city. But he wouldn't have the time to do all that you did."

"True."

"Well, I'll call him now."

I called the central police station, gave the operator my name, and asked for Superintendent Hong. It was several minutes before he answered.

"Hello. I heard you were back."

"I hoped we could meet. Are you free for *yam cha*?"

"That sounds good. I haven't had time for lunch today. About two – two-thirty. Is that too late for you?"

"No. That will be fine."

"You're at the Fortune Hotel, correct?"

"Yes."

Of course, he knew which hotel I was at. All hotels were required to report foreigners who registered at their hotel.

"I'll come to pick you up."

"Do you want to eat at the hotel," I asked.

"Why don't we go to a quiet place, away from the hotel?"

"Okay. I'll meet you in front of the hotel."

"Good."

He sounded amiable.

"That's taken care of. Now, there's some things I'm going to need, Ahn. If you have time, you can get these this afternoon."

"What do you need?"

"I need a recorder. A very good one that can pick up voices clearly."

"No problem."

"Also need some strong plastic tape. Industrial grade."

"What else?"

"A cell phone – a throw away."

"That's easy."

"Good. Also need a Harbin-Changchun train schedule."

"Okay."

"If I'm going to travel by train, I don't want to be too easily noticed. Can you get me clothes like locals wear? And a hat. It's the rainy season so I'll need a raincoat or one of those yellow plastic sheets. And a pair of gloves. Thin ones. Like driving gloves. Pants and shirt and a jacket. Also, see if you can get a bag to carry these items. Here's money to get these things and three hundred dollars for your friend."

I gave him six hundred dollars.

"I'll be back later this afternoon," he said.

"About six? Call my cell phone number if you're tied up."

"Okay."

I went with him down to the lobby. I checked the money exchange rates at the hotel cashier station and bought three hundred US dollars worth of RMBs – about twenty-four hundred RMB.

Back in my room I sat looking out the window and thought about the trip to Changchun. I had never been there and so I wasn't familiar with street names or able to fix my location with known landmarks. I could hire a taxi and drive around where the Shin brothers had their business. Probably better to take a bus. Ahn would know which one to use. They lived in Jilin City, so a reasonable way to make certain they would be at their office in Changchun was to call and make an appointment.

A few minutes before two I went down to the lobby. The concierge stopped me and asked how my accommodations were and if there was anything I needed. I told him everything was fine and thanked him for asking. The doorman smiled, tipped his hat, and opened the door. Dark rain clouds were gathering over the city. Rain was forecasted. Heavy at times. It was the rainy season, so everyone said.

In a few minutes I saw Hong drive to the front of the hotel. He got out and came around the car, shook my hand, and opened the car door for me.

We went to a noodle shop that was filled with the pleasant smell of chicken/pork soup. The owner was a Korean. Hong introduced me and told the owner I was a Korean from America. This brought the owner's wife out from behind the counter to shake my hand. I was the first American to eat in their shop.

We found a table off to the side and soon two steaming bowls of pork noodles were brought to us. The owner himself delivered them. The soup was delicious. I wondered why they didn't serve *man du*, the famous Korean dumplings.

"How long do you intend to stay this trip?"

"I don't know. I'm going to attend the gravestone ceremony and visit some chicken farms. As you know, I deal in beta glucan, an immune additive to help fight off the bird flu. It was the reason I first came to Harbin."

"A long trip for just that."

"The gravestone ceremony helps to bring closure. And I can use the trip to see if there is any new business."

"I see." He didn't believe me.

"How is the investigation going?"

"We have some leads, but nothing definite yet."

"You think the killer is from out of town?"

"Possible."

"Anything definite?"

"No."

"You have her car and know how it was damaged. Maybe you can try to find a damaged truck."

"Do you have any idea how many trucks there are in Harbin and surrounding cities."

"Sounds hopeless."

"Difficult, but not impossible."

"Do you have any new thoughts about the motive? Or do you still think it involves me and Choi?"

"I cannot think of any other reason some one would deliberately smash into Ms. Ma's car. She had no enemies."

"You think the North Koreans hired someone to do this?"

"Also possible, but indirectly. Even they wouldn't be that open."

"Still, Choi's death is connected to this somehow."

"Yes, but proving it is another matter."

"If people from another city are involved how much more complicated will matters become?"

"Police in all cities cooperate in these matters. There is also a national police that can become involved. Similar to your FBI."

"Are they involved?" I asked.

"They're not directly involved yet. We don't have sufficient evidence pointing to any suspects. If there is a tie to the North Koreans the whole matter becomes an international affair and very complicated. But, we are only assuming."

"So, for now, there are only conjectures and suspicions."

Hong had nothing. He was groping in the dark.

"That's the nature of police work. We look for solid evidence. Sometimes we might feel something to be, but cannot prove it."

"Sounds like a dead end."

"Not always."

"Well, Superintendent Hong, it has been most enlightening. I do appreciate your candor."

He looked at me and sighed.

"Have you learned anything about this affair?" he asked.

"No. Only lots of speculations. My supposed involvement with Choi's killing seems to be a part of this. I also believe someone hired a person or persons to kill her."

He continued to stare at me. I returned his stare, then turned away and looked out the window. He heaved a sigh.

"I'll be frank. I think attending the gravestone ceremony is a ruse. Have you found out something? What is the real reason you are here?"

"I have been in America and most recently in Vietnam on business. How could I find out anything? Believe me, I am here to attend the ceremonies and check on possible business opportunities with chicken farms."

"It would not be wise to become involved in any way. I caution you as a friend and a policeman – do not become involved. I think you would get the same advice from your friends in Beijing."

"Do the people in Beijing know what is happening here?"

"People in Beijing know everything." He had a resigned look. The power of the central government was undeniable. "If you know something I am asking you to tell me."

"Right now, I'm no better informed than you are. We're both only making assumptions based on what we believe to be true but cannot prove. So what can anyone do about it?"

"I have to work within the system," he said.

"Well, I'm really only a bystander."

"And you must remain a bystander."

"Of course, there are times the spirit moves you to act," I smiled.

"That would not be wise."

"Spirits are difficult to control, Superintendent. You know, Ms. Ma used to talk about *karma* and things happen because they were meant to be."

"What does that mean?"

"Just that we weave the web that is our *karma*."

He shook his head and heaved a sigh.

"Forgive me, but that's all bullshit."

I laughed. He smiled at me.

"You're probably right."

He waved at the owner for the check.

"Please, allow me to treat you to this lunch."

"No. You are my guest here. This is Harbin, my town."

He paid and I thanked the owner and his wife for the wonderful lunch. They walked us to the door, bowed, and thanked us for coming.

Hong believed that I knew something and wasn't telling him. More than that, he was worried that I would do something rash. Just what did he think I would, or could, do?

We rode back to the hotel without much conversation. He parked at the entrance driveway and got out to shake my hand.

"I will be out of town tomorrow and part of the next day, but you have my cell phone number. You can call me any time – day or night."

"Thank you and good bye, sir."

At the top of the stairs I turned and looked back at him. He stared at me for a moment, then got in his car and drove off.

Choi's killing and BJ's murder had forged a bond of sorts between Hong and myself. Unfortunately, there were times when we were on opposite sides of the fence. This was one of those times.

50

AHN ARRIVED AT SEVEN o'clock with a large plastic bag containing the items I had asked him to get.

"I got two rolls of industrial plastic tape. I don't know how the clothes will fit, but they should be okay. I guessed at your shoe size, so these might be big. But better big than too small. The gloves are new – patent leather and form fitting. The recorder is the newest one on the market. The cell phone will work for about thirty minutes without a recharge, if you don't talk too long each time. This is the wire for a recharge. This yellow sheet of plastic with a hole in the middle is a poor man's rain coat. You put your head in the hole and it covers you pretty good. It's like all the others on the street. The hat is the kind everybody wears in the rainy season. Pull the rim down and it covers your face and keeps the rain off your face and neck."

"Looks great. Thanks."

I held up the shirt and pants against me. They seem to be the right size. I tried the jacket. It was a good fit. The shoes were a bit loose, but comfortable. I turned on the mini-recorder. It was a Korean made LG and had too many buttons for what I had in mind. I wondered who used all these fancy attachments. I never did. After a few trials and lots of mistakes, I learned what buttons to press.

"You have the telephone number for Shin's office?"

"Yes."

"You can call them tomorrow morning and make an appointment for late afternoon. If it's the last meeting of the day there won't anyone else coming in. I need time alone with these guys."

"Okay."

I spread the train schedule on the bed.

"Let's check the train schedule. I'm looking for a non-stop."

"There's one that leaves at 11:16 – train number D174. Gets to Changchun at 15:04 PM. It's about an hour and forty-five minutes ride. I took that one. Remember to get the soft seat ticket."

"If we can make an appointment for around five, it should work out. How much time do I need to get to their office from the train station?"

"Maybe forty minutes. I think the buses runs every twenty or thirty minutes. I rode the Number 18 bus that goes right by their office. Their office is at 73 Tongzhi Lu. You'll see an empty lot in back where they park a couple of trucks. There's a sign painted on the window. 'Tumen Transportation Company,' written in Korean and Chinese. You can't miss it. Watch for the street signs."

"Okay. Now, getting back."

"There are a couple of trains at night. One leaves at 21:03, gets to Harbin at 22:49. If you miss that one, the next one leaves at 22:23 and gets in at 01:09. No late non-stop trains coming back to Harbin."

"I'll try for the 21:03 train. If I miss that, the one at 22:23 will have to do. You have a taxi contact in the city, correct?"

"Yes. I have a number you can call."

"Well, that's it, then."

"Getting there isn't a problem. Coming back depends on what happens when you're there."

"That depends on what I find there. I don't know if there'll be other people around or just the two brothers."

"They don't have any clerks or other workers. They handle things themselves. It's not a big business."

"If it rains that'll be a help."

"I can go with you."

I hesitated and sighed.

"Ahn, you live here and have a family. I don't. Anyway, it's something I have to do alone. You've been involved enough as it is."

"I consider this to be family business."

"I'm pleased you think of this as family business, but if something happens to me, you're the only one who can take care of things. Here's a list of people and where to contact them if I don't make it. Names include my children in the US."

"I can handle that, but still, I would like to go."

"I know. But, not this time."

After all he has done to find the Shin brothers, did he have a right to go? I knew I would feel that way. But, he had too much to lose if things went wrong. Sorry, Ahn.

"Are you working tomorrow?"

"Depends. Why?"

"I'll need a back up story for tomorrow. I told Hong I was checking on chicken farms in the area. So, if anyone asks, tomorrow you and I would be driving around the country looking for chicken farms. But, except Yuan, I don't know any chicken farmers. Some other story might be better. Whatever, I have to be unnoticed tomorrow."

"Is Hong watching you?"

"He said he was going to be out of town the next two days, so he'll be busy. I don't think he has anyone following me."

"Well, I don't have to be anywhere special. Have some guys I can be with who will say what is necessary and I can disappear for awhile."

"Good. Might not need any back up story, but best to be prepared."

"Not a problem."

"Do you have time for a bite to eat?"

"I have to take the night shift tonight. One of my drivers has to take care of his wife. She's going to have a baby. Maybe already delivered."

"Okay. What time will you call the Shins?"

"After eight in the morning. If they can't make a meeting at five, may have to change your train schedule. Of course, if they're not available tomorrow, you'll have to go day after tomorrow."

"Well, let's hope they're available."

"I'll come to get you about nine-thirty. Don't wear these clothes. You can change at a small office I use sometimes."

"Good thinking. I don't want to go through the lobby dressed in this outfit."

"Think about my going with you."

"I have. See you tomorrow."

It would have been a great help to have him along and I was tempted to take him with me. But, this could turn into a fool's errand and Ahn doesn't need that kind of trouble.

It was almost eight and I was hungry. There was a large buffet offered in the restaurant but the dining area was crowded and noisy. I needed some solitude. I remembered the Korean noodle shop Hong took me to and decided to go there. I asked the doorman if he knew where that was. He thought he did, but would ask the taxi driver. The taxi driver knew. A light rain was falling.

The Korean owner and his wife were overjoyed to see me again. There were about six diners, probably regulars, having their dinner. I took a seat at the window table where Hong and I ate. I ordered pork noodles again.

The owner brought me a bottle of Tsingtao beer.

"Compliments of the house. For the first Korean from America to eat in our restaurant." He looked around and then said, "We know who you are. We heard about your problems."

"Thank you. I appreciate it."

"We are pleased you have come to our house."

He didn't comment on my last visit with police Superintendent Hong.

"Thank you, and thank you for the beer. It will go nicely with the wonderful noodles. By the way, I was wondering why you don't have *man du* on the menu."

"Ah, yes. Unfortunately, the filling for *man du* is expensive and takes too much time to prepare."

"I see."

"Are your parents from North or South Korea?"

"Father from Seoul and mother from Pusan."

"Ah. Then you know a different kind of *man du* from what we eat here and in North Korea. Also, the soup is different. "

"Well, your noodles are not too different from what I know."

"It is a mixture of north and south Korea, north and south Chinese, and a little bit Japanese and Manchu. I guess you can call it Harbin style." He laughed.

"Whatever, it's good."

"My wife makes the soup. She was born in Harbin but her parents are from Pyongyang."

"I see."

Pork noodles are very important in most Asian cultures. I thought about the various cultures involved with Harbin pork noodles. The noodle dish was a good mixture of cultures. The noodles were cooked al dente and the chicken and pork for the soup had been boiled for the exact amount of time. It was definitely Chinese and Korean.

There was double the usual number of barbequed pork slices in the bowl. Pays to know the owner.

The sky grew darker and soon ominous clouds began to drop their heavy load on the city. In a few minutes, the rain was coming down hard and large drops splashed against the window. People were running from one awning cover to another with whatever they could find to cover their heads. A few fortunate ones had umbrellas. Several customers came in and shed their wet coats. Some wore yellow plastic parka rain covers but others had nothing to ward off the rain. Most of the men wore hats, as did some women. Other women had scarves wrapped over their heads. I wondered why the locals were not better prepared for the rain. They must know this is the rainy season. Even I knew that. I hoped it continued to rain tomorrow.

Since I didn't know the daily routine of the Shin brothers, I had no idea of what I would encounter at their office. If both were there and they put up a fight, I may have to kill one or both of them. That didn't bother me. It was not a moral issue. But, from a practical point of view, if I killed one or both and was caught, the Chinese government would execute me as a murderer, which I would be.

I also wanted to tape a confession that they killed her. I wanted to know who contracted them to do the job. I had to be careful and not act in anger. Was it a busy neighborhood with people walking about? The silencer pistol was going to be a real help.

If Ahn arranged a meeting at five and things went my way, I could be finished before six. There would be a three-hour dead period, waiting for the train. If the police found the Shins before I left town, they would be looking for a person who was a stranger in the neighborhood. I needed a safe haven.

I remembered I knew someone in Changchun. Her name was Jin Yong and I met her in Harbin. She was the hooker with a name card. Would she help?

I thought I still had her name card somewhere in my wallet. I looked and found cards from people I rarely saw or heard from. Her card was there. Push came to shove, it was a place for me to hole up, and the in-between time could be spent with her. I didn't feel guilty about making use of her. It was expedient and a matter of survival, I said to myself. The same rationale I used often.

I took a deep breath and looked out the window. I saw my reflection in the rain splattered window and wondered who I had become. I had purchased a gun and planned to use it on two people I didn't know. Based on Ahn's information, I was convinced they were BJ's murderers. Without any proof I had begun a chain of events that could end up with one or two people dead. If things didn't go right, it would mean trouble for me with the government that no one could fix. Not Kam Wah, not even Chang or Lai.

It wasn't too late to forget this whole business. I could pay my respects at the gravestone ceremony and leave Harbin. But, I had committed myself to this. Was all of this worth my life? Maybe I was at the far end of reasonableness.

It was Hong's job to find them, but he might never find the killers. I believed somebody murdered her as a way to get at me. This had become my job because I rationalized that it was the right thing to do. Or was that just rationale for absolving myself from guilt? Neither was much of a reason to kill someone, but it was the only ones I had. Regardless, it was something I had to do. This was my *karma*.

I gave up trying to justify my motives. I paid for the noodles and received shouts of thank you from the owner and his wife. They invited me back and walked me to the door. Luckily a taxi was driving by and I waved him down. It was raining hard.

Henry saw me come into the lounge and had a glass of scotch waiting for me. I brushed off the rain and took the last empty stool at the end of the bar. It was a busy night and two waitresses were helping Henry with the crowd. The heavy rain kept most hotel guests from venturing out and the lounge was the most convenient place to hang out. I finished a second drink and went up to my room. I wanted to get away from the crowd and noise.

I put away the package of clean laundry and checked the television schedule. On top of the television was the brochure advertising massages in the hotel. They were open until midnight. A good idea. I went to the massage parlor and had a soothing rub down. The young woman working on me was from Liaoning. She hummed a Chinese song while doing her thing. It was a nice tune. I gave her an extra tip for the serenade.

After the fifty minute massage I went back to my room, showered, had a mini-bottle of gin, and got into bed. I laid awake for a long while. I hoped I was prepared for the coming day's work. If not prepared, whatever state I was in had to do.

51

A FTER A FITFUL NIGHT and only a couple of hours of sleep I woke
at five. The gym was not open until six so I made coffee and
watched the news on television. Rain was predicted. It was the
rainy season, the weatherman said. At six I went up to the gym and
worked out on a couple of different machines for an hour and a half.
Back in my room I went through my morning routine of showering,
shaving, and sending my laundry out.

It was time to prepare for my day. I loaded the magazine with nine
rounds and put the gun and the rest of the cartridges in the small sack
the Russian had given me. I stuffed them all in the tote bag. I checked
the clothes and shoes I would wear and put them into one of the hotel's
plastic laundry bags. I wore the jacket. By eight was I was packed and
ready.

I went down to the coffee shop. For some reason, I was hungry. I
ordered two scrambled eggs, hash brown potatoes, two slices of bacon,
and two pieces of toasts. More breakfast than I usually eat. It was what
Yasha might have. I thought about her again. I missed her.

Strange that I had stopped thinking about BJ as a person. She was
a memory and the reason, I told myself, that I was on my mission.
Memories from the past had become vague and the reason for my
vengeance was often blurred.

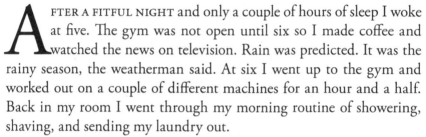

As I was finishing breakfast, my cell phone chimed. It was Ahn.

"I called the Shin brothers and made an appointment to meet them at four-thirty. I told them I wanted to hire them to make weekly deliveries to Shenyang. They're anxious to meet."

"Good."

"I'll be there in about thirty minutes."

"I'll meet you outside."

"Okay."

I went back up to my room and took two thousand US dollars out of the safe. It would be back up to the RMB I had. I thought about wearing the shoes Ahn had given me, but decided against that. I put them with the clothes into the laundry bag. The tote bag was just large enough to pack everything in it. I checked around the room once more and then went down to meet Ahn.

The door man saluted me with a good morning greeting. He opened the door and commented on the coming rain. The sky was gray and dark clouds were coming in from the northeast. It was going to be another rainy day. Why not? It was the rainy season.

Ahn was waiting. We drove to a small office about twenty minutes away. He unlocked the office door, and motioned me inside. It was space large enough for a desk and two chairs in the middle of the room. There was a telephone on the desk.

"There's a bathroom over there." He pointed to the back of the room. "You can change in there."

I went into the small bathroom and changed. I put my regular clothes in the laundry bag and came back into the office.

"You look like a local."

"I feel like one."

"Take Bus 18 from the train station. Watch for Tongzhi Lu. It's a major street. The bus will go right by the place. Number 73. Look for the company sign on the front window. There's a wide driveway on one side of the building. They park their truck and a pickup in the back. The large truck is the one I saw with dents and paint on the left front fender."

"How big is the office?"

"Not very big. There's a front office and a wall that separates it from a larger space in back. There's probably a bathroom back there. I'm sure there's a back entrance."

"Okay. One thing you should know. You remember the woman I met here in Harbin about a month ago? We gave her a ride to the train station. She's not hustling me and she knows I'm not a customer. But, if I have to wait several hours for a train she can keep me out of sight."

"Will she want to know why you're in Changchun?"

"I'm sure she'll ask."

"If something happens to the Shin brothers and news is out, she might connect you to them. Coincidences like the Shins getting hit and you showing up aren't easy to ignore."

"I know. But, it's a place I can go to. And I have a good feeling about her. Another alternative is the train station, but hanging around there for three hours may not be a good idea. I'll just have to see how it goes."

"I can drive down to get you."

"Not necessary. I'll be okay."

"Remember to buy the soft seat. It's almost a two hour ride and the hard seats are just wooden slats."

"Let's go." I put on my rain cover and hat.

The Harbin railroad station was busy and trains came and left every fifteen or twenty minutes. It was crowded and hundreds of people were departing or arriving. I went to the ticket counter and bought a ticket on the D174. A soft seat cost 98 RMB, about thirteen US dollars.

The train was on track seven. A woman train conductor punched my ticket as I boarded the second car. I had a window seat near the back. The soft seats were in cars that had air conditioning and smoking was not allowed. It was comfortable enough for two hours, but might not be for longer trips.

A few minutes after I was seated the car lurched forward and slowly rolled out of the station. I was on my way to Changchun.

———————————

D174 was a non-stop express train and arrived in Changchun right on time. A light rain began to fall as we pulled into the station. I walked out of the station and saw the bus parking area across the street. I found the sign for Bus 18. There was a short line under the sign, waiting for the bus to arrive.

After a fifteen minute wait a bus rolled in and unloaded passengers.

I followed the waiting passengers into the bus. They paid the fare in a coin machine next to the driver's seat. I didn't have change so I gave the driver a ten RMB bill. He took it and gave me change. I didn't know how much to pay. The passengers were impatiently waiting behind me so I dropped one *jiao* in the slot and hoped it was the correct fare. It was. I took a window seat in the fifth row.

There were no stops for about fifteen minutes. After that the bus stopped at every other cross street. About forty minutes later the bus turned right on to a wider street. At the corner was a street sign that read Tongzhi Lu. The numbers on the buildings were not all visible from the bus. After the second stop on Tongzhi Lu, I saw a one-story building with a wide driveway next to it. The number over the door was 73. "Tumen Transportation Company" was written on the window.

I waited until the bus made two more stops. On the third stop I got off. I pulled my hat down lower and merged into the mob of people dashing to find cover from the rain. The rain became heavier as I walked the three blocks back to Number 73. It was a few minutes before four-thirty.

52

I LOOKED IN THE rain splattered front window at Number 73. There was no light in the outer office so visibility was limited. I could make out a desk, a chair, and a phone in the office. A wall approximately five feet high divided the front and rear areas. There was a three feet open space in the divider wall without a door. A light was on in the back. I saw someone moving about. I put on my dark glasses and gloves.

I tried the door. It was unlocked. Fortunately, the door had a manual lock. I shut the door, turned the lock, and walked toward the opening in the wall.

"Hello. Anyone here?"

A man about five feet six inches tall, wearing jeans and a crimson T-shirt with Harvard University printed on it in yellow, came out of the back room. He was slightly built, probably not more than a hundred and thirty pounds. A pronounced feature was his large ears, protruding on each side of his head. He had a boyish face, smooth, and probably didn't need a daily shave. I assumed this was the younger brother, Jung Sam.

He paused, looked at me a moment, and frowned. He probably wondered why I was wearing dark glasses on a dark rainy day.

"Are you Jung Sam or Jung Hee?"

"I'm Jung Sam."

"I called earlier this morning for an appointment."

"Oh yes."

He remembered someone had an appointment today. But he

hesitated, wary and uncertain. I think the dark glasses bothered him. He backed away from me.

I looked into the backroom. He was alone.

He was standing in the entryway holding a clipboard. I came up to him very fast and hit him in the throat, knocking him down. He fell on his back, gasping, and grabbed at his throat with both hands. His eyes were bulging. He was choking and trying to swallow.

I rolled him over onto his stomach and taped his feet together. I sat on his back and pulled his right arm behind him. He tried to pull his arm back. I hit him on the side of his face. He stopped resisting and lay still. I crossed his left wrist over this right wrist and taped them together. When I was certain his hands and feet were firmly taped I rolled him on his back. I kicked him hard in his side. He let out a scream. I put a piece of tape over his mouth and kicked him again. I cracked one or two of his ribs. He made a muffled sound and fainted.

The back room had shelves full of spare auto parts and other products the Shins sold. Temporary plywood walls enclosed a toilet and sink in the right hand corner of the room. Two wooden chairs and a small table were in the center of the room. A desk lamp plugged into an extension cord provided the only light in the room. A door in the far wall led to the parking space in the rear of the building. There were no windows.

Jung Sam was beginning to regain consciousness. He was confused and didn't know what had happened. When the initial shock wore off, he felt the pain in his throat and side. He also became aware that his hands and feet were bound. He jerked his arms and legs and tried to sit up.

I dragged him to the far wall, next to the back door, and sat him up with his feet out in front of him. I wrapped tape around his knees and pulled his knees up against his chest. He was totally immobile.

I found an elongated tire wrench, about twenty-four inches long, used on truck tires. I leaned it against the wall next to the door.

I moved one of the chairs in front of him and straddled it. He was wide eyed, staring at me. He only saw sunglasses under a hat. The pain in his side had become acute. He was terrified, just as I wanted him to be.

About ten minutes later I heard a vehicle drive into the back parking area. It was Jung Hee in the pickup truck. I picked up the tire wrench and stood against the wall, next to the door. He came in and started to take his hat off. I hit him hard on his left foreleg with the tire iron and broke his shin bone. I slammed the door shut.

He let out a cry and fell forward. I sat on his back, grabbed his head with both hands, and smashed his face into the concrete floor. He let out a cry and tried to lift his head. I smashed his face into the floor again. He didn't move and fell silent. His nose was broken, as were several front teeth. His lips were split and bleeding. I taped his hands behind his back and did the same with his feet.

Jung Hee was dressed in a flannel shirt and regular trousers, much as I had on. He wore a hat and plastic coat with a zipper front. He was bigger than his brother, about five feet seven or eight inches tall and weighted at least a hundred and sixty pounds. He had a round chubby face that was marked with small scars. Probably the after effects of small pox. He had a full head of hair, black and coarse.

I dragged him next to Jung Sam and sat him against the wall. I taped his knees together and pulled them up against his chest. He was bleeding from his nose and mouth. He didn't yet fully feel the pain in his leg. He was regaining consciousness. Before he could speak, I taped his mouth. Jung Sam looked at him and at me. He was panic stricken. He wet his pants.

Several minutes later Jung Hee came awake. He looked frantically around the room and then realized his brother was tied up next to him. He could not imagine who I was or why I was doing this to them. Nothing made sense. The pain in his leg began to intensify. It was a nightmare of gigantic proportions.

When he appeared to be conscious enough to be aware of things, I reached into my tote bag and took out the gun. I inserted the clip, chambered a bullet, and put it in the manual mode. Both became frantic and pushed back against the wall, trying to get further away from the gun. For effect, I fired a shot between them. Bits of plaster sprayed on their faces. The gun was on the manual mode so I had to manually eject the shell. They were convinced that I did indeed have a real weapon. I wanted them to believe that I would kill them in a heart beat.

I took the mini-recorder out of the tote bag and set it on my chair between my legs. I didn't turn it on.

"Can you hear me? Nod your heads yes if you can hear me. Can you hear me?"

They looked at each other, and then back at me. They both nodded their heads.

I tapped the Jung Hee on the head with the gun. He looked up at me with wide, frighten eyes.

I spoke slowly, making certain my words were clear and distinct.

"I'm going to take the tape from your mouth. You will not speak except to answer my questions. I will ask you some questions and I want you to answer them loudly and clearly. If you do not, I will shoot you in various parts of your body or your brother's body. Do you understand me?"

He nodded yes. I leaned forward and took the tape from his mouth. He licked his lips and took a deep breath.

"Who are you? What do you want?"

I leaned forward and put the tape back on his mouth.

"You're supposed to only answer my questions."

I shot the younger brother's left ear. A small bit of the bottom part fell off. The tape muffled his scream. Jung Hee made guttural sounds and looked at his brother. I waited. He stared at Jung Sam's ear and back at me. He closed his eyes. I waited for all of this to register in his mind. His brother's ear was bleeding and blood was dripping on to his shoulder. Jung Hee's leg began to throb with pain. I ejected the shell.

———————————

"I will start again. You will not speak except to answer my questions. Do you understand?"

He nodded his head. I took the tape off his mouth and turned the recorder on.

"What is your name?"

He closed his eyes and took a deep breath.

I reached for the tape.

"My name is Jung Hee Shin," he said quickly.

"Who is he?" I pointed at the younger brother.

"He's my brother, Jung Sam."

"Is this your place of business?"

"Yes."

"What is the address of this place?"

"73 Tongzhi Lu."

"You deliver goods to different cities, correct?"

"Yes."

"To Harbin?"

"Yes."

"Do you remember going to Harbin on Saturday, June 15th?"

He was puzzled. Why I was asking about that date? He looked at me and frowned, trying to remember what happened in June. Then he remembered. His eyes widen and he realized what I was referring to.

"I can't remember," he stammered and looked at his brother.

I shut the recorder off and put a new piece of tape on his mouth. I shook my head.

"That was the wrong answer."

I aimed at Jung Hee's right foot and shot him where his toes were. His upper body automatically jerked up. I ejected the shell and pushed him back and held him down. Blood was beginning to seep out of his shoe. For the time being, the shock was greater than the pain. After a few minutes his body went limp. He put his head down and began to cry. His brother was sobbing. I waited until he regained some composure.

"Now. We'll try again. Are you listening to me?"

He nodded his head. I turned the recorder on and pealed the tape from his mouth.

"Once again, Jung Hee. Did you go to Harbin on Saturday, June 15th?"

"Yes," he whispered.

"Louder, please."

"Yes," he said.

"Louder."

"Yes," he shouted.

"Jung Hee, listen to me. I want you to speak loud and clear. I will ask one more time. Did you go to Harbin on Saturday, June 15th? If you did, say you went there on that day."

"Yes, we went to Harbin on June 15," he shouted.

"Why did you go to Harbin on that day?"

"We were told to go there."

"Why were you told to go there?"

"We were to follow a woman."

"Who was this woman?"

"I don't know. We just had a name and an address. We followed her all day. She went to a farm and then came back at night"

"Why were you told to follow this woman?"

"There was no reason given."

"You were told to just follow her?"

"We were to scare her."

"How were you going to scare her?"

"With the truck. Run her off the road."

"Scare her by running her off the road."

"Yes."

"What happened?"

"It just happened. We didn't mean it to be that way. She ran into a concrete wall."

"She ran into the wall or did you push her into the wall?"

"We were bumping her car so I guess we pushed her into the wall. But, it wasn't supposed to be that way. We didn't know the wall was there. We were only trying to scare her."

"When her car crashed into that concrete wall, did you stop to check to see if she was hurt?"

"No."

"Didn't you think she might be hurt?"

"We didn't think anything. We just left."

"That woman died," I said quietly.

He dropped his head and closed his eyes.

"That's what we heard. But, we didn't mean to do that."

I turned the recorder off and waited for my anger to subside. Times like these I wished I still smoked. A good cigar would be soothing and a drink would also help. After several minutes, I turned the recorder on again.

"Who told you to do this, Jung Hee?"

"We don't know. It was just a voice that called us."

"A voice?"

"Yes. He said he knew where our parents lived."

"What did he say about your parents?"

"He said he would have them put in prison or worse. He knew everything. He knew things no one except our family knows. He knew where my older sister and her family lived."

"Your family lives in Musan, correct?"

"Yes."

"You have a sister that lives with your parents and another who's married and has two children."

"Yes."

"You have an uncle who works for the North Korean government."

"Yes."

"Did this uncle talk to you about this woman?"

"No. Only the voice."

"Does your uncle know this voice?"

"I don't know."

"Does your uncle live and work in Musan?"

"Yes."

"Does he come here often?"

"No. Well, maybe once a year."

"What is your uncle's name?"

"Shin Dae Hyun."

"What is your father's name?"

"Shin Dae Mun."

"Did you talk to your uncle about this woman?"

"No."

"If you're lying to me, I will find out."

"No. I swear."

"Tell me about this voice."

"I don't know anything except what he said to me on the phone."

"What, exactly did he tell you to do?"

"The voice said this woman must be taught a lesson. She had to know who had the power."

"The power? What does that mean?"

"I don't know. He just said she had to know who had the power."

"How did you know he knew your family?"

"He sent photos of my father and mother and sister. He also sent photos of my older sister and her family. These were recent photos."

"How did he send these? By mail, Email, fax?"

"He sent photos to my cell phone."

"Where is this voice? In Changchun, Jilin City, Harbin? Pyongyang? How do you make contact with him?"

"I don't know."

I turned the recorder off and reached for the tape.

"Wait! Wait." He gasped. His mouth was dry, but his lips were bleeding. He wiped his lips with his tongue.

I put the tape down and switched the recorder on.

"He gave us a phone number to call."

"What is the phone number?"

"It's in my cell phone."

"Where is your cell phone?"

"In my pocket." He nodded his head down to his chest.

I patted his chest and found the phone in his shirt pocket. I pressed the menu button and found the phone book. There were several dozen numbers listed.

"Which number is it?"

"It's a Harbin number. It's number nine on the quick dial."

On the quick dial I hit number nine. I showed him the number.

"Is this it?"

"Yes."

"Are the pictures of your family still in here?"

"Yes. They're in the photo section."

I fiddled with the buttons and finally found the pictures.

"Are these the pictures of your family?"

"Yes. The first three are my parents and younger sister. The other two are my older sister and her family."

"Tell me more about this voice. Was he Korean or Chinese?"

"Korean."

"Is he a policeman or an agent of the government?"

"I don't know."

"When did you last talk to him?"

"The day before that Saturday."

"You have not talked to him since?"

"No."

"Were you supposed to report to him?"

"Only if we had a problem."

I shut the recorder off. Shin verified everything Hong and I suspected happened that night. What was new was a voice that could get pictures of the family in Musan.

But, what was the reason for the attack on BJ? He said she had to know who the power was – what was that about? Why was the contact made via phone? No professional would use people such as the Shins. Something was very wrong here. It all began to appear flaky.

I walked to the front office. The rain was heavy and steady. Rivulets of water came down from the roof and sides of the buildings and dumped into the gutters. The workday was coming to an end and people were rushing about in the rain, on their way home.

I went back into the room and looked down at the Shin brothers. What more could I get out of them? Along with their confession, I had a phone connection to the person who set this all in motion.

If I left these two alive, when would their families began to wonder where they were? Would they come to check or call someone nearby to come to the office? If the Changchun police found them, what would they tell the police? The Shin brothers confessed to me that they killed a woman in Harbin. Would they tell that to the police?

They were just two dumb clods who accidently killed her. In fact, the person who pressured them to "scare her" didn't actually plan a murder. Instead of real killers, I had these two stupid idiots and a voice. Were they worth killing? I believed they deserved to be killed. They were still alive and BJ was dead.

Killing them would make me feel better, but it would also create a whole lot of problems. In time the Changchun police would be in contact with Hong, who knew me and all about BJ's murder.

I still had to find out who this voice was. Killing the Shins might create problems and keep me from that effort. I decided that finding the voice was more important than killing them. I needed more time.

My choice was a practical one, not based on morality. Whatever, the Shin brothers lucked out.

"What is your home phone number in Jilin City?"

"Dial three on my cell phone."

"I'm going to call your wife and if you're lucky, your wife will come and take you someplace to get medical attention. But, understand this. If I cannot find the voice who told you to do this thing, I will come back and kill both of you, your wives and children, both of your parents, and your sisters. Do you understand?"

They nodded yes. I took the tape from Jung Sam's mouth. He took in a deep breath and exhaled. He had stopped crying. Suddenly he vomited.

The tape I used was commonly found everywhere. Not really traceable. I wore gloves so there wouldn't be fingerprints on anything. I had fired three shots. Two slugs were in the wall and the third was in the cement floor under Jung Hee's shoe. I dug the three slugs out with a screw driver I found in a tool kit. Nothing was left behind except holes in the floor, in the wall, and in their bodies. I picked up the empty shells and put the unused tape into the bag.

I put Jung Hee's cell phone in my tote bag and checked my watch. It was five-fifteen. Another three and half hours until the train leaves at nine o'clock. I put the recorder in the tote bag and looked around and made certain I had all my things.

I turned the light off and went to the back door, opened it slowly, and looked out. The rain had driven everyone in-doors and only a few lights were on in the buildings on either side. I took one last look at the Shin brothers. Jung Hee looked as if he was going to pass out. Jung Sam was softly crying again. That's how I wanted to remember them. I closed the door after me.

I examined the truck and checked the front end. It was damaged and had paint marks on it, just as Ahn said. I walked to the edge of the parking area and out to the street. It had begun to rain harder. People were rushing about in the rain with heads down and no one noticed me. I was just another guy under the hat and yellow plastic rain cover, trying to stay reasonably dry.

When I was a block away I stopped under a storefront awning. I punched number three on the quick dial on Jung Hee's cell phone. After five rings a woman answered the phone.

"*Ye bo sae yo.*"

"Mrs. Shin?"

"Yes."

"Listen carefully. You must come to your husband's office in Changchun immediately. He is badly hurt and needs your help."

I hung up. In forty-five seconds the cell phone chimed. I knew she would call. I let it ring for several minutes. Then I hit the talk button.

"Mrs. Shin?"

"Yes."

"Pay attention to me, Mrs. Shin." I waited a few seconds. "Are you listening?"

A frighten voice said "Yes," in a loud whisper,

"If you do not come to help your husband immediately, he will die."

Now she knew I had her husband's cell phone. She'll try calling the office phone and when no one answered, she'll call Jung Sam's cell phone. She could try calling Jung Hee's cell phone again, but I had shut the phone off. With no way to contact her husband or brother-in-law, she had to come to the office. It would be over an hour before she would get there. Or longer.

Their physical pains will be insignificant compared to the problem of explaining how they got their wounds. The police would be very interested, especially since they were bullet wounds. A bundle of trouble was facing them, but it was a helleva lot better than being dead.

53 ———————————————————————

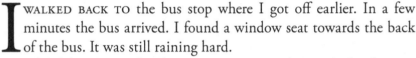

I WALKED BACK TO the bus stop where I got off earlier. In a few
minutes the bus arrived. I found a window seat towards the back
of the bus. It was still raining hard.

I didn't know exactly where I was going or what to do for the next
three hours before the train left. I could call Jin Yong. It was early
evening and she might not have a client yet. But there didn't seem to
be any rush to find a hiding place. It would be over an hour before Jung
Hee's wife got to the office. Riding the bus for a couple of hours was also
an option. It might be better not to get another person involved.

When the bus arrived at the downtown section of Changchun I
got off. It was still raining and wandering around window-shopping
only resulted in getting very wet. Who would be window shopping
in this weather? There were habits and mannerisms unique in every
community and while I was dressed to look like a local, I couldn't fake
local mannerisms for long. I began to feel self conscious.

I finally decided to go to the train station and wait there. Most of
the people there would be waiting for trains so hopefully I wouldn't
be noticed. Seemed reasonable. I asked a man standing at the bus stop
which bus went to the train station. He said most did, but bus Number
98 was an express bus with fewer stops. I thanked him and looked for
a bus stop with a roof.

It wasn't a long wait before bus Number 98 showed up. I sat in the
middle of the bus next to a woman who slept and snored most of the
way to the train station. The bus made five stops. Most of the passengers
remained on the bus until we got to the train station.

In many major cities throughout the world, train and bus stations are havens for the homeless who sleep there and make use of the restrooms. In Changchun, police patrolled these areas and if someone stayed too long or appeared to be a transient, they were questioned. I was dressed as a local but any questioning would quickly reveal I was not Chinese. A foreigner would probably not be questioned. So my disguise could turn out to be not a disguise at all.

I watched two uniformed police officers strolling through the station. They knew who was a passenger and who wasn't. It wouldn't take long to find out I was not a local or even Chinese.

I went to the ticket window and purchased a soft seat ticket on the D177 train to Harbin. It was a few minutes after six o'clock. Three hours before the nine o'clock train.

It was time to call Jin Yong.

I walked out to the street and called her on my throwaway cell phone. She answered on the fourth ring.

"*Ye bo sae yo.*"

"Hello, Jin Yong."

"Who is this?"

"I told you I would come to visit you one day and today is that day."

"The Korean from America! Where are you?"

"I'm in Changchun."

"You're here?"

"Yes. I have short lay over. I'm waiting for a train."

"Come to my house."

"I only have a couple of hours."

"Never mind."

"Okay. What's the address? Your name card doesn't have an address. Just your phone number."

"Stop a taxi. Give him your phone and I'll tell him where to bring you."

I waved to the taxi next in the queue and handed him the phone.

"She'll give you the address."

He listened, nodded, handed the phone back to me, and opened the back door. It was a fifteen minute ride. When I arrived she was standing in the doorway. I paid the taxi driver and got out. She held an umbrella over my head and hugged me.

"Come," she said as she pulled me into the hallway.

We went up a flight of stairs to the second floor. She gently pushed me toward the first door on the left. It was a one bedroom flat with a bathroom, kitchen, living room, and a dining area next to the kitchen. The furniture looked comfortable and appeared to be fairly new. There was a pleasant incense scent in the air.

Seeing her again reminded me what a very attractive woman she was. She had on a light blue silk outfit with peony blossoms on it. Her pants were tight, but not too tight. The top was a well fitted shirt with a Mandarin collar that showed her ample breasts nicely. She had on silk slippers that matched the color of her outfit. Her makeup was just enough to add a nice color to her face – eyes were highlighted with dark mascara. The color of her lipstick matched her nail polish. Even at home, she was more than just a pretty face.

"Have you eaten? Of course, you haven't. You just got off the train. I'll call and have some food delivered. There's a place near by that delivers delicious Chinese food. Not Korean food, but it's good."

She ordered food and went to the kitchen.

"You want something to drink?"

"Sure."

"I have wine and vodka."

"The wine will be fine."

She poured two glasses of a red wine. She sat next to me on the sofa, grinning, obviously pleased that I came to visit.

"Salute," she said and raised her glass.

"Salute," I answered and clicked her glass.

"Now, tell me how you come to be here?"

"Long story. I was going to Harbin and thought I would ride the train from Beijing. I've never done that before. Saw lots of China I have never seen before."

She sipped her wine. She raised one penciled eyebrow.

"That's bullshit," she said, smiling.

I laughed. She was far too intelligent to believe any kind of fabricated story. It was better to not say anything. Silence she could accept, but a concocted story insulted her intelligence.

"I will never be able to lie to you."

"You can try."

"No. That's a losing battle."

"You don't want to say why you're here."

"I came to visit you."

She tilted her head and looked at me. She knew something was not right, but, she accepted things as they were.

"Is this the reason you're dressed in that ridiculous outfit?"

"Oh. You noticed?"

"Hard to miss."

"Well, the next time we meet I'll be more properly dressed."

"Next time?"

"Always can be a next time."

A bell chimed, announcing the arrival of food. She leaped up and grabbed her purse.

"Please, I'll get this." I reached for the money in my pocket.

"No. It's my house."

She ran out the door and down the stairs. She came back with two bags of something that was steaming and smelled delicious. She put the bags on the table and brought out two dinner plates and Korean style silver chopsticks.

"Come. Bring your glass."

There were dishes of stir-fried vegetables, chicken, pork, and fried rice. She poured more wine as we sat down to eat. It was a great meal and her cheerfulness made it that much better.

"How are things with you now?" I asked.

"Good. I have two friends who are in the business also." Meaning her escort service. "We have talked and have decided to pull our money together and start a new business. None of us is getting younger."

"That sounds great. What kind of business?"

"I guess what we should do is open a high style whorehouse. We know the business." She smiled.

"Always good to know what you're doing."

"Actually, we're going into the dress making business. One of my friends has been a seamstress since she was a young girl. The other friend's parents work in the fabric business. The company they work for dyes silk fabric. So she'll get the materials and help with the sewing. I've done some design work in the garment business so I'll meet with clients and do custom designing. And I'll do the marketing. You know, make contact with local stores and women who want to buy custom made clothes. A big market is weddings and New Years."

"How can I help?"

"Can you sew?"

"No."

"Well, I'll think of something you can do," she said, laughing.

"Like sweeping the floor?"

"There is that."

"Seriously, I want to help." I thought a moment and remembered the extra money I brought with me. "As a start I'll invest two thousand US dollars to help you get going."

I took the money from my pocket and handed it to her. She leaned back and squinted at me. She brushed my hand away.

"What are you doing?"

"I'm investing in your business."

"I don't have a business yet."

"This will help get it started."

She looked down at her plate and put her elbows on the table. I put the money on the table next to her wine glass.

"Why are you doing this?"

"I believe in you. I haven't had too much to believe in lately."

"I can't accept this."

"Yes, you can. I want you to have it."

"You don't know me. We've only met twice and that's only for a few hours. You won't even sleep with me. My God, I don't even know your name."

"That's all right. Doesn't matter. This is as much for me as it is for you. And it's far better than other things I've done lately."

"I don't know what you mean."

"Doesn't matter."

"I don't understand any of this."

"Just make good use of the money. I want you to succeed."

She took in a deep breath and sighed.

"When will I see you again?"

"I don't know."

"Stay the night. Go tomorrow."

"I would truly love to stay, but I have to attend to some things. Some urgent matters."

"Business or personal?"

"Just things that have to be done."

"What do I call you?"

"I told you before. Whatever you want to call me."

"Enough of these games. You have a name, tell me."

She was angry and I couldn't blame her. The whole business of not telling her my name was stupid. People in Harbin knew what my name was and she could find out with a few phone calls. But, for now it was better that people in Changchun didn't know my real name.

"I'm sorry. You're right. Call me Jay."

"Jay? That's not a Korean name. Is it your American name?"

"Only a few people call me by that name. Special people."

"I suppose you'll tell me the rest sometime."

"I promise I will."

"Jay," she said. "Sounds nice. Close to my name, Jin. I like that."

"That makes us closer."

She took a deep breath.

"Why do you say things like that?"

"Probably because I'm trying to seduce you."

"I'm very difficult and do not give in easily. To get me in bed, you have to ask me." She smiled and gave me a haughty look.

"I'll work up to that."

She touched my hand.

"You know I'll find out your real name. I can, you know."

"I know. Until then, I'm just Jay."

"There's a reason for all this mystery, isn't there? Alright. We'll let it go. For now."

"You have a computer?" I looked around the room.

"Not yet. I use a computer at a local coffee shop."

"You have an Email address?"

"Yes."

"Write on the back of the card." I handed her the card and she wrote her Email address. It was jinyong1975@hotmail.com.

"I just got this Email address."

"1975? The year you were born?"

"Yes."

"I'll call or send an Email and you can let me know about your new business."

"You give me these things and you really don't know anything about me."

"I know all I need to know about you."

"But, I don't know who you really are," she said.

"Right now, it's better this way."

"Are you hiding from someone? From the police?"

"No." I answered too quickly.

She looked at me and frowned.

"Are you in some kind of trouble?"

"People like me are always in trouble."

"You need help?"

"For now, being here is a big help."

I looked at my watch. Eight-ten.

"I need to catch a train. In fact, the train leaves in about thirty-five minutes. Can you call me a taxi?"

"Okay." She called and asked for a taxi. "About ten minutes."

"Thanks."

"I'm serious. Do you need help?"

"You have helped. And you made me feel good about things."

"I don't understand what all that means."

"No need. I appreciate being here with you, more than you know."

"How long will you be in Harbin?"

"About two days."

"I can come to see you."

"I'll be very busy. I have some things I must finish, so I don't have much time."

"I don't need much time."

"We had a great time tonight. It was a wonderful dinner and I really enjoyed this visit. I'll remember it."

"Have one more glass of wine."

"Your plan to get me drunk won't work."

"I can always try."

"Not a big problem. I'm also easy."

She poured another glass of wine and we sat quietly and sipped our wine. She reached over and took my hand and smiled.

The taxi arrived and honked his horn. I finished the wine and stood. I put my tote bag strap over my head and slipped on the plastic rain cover. I pulled the hat on.

"You do look silly," she smiled.

"It's all the rage now and what the 'in' people are wearing in Harbin."

"I'll have to get the name of the designer."

"I warn you, it's expensive."

"That's okay. I have a rich Korean friend from America."

"Always good to have one those."

The taxi honked again. She looked at me and smiled. I gave her a hug. She kissed me. It was a warm, affectionate kiss. Her lipstick had a cool sweet taste. I'll remember it.

She grabbed the umbrella and led me out the door and down the stairs. She gave me a peck on the cheek and held my hand.

"Remember me."

"I will. Good bye, Jin."

"No. Not good-bye. *Na-jung-e bwae-y.*"

"Okay, Jin. See you later."

I stepped onto the sidewalk and she released my hand. It was not raining hard but it was a steady rain. I ran to the taxi and told the driver to take me to the train station. I looked back through the rain-streaked window. She was standing in the doorway. She waved as the taxi pulled away from the curb. I wondered if I would ever see her again. She was a special person.

I arrived at the train station and boarded the train with only a few minutes to spare. I found a window seat in Car #5 and settled down for the hour and half ride to Harbin.

54 ———————————————————

LOOKING OUT THE TRAIN window in the wet darkness I could see images of the Shin brothers as I left them. One with part of his left ear shot off, bruised throat, and broken ribs and the other one with a busted nose and mouth, broken shin bone, and a bullet hole in his right foot. I left them in pain and bleeding.

Life would never be same for them or their families. But that was fitting. Because of them, life for the Ma family had changed forever. It was my version of justice and I felt no remorse or had any doubts. I suppose some would argue that I should have turned them over to the police. What a good citizen would do. But, I made my own rules and I didn't give a damn what a good citizen does. Why am I into this meaningless rationalizing? I made my choice and I'm satisfied with it.

My next problem was to find the voice. The only lead I had was his cell phone number. If he were a professional he would have disposed of the cell phone and left no traces to himself. But, would a professional use the likes of the Shin brothers? Not likely. Based on what I knew, I wasn't dealing with a professional. Then, what was this voice?

I took out Jung Hee's cell phone. I wanted to call because I wanted to hear his voice. But, what would I say? A phone call would only spook him. Then I would never find him.

With his official resources, Hong could trace the cell phone number and find out who the voice was. I didn't have those resources so I had to do it another way.

I was less than an hour from Harbin when I called Ahn.

"It's me. Arriving at 22:49."

"I'll be there."

The rain had stopped when the train pulled into the Harbin station. I made my way pass the disembarking passengers into the waiting room and out the front entrance. Just outside the sliding doors Ahn was waiting.

"Good trip?"

"Yes."

"The car is parked across the street."

"You know, I'm really impressed with the railway system here. The trains actually run on time."

"Not always, but this one was right on time. Have you eaten?"

"Yes. Had a bite."

"I'll take you back to the office and you can change there."

We drove to his small office and I changed back into my regular clothes. I kept the tote bag with the gun and ammunition and left everything else in the laundry bag.

"Well that part is done." I let out a sigh and sat in the only chair in the place. Ahn noticed my weariness.

"You need a break. Want some North Korean beer?"

"Sure."

"There's Korean place that I go to often on late night shifts. It stays open all night. Taxi drivers hang out there."

The small café Ahn took me to served a variety of short order dishes. The smell of *kimchi* was proof that real Korean food was available. It wasn't crowded and we got a table in the back, near the kitchen.

"I'll get that North Korean beer."

"Sounds good. I've never had North Korean beer before."

He went to the counter and brought back two bottles beer and a small dish of *kimchi*.

"This beer is made in Pyongyang. It's called *Taedonggang*."

It tasted like ale and was surprisingly good.

After we finished the beer we drove back to the hotel. Except for the janitors cleaning the floors, no one was in the lobby. We went up to my room.

I recounted my encounter with the Shin brothers. He listened to the taped confession several times.

"Well, that's pretty clear."

"I think it is."

"But you didn't kill them?"

"No."

"That's good. Could have been many problems if you did."

"I know."

"What about the woman? You trust her to keep quiet?"

"Yes. She helped me and didn't ask questions."

"Whatever, being with her was a helleva lot better than getting questioned by the police at the railway station."

"Yeah, she was okay."

"With the taped confession you have proof of what actually happened."

"They claim they were only trying to scare her, but things got out hand. Also, the person behind all this is a Korean here in Harbin."

"They give a name?"

"No. They claim they don't know who he is. He was only a voice on the phone. This voice said the Shins' mother, father, and sister could be put in prison or worse. To prove this, pictures of them and the married sister and her family were sent to them. These were recent photos. They're in Shin's cell phone. Here, you can call up the photos."

I gave him Jung Hee's phone and he found the pictures. He looked at the photos carefully.

"Looks real," Ahn said. "The houses in the pictures are typical North Korean structures. And they're dressed like people from there. They didn't pose for these pictures."

"Whoever this voice is, he has the ability to cross the border at will. Or there's someone in Musan who's connected to the voice. Photos can be sent by texting on cell phones so everything can be done in minutes. And remember their uncle works for the government."

"Do you think the uncle is in Changchun or Harbin?"

"The Shins say no. I don't think they lied to me."

"So, you have a voice, but no name."

"Shin has the voice's cell phone number in his phone. I just hope he hasn't destroyed the phone."

"That's what I would do."

"Any professional would. But, there are a lot of things that don't add up. The idea was to frighten her, they said. Why? What could they gain with that? If I was the reason for all this, why not just kill me? I don't think the North Korean police are directly involved. It's all too irrational. Even for them."

"So now what?"

"The cell phone number is all we have. We can call the number and see if anyone answers. We'll use Jung Hee's cell phone and that number will show up as the caller."

"Why would Jung Hee be calling?"

"Because they're in trouble or at least think they're in trouble. What time is it? After midnight. A late night call is more like an emergency. The Shins can say they're frightened because the police were at their office asking questions. And the Harbin police stopped them on their last delivery here."

"If this voice is a Korean in Harbin, he knows the police are investigating this as a murder. All Koreans know about Ms. Ma's death and the burial was written about in the local Korean newspaper. There have been reports and updates on a regular basis."

"You make the call, Ahn. My Korean is with an American accent. If I called he would know it wasn't the Shin brothers. He could disappear."

"True. Your Korean is okay, but you do sound like a Korean from America."

Ahn keyed in number nine on Jung Hee's cell phone. It was ringing. He gave me thumbs up. The phone rang for five minutes. Ahn looked at me and shook his head. He hit the stop key.

"No answer. Think he dumped the phone?"

"Maybe he's asleep. Wait a minute and try again."

We waited a few minutes. Ahn pressed the redial key and the ringing began again. After ten rings someone answered. Ahn smiled and gave a thumbs up.

"Who is this?" the voice said.

Ahn put the phone against his face and whispered, "This is Shin."

"What?"

"This is Shin."

"Why are you calling me?"

"The police were here tonight. They questioned me and my brother for two hours."

"What did they want?"

"They wanted to know where we were that night."

There was a long silence on the other end. Ahn gave me a puzzled look and shrugged his shoulders.

"Did you hear what I said? Hello. Are you there?"

Finally, the voice asked, "What did you tell them?"

"We said nothing. But we need help. You said to call if there was a problem."

"How did the police find you?"

"They talked to us about deliveries to Harbin. They know something."

"What can they know?"

"They know something. Why else are they asking us questions?"

"What questions?"

"What our business is in Harbin. Most especially where we were on that day. It was a Saturday and they knew we don't make deliveries on Saturday. But, somehow they knew we were in Harbin that day. The Harbin police also stopped us on our Monday delivery to Harbin. You said there would be no problems."

"What did you tell them about that day?"

"We said we made some special deliveries to Harbin."

Another long silence ensued. Ahn made a face and waited. He was about to ask if they were still connected when the voice spoke.

"I'll call you back." The voice hung up.

"He said he'd call back." Ahn closed the phone.

"He wants to check to see if this is Shin's phone."

"Well, one thing's for sure, he's the guy."

"Now we wait."

While we waited, Ahn listened to the taped confession again and looked at the photos.

"With these pictures of their parents and sister the Shin brothers would believe the voice had the power."

"Yes, they believed him." I thought about it. "I would."

Suddenly the phone chimed. Ahn picked up the phone and hit the receive button. He didn't have an opportunity to speak.

"Listen to me carefully," the voice said. "You and your brother will come to Harbin tomorrow. Take one of the early morning trains that gets to Harbin by seven. Call me as soon as you arrive and you will receive further instructions."

The voice abruptly hung up.

"He wants to meet the Shins here in Harbin," Ahn said.

"That means he's going to show his face."

"He has no choice. He has to deal with the Shin brothers directly."

"Yes. I think he's decided to eliminate them," I said.

"He has to if he wants to keep his identity a secret."

"What's the train schedule like?"

"He said he wanted them to be here by seven. He must know the schedule." Ahn spread the train schedule out on the table. "There's one that leaves at 5:32 and gets in Harbin at 7:42. An earlier train leaves at 3:58 and arrives at 6:52."

"The one getting in at 6:52 is probably the one he has in mind."

"Okay, we can call him at seven."

I got a mini bottle of gin and took a swallow. I was beginning to feel very tired.

"Well, we have about six hours so why don't you go home and get some rest. I'll do the same."

"Things are coming to a head."

"Yes they are. I want to finish this once and for all."

"I'll pick you up about six."

"Good. We can make the call from your office."

It was almost over. I had the confession of the ones who committed the crime and in a few hours I would meet the person who ordered the killing. But, something was missing. The voice, whoever he was, had to have a motive.

If my reputed involvement with the Choi killing was the reason for all this, it would have been simpler to make a direct hit on me. I was a regular visitor to China and my visits were certainly not secret. A professional could have killed me in Harbin, Guangzhou, or in a number of cities.

Obviously, the voice was a part of the Korean community in Harbin. Did I meet him on one of my trips? He obviously knew about BJ and me. How was all this tied up with Choi's death? I was certain everything was connected. But, how?

After a hot shower, two more mini-bottles of gin, and another hour of tossing, I finally drifted off to sleep.

I woke before the alarm sounded, a few minutes before six. It was going to be another long day. A shower and shave helped. I threw my dirty clothes into the laundry bag and called housekeeping.

I put the gun in the tote bag and went down to the lobby. The doorman saluted me and opened the door. Ahn drove up as I walked out of the lobby. He was not driving his taxi. It was a four door Nissan.

"Not driving the taxi today?"

"Thought it better to not use the taxi. Too easy to remember. There are thousands of these cars in Harbin. No one will think anything about seeing this one."

"Sounds reasonable."

It started to rain again. Not heavy, but enough to wet the streets and people out walking.

At the office, I put the hat, gloves, and yellow plastic rain cover in the tote bag and set the other clothes and shoes aside. I loaded the nine round clip and put the gun and a dozen extra cartridges in my pocket.

"Have to destroy these clothes."

"Not a problem. I'll burn them."

At seven Ahn looked at me and held up Jung Hee's cell phone. I nodded.

He dialed the number and waited for an answer. After five rings he raised his head and gave me thumbs up. Before he could say anything, the voice spoke. Ahn listened and reached for a pen and paper. He wrote something down.

"His instructions are to come to this address immediately."

"You know where it is?"

"It's on the edge of the city. Government is trying to develop an industrial park out there and declare it a special economic zone. Right now the older abandoned buildings are ready for demolition."

"I think he's planning to kill the Shin brothers."

"That would be a place to do it. No one around. I wonder what this address is. Some kind of office or small shop. Whatever it is, it'll be empty."

"How long will it take to get there?"

"At this time in the morning, less than an hour if traffic is good."

"Let's go."

The voice must know that under pressure the Shin brothers would tell the police how they came to be involved and that would lead to him. I was certain the voice was planning to kill the Shin brothers.

The last part of the puzzle was to find out why he killed BJ.

55

THE MAJOR STREET RUNNING through the center of the abandoned complex was paved but was in a state of serious disrepair. The buildings on both sides of the main street were empty shells. The windows were broken and most were without doors. Many of the buildings were built by the Japanese in the late 1920's and early 30's. Narrow roads between the buildings connected a street that was parallel to the one we were on. There was only one new building partly completed. Work on the interior had just begun, but the exterior walls and roof were finished.

The entire complex was deserted. It was still raining and workers who worked on the new building would come to work later in the day, when and if the rain stopped.

Ahn drove slowly down the street, stopped, and pointed to a door on the right. It was a one story structure, probably used as a small retail shop at one time. It was one of the few buildings that were still in relatively good condition.

"That's the one. Number 21. There's a car parked next to the building."

A two year old Toyota sedan was parked in the driveway between two buildings.

"That must be his car."

We drove past the address and parked at the end of the block. I checked to see that I had everything. The recorder was in my inside coat pocket and the gun was stuffed in my back waist. I put on the hat and plastic rain cover and slipped on the gloves. I considered leaving the sunglasses off, but decided to wear them.

"Want me to come along?"

"No. This is between him and me. If something goes wrong and I don't make it, you can put the police on the right track to him. And you have numbers of people to call."

I walked quickly to the door marked Number 21. The lower half of the glass window was covered with old faded newspapers. I tried the doorknob. It was locked. I knocked loudly and took a step back.

A minute passed. I knocked again. I heard footsteps coming toward the door. A pair of fingers moved a corner of the newspaper covering and an eye peered out. No one but the person he talked to on the phone knew he was here, so he would assume I was one of the Shin brothers. I heard a clicking sound and saw the doorknob turn.

I rushed the door and forced it open. The person on the other side of the door let out a cry and fell back on the floor. I quickly stepped in and closed the door. The man on the floor started to rise. I kicked him in the face and cut his lip. He began to bleed from his nose.

What little light there was came from the upper half of the front windows not covered with newspapers. Everything appeared gray. The dark glasses didn't help. It took a several seconds to focus.

I ran my hands over his front, back, and sides. I took a wallet and cell phone from his inside coat pocket. He had a pistol in his side pocket. The gun was a snub nosed 32 caliber S&W revolver. Probably bought from the Russian, our friendly neighborhood gun dealer. How many black market guns were floating about in Harbin?

I grabbed the back of his coat collar, lifted him up, and pushed him toward several wooden crates in the center of the room.

"Sit," I said.

He was a short rotund guy, weighing about a hundred and sixty pounds. Receding hair was combed straight back. A round chubby face, with small eyes, flat nose, and thin lips. He wore a gray suit and his white shirt was opened at the collar. He probably wore a tie on normal business days. A raincoat was draped on one of the boxes. I didn't see a hat. An umbrella was leaning against the raincoat.

He put his hand to his nose and lip and wiped the blood with the back of his hand. The physical attack was totally unexpected, which added to his confusion. He expected two people who feared him. Obviously, I was not one of the Shin brothers and I didn't fear him. He suddenly realized I had control. He didn't know how to react.

I put his gun on one of the boxes and placed the mini-recorder next to it. I switched it on.

"Who are you?" he demanded. "What do you want?"

I put one foot on a box, leaned forward and looked down at him.

"Never mind who I am. The Shin brothers sent me."

"Where are they?" He looked again toward the door.

"They're busy right now."

"I told them to come."

"For now, you'll deal with me."

I took out my gun. He drew back, looking at the gun and me. He might be wondering if the Shin brothers had sent me to kill him.

I opened his wallet and took out his name card. The name on the card was printed in Korean and Chinese – Yi Im Chul.

"This says your name is Yi Im Chul."

He looked defiantly at me.

"Is your name Yi Im Chul?"

He turned his face and looked at me and sneered. He pissed me off when he sneered. I put a shot between his legs, close to his crotch. He instantly put his hands and arms up, covering his face. Strange he did not cover his genital area.

"The next shot will blow your balls off. Now, tell me your name."

"Yes. I am Yi Im Chul," he croaked hoarsely.

"Yi Im Chul. You're the voice the Shin brothers told me about."

"They know nothing about me. They don't even know my name." He sneered again.

"No, but they knew enough for me to find you."

He glared at me. Lots of hatred there – along with some fear. He knew I had control, but he still remained defiant. I thought about shooting him in his leg to reinforce my position.

"The Shin brothers said you instructed them to kill a woman."

"What woman?"

I pointed the silencer between his legs and shot at the lip of the box he was sitting on. Bits of the wooden box flew up and against his thighs. He cried out and pushed as far back as he could, almost standing. He knew the next shot would be somewhere on his body. He lost much of his bravado and was visibly shaken. He covered his face again.

"Put your hands down."

He slowly lowered his hands to his lap and blinked nervously.

"They were stupid," he shouted. "They were told to scare her, not kill her."

No denial. He was confident of his authority.

"You were the stupid one. You sent amateurs to do the work of professionals. You made a big mistake."

He started to respond, but held back. He began to stir nervously. He twisted and looked to his left and right. Was he estimating his chances of making a move on me?

I looked at him with some disbelief. Who the hell was this guy? Considering how inept he was at arranging the assault on BJ, I couldn't believe this pudgy bastard was a North Korean agent. A far cry from the North Korean agent Choi. Were they scraping the bottom of the barrel?

"Why did you tell them to attack the woman?"

Obviously, he was not accustomed to being pushed around. He appeared to be a pampered self-centered ass that may or may not be a person of importance. Would he break?

"Tell me or I will shoot you. Not to kill you, but to cause you great pain." I pointed the gun at his face.

He took a deep breath and held it. He closed his eyes and sat upright, back stiff and straight. Was he waiting for me to shoot him? He admitted he instructed the Shin brothers to attack her, resulting in her death. Was he expecting punishment?

I needed to know why he killed BJ. I would always wonder. Was

BJ really the target and her murder had nothing to do with me? Was it personal? I hadn't thought about that.

I thought again about shooting him in various parts of his body. But all that could become very messy. He could pass out or even die and I would learn nothing. Was he that tough? Maybe there's another way.

"The Shin brothers have identified you as the one who gave the order to attack the woman. Your admission that you were the one who planned the attack of the woman is recorded on this tape. I will broadcast this taped confession of the Shin brothers and your words to the world. Everyone, especially the Korean community here and people in Pyongyang, will know you are a coward who kills innocent women."

He wet his lips, became agitated, and twisted nervously. His status in Pyongyang and here in Harbin – was that a key to his mental and emotional state? Was what the North Korean government thought important to him? Was this fat jerk tied to Choi? What was the connection? If there was one.

"I knew another North Korean who was also a coward. He killed women too. His name was Choi."

His head snapped up and eyes narrowed to the point of disappearing. Aha! I had hit a nerve. Choi was somehow involved.

"Yes. Most Koreans knew Choi was a coward who betrayed his own countrymen. Everyone celebrated when he died."

"He was murdered!" Yi shouted and started to stand.

I jabbed my gun hard into his chest, pushing him back down on the box. He glared at me. He was breathing heavily and his face was flush with anger. So, there was a real connection.

"Murdered? Who murdered him?"

"The traitor from America murdered him. A Korean lackey working for the American CIA. He is the assassin."

If he had seen me before he didn't remember me. Or the dim light, the hat, and the dark glasses hid enough of my face to prevent recognition.

"Really? An assassin who worked for the CIA? And how do you know that?"

"My brother told me about him. My brother ..." He bit his lower lip.

Choi was his brother. Now I knew all about him.

"Choi, the North Korean coward, was your brother?"

He started to stand.

"Sit!"

I jabbed him in the stomach with the gun and he sat back down. He turned toward me with a defiant look.

"Yes. I'm proud to say he is my brother." He took a deep breath and thrust out his chin. "He is a hero and patriot. He is fighting for the Fatherland. My duty is to help him."

He spoke in the present tense, as if his brother was still alive. And yet, he spoke of Choi's assassination. He knew Choi was dead, but he couldn't admit it. He was in denial.

"You only think this Korean from America killed your brother. You really don't know."

"Yes, I know. Everyone knows. The Chinese government knows. But they won't do anything. Even my government will not do anything."

"Your government? You mean the fools in Pyongyang? So, like your coward brother, you're an agent of the North Korean government. You work for that other coward, Kim Jong Il."

"I am loyal to the Dear Leader," he said more calmly. "All patriotic Koreans are loyal to the Dear Leader."

He was not a professional nor in the service of the Pyongyang government. He was Choi's mole who spied on the Harbin Korean community. He had no official status in North Korea. There was no sinister plot or any kind of government involvement in BJ's murder. The whole business was a badly concocted revenge scheme of a neurotic who worshiped his brother. How bizarre can this get?

"If this Korean from America killed your brother, why didn't you just kill him? Why harm this woman?"

"She was his woman," he shouted. More quietly he said, "And he was not here."

"That's an excuse only a coward would use. Like your coward brother, you make war against innocent women because you're afraid to directly confront the Korean from America. You and your brother are cowards."

His eyes suddenly grew large and spittle started to flow out of his mouth.

"My brother is a hero," he shouted. "He will deal with the traitor from America."

"Your brother is dead. And you are too much of a coward to face the person you claim killed your brother. No one believes you. You made up this story about the Korean from America. You're not only a coward, you're also a liar."

"The traitor from America assassinated him!" he shouted again.

"Do you know him?"

"I will know him when I see him."

"So, you really don't know this person."

"I will know him. I will know," he said in a fading voice. "I will know," he said in a whisper.

It was something he told himself many times. He believed he would know me when I appeared. He had been waiting, but didn't know what he would do, if and when I materialized.

He sat with a fixed stare, looking at nothing. He was unsure of himself and his defiant attitude was rapidly fading. Choi gave him the confidence to be arrogant and feel superior. But his hero was gone and his life's purpose no longer existed. He was lost, without a definable mission. His world had collapsed.

On the surface, he was just another Korean immigrant from North Korea. His role in the Korean community had been to "help" asylum seekers. He was the friendly conduit that transmitted information to and from relatives in North Korea and doled out some financial aid to new comers.

As the good Samaritan, he learned who was working the underground network in North Korea and identified new refugees who came across the river into China. He found out who took the southern route into Vietnam or Thailand and who tried to go directly to South Korea.

With this information Choi hunted them down and punished relatives still in North Korea. Giving this information to his brother instilled in Yi a feeling of power and worth. He believed he was a "patriotic hero" because of his work in finding the "traitors." Koreans in Harbin didn't know who he was. It was a secret. Because no one knew, he felt even more powerful.

There was no end to this patriotic crusade. He believed he was performing a sacred duty.

Unfortunately, it all ended when his brother was killed. He wanted to avenge his brother's death but didn't know how. The North Korean government wouldn't help him and the Chinese government absolved the accused killer. Frustrated and confused, he plotted an attack on the woman said to be close to the person he believed was the assassin. That plan only resulted in BJ's accidental death.

"I have heard this Korean from America is held in high regard among the Koreans here in Harbin. Quite different from how they thought about your brother. They felt nothing but contempt for him."

"They are traitors."

"When they find out that you were giving information to your cowardly brother, they will know you are the enemy of the people. You are the traitor."

"My brother will …," he stopped in mid-sentence. He looked befuddled and lost.

"Your bastard brother is dead!" I shouted at him. "He's dead and good riddance."

He became agitated and nervously looked from side to side. His brother would have the answers, but his brother was dead. Yi Im Chul was on the edge.

"Let me explain what will happen after I give this evidence to the Korean community here in Harbin. They will know you informed your brother Choi about Korean refugees who risked their lives to escape from the Hell in North Korea. The people will know you for what you are, a traitor to the Korean people. Your life in Harbin is over.

"By your own admission, and supported by the confession of the Shin brothers, you were directly involved in the murder of a Chinese citizen. You will be arrested, tried, and convicted for this murder. The trial will enjoy great publicity and the world will know about your despicable deeds."

He listened passively. He looked down at his hands. He interlocked his fingers and sat as a child being disciplined. He had failed in his mission to avenge his brother.

Tears formed in his eyes and rolled down his plump cheeks. His shoulders sagged and his arms went limp. I turned the mini-recorder off. I left his wallet but took his cell phone and the two shells from the shots I had fired I looked around. Nothing more to clean up. I left the slugs I had fired in the boxes. It no longer mattered if the police found them. I picked up his gun, swung the cylinder out, and dropped the cartridges on the box.

It was over. I knew everything. I wanted to kill him.

He looked up at me and finally asked, "Who are you? You're not from here. Who are you?"

"I'm the voice of all the people you have betrayed."

He continued to stare at me. Suddenly he knew.

"You're him."

His face had a look of relief and resignation. He spoke in a quiet voice.

"I've been waiting for you. When your woman was killed I knew you would come and kill me, just as you killed my brother."

Had he planned this or just hoped it would happen? Part of his fantasy was to die on the field of combat, as he imagined his brother did.

"Why don't you kill me?"

"You are truly a miserable bastard and I want very much to kill you. But, killing you would be too easy. Exposing you to the world will cause you far greater pain. I want you to live and feel the people's contempt every day of your life. You and your brother will be publically shamed and disgraced here and in Pyongyang.

"You want a soldier's death. I will not give you that honor. Instead I want you to live a life of public disgrace. Keeping you alive is my revenge."

He closed his eyes and sat with his head down and softly cried. He looked up as I walked to the door. He picked up his gun and inserted a cartridge into the cylinder.

He pulled the hammer back and put the pistol barrel into his mouth and pulled the trigger. There was only a click. An empty chamber. In frustration he pulled the trigger without cocking the hammer. In his agitated state the gun was pointed at the right side of his chin when the firing pin struck the cartridge. His head was thrown back and blood gushed from under his chin. The slug didn't exit and remained lodged in his head.

I watched him die with satisfaction.

"Welcome to hell, Yi Im Chul. Your brother's waiting for you."

56

A HN WAS OUT OF the car and coming toward the door when I
came out.
"I heard a shot."
I nodded and walked to the car. I looked back at the newspaper
covered windows.
"Let's get outta here."
"Okay."
"What time is that gravestone ceremony?"
"Should be starting around ten. The rain is light today, so probably
won't postpone it. Really doesn't make any difference. Have to put the
stone in place, rain or shine."
"Let's go to the cemetery."
I took off the hat and yellow plastic sheet. I wiped the gun, clip, and
shells and put them in the bag, along with the gloves.
We drove past the decaying buildings and out to the expressway.
The rain was letting up. Traffic began to build up as we came closer to
the edge of the inner city.
Ahn waited patiently for me to start.
"The voice the Shin brothers feared was a man named Yi Im Chul.
But his real name was Choi. He was the brother of the North Korean
agent, Choi."
"Choi was his brother?"
"Yes. That was a surprise, but explains a lot of things. I don't know
what Yi did for a living, but he must have been active in the Korean

community for several years. He was Choi's snitch here in Harbin and he kept Choi informed about Korean immigrants."

"Yi Im Chul? Yi. Yi Im Chul. Yes. I know that name. He runs an herb shop. Sells Korean ginseng."

"Does he have a family?"

"I don't think so. The shop he has isn't big. Many Koreans go there to buy herbs and Korean ginseng from North Korea. I've bought ginseng there. If he was Choi's brother, that might be how he got the ginseng. Korean ginseng is hard to get, even this close to the source."

"Well, people will have to find another source."

"So, he wasn't a government agent?"

"No. He was just a source of information for Choi. I imagine many will be upset to learn that he was the one who betrayed them."

"Yi knew about you because his brother told him."

"Yes. My problems with Choi go back to before I came here last December. Choi must have told him about the young man and his sister I was trying to help defect from North Korea. Yi believed I killed his brother, so he thought killing her was a way to punish me. He believed he was avenging his brother and serving the Fatherland and the Dear Leader. It was all part of his fantasy world."

"It doesn't make any sense."

"He said BJ was killed because I wasn't here. He went after the person who was close to me. Getting the Shin brothers involved was just Yi's way of trying to be clever. The Shins didn't know what they were doing. They were only afraid of what might happen to their parents in Musan. The whole thing was very stupid."

"Then she was killed for no reason."

"No reason at all."

"Did you kill him?"

"No. He did that himself. With his own gun. Choi was the strong one and gave Yi everything he had. All that died with Choi. Now everyone can learn who he was and what he did. Yi just couldn't face that kind of exposure. Whatever the reason, everyone's better off with both brothers gone."

"That leaves the Shin brothers. What do you think happened to them?"

"I don't know. I called Jung Hee's wife in Jilin and told her to go to their office. If she did and got them some medical help, they'll be okay. I don't know if they could find medical help without going to a hospital. If they did go to a hospital, they'll have to talk to the police. Don't know what kind of story they'll tell them."

"You have everything on tape. The reason the Shins were involved may not be clear to the Changchun police, but Hong will know. Are you going to give the tape to Hong?"

"I thought I would, but now that Yi is dead, I don't think I will. Hong can figure out how the Shin brothers were involved without my help. He has to connect Yi with the Shin brothers and that will be difficult. When he learns Yi was Choi's brother, things will become very clear to him. I don't know if I can avoid being involved if that happens. If I get involved you might also become involved. I don't want that to happen."

"So we'll wait and see what Hong comes up with."

"I have to get rid of this gun."

"No problem. Give it to me. I'll take care of it."

"It can't be just thrown away. It has to be completely destroyed. Broken into small parts and scattered all around."

"I know."

"And everything must be wiped down. No fingerprints on anything. I fired two shots in the box Yi was sitting on. The police will find the slugs. They're Chinese ammo, so can be easily identified."

"They won't find anything else."

"All that's left are the tapes and two cell phones. This is a bit messier than the Choi business, but, it'll have to do."

When we arrived at the cemetery the rain had stopped and, as if planned, sun rays beamed down on the gathering around her grave.

Mr. and Mrs. Ma fussed with the stone, brushing off the early morning rain. It was a very nice gravestone. Her name and appropriate dates were engraved under a very nice photo of her. Flowers were in a vase in front of the gravestone and a standing wreath was to one side. I should have sent flowers.

BJ's mother and father saw me and called me to come to see the gravestone. She gave me a hug and her father shook my hand.

"The picture is very nice," I said.

"We're so pleased you could come."

She said this as if I drove over from a neighboring town. But that was all right. It made her feel better. BJ's son was holding his grandfather's hand and wondered what all the fuss was about. He probably didn't fully understand yet that his mother was gone forever.

I wondered if the Ma family would tie the pieces together and figure out how BJ was involved with events of the past week. Hong told them BJ was murdered. Someone who was very curious and took the time, the connection between me, BJ, Choi, the Shin brothers, and Yi wouldn't be that difficult to figure out.

BJ said her involvement with me was her *karma*. Would her mother accept that? Could Mrs. Ma forgive me? That would always be on my mind.

While Mr. and Mrs. Ma turned to thank the others who came, I eased my way away from the group. I left without further good-byes to the Ma family.

"Hey." She came running after me. "Thought you would get away without saying hello or goodbye? You can't leave without a word."

"Hello Mulan."

"When did you arrive? How long will you stay?"

"I got in day before yesterday and leaving tomorrow morning. Just came for this one last thing."

"Have you had a chance to see Mr. and Mrs. Ma?"

"Yes."

"When are you coming back?"

"I don't know."

"Everyone wants you to come back." She looked down and shifted her feet. "And I'm here."

"We'll see."

She came up to me, put her arms around my neck, and kissed me. "I want you to come back."

I eased her arms from around my neck and held her hands.

"Take care." I smiled. "Give your parents my best."

"I'll Email you. Please answer."

"Good bye, Mulan."

As we drove out of the cemetery I looked back and saw her standing with her hands behind her back, watching us leave. The group around the grave grew smaller as we drove further down the street. In a few seconds, everything faded and the figures all disappeared from view. I wondered if I would ever see any of them again. Probably not.

57

WE DROVE BACK TO the hotel without much talk. Dark clouds had moved over the city and it looked as if it would rain again. The weather during the past few days proved that this was Harbin's wettest time of the year, as I had been told several times by everyone. The dark and rainy days provided an appropriate backdrop for the events of the past few days.

Ahn asked me again to come to his home for dinner. I thanked him and declined. I knew I wouldn't be pleasant company tonight. I told him I would call to let him know when to pick me up tomorrow. I wanted to make the plane reservations because I needed some mundane task involving things like time schedules.

I went to the business center and found a computer not being used. I was going to Guangzhou, as I had promised Kam Wah. I needed to talk to him. I looked for a schedule from Harbin to Beijing to Guangzhou.

All of this required making decisions about how much time I wanted to spend waiting in airports. It was times like these when I missed Yasha. She could do this in a flash. The hotel probably had a travel agent who could make the arrangements, but, I decided to do it myself. Needed to be busy.

After an hour of going through schedules I decided to take the 10:30 AM Air China flight from Harbin to Beijing. It got in at 12:25 PM. I booked the 3:00 PM Air China flight from Beijing to Guangzhou that got in at 6:00 PM. All of the seats were First Class. That pretty much exhausted my credit card account. The last leg of the trip would be from Hong Kong or Shanghai to SFO. I decided to book that later. I didn't know how long I would stay in Guangzhou.

I could forget all of this and go directly home. There was a non-stop flight from Beijing to SFO on Air China. But what was my rush? And I might be able to figure out a way to see Yasha again.

I called the airline to confirm the schedule I had worked out and asked them to sent confirmation to the hotel. I paid with my credit card and was relieved the card was not rejected for lack of funds. As a reward for my efforts in arranging my own plane schedule I went to the bar for a drink.

"I'm scheduled to be in Guangzhou tomorrow evening at 6:00 PM. Can Wong pick me up?"

"I will come to the airport."

"Good."

"You have finished your business in Harbin?"

"Yes."

"Is it all done?"

"Yes. It's all done."

"*Hen hao.* Where do you want to stay in Guangzhou?"

"I think the White Swan."

"I'll book a room. How long are you going to stay?"

"I don't know. Three or four days."

"I'll book four days."

"Okay."

"You could stay longer. See all the family. I know Su Lin and Amanda want to see you. Now you have the business in Harbin finished, it's time to think about more important things. Like taking a wife. Su Lin or Amanda will make very good Chinese wives. Pick one. Or pick both. It is fashionable again in China to have one wife and one concubine. Or two wives. Or two concubines." He was laughing.

I had to admit it was an idea.

"I'll see you tomorrow."

"We can have a good Chinese dinner tomorrow. I know you need it."

"I know the dishes will have your herbs in it."

"Of course. Without the herbs, it would not be a real Chinese dinner."

"See you tomorrow."

"Remember what I have said."

"I will."

"So you say."

"Good bye, Kam Wah."

He would never change and I wouldn't have it any other way. He always looked after my best interests, so I can't complain.

I sat at the end of the bar and ordered a *Yoichi* scotch drink. After I finished the drink I went back to my room and thought about going to the gym but decided against it. My laundry was on the bed in a neat package.

I noticed the red light on the room phone was blinking. I didn't tell anyone where I was staying so whoever was calling must have a way to find me. Most knew my cell phone number, but until I called Kam Wah, I had it turned off. When I arrived in Harbin I used a cell phone with a throw away number. A number of people were probably upset with me for cutting myself off from the outside world. If Hong wanted to see me he knew where to find me. And he said he was going to be out of town today.

I checked the room safe and counted what was left of my money. I had almost seven thousand US dollars. I planned to give Ahn five thousand. The hotel bill, Guangzhou expenses, and plane tickets would use up the rest. I spent all my consultant fees. I was broke – again. Things were back to normal.

58

A S MOST MAJOR HOTEL restaurants in China, dinner at the Fortune Hotel was an elaborate buffet. I could order ala carte but decided that would be too much food. Better to pick a few items from the buffet. My rationale was I would eat less, but I seemed to always end up with more food than if I ordered ala carte. It was a losing battle.

A cornucopia of Chinese and western foods were available, including a large rib roast, a giant ham, and a roasted turkey. I walked around the steaming pans of food and decided to start with a salad. I could get meat and other items later. Three different kinds of lettuce, tomatoes, cucumbers, olives, bell peppers, pickles, and all the other ingredients of a salad were cut up and placed in individual trays. They all looked fresh. Avocado slices were available and at least five different salad dressings. I was hungrier than I thought.

It took both hands to carry the giant salad plate back to my table. The waiter had set my glass of an Australian Penfolds Cabernet Sauvignon on the table and waited for me to taste it. I did and nodded my approval. I looked forward to a quiet and pleasant meal.

Before I started with the salad, my cell phone started to chime. I looked at the small screen. It was Ahn.

"Yes?"

"I was paid a visit by Hong."

"He came to your house?"

"Yes."

"What did he want?"

"He wanted to know where you had been the past two days. I told him I drove you around the city and to the cemetery."

"And?"

"He knows something."

"Could he have found Yi?"

"He didn't say."

"Think anyone saw us there?"

"I don't think so. I didn't see anyone."

"There were phone messages on my room phone. I didn't check who called, but I guess it was Hong."

"I think he'll show up at your hotel."

"Well, I won't be hard to find."

"Want me to come over?"

"No need. I'll see you tomorrow morning. Can you come about eight? My plane leaves at ten-thirty."

"No problem. Call if you need me tonight."

"I will."

So it was Hong who called. I knew he would come to the hotel.

I saw him coming into the dinning area as I was finishing my salad. He looked around the room and finally found me. He was dressed in his police uniform. I got out of my chair and stood with my hand extended. He shook my hand and looked around at the dinner crowd. He was embarrassed about interrupting my dinner.

"Hello, Superintendent Hong."

"I'm sorry to interrupt your dinner. I should have waited."

"Not at all. I'm pleased you're here. It's my last night in Harbin and you are most welcome. Please. Sit."

I waved to the waiter, who rushed over to the table.

"Please. A table setting for the Superintendent."

Obviously, the waiter knew who Hong was. He called another waiter and together they set napkin, utensils, cup and saucer, and plate before him.

"I was preparing to go back for some delicious roast beef. Please join me for dinner. The food is quite good. Come and get a plate of something."

My disarming attitude made him feel a bit more at ease. He looked about the room again and finally decided to accept my offer.

"Thank you. I will."

We went to the buffet and loaded up with different kinds of meat, rice, vegetables, and whatever else would fit on the plate. As I passed the waiter I asked him to bring the bottle.

The waiter poured a glass for Hong and myself. I asked him to leave the bottle. I proposed a toast and drank to Hong's good health. I was at my disarming best.

We talked about the weather and how this was the wet season in Harbin. I described the gravestone ceremony and my visit to the cemetery. I mentioned trying to contact some chicken farmers without success. I don't think he believed me. Finally, Hong got to the point of why he came to see me.

"I'm sorry to bring up this subject now, but feel I must."

"What is it?"

"I was informed by the Changchun police that two Korean brothers are being questioned about serious gun shot injuries they had suffered. This is the reason I came back from my trip today."

"And why is this of concern to me?"

"You and I have discussed the possibility that Koreans from another city might be responsible for the death of Ms. Ma. I talked to the Changchun police about this and they have been on the alert for possible suspects from that city. Now, suddenly, someone attacked the two Korean brothers with a gun. They were seriously injured, possibly tortured."

"Tortured?" I frowned. "Who did the Korean brothers say did this?"

"They say they were beaten and robbed by criminals."

"If they were attacked by criminals why should I be concerned? Are they suspects in Ms. Ma's murder?"

"Do you know anything about this?"

"What would I know about Changchun and criminals who rob people? I'm afraid I can't help you with the two brothers. What's their name?"

"Shin."

"Well, I don't know anyone from Changchun named Shin."

"If you do know something, it would be in your best interest to tell me now."

I wished I could tell him, but, getting involved with the criminal system in China was not wise. Especially for an American. It would be even more difficult if it involved the North Koreans. And there was the matter of the gun. Even with friends like Chang and Lai, it would be difficult.

I put my fingers together and pressed my lips. He stared at me, waiting for me to say something. We stayed silent for several minutes. He finally looked down, folded his napkin, and put it on the table.

"Thank you for the dinner. I hope you have a good trip." He pushed his chair back, stood and put out his hand.

I stood and shook his hand.

"Good bye. Thank you for your help." I truly meant that.

"Good bye." He walked out without looking back.

I sat back down and poured another glass of wine.

The Shin brothers had gunshot wounds so the police would be looking for someone in Changchun who had a gun. It wouldn't be long before the Changchun police and Hong found out that the Shin brothers made regular deliveries to Harbin. Their truck would be examined and Hong would deduce the obvious. Would he be able to connect them to Yi and Yi with Choi? Did Hong know Yi was Choi's brother? Whatever, I was certain everybody would be pissed at me, especially Hong.

But, they still hadn't found Yi.

I finished the wine, signed the check, and went back to my room. As I entered the room, the phone rang. It was probably one of the people who left messages earlier. I didn't answer and when it stopped ringing I called the operator and told her to not ring my room until tomorrow. I should have answered the phone, but I didn't feel like talking to anyone tonight.

It was after one in the morning when my cell phone began to chime. Why would someone call me at this hour? I turned on the bed lamp and looked at the cell phone screen. It was Andre.

"Hello."

"Hello, my friend. Are you awake?"

"I am now. What's up?"

"Where are you?"

"In Harbin."

"Harbin? Is this to do with your problem?"

"No problem. Just wrapping up some loose ends here."

"Okay. You'll have to tell me about all this."

"Nothing really to tell, Andre. Things are normal."

"When will you be coming home?"

"I don't know. In about a week. Why?"

"Have some thing that I need your help with."

"What is it?"

"Need to use your contacts in Vietnam. I can tell you about it when I see you."

"Okay."

So, he didn't want to talk about it on the phone. It was one of those things he had to talk about in person.

"I'll be in touch when I get home."

"Very good. Take care."

"I will."

"*Adieu*, my friend."

"Good night."

Whatever it was, it must be important to him. He called to be certain I was coming home and available. Another job? Hope so. I needed some winter income.

It was almost two in the morning. Sleep was not in the cards. Finally, I gave up and found a mini-bottle of gin.

Suddenly my cell phone was vibrating and chiming. I looked at the screen. It flashed "Yasha."

"Yasha. I was thinking about you."

"I tried your hotel last night and your cell phone number was off."

"I'm glad you called."

"I miss you."

"And I miss you, Yasha."

"When will I see you?"

"Depends. I'm leaving tomorrow. To Beijing and then on to Guangzhou. From there, I don't know."

"I'll be in Guangzhou tomorrow."

"Are you leaving Vietnam?"

"I'm flying out of Hanoi tomorrow morning and will be in Guangzhou by mid afternoon."

"Don't you have cities to visit?"

"Have visited three cities already. I've seen enough here. It's up to them to decide which city. They're all acceptable, but Nha Trang is the best. Ms. Ngo has been very helpful. She's also in favor of Nha Trang. Everything has worked out. But, you knew that, didn't you?"

"Not really. As I said before, you're a success all by yourself."

"One day you'll have to tell me."

"Not much to tell."

"Anyway, I'll meet you in Guangzhou tomorrow."

"Okay. I'll be at the White Swan. My friend Kam Wah is arranging for a room."

"I'll call the White Swan and rebook you with me in a suite."

"With you? In a suite?"

"It makes no sense to be in two separate rooms."

"I guess you've already decided."

"Yes. You can decide if it's okay after a couple of days."

"It'll be difficult to decide."

"I'll help."

"I need all the help I can get."

"How long will you stay in Guangzhou?"

"I don't know. Depends."

"I'll provide the reasons to stay."

"Well, that could mean a lot of things."

"I'll have everything arranged."

"Everything?"

"Yes."

"You know it's after two o'clock, what are you doing up so late?"

"Trying to get a hold of you."

"Glad you didn't give up."

"You should know by now, I never give up."

"Well, can't say I haven't been warned."

"Not to worry. You're safe. I guarantee it."

I laughed and for the first time in awhile felt good about things. Yasha had a way about her that made me feel good.

"Okay. I'm in your hands."

"Finally."

"See you tomorrow at the hotel. Kam Wah said he will pick me up at the airport. My plane gets in at six so it should be about seven when I get to the hotel. We can have supper."

"I'll have that arranged too."

"I'll invite Kam Wah to dine with us. Of course, he will think he invited us to dinner."

"Whatever. Time I met him."

"Well, good night."

"Take care."

"Always trying."

"I love you," she said.

"That makes my day."

"Remember that."

"I will."

All the business in Harbin separated me from my past. But, where did that leave my children? Am I separated from them too? How, exactly, am I tied to America? Those ties were becoming tenuous.

The past few weeks wrecked havoc with my usual thoughts of self and identity. Was I a different person? Yes, I thought I was. So, was this my *karma*?

59

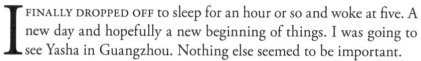

I FINALLY DROPPED OFF to sleep for an hour or so and woke at five. A new day and hopefully a new beginning of things. I was going to see Yasha in Guangzhou. Nothing else seemed to be important.

At six I went to the gym and spent an hour on the treadmill. I came back to my room, had a long hot shower, and got dressed. I cleaned out the room safe and set five thousand dollars aside for Ahn. It should cover some of his expenses and time. Hardly enough for what he did. There wasn't any way I could ever repay him.

It took five minutes to pack. I had the door open when the phone rang. I hesitated a moment. I told myself I would deal with phone calls later and closed the door after me.

Not too many check outs that morning. I paid for the room in cash and wandered into the coffee shop. It was busy but I found a table that seem to be placed there as an afterthought. There were two chairs on each side of a small table that was hastily set up to take care of the overflow crowd. It was next to the window overlooking the street.

I sat down and watched the hectic traffic scene. The street was jammed with cars, bicycles, motor bikes, and pedestrians. The rushing mass of humanity made me tired. Just watching them was exhausting.

A young waitress came to the table with a coffee pot. She asked if I wanted the buffet breakfast. I said I only wanted a cup of coffee. She turned my cup over, poured the cup full, and was gone. I didn't get a chance to ask for regular or decaffeinated coffee. I got what she had in the pot. I touched the cup. The coffee was just barely warm. It was going to be one of those days.

A few minutes before eight, Ahn came to the entrance and spotted me.

"Want some breakfast?"

"No thanks. Had breakfast at home."

"How's our time? Plane leaves at ten-thirty."

"Plenty of time. Have breakfast if you want."

"The place is busy today. And I'm not hungry."

"Did Hong find you last night?"

"Yeah, he did. We had supper here."

"And?"

"The Changchun police found the Shin brothers. I guess they went to a hospital. They explained their wounds by telling the police they were robbed."

"Don't know how that story will hold up."

"The Changchun police called Hong about it. Apparently Hong has been talking to them about BJ's death. Hong suspects I was involved with the Shins."

"Is he going to push it? Will he tell Changchun about you?"

"I don't know. If he wants to get the Shin brothers for her murder, he'll have to tell them. "

"I still have the cell phone you used."

"Destroy it. In fact, destroy everything I have touched. Hong will probably question you and it won't be pleasant. The Changchun police will probably also talk to you. Sorry to leave you holding the bag like this."

"Not a problem."

I looked for the waitress to get the bill. All of the waiters and waitresses were busy. I stood and grabbed my bag.

"Let's go."

I didn't drink any of the lukewarm coffee and didn't pay for it either.

Ahn pulled up to the loading zone at the airport. He came around and got my bag from the back seat. We stood on the sidewalk and looked at each other. I didn't know what to say. "Thank you" seemed so inadequate.

Finally, we grinned at each other, like two teenagers who pulled a fast one.

"It was a helleva ride, Ahn."

"Yes, it was. Something I won't forget. In time, there will be many stories told about this."

"I suppose so. Most of them won't be true."

"Doesn't matter. Everyone will have their own version of what happened. You might end up a hero."

"I hope there won't be too many stories about her."

"Can't be helped. You and she are the center of all this."

I heaved a sigh.

"Well. It's time. Please give my very best to your wife. Tell her I promise the next time I will come to eat some more of her cooking."

"She'll be expecting you."

"Take care, Ahn."

"You too."

I stuffed the five thousand dollars into his shirt pocket. He looked at me and shook his head.

"Not necessary."

"It's not enough, but for now it's all I have."

I gave him a hug, tapped him on his shoulder, turned, and walked toward the entrance. At the door I stopped and looked back at him. He waved. I wondered if I would ever see him again. He was some kind of guy.

He was right about the aftermath. There'll be dozens of stories told. None will be totally true. Whatever, my adventures in Harbin was now history.

It was a mid-morning flight and most of the passengers were business men and women on their way to Beijing. There were two rows of seats in First Class and only two passengers. I had an aisle seat in the second row. I put my one carry on bag in the overhead compartment. The flight attendant asked if I wanted tea or coffee. I had coffee and a breakfast biscuit. Both were only warm. I was beginning to think hot coffee was never served in China.

We arrived in Beijing a few minutes before the scheduled time. I had a two and half hour lay over, but waiting wasn't too bad. I went to the Plaza Premium Lounge, a pay-in lounge. I had a membership, which entitled me to access to lounges in cities in Asia and Canada. I thought about tonight's dinner with Yasha and Kam Wah. Thinking about the two of them meeting for the first time made me smile.

After a while I went to the refreshment center and got the Beijing version of a *cha shu bao* and a couple of *shu mai*. A bottle of Tsingtao beer was available. I took these back to my seat and watched the planes arriving and departing.

I remembered Kam Wah and Yasha were both making room reservations for me. I called Kam Wah to tell him what was happening. I caught up with him in Huangpo.

"Kam Wah, it's me."

"Where are you? Are you on schedule?"

"Yes. I called to let you know that the lady I was working with in Vietnam is coming to Guangzhou. She is making reservations at the White Swan, so not to worry about a room."

I could hear him lighting a cigarette.

"She is Chinese, correct?"

"Yes. I told you about her. The company she works for has the project in Vietnam."

"You have not told me her name."

"Her name is Yasha Hsiao."

"Yasha Hsiao? From Shanghai?" He thought for a second. "It's an okay name. You are close to this woman?"

"I don't know what you mean by close, but we are very good friends."

"I shall want to meet this woman."

"You will. We will have dinner tonight. You'll like her."

"She is Chinese, so she can be a good wife for you."

"Not in the cards, Kam Wah."

"But, you have been with her."

"Been with her? What does that mean?"

"You have pillowed her."

"Kam Wah, I don't talk about my relations with women."

"Yes, I know. But, it sounds as if you have feelings for her. That is a good sign."

"I'll see you tomorrow."

"This news has given me hope that you are coming to your senses."

"Good bye, Kam Wah."

Pillowed? Where did he get that? I remembered an English author used that term in a novel about Japan. Did they use the term in Chinese novels? Hell, the Chinese probably coined the word.

The sleepless night caught up with me and I began to doze off and I napped for a half an hour or so. While I slept the lounge attendant had cleared the dishes and the empty beer bottle. I looked around and noted more passengers had come into the lounge. It was almost two. Another hour. I thought about walking around the airport.

There were only two people who could find me in the Beijing airport without any prior word that I was flying in that day. Chang and Lai. Sounded like a name for a comedy team or a law firm.

I saw him coming into the lounge and he walked directly toward me, as if we had an appointment to meet. I would never know how he knew I was in the Plaza Lounge. I stood, smiled, and put out my hand.

"Mr. Lai. What a pleasant surprise."

He shook my hand and smiled.

"Please sit," he said and took a seat next to me.

"Are you here on business?" I asked.

"Yes, I am. In fact, you are the business that brings me here."

"Me? Really?"

What part of the business in Harbin did he know? The Shin brothers? Have they found Yi?

He came directly to the point.

"You know about the two Korean brothers in Changchun."

"Superintendent Hong told me about them. I understand they were beaten, shot, and robbed."

"That's their story. The police will find out what really happened."

"I'm sure they will."

"Another Korean, named Yi, was found today in Harbin. He did not open his shop this morning and was reported missing. Workers in a construction site found his car parked next to an abandoned store. They found him inside. Apparently he shot himself. He was one of three brothers named Choi. Yi was the brother of the North Korean policeman who was assassinated last December."

"If he was Choi's brother, why is he called Yi?"

"It was a name he assumed to hide the fact that he was Choi's brother. We have known about him for while. However, he did not break any of our laws and apparently was accepted by the Korean community. But, because he was Choi's brother we kept him on a list of possible foreign agents."

"You said there are three brothers."

"The third one is a recent arrival from North Korea. We do not know of his present whereabouts."

"Why are you keeping track of these people?"

"The two brothers might have planned to avenge Choi's death."

"Avenge his death?"

"You know you were considered a primary suspect in the assassination of Choi."

"Superintendent Hong has advised me of that."

"The Chinese government can only act on provable evidence and there was none in your case. The North Korean government knows this and has accepted our conclusions about your non-involvement. However, the Choi brothers are not required to accept our word."

"I haven't been attacked or even confronted by anyone."

"But a woman with whom you were closely associated was murdered."

"Do you think the Choi brothers were responsible for her death?"

"That's under investigation by Superintendent Hong. We do not want you to become a target of their vengeance. Especially, not on Chinese soil."

"That's comforting to know."

"Please understand. We can only act in China where we have authority."

"I know what you mean. So, that leaves the third brother."

"We're looking for him now."

"I'm sorry, but I can't help with that. I didn't even know Choi had two brothers."

"You are going to Guangzhou. How long will you stay there?"

"I haven't decided. I guess it could be three or four days. Not too much longer than that."

"Guangzhou's Chief of Police Wu has been advised of the situation and he is taking steps to provide some protection for you."

"Protection? Is this third Choi a professional?"

"He's not a policeman, as his brother was. As you know, the elder Choi was a well known professional." Lai hesitated and said off handedly, "That's what made us wonder how he was assassinated."

"Anybody can be assassinated."

"True. And you must understand the remaining Choi brother could be a determined vengeance seeker. It makes him very dangerous."

"Well, Mr. Lai, so far we know the following. The North Korean government has no interest in me because the Chinese government feels there is no evidence linking me with Choi's death. Two Koreans in Changchun have been beaten, shot, and robbed by a person or persons unknown. One Choi brother, who called himself Yi, has killed himself and no one knows why. This leaves a third Choi brother who may attempt to kill me because he is convinced I killed his brother. And the collateral damage to all this was the murder of an innocent woman in Harbin."

"Yes. That sums it up."

"Kind of stupid, isn't it?"

"Yes. It is. But, it's what we have to deal with."

"I guess you would like to see me leave China."

"No. I want to see you safe and the last Choi in custody."

"I can't help you with any of that."

"I know, but I wanted to let you know what the situation was. We are doing our best to control matters."

"Control matters? What does that mean?"

"Police Chief Wu will probably meet you at the Guangzhou airport.

I don't know what Chief Wu will do. I suggest you listen to what he has to say. It will be for your own protection."

"Well, I should be getting to the departure gate." I rose and grabbed my bag.

Lai sighed and stood.

"Remember. As you said, anyone can be assassinated."

"I'll remember that. Thank you for coming and letting me know about all of this. And I appreciate your concerns. But, with all the precautions being taken, I doubt I'll have any problems."

"I urge you to be careful."

"I will."

I shook his hand, grabbed my bag, and went out of the lounge. At the door, I turned and looked back at Lai. He was watching me. He nodded at me and then put the cell phone to his ear. I wondered if there were police watching me.

A third brother. That's a surprise. Was he in on what happened to BJ? Does he know Yi is dead? Police Chief Wu in Guangzhou was now involved. If Lai knew about all of this I was certain Chang knew.

Anyone could attack and kill a foreign traveler, even if he was being watched by the police. Been done before. Could he get a gun? Why not? I did. And there are other weapons he could use. Where could he try to kill me? If Chief Wu and the police were at the airport, would be difficult to try there. On the streets or at the hotel?

Does the third brother know I'm on my way to Guangzhou?

I wondered what Kam Wah would say about all of this. I wasn't sure how Yasha would react. I didn't want either of them involved.

I thought things had been taken care of and the Harbin affair was finished. Obviously, it had not yet ended. It wouldn't be over until the last Choi or I was dead.

60

THE FLIGHT LEFT ON time and twenty minutes after take off an early dinner was served. A shrimp casserole was on the menu. Because of the scheduled dinner with Kam Wah and Yasha tonight, I passed. I had a glass of Chinese red wine. I also tried their coffee and it was hotter than the others I had that morning. There was hope.

We landed on schedule. First Class passengers were the first to disembark and since I didn't have baggage to recover, I was out in the lobby ahead of the other passengers.

I saw Kam Wah and Wong standing in back of the crowd of people waiting in the lobby. Wong pointed at me and Kam Wah waved. I looked for Chief Wu but did not see him. Maybe things were not as bad as Lai thought.

"Welcome home," Kam Wah said as he shook my hand.

"Welcome," Wong said. I shook his hand and he took my bag.

"I checked with the White Swan," Kam Wah said. "Your lady friend has booked a suite. Why do you need a suite?" He shrugged. "Anyway, we can have dinner after you check in. Will she come to dinner with us?"

"She was planning on that."

Dinner was Kam Wah's thing. It was not Yasha's dinner or my dinner. Obviously, neither Yasha nor I would have anything to do with choosing the dishes. Things were back to normal. Felt good.

I looked around the arrival area and noticed several policemen walking about. There were too many and too obvious. It was not normal. Was all of this for me?

The uniformed officers were armed with the Type 81 assault rifle, a later version of the Type 57, a copy of the Kalashnikov AK-47. Something new. Lots of fire power. Were heavily armed policemen going to follow me around?

We started toward the door, with Wong leading the way. Kam Wah was a few steps ahead of me and I brought up the rear.

I felt he was there, but didn't actually see him. He was coming toward me on my right, almost running as he neared me. About twenty feet from me his arm swung up. He fired when he was fifteen feet away. I felt the bullet just below my right shoulder before I heard the shot. I started to fall before I felt any pain. I didn't hear or feel the second shot.

The last thing I remember was Kam Wah kneeling beside me, calling my name. Then everything went blank.

61

UNIFORMED POLICEMEN WERE ASSIGNED *to watch the special passenger with Kam Wah so they became eye witnesses to the shooting. It was a few seconds before they realized the shooter was someone dressed as a police officer. One officer opened fire on the shooter and continued firing. The assassin was hit five times and was dead before he fell to the floor.*

While several officers rushed to where the assassin lay, two others came quickly to where the shooting victim fell. They firmly moved Kam Wah aside and looked at the victim's wounds. He was still alive. One was talking on his intercom, calling for an ambulance.

The officers verified the assassin was dead and searched his pockets, looking for identification. No one knew why he was wearing a police uniform. What could have been a panic scene was not. The police were well trained and order was quickly established. The entire area was immediately cordoned off.

Within minutes Police Chief Wu entered the terminal. He was briefed by the officer in charge. He came to where the shooting victim lay and spoke to Kam Wah.

"An ambulance should be here in a few minutes. We'll take him to the Guangdong Provincial People's Hospital. They handle major emergencies there."

"Who is the man who shot him?" Kam Wah asked.

"I'm sure it's the person the Beijing authorities warned me about."

"He was dressed as a policeman."

"Yes." The Chief heaved a sigh. "We'll have to find out about that."

The assassin was dressed as a policeman and Chief Wu would have to provide an explanation. This was a major problem for the Chief. He had been warned an attempt on the victim's life might be made and the victim was shot on his watch. Moreover, the victim was a friend of the Chief as well as a close associate of some important people in Beijing.

Less than ten minutes later the ambulance arrived.

"Ah. Here's the ambulance," the Chief said, pointing to the curb.

The ambulance backed up to the door. Paramedics leaped out of the back and wheeled a gurney into the terminal. They examined the victim and did what they could to stop the bleeding. An IV was inserted into his arm.

The Chief walked to where they were working on him and watched for a moment.

"How bad is it?"

"It's a bad one. He was shot twice. Once in the upper right chest and once in the mid-abdominal area. He's bleeding badly. If we can stop that he'll stabilize."

"Is he going to make it?"

"Depends on what damage there is inside."

"Do everything you can. Spare nothing. Understand? I'll be at the hospital soon."

"Yes, sir."

Chief Wu dialed a number on his cell phone. It was a private number. The call was answered immediately.

"Hello. Dr. Zhang speaking."

"This is Police Chief Wu. There is a special emergency that will be at your hospital in a few minutes. It is a shooting victim and the paramedics say it is serious. The victim is a very close personal friend. There are also some people in Beijing who will want to know what his condition is. I mention this because his welfare is of great concern to certain people. We will all appreciate the very special attention you can give to this."

He waited while the person on the other end of the call spoke. The Chief nodded and said thank you. He closed his cell phone and turned to Kam Wah.

"I just spoke to the hospital director. He'll get the best care."

"I'm going to the hospital."

"I'll be there shortly."

Kam Wah shook the Chief's hand and went out to where the van was parked. Wong was waiting with the door open.

"We go to the Guangdong Provincial People's Hospital."

He got in and lit a cigarette. He stared ahead and thought about his friend who had just been shot and in an ambulance on his way to the hospital.

"Why was he shot? What's happening?" Wong asked.

Kam Wah took a drag of his cigarette and blew the smoke out the window. He sighed and shook his head.

"It began last year with a diamond deal in Beijing. But it got very complicated and involved people from North Korea. You remember that girl you and he tried to get out of that hotel and on to a train to Hong Kong?"

"Yes. He bought a Hong Kong residence card from a woman for five hundred US dollars. The girl was going to use it get into Hong Kong."

"Well, as you know, that didn't turn out too well. The girl and her brother were arrested and put in a North Korean prison. She killed herself there. All of that was caused by a bastard named Choi, a secret policeman from North Korea. He hunted Koreans who escaped from North Korea. Last December Choi was killed in Harbin and some think our friend killed him. Because of that, a woman in Harbin was murdered."

"What did the woman have to do with this?"

"Nothing. Her problem was she was in love with him."

"She was killed because she loved him?"

"Yes."

Wong shook his head and stared at the road ahead.

"You know, he's that kind of guy. It's like when we went to get Su Lin away from that bastard moneylender."

"Yes, he is a special person."

"This shooter at the airport thought he killed the secret policeman from North Korea?"

"Yes."

"Well, he's dead."

"Now we have to find out if our friend is alive."

They fell silent and each thought about the man at the hospital and the many adventures they had shared with him.

The hospital was on Zhongshan Er Road. It was a well known emergency center. At the hospital entrance Kam Wah got out at the curb while Wong parked the van. Kam Wah went quickly to the emergency reception desk.

The receptionist told them the patient was in surgery. She suggested they wait in the lounge. Ten minutes later Chief Wu came into the lounge.

"I checked with the hospital director. They have the best people working on him. May take some time."

"You know who the shooter is?" Kam Wah asked.

"Yes. Beijing says he's the brother of the North Korean policeman who was killed in Harbin last December. We don't know yet where he got the gun. He stole the uniform at the police station. He got in by posing as a custodian," Chief Wu sighed. "People from Beijing will be coming down. These are powerful people. The shooter was a North Korean so the North Korean government will get involved as well."

"This shooter is the North Korean policeman's brother?"

"Yes. Beijing says there was another brother in Harbin who killed himself yesterday. I don't know why."

"So, all three brothers are dead."

"Yes. How they were tied up with our friend in there is not clear. We may never know. Well, I have to check in at headquarters. I'm sure Beijing will be calling."

"I'll wait here."

"I'll be back later."

The Chief was answering his cell phone as he left the lobby.

"It might be a long wait. You want to get some tea?" Kam Wah asked Wong.

"Okay."

"I know a place close by. They will let me smoke."

Kam Wah suddenly stopped and said, "I forgot about the woman at the White Swan. She must be wondering what happened."

"If she has the television on she must have heard something."

"I don't want to talk to her until I know more about what's happening with his surgery. I'll check after we come back."

An hour later Kam Wah and Wong returned to the hospital. Kam Wah looked up at the clock on the wall.

"He's been in surgery for two hours."

Kam Wah looked around and went to the reception desk and asked to speak to the hospital director. The receptionist called someone on the phone and soon a man in a white gown came to the lounge. Kam Wah quickly rose and went to him. He spoke quietly for a few minutes. Kam Wah nodded. He turned and waved at Wong to follow him and walked out of the hospital.

"Take me to the White Swan."

Kam Wah lit a cigarette and rolled down the window. He sat silently and smoked his cigarette. He stared out at the dark streets. Wong knew him well enough not to interrupt his thoughts. They did not speak during the thirty minutes it took to get to the hotel.

He entered the lobby and went to the counter where phones were available for in-house calls. He asked the operator to ring Ms. Yasha Hsiao's room.

"Hello."

"Hello, Ms. Hsiao?"

"Who is this?"

"My name is Kam Wah Cheung."

"Oh. Mr. Cheung. I've been trying to find out where you all were. I called the airport and they said there was some problem there, but no other information. His plane landed two hours ago. Where is he?"

"You have not been watching television?"

"No. I've been working on the computer. Why?"

"Ms. Hsiao, I wonder if I may have a word with you."

"Is something wrong? Where are you?"

"I am in the hotel lobby."

She was suddenly very frightened.

"I'll be right down."

Kam Wah reached for his cigarettes. Then he remembered smoking was not allowed in the hotel. He put his hands behind his back and paced in front of the elevator. In a few minutes he heard a bell chime, announcing that the elevator had arrived. The doors slid apart and Yasha rushed out.

She immediately knew he was Kam Wah. She was visibly upset. She looked around and past Kam Wah, thinking she would see him. He stood with his hands behind his back. She looked at his sober face and took in a deep breath.

"Something bad has happened to him, hasn't it?"

"Yes."